BELVEDOR AND THE TRAIL OF FIRE

BOOKS IN THE
OLLEB-YELFRA UNIVERSE
BY ASHLEIGH BELLO

A Myrmaid's Kiss

The Belvedor Saga

Belvedor and the Four Corners

Belvedor and the King's Curse

Belvedor and the Desert of Secrets

Belvedor and the Trail of Fire

Belvedor and the Golden Rule

BELVEDOR AND THE TRAIL OF

FIRE

ASHLEIGH BELLO

Not all that burns is evil.
Not all that burns is good.

First Edition: February 2022

Originally published as:
Belvedor and the Golden Rule (parts one and two)
February 2020

Cover design by Mirella Santana.
www.mirellasantana.com.br
Cover photography by Jessica Truscott (Faestock).

Other publications by Ashleigh Bello in the Olleb-Yelfra Universe:
Belvedor and the Four Corners
Belvedor and the King's Curse
Belvedor and the Desert of Secrets
Belvedor and the Golden Rule
A Myrmaid's Kiss

For more information, visit: www.ashleighbello.com

ISBN-13: 978-0-9987974-7-2
ISBN-10: 0-9987974-7-2

10 9 8 7 6 5 4 3 2 1

To all the people who have ever lost someone they loved.
You're not alone. Keep going.

CONTENTS

CITY OF THE FOUR CORNERS
THE JAR OF STONE
UNDOR
Agrarian's District
Healer's District
Vanishing Tunnels
Creator's District
Warrior's District
Tombs
Draminet
NICORA FOREST
BLACK SAND DESERT
BELGRADIA
Fate's Pool
KAMPAULO
MORIAMO
HIGH CITY OF SAINDORA
SEA OF SAINDORA
Empress Isle
OLLEB YELFRA
NW N NE
W E
SW S SE
LIZARD INK

BLANCOREN MOUNTAINS
NORTH LUOSE
SOUTH LUOSE
ZAMBIENTH
The Greenhouse
LANZATARÉ
Island of Idris
IMPENETRABLE FOREST
The Treehouse
Starr Caverns
GUANAMARA

*"All wounds heal with time. Don't let the pain control you.
Instead, you must learn how to wield it into power.
Pain is a feeling of the past, and the past is only meant to
guide the future… not govern it."*

– Diveena, Impenetrable Forest

PART ONE

DIVIDED

ELI PACED THE ROOM, rubbing at his neck where the point of Solomon's sword had pricked his skin not even an hour before. "We have to go after her," he said in a panic. "She saved me. She sacrificed herself for us. We have to go now, or…"

He couldn't speak the words aloud, but Lessa knew what he wanted to say. She had her own wounds left by Solomon, the lingering stings reminding them both of what they had cost the guardians, of who they'd lost—Arianna Belvedor.

"We can't," she said with trembling words. She had resigned herself to the hard choice of separating from Arianna the moment she and Eli had followed Noah to safety under the cover of the blizzard. There had been no alternative.

With cruel clarity, Lessa remembered backing away from where Solomon and Arianna stood, shaking her head with each slow step; Arianna had stayed her ground, chest lifted high, even with Solomon's sword at her throat. She had kept Solomon's attention so that they could escape. Once again, she'd placed her life at risk to protect those she loved.

Though Lessa felt fear clouding her senses with Arianna gone again from her side, this time she could see the reasons…

Arianna had never really been able to cope with the fact that those she deemed family could be harmed on the dangerous path toward freedom. If given the choice, she might gamble her own life—but the lives of her friends were *not* something she was willing to risk.

In their most recent battle, Solomon had gained the advantage; Arianna's surrender had been the only way for the rest of them to stand a fighting chance on another day, and she did so without hesitation.

"There was nothing you could've done," said Noah, pinching himself as if he might wake from a dream at any moment. "No one can beat General Bell. Arianna trained under him for nearly half her life, and she still… *still* hasn't outdone him yet, has she?"

His lip quivered. "He would've slaughtered you, mate. He nearly did. She saved your lives."

Lessa played with a long, bronze key, twisting it between her fingertips as she relived the last few hours over and over in her head. If she let her thoughts wander too far beyond the here and now, her heart would feel the sharp ache of loss, and not just for Arianna…

No matter how hard she tried to focus, her stomach continuously churned at the memory of her final moments with her late master and friend, Talis Churry, on an otherwise beautiful beachfront in the pyramid city of Zambienth.

"There's nothing we could've done," she repeated to herself, forcing her mind back to the present before it could get lost in any more pain; her head was still pounding from the mind magic done to her to suppress her memories. But with Arianna gone now, any anger she'd harbored toward her for her part in that had evaporated into thin air.

I understand now, Ara. You did what you had to do. Please, stay alive.

She took a deep breath, not letting herself spiral again. She had to remain calm, for their leader and friend was no longer there to guide them. *She's gone…*

They had to continue on without her—that's what Arianna would've demanded.

Eli was shaking his head, staring at his hands. "But maybe if we—"

"*No,*" said Lessa, more firmly, "we can't go after them, Eli." She put her attention on their badly battered avatar companions, shifting the key into her pocket. "Solomon is too strong for us, and just look at Sano and Solza. They can hardly even stand. We couldn't win now."

The silver magic was beginning to fade from the avatars' eyes.

"Arianna must've seen our message," she said, nodding to herself. "The guardian dragon enchantment lit up the sky, even during such a storm. She'll know we're all right, and she'll find the strength to fight Solomon. I know she will… somehow."

She went to tend to the avatars' wounds; she had to do something other than just sit.

Solza had since shifted back into her favored snow leopard form from yet her third avatar transformation—an owl with command over the air element—a grand surprise during the battle with Solomon; she was curled up in the corner of the room.

Lessa worked on her with gentle hands, saddened at her state; it was painfully clear that the normally strong-willed avatar wasn't just weak from battle… she was weakened by a broken heart, separated from her master.

Lessa thanked the gods that she and Sano hadn't met the same fate. And she thanked them that Solza was, at least, still breathing—it meant that Arianna was still alive.

When she was done with Solza, she went to check on Sano;

he was back to his old self now too, changed from the glorious white wolf that had saved their necks on the dueling grounds to a small monkey that fit perfectly on her shoulders.

As her healing magic wiped away the avatars' ailments, Lessa's focus shifted to the howling winds outside—they pounded on the doors and windows of the room that sheltered them, demanding to be let in. It gave her the uneasy feeling that until this fight was over, there would be no place they could deem 'safe' again…

Their short-lived glory as highlifes in South Luose had been swept away in a single moment. And their days basking in the sun on the Island of Idris had proved a nearly catastrophic misadventure in the end.

Their sanctuary in Zambienth had fallen to the darkness just the same, and now Lessa was without the person she trusted most of all to get her out of the Four Corners alive… *again*, their oasis in the Vanishing Tunnels forever compromised.

She glanced from Eli to Noah and back—she was surrounded by an entirely new group of friends to count on in these desperate times; Demetrius and Jeom had escaped on the sea—to freedom or to death was unknown… for she knew how fickle water could be—and Arianna had been taken hostage.

No one will be coming to our rescue.

With the unknown fates of her family looming at the forefront of every thought, it was undeniable that this fight, this war, was just beginning.

Lessa Thur was a Guardian of Gold, an escaped slave of the districts returned home to the start. And although she had every hope that her friends had survived these trying tests, she couldn't rest for a second in pushing forward toward the goals they had all started out to achieve together.

The warmth of a tear brushed her cheek as this realization settled with her. *My friends are strong, so I must stay strong.*

She took another deep breath, considering the room…

"It's like time stood still here all these years," she muttered.

So much has changed.

This place had been a refuge to her before, when she'd needed to evade her district regulators after they'd learned she'd broken the rules. And within these walls Lessa had uncovered a history of magic and the Golden Age, alongside Arianna.

This had been just a temporary home for her then, but fond memories lingered—Talis had often visited with stories from the Healer's District, new scrolls for them to devour, or lessons to impart. Here, she had begun her studies in healing with magic.

It was also where Lessa had first witnessed Arianna's talent as a warrior; she'd regularly watched her and Solomon spar, mesmerized by their dance with swords around the private training room.

That was before Bell had gone dark. *Before...*

So much had happened before.

Lessa took the rusted key back out of her pocket, examining it closely. In all this time, she'd never been able to part with this token from the Warrior's District.

She had stolen the key from Caretaker Cyn, slipped it away from right under her nose. Then she and Arianna had snuck out for a night to remember, getting to know each other better beneath a rare, clear sky in the Dueling Arena.

They'd shared their strengths and fears, and what 'freedom' meant in their hearts—something that had long since exploded from a focus on purely surviving the Free Falls Festivals to solving an unfathomable puzzle with Olleb-Yelfra's very existence at stake.

Lessa squeezed her eyes shut, wrapping her palm tight around the key that had unlocked the door to so many adventures. She could nearly taste the frigid air of the very evening that had thrown everything else into motion... the night sky lit up in a blaze as a mighty star fell from its place in the universe.

It had passed over the Blancoren Mountains, landing far beyond the Jar, leaving only the remnants of its soul behind in the

Black Sand Desert, to be found over a year later by wary travelers.

As was her destiny, Arianna had plucked that star's soul straight from the dirt and held it close to her always, confiding in it her greatest desires. And a single wish at a desperate time had ultimately led Lessa back to a room she could've never imagined she'd return to in a million years.

Alas, here she was—clinging to the very key that had ignited their journey to freedom in the first place.

It was in this moment that Lessa grasped the true meaning of 'destiny.' *We've come full circle now.*

"I think this is right where we're supposed to be," she said, standing to face the boys.

With the key still clutched in her fist, she pulled all her hopes and positivity to the surface.

"If I have any faith left at all in this cruel world, trust me when I say that *this*," she spread her arms out wide, Sano scuttling across her shoulders, "is exactly what was supposed to happen next."

She locked eyes with Eli.

"We have to stay focused, if we're to see her again."

Arianna, stay focused.

Eli sucked back his emotions, and a long silence filled with so many future possibilities settled in the air.

"Do you think she really knows we're all right?" he asked after a moment, tracing the golden lines of the dragon etched on his palm.

"No amount of snow could've stopped our dragon from shining," she replied. "Anyone with eyes to the sky would've seen it across all the districts."

"Then… then she must have seen it," said Eli, sounding somewhat reassured. "Arianna can never keep her eyes on the ground. They're like magnets to the stars."

Lessa smiled. "My thoughts precisely."

"I just *can't* believe this," shouted Noah all of a sudden, eyes wide. "I saw…" He threw his hands up. "And Solomon against her? There was nearly a revolt!"

He paced the room as he muttered to himself, pulling his fingers through his mess of fiery hair—his shock had worn off, confusion manifesting in its place.

Noah was no longer the awkward, unpolished boy Lessa remembered but a strong young man with a passion in his eyes that shouted for freedom.

"They've really lied to us," he said, more to himself—Lessa could practically see his memories start to string together to form a clear picture of something that had always seemed so hazy before.

"Now you know," said Lessa. "The King and his followers have lied about everything, tried to suppress a truth they had no right to bury."

She stood to properly introduce herself.

"Noah, I've heard a lot about you from Ara. We met briefly during the Free Falls, when Liam was wounded. I don't know if you'd remember?" She extended her hand. "I'm Lessa Thur, former Healer's District."

"Right you are," said Noah with a whistle, shaking her hand. "I guess they lied about how that went down, too."

He stared at her with a sort of stupor in his expression, as if he wasn't sure whether or not he'd gone mad; Lessa returned a somber nod.

"I see… well, it's all coming back to me now." He let go of her hand. "Pleasure to see you alive and well, Lessa."

He turned to Eli.

"And what should I call you?"

"The name's Elijah Neve," said Eli. "I used to be a Warrior's District slave too, placed in South Luose a few years back after my Free Falls… before meeting Arianna."

"Shame we never crossed paths before all this, then," said Noah with a shrug. "Nice to meet you, Elijah."

They shook hands, looking each other over.

"Just call him Eli," said Lessa. "We're all about to get to know each other very well."

Noah offered him a shaky smile. "Eli it is, then."

He perked up a bit.

"Did *you* know Liam too? Did you see him on the outside?"

The hope was thick in his voice; Lessa shriveled up even more on the inside.

"I'm not sure..." said Eli. He looked to Lessa for help. "Who's Liam—"

"He's talking about Liam Black," she said, eyes cast down. "You remember. Ara would have told you about him."

A sharpness formed in Eli's face, understanding. He hadn't personally known Liam, but he'd witnessed Arianna's emotional scars from the death of her district friend.

Noah continued rambling on, unaware of their exchange.

"He had a tough Free Falls," he said. "Burned pretty badly on the face, but he survived. That was the day the King came to visit. *Epic*, really!" He shook his head at the recollection, his freckled cheeks reddening. "He told me that was his placement too, some city named... how'd you say it again?"

"South Luose," Eli mumbled.

"Right! That's the one. I'm sure of it. I plan to meet him there first thing when I'm free of this place." He cocked his head to the side. "How is the bloke?"

Noah was clearly eager for a piece of the familiar world to stay the same as it crumbled all around him, and Lessa could surely relate; it was more comfortable than facing the hard truths that often came with change.

Yet all the 'truths' that Noah had ever known had already shifted drastically, even if he couldn't quite grasp it yet—now his world was about to sway even more.

Eli cleared his throat to speak but nothing came out; Lessa stepped forward to deliver the tragic news.

"I'm sorry, Noah," she said, head bowed. "Liam, he… didn't make it long in South Luose. Life outside the districts can be just as brutal for some."

Noah stilled, a slight smirk on his face. He looked back and forth between Eli and Lessa as if for the underlying joke; Eli nodded his head in confirmation.

"No," he said, his smile vanishing. "No!"

He stumbled into the wall at his back.

"You're not saying… he's *dead?*"

The light in his eyes was snuffed out just as quickly as it had come.

"Liam…" Noah shook his head. "I won't see him again?"

He turned away from them.

"I'm sorry for you to find out like this," whispered Lessa, laying a gentle hand on his back. "I remember how much you cared for him. It wasn't right."

He shrugged it off and faced her.

"He was my best friend," he said with conviction, sucking back his tears. "Tell me straight. How did it happen? I want to know."

He squared his shoulders, bracing himself for the details, palms pressed upon the stone wall.

"Solomon." Her words were weighted with sorrow and anger. "He murdered him to get to Arianna. She and Liam had reconnected in Luose while we were in hiding, after our escape from the Jar. Solomon sniffed us out with magic and used Liam as bait along the way."

"*Magic,*" Noah breathed, fingertips digging into the wall. "I wish I could go back in time and realize what Liam had already known. He never lost those memories from the night of your escape, but I did. He even *tried* to tell me that last day of the Free Falls when he woke, but I thought he'd lost his damn mind after such a bad beating. I just… dismissed him."

He looked to his hands, trying to catch his breath.

"He seemed so broken when he left… we never really made amends." Noah lifted his eyes to Lessa, searching for something—she was sure it was forgiveness. "Did he at least find what he was looking for?"

He swallowed, trying to keep it together.

"Before he—"

"I think that he did," said Lessa with sincerity. "When we first met Liam in South Luose, he seemed so lost. But a short time later, him and Arianna were the closest of friends again—" she hoped her next words would offer him some comfort "—and she did not let him die alone."

She sighed, shoulders sagging.

"It's not your fault, Noah, what happened to him. He always believed, and that made him strong. Now you can believe too and remain strong in his memory."

"I'll kill Solomon for this," he growled, hands balled into fists by his sides.

"Get in line," said Eli in solidarity. "It's grown quite long, and Arianna is at the very front."

Noah wiped his eyes, shaking his head.

"This was supposed to be my Free Falls Festival, you know? I had already passed the test before you lot were dragged in. I thought… I thought I would finally get to see him again."

He bowed his head, looking to the floor; the Free Falls meant nothing anymore, and everyone in that room knew it.

"What do we do now?" he asked after a moment.

"We fill you in on everything," said Lessa. "Then… I guess, we plan another escape."

She glanced to Eli—he echoed her uncertainty.

"We have no other choice," she said, mustering up her courage. "No mistakes this time. We can't afford any if we're going to make it even a foot out of this district alive." She looked between him and Noah. "And we'll need more than just *us* if we're to be successful."

Eli remained silent, chewing on his lip.

"You know what I speak of, Eli," she implored with a sigh. "We must see the plan through. We were patient before everything fell apart in Zambienth, but now we have to try." She waved her hand. "There's no more time left to sit and *wait* for better options to play out."

Eli crossed his arms at his chest, a sardonic laugh escaping him.

"I mean, all fine and good. You know I'm in. But *what* about Arianna?" he demanded. "Solomon will kill her!"

"He won't," said Lessa, really believing this. "Solomon needs her alive to bring back to the King. I'm sure of it."

She placed a hand on his hand, forcing Eli to unwrap his arms and open up to her.

"You and I need to concentrate on the part of the plan that we've found responsibility for," she said. "No one else but us can do this now, not even Arianna."

"But—"

"This is the *only* way, Eli, please." She squeezed his hand harder. "I need you. Besides, if I know her at all, she'll not make an easy captive to hold... not even for Solomon Bell." Lessa looked to Solza. "And with any luck, we'll all meet again at the finish."

Eli let out a heavy sigh, releasing all the tension in his body.

"I know. You're right," he said. "But it's truly a mad plan if I ever heard one. May the gods keep us in their favor all the way to the end."

"The gods have already proven whose side they're on," said Lessa—she felt the magic burn bright in her eyes as she stroked Sano's fur. "It is *not* the King's."

AS THE BLIZZARD RAGED ON, Arianna's former training quarters doing little to keep out the cold, they huddled together at a table; Eli and Lessa began to catch Noah up on all their adventures since the escape from the Four Corners, centering on their newfound quest to defeat the King. Between the two of them, they were able to detail every major moment that would eventually lead them right to this very spot, not discounting the day they had reunited in Zambienth, the Guardians of Gold gathered once again—just in time for an epic battle with the Shadow Resistance.

Lessa cupped her hands together; they visibly shook from the cold now settling in at the finale of their story.

"*Solza ven immito*," she whispered, blowing into them.

With the magic of her breath, a bright, pink flame sparked between her palms, making their faces glow in the darkness.

Noah stared at her in disbelief, her flame dancing in the reflection of his eyes.

"And then, Arianna made a wish upon a star that she had found in the desert. Its properties contain some of the rarest magic ever known to exist," said Eli in a hushed voice. "That's how we somehow landed here."

He gestured to the room.

"All right, mate," said Noah, scratching his head, "I'll save my questions on the 'how' for later, considering our bigger problems at present. But allow me this… why in the King's name would Arianna wish to return *here*, of all places?"

He raised an eyebrow, still some skepticism lingering.

"The girl I knew only ever had one wish, and that was to escape to a place far from here and never look back. I don't even recognize this person you speak of!"

"That may be so—" said Eli, standing to grab a torch off the wall. He nodded to Lessa for a little help.

With just the flick of her finger, a flame grew there too.

Eli used the torch to light up a dusty fireplace tucked away in the corner. "—but Arianna has changed, and that past is gone."

"She's been… chosen, so to speak," added Lessa. "We all have. And that includes you as you find yourself here with us now, on a different side of history."

"Chosen for what?" asked Noah, drawn to the growing fire.

"To help fulfill a prophecy of old, one that will right the world again," said Eli. "The Golden Rule."

"Light is light and dark is dark, but never shall they live apart," said Lessa, reciting the words to the mantra now burned into her mind.

"I see…" said Noah—he clearly did not. "But what does some riddle have to do with you all coming back here? I don't understand."

"Because," said Lessa, "if we want to rid King Devlindor of his throne, we need bigger power than what our small group can give, more than just the Guardians of Gold."

"*Wait*," said Noah, an incredulous smile replacing his frown. "Are you telling me you want to try and rally the districts behind you?" His voice pitched. "Is… is that what all this is about?"

His question was met with silence.

"I'm right, aren't I?" He jumped to his feet. "You're not just looking to cause a disturbance. You want to actually bring the slaves into an uprising against our king? *Take* the Four Corners?"

Lessa stood to face him.

"It was an idea that was in discussion with the other guardians, yes," she said, "but we were attacked before we could properly prepare. Now that we're here, we have to at least try."

"A true uprising against the King," breathed Noah—his words hung in the air for all to consider. "That sounds like a death wish."

"Maybe," said Eli, eyes brightening. "But just think about what a revolt truly means, Noah. It means that you, me, *all* the enslaved… we fight back to those who have oppressed us, beat us, *killed* us."

He opened his hands wide, as if to weigh the choices.

"With the truths you know now, can you think of any other option? Your choices are to fall back in line and bury your knowledge, flee… or fight." Eli spoke evenly. "We have to get them all on our side and take out the regulators on the way. Our army is right here, waiting to be awakened."

"We didn't come here to run away again," said Lessa, moving to Eli's side. "And we're certainly not going to kneel before the King with our hearts still beating."

Noah was silent for barely a second before his face lit up.

"You don't have to ask me twice!" he sang. "I'd give an arm and a leg for some justice." He put his fists on his hips, standing with a prideful grin. "I'm in! How can I be of service?"

Eli massaged the stubble on his chin.

"We'll need a way to get everyone's attention," he said, thinking out loud, "sway them to our side, *before* the regulators can get wind of what we're doing. I'm sure they're regrouping themselves now after such a commotion at tonight's festivals. Even with magic on our side, I doubt we could take them all out on our own should they find us, or interfere too early." His forehead wrinkled as he thought. "And *pray* no one gets word to someone in the Shadow Resistance before we figure a way out of the mountains."

"Seems an impossible task," said Lessa, also mulling over their options. "They're always patrolling the streets around this time from what I can remember."

"Not tonight they won't be," said Noah—he pointed to the window as snow pelted the frames. "If there was ever a time to sneak out past curfew without getting caught, it'd be now. The regulators will be holed up in Supreme Way. That's on the other side of the district! Besides, from what I saw out there when you all turned everything to shit, they're *frightened.* If I see the truth of magic now and remember what the King erased years ago when Arianna first fled, I'm sure they do too."

Lessa gently stroked Solza as they talked.

"I can't believe Ara's spell really worked," she whispered. "She's been practicing mind magic a lot, but I didn't think…" She shook her head, a smile on her face. "Solza gave her *quite* the boost, to be able to reverse the King's magic on such a scale."

Arianna's power never failed to awe her—it always came when she *really* needed it. And each time it did, it proved stronger.

"Well, whatever she did, it felt like a veil placed over my memories had been lifted," said Noah, shifting a cautious glance toward Solza; Lessa thought she must look terribly frightening to strangers. "Without that little story you just told me, I'd be right out of my mind with even more questions."

He shook his head.

"All you described… it doesn't *really* make sense. But it's at least an explanation as bizarre as everything else I saw." He stared into the fire. "What I'm saying is, I bet you'll have a very keen audience tonight."

"He's right," said Lessa—she recalled just how difficult it'd been to convince Jeom of magic. "But we better do it quick, before they start questioning the reality of it."

"Or before anyone working for the King can get to them and cover up the secret again," said Noah.

"Well, what are we waiting for? Let's get going, then," said Eli, giving Noah a pat on the back. "Glad to have you with us."

He pulled on his cloak, fastened a sword to his hip from the sparring room's ample supply, and prepared to step outside, the others following his lead.

Lessa collected her bow and arrows, slinging them across her back, and she pulled on an extra cloak that was left hanging in the room—hers had gotten soaked from the failed astral projection with Arianna in the tunnels, so she was due to catch a cold at any moment.

"I don't think I've ever been so scared in my life," she said, pausing at the door.

Noah chuckled as he grabbed an axe from the weaponry stash. "After the tale you just told, I've got trouble believing that."

"You were right," said Eli, addressing Lessa with seriousness. "Arianna can't help us here, and we can't help her. It's like you said, we *have* to try if we have any hope of doing some good in all of this mess. It's the perfect timing, the only time. Everyone will remember the magic from earlier tonight. There can be no denying it now, and the King won't have time to stop it from spreading if we play our cards right. This is our chance."

Lessa felt her fear ebb and her hope swell with his reassurance.

"All the slaves will be separated in their quarters, so we can tackle them in small groups," suggested Noah, seeming excited to finally take matters into his own hands.

"Lessa, you have control of magic, so you can prove our story to them on the spot, and I can help lay claim to it," said Eli. "To me, they'll listen because I'm a former warrior-slave and I earned my citizenship, no magic to show except for my loyalty." He gestured to Noah. "And with you, someone they know and trust, I'm sure we can do this."

"All right…" said Lessa, letting Eli's words sink in.

She thought of him fondly now after all they'd been through together; he'd proven himself ten times over as a true guardian and friend, so she was glad he was here by her side.

"I think that's as good a plan as it gets. Let's not waste another breath." Eli and Noah returned firm nods. "Sano, mind shifting back to your new earth form? I think you made quite the impression earlier."

The little monkey jumped off her shoulders to the floor. Upon landing, a colorful burst of magic encircled him—his body expanded until a magnificent white wolf with orange eyes was padding confidently about the room.

Solza got to her feet as well, so big now that Lessa thought she might even clear Jeom in height if she stood on her hind legs and lifted her paws to the air. Together, the two avatars were a powerful pair, their collective magic radiating off them.

Eli knelt down in front of Solza; she nudged him affectionately, her piercing blue eyes filled with worry.

"It's going to be all right, my friend," he said, ruffling her fur. "She'll be safe. And we'll keep you safe until you can meet her again."

"This is insane," said Noah as Sano sniffed him. Then he shrugged. "But... I always knew Arianna was special."

Lessa chuckled. *That's an understatement.*

"Noah, thank you so much for your help back there," she said. "Without you, we would've never been able to reach the Dueling Arena in such a storm."

"Now that I know... now that I remember," he said, "I would do anything to help Arianna and her friends, no matter the rules to be broken."

His eyes traveled past her; something made him stiffen.

Lessa turned to follow his gaze and found a parchment hung on the wall; it was one that papered the districts, in every home and establishment. A message so prominent in daily life that it had eventually melded into the background of her mind—though never to be forgotten and always to be obeyed.

In her months living with Arianna, she had never really noticed it there before, yet she knew its contents by heart:

The Laws of the City of the Four Corners
· Freedom is a privilege earned ·

i. No slave may have contact with another outside of their respective district.

ii. Each slave shall be issued a number upon entering the city and shall be referenced by this number until successful completion of their designated Free Falls Festival.

iii. A bell shall ring in each district for various announcements—its sound shall be obeyed incontestably;
- One ring shall signify that all slaves should begin their schedules;
- Three rings shall signify an assembly in the city center for the morning commendation of the King;
- Ten rings shall signify curfew; slaves must be in their sleeping quarters by the final sound.

iv. Each slave must attend daily lessons at the district Learning Center for basic education as well as teachings of His Majesty.

v. Slave years 5-12 must attend regular group training for general skills.

vi. Slave years 12-17 must attend small group training for specialized skills.
- Exemption: a master trainer may choose to select a slave who has reached their thirteenth year for an apprenticeship.

vii. Each slave must follow their schedules precisely, unless otherwise permitted.

viii. In order to be considered for citizenship to Olleb-Yelfra, slaves must participate in—and survive—the annual Free Falls Festivals at the turning of their eighteenth year.

ix. Defiance of any of the above laws of the Four Corners is subject to extreme punishment or death.

x. If a slave dies, they are thus deemed 'unfit' for citizenship and shall be buried in the Tunnel of Tombs without ceremony.

Noah marched to the wall and tore it down. He crumpled the parchment up and tossed it into the blazing fire.

With satisfaction, they all watched it burn, the fire crackling with a delicious sound that gave them courage; they may be trapped in the Warrior's District for the time being, but it was a place they'd all managed to survive up to this point. And now they knew a whole lot more about the world outside of it.

In fact, as that fire ripped through the foundation of what King Devlindor wrongfully established centuries ago, leaving nothing but ashes behind, Lessa had never felt more assured in all her life about where she stood.

She set the key down on a small table by the window, taking one last look around the room; the Warrior's District emblem caught her eye through a cracked mirror on the far wall.

What's broken can always be fixed, she thought.

A spell fell from her lips, the break in the glass stitching itself back together.

"This should be fun," said Eli with a knowing smirk.

"Shall we?" said Lessa, feeling exhilarated by her magic.

Noah and Eli stepped aside to let her pass.

With the flick of her hand, the door blew open and the howling wind poured into the training quarters, taking it over.

Ready for the final chapter in this war for freedom to begin, they each stepped out into the cold with torches in hand—except Lessa, who still grasped the burning flame in her palm.

GUARDIAN GABRIEL

THE ECHOES OF BATTLE and pleading of the dying were something every citizen of Olleb-Yelfra had experienced in their past, but for Gabriel they had now been renewed. Though his journey escorting the broken and battered Kane brothers across the sea had long since replaced the sounds of war with the sounds of water, the memory of screaming voices and clashing weapons still rang through his mind.

The unforeseen battle in Zambienth—guardian versus shadow—was all Gabriel heard and all he thought he might ever hear again for the rest of his life… a life that was likely to end soon; it had been just a few days at sea, but it felt like an eternity.

Gabriel thought he was the only one with any of his wits left about him after such a tragic separation from the other guardians. Save for the song of the sea as it gently rocked the boat back and forth, there had been nothing but silence soon after they'd fled the shores of Zambienth, forcing him to focus on the voices of his own terrible thoughts…

Demetrius never moved from the spot where he sat, a shrunken version of the young and happy man Gabriel knew him to be. He never lifted a finger to steer the oar, never lifted his head to see the sky, and he never once could meet his brother's eyes.

He was giving up.

Not only had he lost a leg but it seemed he'd also lost the piece of his soul responsible for the motivation to keep on living. His light, one which had always overshadowed the overwhelming darkness, was now just a flicker; without that light, Demetrius was merely a stranger.

Jeom, on the other hand, took on so much guilt for their situation that Gabriel wasn't sure he had room to feel anything else in his heart right now.

He had started countless apologies to Demetrius during their first hours at sea, ceaseless explanations for what he had done with the Axe of Crissy; Gabriel tried to implore that the situation had been out of anyone's control, but Jeom wouldn't surrender to excuses.

"*They were my hands!*" he had screamed back at him, blood still upon his palms.

As the hours wore on, Jeom's apologies inevitably died away along with his voice. Instead of pleading for forgiveness, he threw all his remaining energy into rowing, pushing the boat faster toward a destination that no one was sure existed, no matter the weight of his exhaustion.

Phantom—the horse whose luck proved more profound than most—had also survived the attack on the beach. He created a barrier between the brothers, one on either side. But, like the boys of the boat, even Phantom's luck was running out; he hardly ever stirred.

Gabriel wasn't sure if any one of them could survive another day without sustenance.

They wished for rain, but it never came. And even if he had

the energy enough to somehow summon water using magic, he didn't know a spell to do it. The situation was dire at best.

Gabriel had even considered, more than once, making the hard decision and letting Phantom go to the fate of the sea for the sake of quicker travel…

He couldn't bring himself to do it, because of Demetrius—his hand never left the horse's side. Since day one on the sea, he stroked Phantom mindlessly, as if the action were the only thing in the world that kept his mind attached to his body.

What if it was?

The thought of taking something of comfort away from someone who had lost so much already made Gabriel sick; Demetrius couldn't afford to suffer another loss.

Gabriel put his focus on anything else, rowing faster to ensure they were still moving toward wherever Destiny had planned for them.

He glanced down to the compass; it lay safe on Demetrius' lap—it was the only thing that gave them any security at all on this desperate journey.

The arrow pointed steady toward the east.

At first, Jeom had insisted they follow the South Star, as his friends had done before in the desert.

Gabriel hadn't objected—it was familiar to them all.

However, each time they had tried to steer the boat in that direction, their course would always slowly yield toward the east.

Before long, they'd given up that losing fight.

Gabriel never let his eyes off the compass now, the golden arrow set in the sparkling stones of aura and ora hopefully leading them right to where they needed to be, its peculiar magic known to be one of guidance. Nevertheless, he couldn't help the hum in the back of his thoughts reminding him that magic had a mind all its own. There was no way of knowing where they traveled to now, or if they'd even make it to land before they died of thirst and starvation.

THE SKY WAS GROWING DARK, signaling the fourth night.

"I… I think I see land," said Gabriel, blinking his eyes to ensure he wasn't hallucinating. His voice barely came out, his throat feeling as if he'd swallowed all the salt in the sea. "Yes, I definitely see something. Look!"

It was the first time Demetrius had lifted his head in days, but Gabriel was just glad he could still move at all.

He watched, uncomfortably, as Demetrius and Jeom locked eyes, unable to avoid each other forever in such close proximity.

Demetrius glared with an intensity that could only be described as hatred. It was an unnatural expression for him, maybe one he'd never once shown before in his life.

Jeom looked away, not strong enough to take the weight of his brother's blame.

"You're right, I do see something," muttered Jeom, staring past Demetrius. "We have to find food and water. Then we can start to heal…" He spoke as if to himself.

"Not all wounds can be healed," said Demetrius with a certainty that made Gabriel shiver to his core; they were the first words he'd spoken since the incident.

Jeom froze for a moment, the glimmer of a tear wetting his cheek. Then he put every last ounce of energy into reaching whatever shore they'd discovered.

Gabriel followed his lead, and Demetrius just kept glaring.

Soon, what looked to be a city in the hills grew out of the darkness, the fires of civilization dotting the night like stars in the sky. As the boat met a bumpy shoreline, the flowery smell of nature enveloped them like welcome arms.

A wave of pure relief washed over Gabriel.

We can do this! We just need to find drinking water.

Jeom jumped out of the boat, water to his waist—he pulled

them all a safe distance up the shore. Once the boat was settled, he collapsed to the sand like an axed tree.

"Jeom!" called Gabriel.

Demetrius gasped. "Is he… dead?" he croaked out in shock, eyes rimmed red.

He tried to lift himself out of the boat, but he couldn't do it on his own, his body too heavy for him to maneuver now with only one leg.

Gabriel leaped out of the boat and ran to Jeom. He gently placed his head on his chest, feeling a faint heartbeat there.

"He's still alive but barely," said Gabriel, anxiety twisting his insides into knots; Demetrius was visibly relieved, but they weren't out of danger yet. "We need to find help, and fast, if he's going to make it."

"But… I can't—"

Demetrius choked on his words, glancing down to his lap.

"I'll go," said Gabriel with his best reassuring smile, even though all he felt was overwhelming fear.

Luck had not been on their side these past few days, and Jeom was nearer to his death than either of them could deny.

"You stay here with your brother, and I'll come back for you both."

Demetrius gave a faint nod—he knew he didn't have a choice.

He reluctantly opened his arms to let Gabriel help him out of the boat; it took every ounce of strength he had not to collapse himself as Demetrius leaned all his weight upon him, hobbling as best he could on one leg.

Gabriel sat him down near Jeom in the sand. Then he led Phantom out of the boat, positioning him next to the brothers.

"Protect each other," said Gabriel to Demetrius, clutching the compass tightly. "Don't worry. I'll take good care of this, and I know it will guide me straight back to you." He touched it to his lips, praying his words would ring true. "Just hang on."

"I wish you all the luck that is left to me," said Demetrius, before he set his eyes again on the sea.

Gabriel gathered the last morsels of his strength and tackled this new terrain.

Every step up the shore was a painful one, the black sand of their pasts replaced by a narrow strip of foreign, pink beach that quickly met a blanket of twisty trees.

When he passed the threshold of this new maze-like jungle, he took one last look to the beach where Jeom and Demetrius Kane—escaped slaves of the Four Corners and young Guardians of Gold—lay dying.

They were the family of the notorious Arianna Belvedor, the one who might save them all. And as a guardian who truly believed in her cause, it was his duty to ensure that her family, his newfound friends, would reach safety and be made whole again.

True to the memory of a fallen guardian and fellow agrarian, Tobias, who had introduced him to the honorable rebels of the world, Gabriel would try to make a difference by doing what was right... as best he could for as long as he could.

In this moment, that was reuniting the Kane brothers with Arianna and Lessa—he'd witnessed the gifts granted to the four in their quest to take down the King and his Shadow Resistance, and he knew that they would all need each other's support to have the best chance at saving the Olleb.

Just as he himself had been given a chance not so long ago by the Guardians of Gold, Jeom and Demetrius had long since proven they were part of something so much greater than just the typical path the King had laid out for everyone born under his rule; Gabriel refused to let this wretched voyage be their ending.

The ambush on the beach had exacted a terrible price for the guardians, the Greenhouse overtaken. And true, their South Lu-ose safe haven had also been compromised. But Gabriel knew these were just small battles part of a greater war on the horizon, so he would do everything in his power to ensure that the Kane brothers at least made it to the frontline of the final fight for freedom with all their wits about them.

These thoughts of courage resonated with him for a long while as he walked, following the compass.

They vanished under the haze of growing fear as the trees eventually thickened around him; it was clear now that the city they had spotted from the shore was likely hours more away, not nearby at all.

We don't have that much time left.

If he didn't make it back with provisions soon, they'd all surely die—him in the depths of the jungle and the Kane brothers by the sea.

The moon became blotted out by a canopy of trees overhead, so the only light was from the compass giving off a golden, magic-filled shine; he took a few more steps and felt the ground fall away beneath him.

He tumbled down a steep, muddy hill, landing hard at the bottom—the compass flew from his hand.

Gabriel could barely raise his head, but he laid eyes on the compass just a few inches ahead; the arrow appeared to be spinning about in a frenzy, no sense of direction at all.

A stab of fear paralyzed him further as the sound of leaves crunching underfoot reached his ears.

"Who's there?" he called, the words scratching against his dried throat.

As his eyes adjusted to the dark, he witnessed a pale hand reach down and take the compass.

"No, please. It's our only hope," said Gabriel, crawling forward with his last remaining energy.

He lifted his eyes to the face of a woman with bluish-silver hair and big, green eyes that twinkled like jewels; she knelt down to face him, Demetrius' compass in her hand.

"Who are you?" he said, gasping.

His vision started to blur as his mind fought for him to rest.

And the trees around him seemed to reach like giants toward the sky in a strange sensation, making him dizzier still.

"I am Diveena," she said in a smooth accent as she studied him intently. "I think it's time you closed your eyes."

"I can't," he stammered, thinking of Jeom and Demetrius. "*Please*, no. I have to help them. They'll die if I don't return with water."

She waved her hand across his eyes. "I said, sleep!"

She whispered something in a strange tongue that Gabriel could not understand. His gut told him it was magic.

Her enchantment sank into his mind, and he was unable to resist; the trees seemed to fall away into the blackness of the universe, taking him along for the journey.

"Please don't let us die," Gabriel murmured before finally closing his eyes.

SLAVE TO SOLOMON

ARIANNA JOLTED AWAKE to the vibrations of rock and earth churning over and over beneath her, crushed by the weight of wood and steel.

Thump, thump, thump.

The heavy, melodic sound of hooves from at least two trotting horses reached her ears, and the lash of a whip gave her chills every time the cord snapped against their pelts. The horses snorted against the pain, but they ran faster, obedient to their master's command—*her* former master, Solomon Bell.

She lay crumpled in the corner of a wooden carriage without bars, just wood all around.

The urge to incinerate the entire thing to ashes tickled her thoughts, but a splitting headache, made worse with the continuous bumping along on this uneven trail, didn't leave room for much focus.

Sunrays spilled into the wooden box sporadically through

cracks from somewhere up top, so she could at least see well enough.

Arianna shook her body awake and stretched her limbs, attempting to orient herself. She ached from being squished in the same position for too long, and beads of sweat had gathered uncomfortably on her skin.

Had it been hours? Days even? She had no idea how much time had passed, but even a short while was too long.

There was still a lot of work to be done.

Down with the King.

"Let me out," she murmured, pulling herself up toward the light, pressing her hands against the ceiling to try to peer through the cracks.

Her voice came out scratchy and weak, sounding just the same as her body felt.

She took deep, slow breaths to try to anchor herself to the here and now, dizzied still from the magical beating she'd endured. She pressed a shaking hand against the wall, trying with all her might to make her magic come, to obliterate this cage around her...

It wanted to, but it couldn't yield to her now; that piece of her mind felt locked away, suppressed by an unwelcome force that she was in no state to combat.

When there was no more use trying, her focus drifted over excruciating memories—they came back sharply with each inhale.

Lessa, Eli, Noah. Had the regulators done them in?

Jeom, Demetrius, Gabriel. Did the sea now claim their souls?

Master Tayshin, Cyn... the other guardians who were ambushed in Zambienth. Had the Shadow Resistance finished them off, as they had poor Talis and Tobias?

Arianna's dry eyes began to water slightly, and a choke caught in her throat at the thought of so many potential lost lives, building up on top of the ones that could no longer be saved.

The moments before she had been defeated in the battle of the Four Corners flashed through her mind next.

Solza... Forced to sever ties with her without even a goodbye.

Alive or dead? Arianna had no idea, but she felt the emptiness without her now.

It was painful, to be cruelly denied the endings of these stories she'd witnessed the start of. Not knowing about any of their fates was maybe even a worse agony than if Arianna was certain of their deaths, for it saved room for hope in a situation that seemed completely void of it.

However, there was one positive thing she did recall from that treacherous night, faint though it was—the golden dragon symbol of the guardians, shining bright through the blizzard. *Conjured by my friends, or by my imagination?*

It was hard for her to believe it had been real. Everything at the end was such a blur, but if there was any hope left at all for her to cling to, it was that dragon.

She sucked a breath in through her teeth at a sudden and unwelcome sensation—it felt as if someone was digging into her mind, spying on her fears.

I know the stink of your mind magic by now, she thought.

"Get out!" screamed Arianna.

She lifted her hands to her head, the wood panels vibrating all around her as some of her power seeped through the blockage.

It was only a dull shake and had taken every ounce of the energy she had left.

She slid back down to the floor, defeated; Solomon's magic-resistant precautions were infallible.

As she caught her breath, a flap toward the front clicked open. Sun drenched her cage, stinging her eyes.

"Ah!" she cried, shielding her face—she had to blink several times before noticing a barred space on the wall across from her.

"Save your energy," spoke Solomon. "You'll be needing it where we're going."

Just hearing his voice wrap around her made her feel ill.

She jumped back to her feet, head brushing the ceiling as she peered through the thick, steel bars so that she might lock eyes with him.

She wanted Solomon to feel her hatred, to see the promises of revenge written there in just one sharp look. With her fingers curled around the bars, she gently pressed her face against them, wishing to push her way through to the other side.

"I hope you rot in whatever darkened afterlife awaits fallen souls like yours," she whispered, wondering if her hand might fit through the small space to snap him dead.

"Tell me, child, what do you consider 'dark' compared to a world like this?" he asked with a sickening formality.

"I don't know," she replied. "But the world would certainly be a better place without monsters like you and the ones you serve."

Solomon spun around to meet her glare.

Arianna couldn't stop her rash confidence fleeing back to fear as she saw the magic flare up in his irises, like two dark cups filling to the brims with silver liquid.

She flinched on instinct, afraid at what might come next; she knew that look, the silvery stare of a master sorcerer with powerful magic just itching to discharge…

She knew because she experienced it the same.

But Solomon was too fast, too strong, too practiced. Arianna had already lost the battle with him, as she had lost every time before; she was in no position to challenge him now.

"It's time for you to go back to sleep," he commanded, the magic on his very breath entangling her like the heavy blanket of her district days.

There was nothing she could do but surrender to his will. In an enveloping wave, her body suddenly felt as heavy as stone.

She slumped back to the floor.

How many times had they done this dance before?

The only thing Arianna knew with any certainty was that this wasn't the first time she'd been drugged with sleeping spells on this wretched journey… she was starting to remember.

Each time she woke, she got a little stronger—stayed awake *just* a little longer.

She always tried to fight him, but every inch of her being, both physical and mental, seemed weighted down. Solomon's magic urged her to give in to her dreams and forget this world.

Yet, this time was different than the last; in the moments before her mind succumbed to his magic once more, Arianna had enough wit to grasp an idea that might save her.

"Sleep won't protect you forever," she muttered before her eyes shut tight—though, not before thinking three little words as she felt for her dagger, Aurora, still strapped securely at her thigh.

Solomon had not thought to remove it.

Sensorial depriva tempe.

THANKS TO MASTER TAYSHIN and his quick lesson in astral projection, her dagger *could* be the way out of this mess.

Arianna had long since mastered her dreams, and now she was equipped with the magic and knowledge to become part of her dream world at will. With the aid of the astral projection spell, the second her eyes had closed, her soul fled her body to search for help.

Somewhere in the night, she existed, but nobody knew she was there. Arianna was a ghost, a wandering spirit, a mere thought flickering from one plane to the next.

Aurora, the guardian relic Solomon had gifted her long ago, guided her along the way.

If she could keep control over her mind's urge to roam in the astral plane, maybe she could get a message to someone worthwhile. But it was a magic she had little practice with, and the mind was difficult to govern in an ethereal state, tempted to explore when liberated from the confines of a physical form.

Arianna hovered there for a moment, observing her sleeping self and wondering how long until she might wake this time. As she scanned her body, every cut and bruise she noted made her even more motivated to break free.

Floating through the bars and to the front of the carriage, she positioned herself next to Solomon, wanting to imagine him for what he was to her—*dead.*

She didn't have to stretch her imagination very far to picture him that way.

It had been a long time since she'd been this close to Solomon without holding a sword, but as she observed him now, there was a vacancy in his eyes that hadn't been there before, as if he were lost in his thoughts. So monotonous in his movements, like the tick of a clock, Solomon whipped the reins of the horses and blinked his eyes, nothing more to suggest he might be alive at all.

He seemed void of emotion, an empty shell of who she'd once known. *And they call you a great sorcerer?*

Arianna scoffed.

For all he was worth, Solomon didn't even know she was watching him now, did he?

Arianna wished for a solid body then, to be able to extend her hand and inflict harm on him, end him, and turn the carriage around in the direction of her friends…

It was a wish that didn't come true.

She could only observe him, contemplating her grim situation for a moment that seemed to stretch on for hours; in the astral plane, time felt different.

The thought that came next unshackled her from this cage of anger and worry. It had nothing to do with the distraction of revenge and everything to do with Lessa.

In her brief training about astral projection, Arianna had learned that an experienced practitioner only need think of who they wished to see or where they wanted to be in order to appear there…

Here goes nothing.

She closed her eyes, shouting out for Lessa loudly in her mind, confident that the magic of the aura and ora stones would guide her safely back to her body should she stray too far.

"Open your eyes," came a voice.

In a daze, she looked around expectantly.

"Lessa?"

All she saw was white—a glaring, empty, endless white.

"Lessa… are you there?"

She squinted, trying to see anything at all in this peculiar space.

Solomon was nowhere in sight, and the carriage and the road had vanished. The *world* had vanished, it seemed.

"You won't find her here—" came the voice again.

There was a slow *click, clack,* like shoes on tiled pavement.

An enormous, silver shadow in the shape of a man emerged in the distance.

The shadow raised its hand to the air and snapped its fingers; a deep echo resounded across the area, and with it came a wispy meadow of feathery, white plants, wiping away the nothingness.

Arianna stifled a scream as a boundless field of what she recognized to be snowflowers emerged all around her. They appeared to sprout from thin air and grew tall, touching a bright blue sky with a smiling sun that had surely not been there before.

"And you shouldn't be here either," added the shadow. "But since you are, go on and have a seat. We might as well take advantage of this gift while we've got it."

Arianna couldn't bring herself to speak as the shadow began to solidify into none other than her departed friend and former teacher, Master Talis Churry—the man who had marked the beginnings of her magical future.

He looked years younger than Arianna had ever known him to be. Gowned in cerulean robes that glistened like the ethereal sky above, Talis had the healthy glow of a young and happy man; it seemed the hard and heavy years that had come with a long life in Olleb-Yelfra as a secret Guardian of Gold and revered master of healing had been stripped away in death.

Arianna ran to him without hesitation, hugging him tightly around the waist.

He laughed as he welcomed the embrace.

"I thought…" she stuttered, her words muffled in his silky robes, not able to quite comprehend this moment.

"I know," said Talis, finding her eyes. His twinkled with more wisdom than ever before, and Arianna was sure he had all the answers there that she needed. "I was thinking about Lessa too. Our minds must've connected when you were crossing realms. Funny how the mind and magic work, isn't it?"

He guided her to two cushiony seats which had materialized among the field of flowers.

"Not even the grandest masters have the answers for everything," he added, as if reading her thoughts.

Arianna was certain that he did and always had.

"Are you quite sure of that, Master Churry?"

He smirked. "Sit, won't you? Let's have a chat."

Obedient, Arianna sat down.

She realized only then, feeling the softness of the cushions beneath her, that in this realm she somehow had a physical form—she could feel everything, as if she were back in her own body.

Though something felt off… like it wasn't exactly real.

"What is this place?" she asked, gazing around in awe.

The wide-open sky was a welcome warmth compared to her cold reality, and the soft sway of the snowflowers surrounding them gave her much joy as she recalled the first time she'd ever laid eyes on such exquisite nature—the day she'd escaped the Vanishing Tunnels and taken her freedom.

"Don't you recognize it?" said Talis with a knowing smile, twisting his pearly beard around his finger. "Rumor has it, you've been here once or twice before."

She blinked—Talis was suddenly sipping out of a cup of steaming tea that scented the air around them.

He raised an eyebrow at her, but she just shook her head.

Just like the time he had danced around her questions of what had brought her back to life after the ill-fated Warrior's Challenge with Grinda Risso, Arianna was utterly bewildered; even in this miraculous, unbelievable moment, she wanted to shout at him to be straight with it.

"Child, this is the afterlife," he finally said with a sigh, taking another sip of his tea and crossing his legs. "Close your eyes and see."

Arianna's mouth dropped open to form an 'O', but no sound came out. She sucked in a deep breath, letting her eyes close.

A warm energy rippled all around her, changing with her every thought and feeling. It was as if she had suddenly been transported back through time—Arianna could sense the path she had once followed when this so-called 'afterlife' had almost claimed her soul.

"I see now," she said in a gasp, her other senses heightened.

Maybe it could be depicted as a sea of darkness with only a tinge of light, tempting those to chase it or taunting those forever stuck. Or maybe, it could be an endless field of snowflowers on a sunny day...

She understood it perfectly now. This *was* the afterlife—and it could be everything or nothing at all.

Talis' spirit in the afterlife had manifested in the form of this field of flowers, but with her eyes shut, Arianna recognized this realm in a way that mere sight could not possibly comprehend.

She sensed Talis with her there now, just as she had once sensed Liam Black there with her once before.

"Why snowflowers?" she whispered as she let this inexplicable, exhilarating feeling wrap around her very being.

"It all lies within," he said, his voice an echo. "One's soul creates the truest portrayal of what death means for them, so the afterlife is unique to us all. When the body is stripped away forever and all that remains is the mind, there's no hiding from the truth of who you really are… or *were*. The afterlife is a reflection of that truth, so, depending on the soul in question and the life they chose to lead, it can be full of light or full of horrors."

"Then the afterlife is lucky to have gained such a noble soul as yours," said Arianna. "But you still haven't answered my question, Master Churry."

Talis plucked a petal from one of the flowers and squeezed it in his palm.

"They remind me of Lessa and our time spent together in the Jar," he said with such affection. "She was a resilient, bright presence in the coldest of places, a memory I'll always cherish."

Arianna opened her eyes—tears fell, even if they weren't technically real. "I think that's very fitting, sir."

Talis considered her with a solemn look; there was so much to be said and such little time.

Arianna knew there was a limit on this moment, that her visit to the afterlife was short, so she worked up the courage to truly face the man before her.

"It isn't fair," she blurted out. "Master Churry, I'm so sorry we couldn't save you. That was no way to die." She bowed her head. "I'm sorry you had to die—"

"That was a *fine* way to die, child," said Talis. "My time was well up in that life, and I didn't linger because I had fulfilled my purpose. My destiny was to see you girls as far as I could in your journey and help to secure the future for all those left to live it. I'm prouder of you and Lessa than I could possibly tell you with words, and I'm with you every step of the way. We all are." She looked up to face him, his expression pained with a mix of hope and concern. "We're always with you, watching closely at how this might end."

"He speaks a truth," said a deep voice from behind her.

Arianna was almost too stunned to turn around. When she did, she found a rare and warm smile on the face of Keeper Kassime.

She gasped. "You too?"

"Me too." He gave her a strong hug that she wasn't expecting—the first they might have ever exchanged, she thought.

"But... why this face?" she asked, confused. "Why not show your true face? Why not the face of Ferlon Ragaric?"

He sighed, studying her for a moment.

"I am and always will be both Ferlon Ragaric *and* Helix Kassime. My mask, the mask of the keeper, became a permanent one in the end, after so much time. You know this... you understand."

He placed a hand on her shoulder.

"Just as all you've learned and lived as Aridyn will always reside in your heart. Our pasts reflect who we are; they cannot be erased and they cannot be changed. The afterlife is sure testimony to that."

Talis nodded. His teacup vanished.

"All your experiences, good or bad, are equally precious, Arianna," he added. "They will decide your future, even after death. Remember that."

Keeper Kassime pressed the tips of his fingers together, glancing to Talis. "I also chose to show you this face now because I know it's one you'll trust. No more time can be wasted on formalities. We have a very important message to relay."

Arianna saw they shared a strong connection as she looked back and forth between the two guardian masters. Only now did she remember that Keeper Kassime and Talis had been friends in a past life she was too young to have witnessed, and suddenly she found herself very glad they had found each other again—death didn't have to be journeyed alone.

"Well, what is it?" said Arianna, trying to hide her nervousness.

"You *must* reunite with the ones whom you trust most," said Talis, clearly searching for the right words. "If you're careful, if you do not stray, your road will lead you there."

"And the ones who you don't yet trust," added Kassime, "you must at times find the strength to. Just as you did with me." He had a serious look on his face now that Arianna recognized better than his smile. "Your life and the lives of so many others depend on your courage and faith, so don't let your fears cloud your judgment."

"But how do I do that?" said Arianna.

They both remained tight-lipped.

"Why must everything be a leap of faith?" she said with a howl of frustration. "Can't you just tell me straight for once what exactly it is that I'm supposed to do? How can I get back to my friends?"

Both men chuckled.

"Was she really *this* thick-headed when we sent her on to you?" asked Talis.

"Worse," said Kassime with a sly grin. "We had our ups and downs… didn't we?"

Arianna tried to hold the laughter behind her teeth.

"You could say that," she said, shaking her head at the memories; there were times she used to think she despised him, and now those moments seemed so trivial in the scheme of things.

"I only ever meant to keep you safe," said Kassime, earnestly. *Can they read my mind here?* "Sometimes, it's only in the end when the truth can be revealed."

A tear rolled down her cheek as she thought of how Keeper Kassime had given his life to protect her and her friends, a man she wasn't sure she even liked for most of their time together.

"Promise me you'll remember that for the future."

Arianna nodded.

"Freedom and *faith* are why we fight," said Talis. "Faith in a world that once was and could be again. Believing in yourself and opening your heart to trust, even when it's difficult, is the only way we can take back what's been denied to us all. I remember when Solomon had to remind me of that too."

"I know," she said, looking at her feet. "I wouldn't be here if he hadn't."

"I didn't quite realize it until the final moments of my life," said Kassime, "but my faith does lie with you and your friends, Arianna." He brought his fist to his chest. "You're the dragons I've been waiting for, wishing for. You've awakened the guardians now, and we will not sleep again until this war is won. But we must stick together."

He grabbed her hand, forcing her to look at him.

"You *cannot* do this alone. Not until you're ready."

He maneuvered her hand so that the golden guardian mark was face up—the faint, shimmering lines of a dragon curled in her palm. Then he pressed her hand into a fist with a reassuring squeeze, his eyes settling on hers with gravity.

Arianna contemplated both the brave, lost men standing before her with a heavy heart.

"I hope you're right to put your faith in us," she said. "It's only because of the time and strength you bestowed on us that we're even still standing. You both gave your lives to see my friends and I through."

She held her head high, but she felt the threat of more tears coming.

"I... I only wish you could be here now to guide us. I fear we've failed you. How will I reunite with them again?" She turned her attention to Keeper Kassime. "I *know* I can't do this alone, but I'm lost now. And we're running out of time. I can feel it."

"You mustn't let such dark thoughts consume you," said Talis. "Things may seem broken now, but only through the shattered glass can you see the pieces that were truly meant to be."

"We died for what we believed in," added Kassime. "That's you, and the fate of Olleb-Yelfra returning to something good and strong. Heal her and let the scars of loss serve as a reminder for all—"

He grabbed Arianna by the shoulders.

"Your friends need you now more than ever, and you need them," he implored. "Find them before the King or his Shadow Resistance do. You must reunite. If you try to finish this alone, you *will* fail, with or without your life."

Arianna already knew that the success of this quest had nothing to do with whether she lived or died but, rather, whether the Olleb did. Though, hearing it all from the mouths of two very wise guardian ghosts put everything in an entirely new perspective.

"Kassime..." said Talis with a worried expression.

Keeper Kassime pursed his lips and gave a short nod, letting her go. "I believe in you, Arianna," he said. "We all do."

"We're out of time now," said Talis, grasping Arianna's hand.

The flowery setting began to break apart at the seams as if a pounding wind sought to obliterate it all.

"But there's one last thing..." His voice was nearly drowned out by the sudden chaos. "If fate allows it, find a woman named Diveena," he yelled. "She can help you the rest of the way."

"Where can I find her?" Arianna shouted back, hardly able to see through her hair whipping about her face. She could barely keep her feet on the ground and felt as if her body might lift off at any moment.

"You must trust in those whom you don't yet trust," said Kassime again. "That is all we can say. Then, and only then, will you be guided in the right direction."

"Diveena can only be found if she wishes to be," added Talis, at Kassime's reluctance. "But I daresay that she's ready to come out of hiding. The whole world is ready."

"I'll do my best," said Arianna, tasting the salt of her own tears.

"I know you will," said Talis. "And you take care of our girl now, you hear?"

"On my life, sir. I promise," she replied. "I wish you both only peace now."

"And, Arianna," said Kassime, grasping her other hand—their grips were the only thing keeping her from flying away at this point, "I might not have showed it, but you and your friends have made me so proud. You're the greatest guardians we could have ever asked for. Bring us home now."

She felt their hands slip away, and Keeper Kassime and Talis waved their goodbyes. They faded into the background as the snowflower setting melted back into the glaring white void, taking the fallen guardians with it; a part of her wondered if there wasn't even a higher power keeping them from giving her more guidance.

I cannot do this alone.

Arianna screamed out for them to return, but her voice was lost as her astral body was sucked back into the oblivion from which she'd come.

When she opened her eyes, Solomon was standing over her.

"Do you think I'm stupid?" he spat as she came to, pulling her up by her tresses.

Arianna reached for her dagger, but he had slipped it away from her.

"Who were you talking to? Who did you see on your little adventure just now?" he screamed.

"Nothing and no one," she retorted. "Give me my dagger!"

He looked at the weapon with a sardonic smile. "I believe this belongs to me, so I think not."

"Not anymore," said Arianna, lunging for it.

In one quick move, Solomon had the starry black blade to her throat, as if it were any other day in training, another duel she'd lost. This time, though, she wasn't sure if he would stop the blade before irreplaceable blood was drawn.

"I gave this to you because you had earned it," said Solomon. "That was in another lifetime… look at you now. Do you think you deserve this? Do you think you deserve to stand as a Guardian of Gold? To *fall* like one?" He shook his head. "I'm not sure at all anymore that you're worthy of such an honor. You haven't even discovered the dagger's truest gift yet, have you?"

Her lips pressed into a tight line—she had not.

Arianna knew all guardian relics concealed unique talents, in addition to their ability to assist in astral projection. *What else could Aurora do?*

"That's what I thought," said Solomon, spinning her around to face him.

Arianna could only describe his expression as pity.

"You're still so weak and naïve to the truth around you. How could you help anyone if you can't even help yourself?"

She felt for a moment as if she'd failed the Solomon she had once known to be true and good from her past. For, in that flicker of an instant, she thought she saw him there—truly disappointed.

Her thoughts lingered over their first encounter.

'*I chose you because you are worth choosing,*' he had said on the day he'd named her his unlikely apprentice and gifted her that priceless weapon.

But chosen for what? She *still* wanted for the answer.

"Master Bell—" She forced the words from her mouth as he glared down at her, the winged-pommel of what she now knew to be a dragon grasped tightly in his unwavering grip, the cool stone of the blade making her skin sweat. "—why did you choose me then?" she asked in all seriousness. "For *this?* For death by your hand or by the King's?"

The distant look she thought she had recognized vanished instantly as Solomon shoved her back down; she was flush against the floor, tasting the wood of the carriage, her hair and robes a tangled mess around her.

"Seeing you for what you are now, I really can't remember."

He slammed the door to her cage.

The sun set soon thereafter, darkness stitching to the air—only the steady beat of hooves on the ground let Arianna know she was still one with the earth and not a floating body on another plane.

In her solitude, she forced her mind to reaffirm over and over what was strong in her heart…

I am worth choosing, and I know my destiny. Never forget.

As the hours dragged on, though Solomon's suppressive magic wrapped around her so tight that she could not tangibly conjure her own, the silver shine in her eyes lit the wooden box like a glowing spirit trapped inside her—she knew it would be ready when she called to it in her greatest need, as it always had been, even before she had known what 'magic' was.

More reassuring still, the mighty soul of the star remained safely in her possession, the nearly invisible chain of beach crystals never giving it away; it pulsed warm against her chest with an untapped magic all its own, something that no necromancer, tyrant king, nor two-faced wolf could ever tame.

It was *her* magic and hers alone.

As Arianna clung to new hopes and the conviction in her choices that had already gotten her so very far, she now thought of only one thing… *Find Diveena, and trust no one.*

DRIFTING

SOLOMON DIDN'T BOTHER TO FORCE her to sleep anymore. It was much less draining on his energy to just let her be. Arianna was weak without magic and without the escape of her dreams, so torturing her with the loneliness of confinement proved the most effective punishment.

Having to pass the days consciously was at times unbearable for her; Solomon had ensured she could no longer astral project, though some nights she wished she would never wake from her sleep just to avoid the agony of doing nothing for hours on end. Time moved slowly as she wasted away as his prisoner, yet she knew the horse-drawn carriage barreled faster toward their destination every day.

Arianna made empty wishes for time to *truly* slow, stop even, just to give her a chance at escape before the Palace of Saindora inevitably rose into view. And with nothing for distraction but her own imagination, she wondered what she might do if she did have such grand powers as to control time.

Would she go back to some past moment to save a friend? Or skip through this monotonous chapter of her life to see what might be waiting on the other end? Would she have done things differently, if she were given the chance?

But no matter what story her mind painted of what could be or could've been, Arianna always came back around to the hard truth that *none* of it mattered. The only thing that did matter was the here and now—and it was brutal.

It had been weeks since they'd left the City of the Four Corners, and anything could have happened to her friends since that dreadful night. Their fates were as far out of her control as her own.

After Solomon stopped drugging her with magic, she began to track the days, marking a small scratch in the wood each time she woke; there were many scratches now. Twenty-seven to be exact.

The carriage only stopped out of necessity, Solomon escorting Arianna with a sword at her back anytime he let her out; those sparse moments to stretch her legs and breathe fresh air were the only thing keeping her sane.

From the cage to the bushes and back—she relished every footfall that churned her blood and worked her weakened muscles. It helped her solidify where she was in time.

It had been cold at the beginning of their journey, but the sun grew hotter every day. At first, there had been a bitter familiarity as they traveled on paths she had long ago braved with her friends at her side. Then the air had started to swelter, the scenery shifting into such that she'd never seen before.

There's still so much of the world left to uncover...

Arianna had now unearthed more of Olleb-Yelfra with Solomon as her guide than she had over the last couple years with her friends. She had witnessed sprawling cities across dry and wet lands, rolling hills of green, and forests sprouting tall from beds of flowers that stretched farther than she could see. Mountainous cliffs had enclosed their paths at one point before the land again flattened, and each village they passed through had a character all its own.

The Black Sand Desert had made a reappearance once or twice during their travels—Arianna swore she'd heard the seductive whispers of the fairies again when the carriage drew too near.

There were even times that the Sea of Saindora came into view, raging and roaring against the land as they followed a winding trail along its shore; the trail seemed to reach, uninterrupted, all the way from the north to the south of the Olleb.

Arianna longed to meet those waters, to again explore that sea of wonders. She longed for *anything* but her current situation, not to experience this beautiful world again as a slave.

Her mind drifted to Eli more than once in her solitude.

He'd spent a year of his life in the darkness of the South Luose Dungeon, alone.

Arianna had thought she'd been empathetic to his suffering. She and Lessa had worked hard to help him heal…

Now, after enduring even a taste of what he'd gone through—isolated for so long, without even a need to use her voice—she realized she had not understood even a fraction of his pain.

Arianna had never really understood him at all.

In the months that followed his rescue, Eli had confronted her so many times, trying to get her to open back up to him; these moments seemed so inconsequential to her then. She was focused only on a future of freedom.

But in her loneliness now, they were cast in a new light.

Eli had been incredibly strong to have survived life in the dungeons for as long as he did. And to make room for such vulnerabilities as asking for forgiveness and love proved him a stronger man still.

She had urged Eli to set aside his feelings for the good of the war to come, but he'd refused, pledging his allegiance to her regardless.

What a perfect fool I was to dismiss him.

She'd never quite understood his choices, thought he couldn't possibly comprehend what she'd suffered or what it was she *really* fought for. But with nothing to do now but contemplate each and every memory of that man, she saw how selfish she'd been—to ever think that her pain was greater than his, or anyone's...

How could it be when people experienced life uniquely?

Eli was right all along.

Just like Keeper Kassime and Talis had reaffirmed in the astral plane, hope, faith, forgiveness, and love all went hand in hand— *this* is what she was ultimately trying to secure in this battle toward freedom.

Arianna searched the sky through the broken ceiling of her cage, toying with the stone of her necklace. On the clearest nights, the stars would pour in and soak her in twinkling, soft light; warm thoughts of her friends wrapped around her.

This night, the South Star graced her with its presence, its light so bright that it shone through the cracks in the wood, and through the cracks in her courage. As its light danced around the small space, it met with the soul of the star.

A beautiful reflection surrounded her, dousing the cage in a rainbow of colors as the light refracted around the space. She thought that if the stars could speak through their dazzling display in the dark, they must be saying that everything would turn out all right in the end.

Arianna twisted the impeccable stone between her fingers, making the light twirl in different directions. Her mind wandered with it, over the possibilities—she still had one wish left.

Wish for an escape? Wish for the safety of her friends? Wish for the Four Corners to come together?

There were so many hopes in her heart that she thought for

each tiny star in the sky, she could find something significant to plead for.

She trusted that the soul of the star understood her truest desires, so she didn't wish for anything at all... she knew it wasn't time yet.

No matter the wishes and wants in her mind or on her tongue, her heart had absolute control in the end. Its beat was normally so strong, distinct in its rhythm.

'Don't be brave, little slave. Be a warrior.'

But with the heavy shadows that Solomon had stitched around her, the song was slowly starting to diminish; she couldn't understand her heart now.

The only thing she was certain of was that she wished King Devlindor no longer existed.

She looked down at the necklace, sensing its response.

If only it were that easy...

Arianna knew that this bright star soul, a warrior fallen from the skies, could not defeat the Olleb's greatest enemy; only a warrior of flesh could stand against the King.

She used to be able to imagine herself as the one who might deliver the final blow, but those thoughts felt like such a fantasy now with four walls imprisoning her again.

As the South Star drew closer on their travels, its light brighter than ever before, Arianna knew they were nearing the City of Saindora, nearing the King's lair.

She touched the stone to her lips before drifting to sleep under the watch of the sky, praying for peace of mind in her dreams; she would save her last wish until her life was again truly in jeopardy, a time that would surely come soon enough. This her heart had decided assuredly.

AFTER NEARLY FORTY DAYS AND NIGHTS traveling across the many terrains of the Olleb, the air had grown permanently muggy and worries of snow and cold were a distant past.

Arianna took to practicing the meditation exercises she'd learned from Solomon back in their Warrior's District days, trying to pass the time with her sanity intact. On this evening, as she sat cross-legged in deep concentration, sweat dotting her forehead, the carriage came to a screeching halt.

She tossed forward, rolling onto her hands and knees as the horses cried out.

"Whoa, now," she heard Solomon say to try to calm them.

"What was that?" she shrieked.

Arianna got to her feet, peering through the bars at the front. She saw what appeared to be a tree blocking their path.

Solomon got down from the rider's seat to inspect it, weapon drawn.

Arianna narrowed her gaze. *I miss my swords.*

"That tree was placed there deliberately," he called back to her. "Probably rogue drifters looking to rob the wrong carriage. They've been rampant in these parts the last few years."

His voice grew louder.

"Who goes there? Make yourselves known at once!"

Eli was the only drifter Arianna had ever met, but she wouldn't have considered him 'rogue' nor decidedly 'dangerous' upon first impression; he was well-liked throughout the neighboring cities to South Luose, always paying his dues and working hard to afford his travels.

Later she'd learned that this unrestrained lifestyle was scarce among citizens. Most drifters did not 'drift' by choice to pursue dreams of exploration...

More often than not, those with such labels had been forced to leave their placements and took to breaking the King's laws to get by. There were special places in the dungeons across the Olleb for them—most weren't known to drift too long before getting caught by a regulator for doing something wrong.

They weren't widely tolerated in the cities, so it made perfect sense that they'd take to the outskirts, banding together away from prying eyes or persecution. But every speck of land in Olleb-Yelfra was governed by the King, his laws, and his punishments.

"My, my, *my*," came the shallow voice of a man. He slunk out from the trees and onto the path. "All alone, are we? Now is that anyway to greet a friendly wanderer?"

The man gave a slight curtsy and then swiftly moved to the side—archers aimed at Solomon from the cover of the bushes.

He ducked to safety behind the carriage just as they let their arrows fly.

Arianna followed his lead, dropping to the floor; several of the arrows landed in the wood, but one flew straight through the bars, barely missing her head.

The shrieks of the horses told her they'd not been so lucky.

"Damn it, you idiots! You hit the horses," barked the man. "Better hope they have something worth trading stashed away."

Arianna stood back up with caution, peering again through the bars to watch.

Solomon was crouched near the fallen horses—he put them out of their misery in one swift swing of his sword.

"Show us what you got in the carriage, old man. Let's make this quick," said a woman with a nasty scowl.

She was twisting a rusted, curved blade by her side as she joined the man in the open. Her hair was twisted up into several balls on the top of her head, and she wore rags that left most of her scarred skin uncovered.

"I suggest you all get back to whatever hole you crawled out of," said Solomon. "I'm in no mood to teach tonight."

He stood to face them, and the rest of the gang started to creep out of hiding.

"What you mean, teach?" growled a lanky young man with sallow skin. "We'll teach *you* something."

He dashed toward Solomon with his weapon raised.

Arianna didn't have to see much to predict the young man's swift ending.

There was a snap—the neck she was sure—and the sound of a body hitting the ground.

There was a collective gasp, and then all weapons were drawn.

Solomon remained silent, moving closer toward the carriage.

"Myron!" The woman went to inspect the young man. "He's dead, Chief," she said.

Arianna kept her eyes glued to the danger unfolding, trying to see as much as she could. More and more drifters, all dressed in similar shabby clothing, crept out from behind the trees and the shadows, some lighting up torches to make themselves known.

She counted the number of people that had gathered against them. *Incredible...*

No matter how far the King's reach, there would always be someone willing to challenge his law—it was human nature, this constant struggle for power and life. If a person had to choose between death and breaking the rules to survive, they'd burn the rules to the ground in a heartbeat.

Arianna was proof of that, and so were they.

Even if they battled each other now, ultimately they all shared the same enemy.

She imagined the innocent people these drifters had probably murdered just to get by, but could she blame them? In a world that would just as quickly purge them, forcing them to scrounge for their lives by looting what others had rightfully earned, could she hold them responsible? *No, but everyone has a choice.*

Even drifters—they had a choice of the type of person they turned out to be in the end.

Arianna couldn't blame them, but she couldn't respect them either.

"You killed one of our own!" said the man who had been

dubbed the leader of this misfit group.

"He meant to kill me," said Solomon with an even voice. "Do you mean to kill me too?"

The man puffed out his chest, clearly offended at being challenged in front of his people… though too scared to attack after poor Myron's utter failure.

"We said, show us what you got," he replied, flaunting his weapon. "If it's worth our time, *maybe* we'll spare you."

"So be it," said Solomon. "But I warn you, it's nothing to lose your head over." He walked around to the back of the carriage.

Arianna knew he was just buying time, too many of them to outmaneuver without, at least, a little thought.

However, she'd also heard the smile in Solomon's voice when he spoke; she felt sorry for the inevitable fate of this group.

They had no idea about the sleeping beast they were poking.

"Out you go, then," said Solomon.

He swung open the door to Arianna's cage and offered his hand, a tight smile on his face.

She glared back at him from the depth of her box, and his smile tightened even more, his gaze narrowing—she knew that look for certain.

It was his 'do-exactly-as-I-say' look she'd seen enough times during training in the districts. And it was a look she would have never before disobeyed.

But this was not a practice duel. It was real life, and they were no longer friends.

The voices of Talis and Keeper Kassime rang out loud in her mind as Solomon's palm lay open for her to take. For a moment, Arianna wondered if she had lost her senses completely after being cooped up for so long—or did they actually speak to her now?

It's just a memory.

But it was pulling her attention for a reason.

She tried to untangle what had been their last piece of wisdom to her. *'…trust, even when it's difficult.'*

She sighed, pushing herself off the wall.

While there was no ounce of will left in her to trust Solomon Bell in the slightest, Arianna would again obey her former master, if only to get out of this alive.

A shudder coursed through her body as she grasped his hand, Solomon's cold fingers wrapping around her own.

He helped her down from the carriage, bound her hands behind her back with rope, and escorted her into the open.

They stood on a white, pebbly path that glared under the soft moonlight; more than fifty drifters joined them, surrounding them from all sides.

Despite the danger, Arianna couldn't help but take notice of this new setting—things were jarringly different than when she'd last stepped foot outside.

Spiky bushes and skinny trees with curly leaves decorated the vicinity, and tall, mossy cliffs grew up from the ground, locking them in. This forest seemed to grow only wilder in every direction, but she was sure that the land met the sea again somewhere nearby, if there was any pattern to this journey at all.

"Well, look at what we got here. A prisoner?" A woman whistled. "Someone's in trouble, I'd say."

Arianna kept her head down and her hood up; they started circling her and Solomon.

"Check the carriage," commanded the leader.

"I'll do it," said another eager young man, scrambling around back to inspect it. He returned almost immediately. "Nothing here, Chief."

He sat down on the edge of the carriage, dangling his feet.

"Rumi, check up front," he ordered to the woman by his side. "There's got to be something!"

She hopped into the rider's seating area and began rummaging through Solomon's things—Arianna felt his muscles tense, one hand squeezing her tightly on the shoulder.

Still, he kept quiet.

"Jackpot," screeched Rumi. The sound of metal clanging together filled the charged silence of the night. "These swords got to be worth a fortune, Chief. And this dagger… I've never seen anything like it. Gold too! Enough to keep us for a *long* time, I'd wager."

Arianna went rigid with anger, hardly able to cool the blood beginning to boil beneath her skin.

Solomon gave her another squeeze on the shoulder; he wanted her to keep calm. He had a plan up his sleeve, like always. But those were *her* prized possessions on the line…

She took a deep breath in through her nose—when she exhaled, she was sure that it would appear as steam for how fired up she felt on the inside.

"I think you ought to see this, Chief," said Rumi. Her voice quivered slightly. "This here… this is the King's Crest."

She jumped down with her findings, and Arianna's eyes followed the silver sheen of her swords and the glint of Aurora all the way to the chief's dirty hands; she clenched her teeth together and took another deep breath.

Solomon's old, bronze swords were tossed to the side, but Rumi handed over his cloak—a fine, black-threaded robe with the golden snake coiling all the way from the hood to the bottom hem.

The chief quieted the curious hum of his followers; this pattern was a known costume of the King's Guard.

"Who did you say you were?" asked the chief, turning more serious. His voice pitched a little as he sized Solomon up, his sword at the ready.

"I didn't," said Solomon, a threat building there. "Why don't you ask?"

He squared his shoulders but took a step back. "You part of the King's Guard?"

Solomon offered a slight nod.

"Very good," he said in a soft yet savage voice. "General Solomon Bell, pleased to make your acquaintance."

The chief sucked in a hiss through his teeth, like he'd pinched himself hard to try to wake up from a nightmare—the words 'Wolf of the East' followed in frightened whispers from the bystanders.

"Ah, so you have heard of me, then?" Solomon chuckled, cocking his head to the side. "So what'll it be, Chief?"

"Maybe we ought to let them go," called someone from farther back. "He's got a record, that one. He's got a long list of kills."

"Quiet!" snapped the chief. "We've got him sorely outnumbered *and* hold all his weapons."

He looked Solomon up and down with a smirk, but his uncertainty was palpable.

"He ain't no threat to nobody." He turned his back to Solomon, waving his sword wildly in the air to try to rally his people. Then he looked back at him over his shoulder and spat in his face. "You ain't no wolf anymore. Just a dead dog in the making, aren't you?"

Arianna's mouth fell open. Solomon used his free hand to wipe it off.

Not even the gods' mercy will save that man now…

"Maybe you should listen to your friends," growled Solomon. He took a slight step forward, Arianna forced to follow. "I'd hate for you to catch my bite."

The chief lifted his sword in Solomon's direction, his blade quivering.

"You would just as soon kill us, or have your regulators sweep the woods for us drifters if I let you go." He tried to sound strong, but his façade was crumbling fast.

Solomon took another step forward, and the chief, unsteadily, took three steps back.

"We're just trash to you highlifes, but you're in my territory now, Bell, and ain't nobody even knows you're here."

He turned to his people, pleading for them to fight.

"We let him go, he comes after us. If we do him off, we ensure our safety. That's the best option!"

Arianna heard hooting from the young man now dancing obnoxiously in front of her former cage, and scattered claps of encouragement sounded from the surrounding party.

Though, not everyone looked so confident.

"I assure you, it is not," said Solomon, firmly. "My business isn't with you. If you let us go now and return to us our belongings without resistance, I promise, in the name of the High King, I will not harm you nor anyone else here. And I'll not come for you later." He put his free hand out for the chief to take. "We'll part ways as equals."

The chief looked at his hand, an eyebrow raised as he considered the offer.

"Promises from the King's pet ain't worth much to me!" he said after a moment. "But you know what is?" He glanced to Rumi—she was turning Aurora over in her hands with hunger in her eyes. "Gold, silver, and *steel*."

He turned his sword on Arianna.

"What's your business with this one now?"

Solomon let out a sigh of frustration, his grip tightening on her shoulder.

"Just a citizen who needs reckoning with," said Solomon, growing impatient.

He moved his hand to her neck to show force; Arianna bent her head lower, curls tumbling over her face.

"We could use another citizen fallen from grace in our crew," mused the chief, forgetting his fear and growing cockier by the second. "Or... a prisoner of our own, perhaps."

His followers spoke their support, and Arianna could feel his beady eyes on her, searching.

"Let me see your face, wench," he barked. "Are you worth

saving or enslaving?"

Arianna couldn't help herself, even though the press of Solomon's hand urged her to be discreet. She lifted her head and locked eyes with the chief.

"I'm not the one who needs saving here," she said. She turned her gaze on Solomon. "And I'm *nobody's* slave anymore."

Solomon gave up trying to hide her face from them, and her hood fell down. She took a deep, energizing breath, the wind caressing her cheeks and sweeping the hair away from her eyes.

Just try me. She was dying to get back into practice, and these fools would do just fine.

"You look damn familiar," said the chief, taken aback.

"Why, I don't believe it… that's Arianna Belvedor," shouted the young man by the carriage. "I thought those were just rumors, but that's got to be her. *That's* the slave who they say escaped from the Jar!"

There were excited gasps from the gathering.

"By the gods, he's right," said Rumi, looking up from her pile of stolen treasures. "If that's really the Belvedor slave, her head is worth the highlife reward… *and* immunity!" She pointed a condemning finger toward Arianna. "That would change everything for us."

"You don't say?" said the chief, looking her over with new interest. An unseemly grin spread across his cracked lips. "What did that poster say again? Dead or alive?"

"They don't be complaining much when they're dead," said another girl, nudging Myron in the leg.

"You're quite right," said the chief, twisting the hair at his chin as he thought. "Quite right, my friend." He opened his arms wide, as if he had a grand announcement to make. "Ladies, fellas… our luck just turned right-side up. We won't be hiding for too much longer, I daresay."

He advanced, spinning his sword in his hand—the drifters began closing in behind him.

"What's your plan now, *Master?*" whispered Arianna, growing anxious as so many greedy eyes narrowed in her direction.

Solomon placed his hand on her back; it was unnaturally warm, but she didn't pull away.

The magical force he'd sewn around her, which kept her powers at bay, fell off her like chains being broken. His magic began to surge within her, as if stirring awake her own sleeping powers. She felt as if Solza were somewhere nearby, sending a much-needed energy boost.

I wish it were you and not him, she thought.

But magic was magic, no matter its source, and hers was accessible again.

Arianna inhaled deeply, her powers coursing anew through her veins, free and unhindered; the ropes at her hands burned away with her next exhale, singed to ashes with a fire that had been dying to get out. The only weapon she needed lay within.

The drifters fell silent, coming to a halt as they looked upon her—she knew they saw the bright silver filling her eyes.

"You're right to be afraid," she whispered, glaring back at them.

"Kill her!" said the chief, fear shadowing his expression. "And the wolf too!"

The drifters rushed forward, weapons raised.

Solomon used his magic to call for his unguarded swords and tossed one to Arianna, splitting up the pair; for the first time in a long time, they battled together as one.

The weapon of her childhood felt heavy but comfortable in her hand, like a familiar friend. She tore through her opponents with ease. And with Solomon at her back, Arianna couldn't help the overwhelming feeling of happiness that took over—it was easy to pretend that they were on the same side once again… to pretend this was not the present but the past.

But she knew better than to let nostalgia overwhelm her completely. She *was* Solomon's prisoner—adversary—and after the torture he'd put her through, she could never forget it.

She tried to get as far away from Solomon as possible during the battle, setting her focus on Rumi; the drifters were focused on Solomon, and Rumi was greedily clinging to Aurora and the stash of riches she'd acquired from the carriage.

Arianna slipped away from the onslaught, leaving Solomon behind on the path. She tracked Rumi into the outskirts of the trees.

She hadn't even needed to release her magic yet, relishing the movement of her body as she dodged attack after attack with her sword. But when Rumi lunged at her with her very own dagger, Arianna couldn't resist the fury she felt to see Aurora wielded against her.

Her magic flooded to the surface—she raised her hand to stop the attack before the guardian relic's sharp blade could pierce her chest.

Rumi's arm froze in midair, fingers wrapped around the dragon hilt.

"I can't move!" she screamed, trying desperately to regain control of her arm; Arianna stepped out of the dagger's path.

Levantis bora, she thought.

She let Solomon's sword fall to the ground and lifted both her hands to the air—her magic flowed from her mind to her fingertips, exhilarating every nerve in her body.

Rumi flew off her feet to float among the treetops; she barely had time to scream. The dagger fell from her hand to lie in the dirt as she flailed in the air.

"This belongs to me," said Arianna, plucking Aurora from the ground and wiping it clean. "Walk away, and I'll let you live. I know your struggle is not of your own volition. I'm going to fix that, make things right again."

With the flick of her hand, Rumi crashed back to the earth.

Arianna looked back toward the path to try to locate Solomon; he was still fully occupied with fighting for his life.

"I'll have your head," growled Rumi as she peeled herself off the ground with a groan. She grabbed the discarded bronze sword and lunged for Arianna.

Flying forward on the tails of her magic, Arianna plunged Aurora's blade into Rumi's stomach.

"I gave you a choice," she said without pity as the woman fell to her knees. "Not everyone deserves their freedom."

The battle was beginning to simmer to an end now; the drifters nearest to her, the ones who had seen her use magic, tried to retreat into the trees—she wouldn't let them run.

Cementas cuerpal!

They all stopped dead in their tracks, her magic immobilizing them. Their eyes were the only parts of their bodies she let move.

Arianna walked over to them, at the edge of the woods where the trees met a wall of high cliffs.

"The Olleb is broken," she said, addressing the drifters with a firm stance. "I'm trying to piece it back together. You've seen now that my story is no rumor. I *took* my freedom from the King, and I'm going to free you too."

She slipped the dagger back into its rightful place at her thigh. Then she looked them each in the eyes, trying to memorize their frightened faces.

"There will be a fight to come, a fight bigger than you or me… bigger than anything. When that time comes, you'll need to decide on the person you want to truly be. This is your clean slate, your do-over. When you're called to choose sides, as we all shall be at the end, just remember that I let you live. The King has already taken your life."

She released the spell, and everyone stumbled forward, momentarily shocked.

"I'm *not* your enemy, unless you make one of me," said Arianna as they began to back away.

One man uttered, "Thank you," before they all dashed off into the safety of the forest. And she heard a woman cry out,

"Mercy be the gods!" as they vanished into the dark.

Without a second thought or even looking back, Arianna swept up her priceless swords and sheath that Rumi had also tried to get away with. She secured them across her back and ran as fast as she could, trailing the fleeing drifters into the trees.

"Arianna!" Solomon's voice cut through the air with a vengeance as sharp as his blades.

She felt the force of his magic almost knock her to her knees—a blast of dark, explosive power radiated from the place she'd fled only moments ago.

She was certain everyone still in that vicinity was dead now, and she was sure Solomon was already running after her.

But she was younger, faster, and now full of a magical energy boost of his own offering, not to be caught easily. Arianna pushed onward, tearing through the trees until they swallowed her whole, hiding her from the wolf that hunted her mercilessly.

She had been dreaming of this chance for weeks, and now she had finally escaped his hold. To where, of course, she had absolutely no idea. But she knew in her soul she was headed in the right direction—for there was no going back.

Don't be brave, little slave.

"Be a warrior," she whispered, thankful for the strong rhythm of her heartbeat, guiding her once again.

LEAP OF FAITH

HER CHEST HURT with every breath now, and the aches she'd suffered from the battles of Zambienth started to whine, but Arianna never stopped moving. Deep in the forest, a long, snaky river divided the trees; she let it escort her each step of the way forward.

If not for the threat of Solomon close behind, she might have stopped to appreciate the land in these parts—it was stunning in the early morning light.

Dark green hues of grass padded her feet, and smoky blue water rushed along beside her. The darkness was beginning to fade away into a deep indigo as the first rays of light crept above the high cliffs and trees, illuminating the path to her escape.

Arianna tried to stay hopeful and think of anything else other than her waning endurance, but it was getting harder to breathe. And her clothes, drenched in sweat, clung uncomfortably to her skin, weighing her down.

The sea was also getting closer.

Arianna could hear the faint groan of waves somewhere nearby; the sharp taste of salt settled on her tongue, the air thickening with it.

Though she wanted nothing more than to dive in and put an ocean between herself and Solomon, the Sea of Saindora would mark a dead end in her escape—unless she could miraculously procure a boat.

Solza, where are you? There was no way she could survive those waters alone.

She shoved aside her worries, still keeping pace with the river. She prayed that it might lead her to some kind of shelter before she had to face another obstacle.

At least another hour passed as she trekked through the wilderness—the dense trees started to thin.

Arianna could sense Solomon's shadow drawing nearer as she inevitably slowed; the pull of his darkened magic was palpable, like a magnet to her own, growing stronger as he approached.

Just survive.

She placed one foot in front of the other, pounding the ground. Her lungs throbbed for more air as she tried to stay ahead of him. When she broke through the last row of trees, the land disappeared in front of her eyes.

Arianna skidded to a stop, just in time.

A scream caught in her throat as she teetered on the edge of a high cliff. She stumbled backward to safety, finding her bearings.

The cliff gave way to a water-filled ravine below—far, *far* below. It was as if a gaping hole had been carved across the land, twisting so far out in either direction that she couldn't tell where it might end.

The river she'd been following so diligently before now spilled into the ravine to create a thunderous wall of water, emptying into its depths. Its roar wiped away the heavy silence of the forest, splashing the purplish-brown cliffs with water so that they gave off a spectacular shine.

Arianna had never been very fond of heights, but she felt a rush of excitement now as she leaned forward, peering all the way to the bottom; the river coiled down the side of these cliffs practically from under her feet.

She whistled at the view. *Breathtaking...*

But a deadly drop for certain.

She knelt beside the rushing water, carefully skimming it with her fingertips. She thought if she let her hand dip too far down, the current might take her with it and never let go.

She looked across to the other side of the river and spotted an old sign covered in moss. She could just barely make out the words 'Fate's Pool—Swim at your own risk' carved into the rotting wood.

A laugh escaped her as she noted where the currents passed a large pool of calm water at its center. A line of rocks separated it just before the river tumbled over the cliff.

Only Fate would play such tricks on us.

She thought fondly of Jeom and Eli then, knowing they'd risk such a swim, just for fun; Demetrius and Lessa, on the other hand, would surely try, and fail, to hold them back.

Arianna took in the wider view again and thought everything seemed so small from this high up, everything except for the giant clouds of spray continuously bubbling to the sky as the waterfall thundered down; the early sun glared off the watery clouds, reflecting a rainbow of colors across the ravine.

She'd never seen such a thing before. It was as if the smoky-looking air had been painted with bright, shimmering strokes that flickered in and out with the sun, colorful and alive—it made her believe in magic all over again.

An overwhelming dark energy seemed to overtake the moment, cold bumps running across her skin even on this warm day.

Arianna peeled her eyes away from the ravine, knowing what she'd find. "Solomon," she uttered.

He broke through the trees, finally catching up to her again.

She ran a few paces ahead to where she'd spotted a long, rickety bridge—it connected the cliff she stood on to the land on the other side.

When she reached it, she hesitated.

The bridge was badly battered, surely having weathered many storms. Wooden panels were missing altogether, and it swayed ominously in the light winds.

You can't be serious…

This bridge was absolutely the least lucky thing 'luck' had ever granted her, but what other options did she have?

She took one last longing look at the rainbow streaking the air, gathered her courage, and then tested a foot; she had to hold on tight to the hardened cords on each side to feel even slightly steady.

It didn't break.

She glanced back to Solomon, daring him to suggest she might not risk another step.

"Stop right there!" he shouted.

Arianna slowly moved forward.

"Even if you reach the other side, there's nowhere left for you to run," he yelled after her. "Trust me when I say this."

"How could I ever trust you again?" she retorted.

He walked to the edge of the bridge, placing his hands on the poles grounding it into the earth; Arianna's heart beat faster.

If he wanted, Solomon could rip them out and she would fall to her death—the chase would end.

She lingered over the middle of the ravine now, the waterfall's hum drowning everything else out. Although, her thoughts remained loud and clear.

He's got me… this thing isn't going to hold if I go further.

She couldn't outrun Solomon forever; she was weakened from so much time without exercise or practice, and her lungs and legs burned from the exertion it took just to make it this far. She looked down to the waters and then back at him, trying to come to terms with her options.

"It's over, Arianna," he said. "I intended to bring you to the King alive, but I would still be celebrated if I only delivered your body." The indifference in his voice was like a punch to her gut. "It's up to you. Make your final choice, now."

His grip tightened over the poles.

"There's nothing left for you to fight for. This battle *is* over."

She took another step toward the other side, and the bridge swayed dangerously.

"You're wrong," she said in a hushed voice—she was fixated on the rainbow of light around her and the beautiful landmark she had discovered. "Look around you. This is what I'm fighting for. It's everything. It's *worth* everything."

She gazed down through the gaps in the wood to see the water rolling over itself in vicious patterns. It reached up to her like an extended hand. *Friend or foe?*

She had come to understand water well during her time on Idris, but it was still hard to tell whose side it was on. Just like magic, it had a mind all its own, never to be ruled.

"Don't test me, Arianna. What'll it be?"

Magic sparked across his hands, eager and restless.

"It's not over until one of us is dead." She shed her cloak, making up her mind to keep on fighting.

These robes had once belonged to Solomon, from his time spent as a master trainer in the Warrior's District. She used to put such an importance on their regal appearance, though now they'd been diminished into mere tattered cloth after years of journeying on her back; she had always worn them inside out—the red silk lining displayed on the outside and the white velvet exterior with the golden district emblem hidden on the inside.

Arianna let the silky cloth pool in her hands one last time before she tossed the cloak over the side of the bridge; it billowed down into the ravine with an eerie descent, as if a fiery spirit fell from the skies to be claimed by the water.

"My heart is still beating, so I guess that's the choice I'm making," she said, keeping her eyes on the drowning cloak until there was nothing left of it to see.

She'd carried it for so long since her district days that it had become part of her—she'd never been willing to let go of that piece that connected her to the identity of being slave Twenty-Two. But she was ready to say goodbye to her past now, to face the future without anything else weighing her down.

She turned to Solomon, holding her head high. "You can deliver my body to the King in a box with a bow for all I care. That is, if you can find it."

"Do not play games with me, child," he snapped, eyes glowering and silver.

His energy was so profound that Arianna could feel his magic about to release.

"This isn't a game," she replied. "It's my life, and I *won't* let you have it without a fight. Not as long as I'm still breathing."

She brought the soul of the star to her lips and impressed upon it one last wish from her heart. Then she placed both hands to the ropes of the bridge and hurled herself over the side.

When her feet met the air, it seemed as if the rushing waters might reach out to catch her in their arms. *Friend... I pray.*

She decided to trust the water today.

At this point in her journey, Arianna had conjured up so much faith that it was sometimes uncontainable, boiling over the surface and ready to be shared with the world. And despite the doubts that sometimes surfaced in her darker moments, a rainbow shimmered above her now like a beacon of hope, giving her yet even more faith that she could survive another fall.

The jump might have terrified anyone else. Another soul might have seen their life flash before their eyes, but Arianna couldn't deny the overpowering sense of joy that washed over her as gravity pulled her body downward, away from Solomon Bell.

"Ara, no!" he shrieked, his dark magic racing after her.

She glimpsed him leaning over the side of the bridge, hands outstretched.

She met the water with an excruciating smack, and a huge splash exploded out around her, cushioning her. She was dizzied but still conscious, and Arianna knew that magic had everything to do with it—star magic.

To her glorious luck, whatever spell Solomon had cast to try to catch or kill her midair was outdone by her wish; the star magic had softened the blow when she'd met the water.

Another direct attempt at her life had been thwarted by the enchantments of the universe, willing her to survive.

Arianna's momentary relief turned back to fear of the ruthless creature that water could be—the waves took her.

All she could do now was let them carry her to wherever they would. Whether that was death or yet another chance at life, she'd soon find out.

As the heavy arms of the river bounced her body back and forth across its dangerous path, she held on to one thought…

If I can survive the fall, I can survive the journey.

Solomon's face twisted in her mind as she struggled not to drown. Water rushed her throat every time she gasped for air, and her limbs knocked against sharp stones.

After what seemed like a never-ending period of struggle, everything stilled—the waters grew calm, quiet, and shallow. Nothing but the sound of a tinkling trickle and the water at her back suggested there was even a river at all.

Arianna used the last of her strength to drag her beaten body out of the water and up the pebbly shore. She coughed out the remaining water in her lungs.

She checked on her possessions; to her astonishment, her swords were still strapped to her back, the dagger was at her thigh, and the star was around her neck—though its worth was now spent.

Arianna sighed in relief, letting the ground support her for a moment. Eyes to the sky, trees dotted her vision.

Absolutely worth it.

She pushed herself up, moaning as her injuries started to make themselves known. She thought her arm might be broken from the fall—a large, purplish bruise twisted up from her elbow, running into the silver scar where Solza had left her mark long ago.

Using her dagger, Arianna cut off a chunk of her shirt and tied her arm up in a sling; she mentally thanked Cyn for the tip to quicken healing.

"*Helthra saludis emencia,*" she murmured, mentally thanking Lessa as well.

But she wasn't sure the healing magic would work; she was completely depleted of energy, Solomon's boost long since worn off.

Arianna spotted a nasty gash on her left leg, and noted more bruises and bumps than she cared to count. She tried to clean them up as best she could the old-fashioned way, but eventually she just had to carry on.

She wobbled to her feet and headed straight into the thick of the trees, searching for any sign of direction. Solomon was still out there with a vengeance to be had, so she needed to put as much distance between him and her as possible.

As she limped along, the aches of her body urging her to stop, lightning began to snake overhead, sizzling with each crack. The sky had grown a dark gray, so dark that the sun barely shone through to the ground but instead illuminated the thickness of the clouds, creating a peculiar glow overhead.

In the next flash of lightning, Arianna was reminded of

Solza—of her electric eyes and enduring soul—and felt that all would be all right. She was compelled to stop a moment to watch the storm unfold.

She sucked in the warm air as rain started to drizzle down, soothing her wounds. Long, thick leaves fluttered above her in the growing winds, stemming from spiraling tree trunks; she placed a hand on one of the trees, allowing the rain to rinse her of her worries. It felt like a bubble of protection had formed around her, extending from the tree through her hand, grounding her…

Just a moment without worry, anger, or fear.

The rain started to fall harder, the umbrella-like leaves struggling not to bend under the weight of the water. But Arianna stayed her ground, staring toward the glowing sky that only seemed to blacken.

The darkness closed in tighter, pressing into her bubble of safety. She began to shiver as the winds cooled, sniffling from the onset of a sure cold after being stuck in wet clothes for hours on end.

The sky erupted with a sudden clap of thunder, and Arianna jumped, snapping awake to the reality of her situation.

There's nowhere left to run. Solomon's warning dug into her mind, chasing away any thoughts of positivity.

Her hand fell away from the tree in the same moment, her safe space broken.

Before she could will her broken body to take another step forward, something hard cracked across the back of her head. All sounds turned to an incessant ringing in her ears, and the trees and rain blurred together into a deep gray.

Her knees buckled beneath her, and she fell face-first into the mud.

ARIANNA WAS SLOW TO WAKE, a pounding headache begging her to stay asleep. But something wasn't right. *Open your eyes!*

She tried to move but felt stuck—mud caked her skin and clothes. *It's Solomon, wake up!*

There were hands on her, many, grasping at her arms and legs. They heaved her into the sky with little effort, baring her to the rain like an offering to the gods above.

Her eyes flew open.

The treetops looked inverted from this view, like a dome of shiny, green clouds, though they did nothing to shield against the heavy rainfall. It was as if she were flying, floating above the forest floor like a ghost among the trees.

Arianna squeezed her eyes shut again to block out the large droplets of water falling fast toward her, but there was no escaping them; her head lolled to the side, and her vision went back to black.

When she came to again, she noticed the light of fire bouncing in and out of her line of sight—torches.

She struggled to stay conscious as she was propelled forward through the trees. Yet even in such a state, she couldn't help but wonder at how the torches could *possibly* combat this rain.

She tore her eyes away from the flames and studied the people holding them. *Solomon?*

She could only see shadows for faces, but there was nothing to indicate he was among this group at all; they were camouflaged against the trees so that she could barely tell how many people were actually there.

Another clan of drifters, possibly?

No, she thought.

These people were much more calculated than the drifters had been, quiet and purposeful in their movements as they trekked deeper into the trees.

Regulators, perhaps? *Couldn't be.*

They didn't wear robes binding them to the will of the King. They wore netted wraps of dark green, brown, and gray around their chests and waists.

In the light of the fire, Arianna also saw the same colors of paint or mud smeared across their skin; if not for the flames that lit their path, she wouldn't have seen anyone at all.

They blended right into the forest background.

Whoever these strangers proved to be, Arianna could think of no better way to describe them other than as people of the trees—and they were only visible to her now because they wanted to be.

Though their faces were all covered, many eyes glittered in the firelight, paying her no mind at all. They kept onward with her as their captive.

"Let me go," she muttered, trying to wake up her body, feeling pain every time she attempted to wriggle out from their grasp. "Let me go!"

A shock of magic originated from her gut as her fear surged. It tickled across her skin, snaking all around her body as her water-drenched clothes carved a hungry path—anyone touching her was shocked, forced to release her.

She slammed to the ground with a groan, her head smacking against the forest floor. Her vision blurred in and out again, and she could taste blood swelling between her lips.

Using all of the strength left to her, she rolled over onto her belly and pressed her hands against the ground to try to get up. It was no use, but she felt the sure texture of wood underneath her fingers, hard and veiny.

Another bridge, she suspected.

She managed to lift her head to see what lay ahead of her and found that she'd guessed right. Another bridge—except unlike the last, this one was vastly wide and sat very low to the earth. It was built of the same thick, resilient, cordy spines of the trees she'd gotten to know so well in these parts.

Upon first glance, the bridge didn't seem to cover anything but ground. As she looked closer, it *appeared* as if the earth beneath it had begun to bubble and churn; there was something quite sinister about it.

Arianna also noticed that the forest had thinned out considerably to make room for this path; the trees were more scattered, leaning against one another for support to create a tangled canopy of leaves high in the sky.

She squinted through the foggy haze—the light of what had to be several fires, far away on the other side of the bridge, winked back at her. They flickered in and out from the storm.

In a way, she found the image somewhat comforting… they reminded her of firebugs dancing in the dark.

Fire means civilization. Arianna tried to crawl forward.

"Help me," she groaned, reaching toward the light.

One of her captors crouched down in front of her, blocking out the view. Angular brown eyes peered out at her through a dark green cloth. "Get her up, now."

"No!" she screamed, spitting the blood from her mouth as she fought against the hands trapping her once more. They clutched at her arms, legs, and neck, hoisting her back into the air.

Upside down again, Arianna was able to make out a sign in the darkness nailed to a nearby tree, illuminated by the peculiar pink-flamed torches. It read, 'Beware of Monsters.'

She knew which monsters pursued her, but which ones had her in their grasp now?

"Welcome to Moriamo," said the brown-eyed girl.

She blew a blue powder in Arianna's face; she couldn't help but suck it in with her next breath, relaxing into its calming effects.

Before Arianna completely lost consciousness, she watched the girl lead the way across the bridge, toward the twinkling, firebug-like fires in the distance.

SHADOWLEAF

"GET UP," SAID A YOUNG WOMAN. "Get up, now." It came sharp, piercing the haze of sleep that had enveloped Arianna.

She blinked open her eyes to a soft light, a warm wind tickling her senses awake.

"Up!" she barked again. "You've had enough sleep to last you a lifetime."

Arianna found brown eyes glaring down at her, ones she immediately recognized—they belonged to her newest captor.

"Where am I?" she said, becoming alert.

"The Swamp of Moriamo," replied a new voice.

Only now did Arianna notice a bronzed and brawny young man sitting at the side of her bed. When he stood, she couldn't help but be humbled by his size.

A worthy opponent to Jeom, she thought.

Colorful tattoos scrawled across his chest, and the sun glared off his bald scalp.

"You need to tell us who you are, right now," said the girl, drawing back her attention.

Arianna studied her, trying to make sense of her situation.

Silky, black hair was fashioned into two tight braids that fell long to her waist, and pale white skin proudly displayed scars from past struggles. And like her companion, the young woman also boasted colorful tattoos all over her body.

She was fit too, the definite make of a warrior, complete with a spear in one hand; Arianna felt as if she looked upon her reflection.

"We know who she is," said the young man, clearly uninterested in this exchange.

"Hush!" hissed the girl. "We don't know anything, except that she was trespassing."

They began to bicker.

Arianna took advantage of their lapse in concentration to inspect the rest of her surroundings.

She sat up and looked around—the room they were in was completely open to the outside, allowing the sun to sprinkle in and eliminating any privacy.

An entire bustling village spread out before her eyes.

With the aid of the daylight, it seemed that the area had wholly transformed after the storm from the night before; Arianna saw that the wide bridge she'd seen actually branched out in endless directions, disappearing behind a wall of trees. And it didn't sit atop the ground, as she had at first thought, but over what looked to be a sort of marshland.

Small, crooked buildings poked up everywhere in the vicinity and beyond, following along with the sporadic pathways of the bridge. They appeared protected by the forest, not a single one clearing the treetops.

The trees along the marsh were decorated in lavender-colored moss, as if they'd been dressed for a party. And canoes meandered along the thick waters, drifting through tall, swaying grasses; their rowers gently guided the boats this way and that, carrying passengers to unseen destinations.

What is this place?

Arianna had seen nothing like this village so far on her journeys. She drank in the new setting, trying to understand it all in a single minute.

The people in her line of sight began to take notice of her.

Arianna's cheeks ran hot as they walked back and forth past her hut, sneaking glances her way; it appeared they were just as curious about her as she was of them.

She could sense she was stirring up much gossip in this closed community, though the people averted their eyes quickly—had they captured her for the highlife reward the King promised?

She assumed as much.

Still, there was something odd about this place that she couldn't quite put her finger on in her foggy state.

She *never* would have imagined that such a lively village could be hiding so deep in the wilderness; she had wandered for hours without seeing a single soul.

How can they thrive here, so separated from the rest of the Olleb?

"Look, Mother!" she heard a small voice shout.

Mother? Arianna felt as if she'd been slapped awake, the fog over her mind instantly vanishing. Her mouth fell open as she laid eyes on the most curious thing of all about this mysterious place—a child.

In fact, as she started to really *see*, there were many children running up and down the village trails.

The only Opalls she knew of were located on the outskirts of the Blancoren Mountains, fostering the babies of the Olleb until they became of age to be herded into the districts. And an Opall Mother certainly would not have condoned such playful, free-spirited behavior as what she was witnessing now.

"Could I be dreaming?" she muttered.

Her eyes hungrily followed the bright faces of youths who, by the King's law, should be locked away in the Jar until rightfully earning their citizenship.

Yet here they were—bouncing around with dirtied hands and faces, a playful innocence about them as men and women ushered them along. They gawked at her excitedly, whispering and giggling all the while.

"What have you done to me?" demanded Arianna in a panic, not believing what her eyes surely saw.

"We'll be asking you the questions here," snapped the girl, abruptly ending the debate with her friend. "Now, *please*, do get up!"

Arianna noticed only then that ropes bound her hands at her front; she tried to remember the last time she hadn't woken up as somebody's prisoner.

"Yes, let's get going," said the young man, his voice much gentler than his look.

Arianna slowly moved to her feet, expecting to feel pain—she felt nothing but the normal dull aches that came when trying to wake her limbs after a long, deep sleep.

She inspected her body for the injuries she'd earned during her escape from Solomon, but there were no wounds to speak of. Not even the broken arm remained.

Someone from this village has healed me...

Completely, and quickly. So quickly that Arianna thought their access to curatives must be of the extraordinary sort.

Her bones creaked and cracked, like she hadn't moved in days. She welcomed the firmness of the wood beneath her toes, grounding her in the present.

"How long have I been here?" she asked.

"Too long," said the girl, clearly annoyed.

She leaned against her spear, eyes probing, impatiently waiting for Arianna to find her bearings.

"We healed you, but you took a while to wake," added the

young man. "It's been several days since we found you in our forest."

"You mean, attacked me…" said Arianna, finding his gaze.

The girl snorted. "If you're well enough to speak so much, you're well enough to walk," she said, slamming the butt of her spear down on the ground. "Get moving."

Arianna obediently followed her and her companion out into the clearing and into the sun.

The people nearest to them scattered, but others in the distance waited and watched with interest; she observed the villagers observing her, and she admired everything about them—this place had no rhyme nor reason, not anything like the cities she'd traveled to before.

It felt otherworldly.

Children chased large, hopping frogs into the thick of the trees, and men and women carried baskets of fruits and vegetables atop their heads, passing them out generously as they walked. Many people sat around low-burning fires, eating what looked to be some kind of meat, while others picked apart the brightly colored fruits of plenty. Giant, white birds touched down now and then, trying to get at the scraps, before smaller creatures of the woodland scurried out to claim them.

Even the style of clothing here proved peculiar; no discernible status or skill could be determined just by looking at the cloth on the villagers' backs. Aside from the sure warriors who escorted her now, Arianna had no way of knowing what anybody else might contribute to the Olleb's society under the King's regime.

The patterns and dyes of the garments were unique to every person she passed. Some of the villagers even wore colorful wraps about their heads, and their clothes flowed free and loose to accommodate the muggy weather. *Absolutely beautiful.*

The only people Arianna could make any assumptions about were those covered in elaborate tattoos, each with their own distinct designs yet all of the same style—she guessed these were her captor's warrior-like peers.

She plucked at the fabric on her own skin, taking note only then that the clothes she wore now were not her own. They blended right into this peculiar village, light orange patterns decorating the cloth.

Someone must have bathed and dressed me.

She patted her thigh where her sheath and Aurora should be and was unsurprised to find them missing.

"Where are my belongings?" she asked, glancing back to the hut.

"You ask a lot of questions," said the girl. "Maybe you'd be quieter if we removed your tongue?"

Arianna closed her lips tight but struggled slightly against the ropes; the girl forced her forward, her spear at her back.

The young man walked ahead and they followed him through the center of the village and onto the main path of the bridge. Arianna was drawn to the mossy waters—beady, dark eyes glared back at her from below.

"Meet the monsters of the swamp," said the girl, a hint of a smile in her voice; Arianna slowed to look. "If you don't have a good reason for infringing on our territory, they will be having you for dinner."

She shoved Arianna forward against the rail. From this angle, many scaly creatures were made visible. They roamed eerily about the waters, thick tails flicking back and forth and teeth bared; it appeared as if they were content to patiently wait for their next meal to come to them.

In bizarre contrast, tall, stick-thin birds stood so still atop the monsters' heads that they blended right into the trees jutting out from the water; Arianna couldn't help but think that they must be the bravest birds alive, for they perched upon some of the most sinister creatures she'd ever seen.

"Where are you taking me?" she said, trying to sound unperturbed. She moved away from the rail.

No one responded, resuming their journey across the bridge.

"At least, tell me your names," said Arianna after a while, growing aggravated with the silence.

The girl sighed. "If it will shut you up, you can have my name."

Arianna nodded, desperate for any piece of information.

"I am Kayode," she said after a moment.

"Like the animal?" mused Arianna, glancing over her shoulder to lay eyes on her. "I've met wolves before, you know. You don't look like a wolf to me."

"A *coyote* is not a wolf," she said, pressing the tip of her spear forward.

Arianna picked up the pace. "Same family," she muttered.

Kayode snickered. "Different bite."

Arianna couldn't help but smirk a little at the banter, though this girl didn't know the wolf that hunted her; if Solomon couldn't pin her down and hold her close, neither could a coyote, however cunning. *Just survive.*

"Can you please just tell me where we're going?" said Arianna, again fidgeting with the ropes. "I promise I'll be quiet if you do."

She was trying to decide if she should use her magic to attack them here on the bridge or wait until they got to wherever they were going.

The brawny boy looked back over his shoulder.

"We're taking you to see the village mother," he said, one hand on the hilt of his sword. "She'll decide whether you can stay or—"

"Shut your mouth, Tayo!" said Kayode.

He huffed, shrugging his shoulders. "You're always so dramatic."

They continued on in silence.

Arianna decided to take her chances with the village mother, though she grew more uncertain with each step. What might happen if this person deemed her unfit to stay in what was surely a place that had been carefully hidden?

What is it, Fate, that you have in store for me this time?

From just one look around, Arianna knew in her gut that the Swamp of Moriamo was one piece of Olleb-Yelfra not ruled by King Devlindor.

THEY FOLLOWED THE WINDING BRIDGE over the swamp waters and back to solid land. A high hill greeted them, and Arianna was forced to climb to the very top; she thought her knees might buckle, her stamina wavering in the humidity after so much time without proper exercise under Solomon's watch.

At the top of the hill, a giant, black marble statue of a woman rose into view. It was decorated with wreaths of white flowers, like a gravesite. When they reached level ground with the statue, Arianna was able to make out a name scrawled in big, golden letters across the base—it read 'Moriamo.'

Never before had she seen a centerpiece of a town, village, or city as anything other than King Devlindor's face, his snake coiled about his shoulders and the emblem of the Four Corners somewhere nearby. In fact, the only comparison she could draw to this grandiose tribute lay in the forgotten City of Undor, a statue of the dwarves' fallen king raised in remembrance.

Moriamo's palms were carved to be forever reaching toward the sky, and she knelt on both knees, as if in prayer to the gods. A lion with a brilliant beard nuzzled up against her legs, fierce and protective.

The base they were erected upon was painted in striking designs of blue, green, purple, and red—all intermingled together until they became one in the center as a pool of gold.

Curious…

The design reminded Arianna so much of the symbol of the Four Corners, though it clearly was anything but.

Still, the most striking thing about the statue was Moriamo's eyes—they were painted a glossy silver, as were those of her lion companion.

Kayode and Tayo led her around the back of the statue; large, silver dots painted in a circle around Moriamo's hip struck Arianna as odd.

She craned her neck to get a better look. "Those aren't meant to be… bite marks, are they?"

"Eyes forward," said Kayode, guiding her toward a building positioned atop yet another hill—it loomed over the Moriamo tribute, forever keeping watch.

Stairs were carved into the earth here, so it was a much easier climb to the top.

When they reached level ground, Arianna had to stop a moment. The vast structure must have been built with care by the hands of a great creator—probably the very same who had constructed the statue. Thick pillars created an archway at the entrance, and complex designs had been chiseled into the stone from the top of a dome-shaped roof down to its base; it was much more sophisticated than the huts and cottages she had glimpsed on the other side of the village.

She began heading toward the entrance, but Tayo veered off to the left, leading them to the rear of the beautiful building—there, the land tapered off and a sharp cliff met the open sky.

Arianna's heart skipped a beat. She was gazing down at the very ravine she had dived into during her last encounter with Solomon; the bridge she'd thrown herself from was now broken in two, planks of wood barely hanging on to life as they dangled over the side of the rock.

From this height, there would be no chance of survival if she should fall again. She was much higher up now than at her first view of that waterfall.

Solomon would have to fish my body out in pieces.

Her hair whipped violently about her face as the wind picked up, and she thought a bigger gust might fly her right off the edge. She breathed in deeply, the crisp air sharp against her lungs—her magic stirred inside her, revitalized.

In case she needed to protect herself against an attack from these strangers, she was ready.

Arianna scanned the skies, the sun heavy on her skin and the clouds doing little to stop it—she wondered what another night-fall might bring as she considered this new chapter in her life.

"Sit," came a new voice, interrupting her thoughts.

Arianna glanced to her right, finding an old woman there. She hadn't noticed her before, amidst the picturesque backdrop.

The woman gestured to a fallen tree trunk opposite her.

Arianna hesitated. *So this is the village mother to decide my fate?*

It was not who she'd expected to meet.

The old woman was wrapped in a cloak of soft green with gold and black patterns. She was working carefully to create some sort of mixture, pressing the ingredients into a chalk-like paste; her dark skin crinkled with every slow movement.

In Olleb-Yelfra, old age was not long-lived, for the King deemed the elderly to be weak. But Arianna could sense something incredibly strong about this woman—and she was certainly the eldest woman she had ever met.

"Go on," said Tayo, offering her a reassuring smile; Kayode removed the ropes from her hands.

They both stood back, urging Arianna forward.

The old woman continued to mix in her pot, never lifting her face to them.

Arianna contemplated making a run for it as the winding paths in the distance came into view.

But she was so tired of running.

"I said, sit," said the woman again, more forcefully.

She lifted her eyes to Arianna's—they were dark brown and rimmed with gold as they caught the bright light of the sun.

Arianna felt her knees go a little weak; she found herself seated atop the tree trunk and couldn't decide whether or not it had been a doing of her own will, or a force from something else.

Could these people wield magic? The thought had just plopped into her mind.

Logic made her want to deem it an implausible one—especially considering how close this village lay to the City of Saindora, the epitome of no-magic zones—but it was hard to shake.

Her exhausted mind was slow to catch up to the truth she felt in her soul, and had seen plainly in just one look at the silver eyes on the statue of Moriamo. The existence of free children alone was all Arianna needed to know that she was right to assume that magic had found a way to flourish here.

The woman stood and removed her cloak, revealing most of her back. She held it out for someone to take, and Kayode bowed slightly as she stepped forward to accept it.

Arianna gawked; the woman's skin was covered in strange markings… scars of silver.

"Those scars," whispered Arianna. "Where did you get them from?"

The woman laughed, sitting back down.

Arianna realized she wasn't dealing with just any citizen of the Olleb, wasn't held captive by a villager out to sell her for the highlife reward. This was someone with a history quite like her own. And, given the woman's age, she probably knew a lot more about the enchanted secrets of the world than Arianna did herself.

Moreover, it appeared this *entire* place was one of the very treasures the King had tried—and failed—to drown out of history.

Arianna was humbled, her curiosity winning out over her

worries. "Who are you?" she whispered, afraid and excited all at once.

"I am the keeper of this swamp, Mother of Moriamo," she said, indicating everything down the hill and beyond.

"A keeper?" replied Arianna, raising an eyebrow.

"A keeper indeed, but by choice," answered the woman. Even just the depth in her voice suggested old knowledge. "I belong to no king and neither does this village. It's been left to my care after the passing of the last two mothers. Before them, it was governed by Mother Moriamo herself, if only for a short while. And soon, it shall be passed to another worthy soul, until the prophecy comes to be."

She went back to stirring her concoction.

"So it's true, then!" squealed Arianna, leaning forward. "The King doesn't rule here... but how?"

"I imagine it's much like the way the King does not rule you," said the woman, focused on her pot. "I know who you are, Arianna Belvedor, Guardian of Gold. Your story precedes you."

"Then are you... a guardian too? How could you know of my story?" Arianna was too intrigued to remember she was still a prisoner. "What do you think you know of me?"

The village mother smiled, still stirring her concoction.

"Those of Moriamo do not wear the mark of a guardian," she said, gesturing to her palm. "Though we are allies just the same, friends even." She glanced up. "It's been many moons since I've heard anything more of your whereabouts or the guardians'. Master Tayshin and his apprentice, young Gabriel, came to sing of you not so long ago."

Arianna couldn't help but gasp—any connections to her friends was something to rejoice about.

"They say you'll rise against King Devlindor, that you're the second chance our world has been waiting for." She reached out and touched a strand of Arianna's hair, her expression etched with doubt. "They speak of your triumphs, of your escapes... of the fact that you still *live*. That alone is a magical mystery."

She set her attention back to her pot.

"They say you're willing to fight, a true warrior of Olleb-Yelfra, indeed. That you may be what sparks the prophecy to again ignite and put things back on track—"

She dipped her fingers into the mixture and tasted it.

"Yet, here you are, stumbling broken and beaten into our swamp, so close to the City of Saindora where the King lies in waiting." She smacked her lips, her nose wrinkling. "It's hard for me to see how these rumors speak a truth when it seems you barely have a leg to stand on."

Arianna sat up straighter, affronted.

"At least, I am still standing," she said after a moment, trying to decide whether or not this woman could be trusted.

The village mother shrugged, evidently unimpressed.

"I daresay your story is coming to an end," she said, matter-of-factly. "Wouldn't you?"

"As is inevitable," said Arianna.

She felt compelled to justify her life's choices in the face of this elder who plainly passed judgment.

"I've journeyed far, merely following the paths laid before me."

She gazed to the sky, trying to find the right words.

"Honestly, I don't know if I'm the answer to anything… as Master Tayshin, Gabriel, and so many others have deemed me to be. But my life is no longer my own." She looked back to the village mother, and the woman finally gave her full attention. "Until I die, I'll use it to shed as much light as possible on the darkness the King has brought to this world, a world which has shown me such mercy and so much beauty—"

"They say you control avatars, but I see none with you now," said the village mother, scrutinizing her further. She cocked her head to the side. "Are these lies?"

"What do you know of avatars?" retorted Arianna—her heart

was pained with thoughts of Solza, wanting to protect her loyal friend even from afar.

"Surely a wealth more than your young mind could hold," she said, evenly. "But I'm willing to share my knowledge with any honorable soul." She narrowed her eyes. "Can I trust you, Arianna Belvedor?"

She considered this a moment, what trust meant to her. Then she tugged on the collar of her clothing so that her upper arm was made visible, showcasing her own silver scars; Solza's claws had made a lasting impression there, the marks stretching across her arm from her shoulder to her back.

There was a time when it had bothered her, a solid reminder of the excruciating pain Solza had caused her that dreadful night, but now it was anything but a negative memory; Arianna recognized this scar as a token of a friendship and bond she'd never trade for anything—an invaluable gift.

"I don't lie about who I am nor where I intend to go," she said with her head held high. "Trust at your own risk, but I ran away from the Four Corners so that I could take back my name and shed the lie I was given. *That* is my truth. I didn't ask for this life, but it's mine—"

She felt the threat of oncoming tears swell up inside her chest, but she didn't permit them to fall.

"My avatar and I were separated during battle against Solomon Bell and his regulators, back in the Jar, but I'll find her again." Arianna took a deep breath as that promise settled with her, hoping with all her heart that Solza still lived. "And you, how were *your* scars earned? I know an avatar's touch when I see it."

The woman smiled, so warmly, countless lines wrinkling her forehead and the sagging skin around her eyes.

"There were many battles to be fought when I was even a younger girl than you," she said, clearly tasting a delicate memory. "A child, really. A budding witch when magic was still being fought for toward the end of the Golden Wars."

She looked Arianna up and down.

"I'm glad to see the sun hasn't yet set on that battle…"

She gazed to the ravine, a sereneness taking over her expression; Arianna wondered what reflection of her past she saw in those waters.

"My scars were earned fighting to protect those around me. I fought well, but a novice witch couldn't last long against the Shadow Resistance. You see, I was one of the lucky ones…" A shadow crossed her face. "My wounds were healed by an avatar and her master, the one we call our first village mother—Mother Moriamo." She let out a heavy sigh, sounding as if she released all her burdens. "I'm much stronger than I used to be then, but my scars humble me always."

Arianna's mouth went dry as she tried to grasp what she'd said.

Another avatar master is known.

"Moriamo…" she stuttered. "The statue down below with the lion… so she *was* an avatar master?"

The village mother nodded.

"I knew it!"

Arianna whipped around to look at Kayode and Tayo, feeling that everyone must share in her excitement—they remained stone-faced.

She turned back to the village mother. "So you knew her then?"

"Why, of course," she said with a chuckle, as if Arianna had asked the silliest of questions.

Every worry flew out of her head about whether or not to trust this woman—all she wanted was more answers.

In all her lessons of the Golden Age, or even references to times before, she'd been unable to obtain any trace of others like herself or Lessa, avatar masters in the new age. The Guardians of Gold had shared only vague stories, whispers of a history that alluded to avatar masters being scarce and eventually wiped out during the wars, save for King Devlindor and his avatar, Raja.

That is, until Solza and Sano came to be.

Arianna pressed her hands upon her cheeks, trying to steady her whirling mind.

One minute, she was running for her life. The next, she was learning about an avatar master born of the Golden Age with healing powers, possibly similar to Sano's, on a hilltop in the middle of nowhere—it was all too unfathomable to consider.

Lessa, I wish you were here. She would know the right questions to ask.

Arianna started with the most obvious one. "What was she like?"

"Well, she was the last of her kind, besides King Devlindor. *Or* so we thought. Then we heard word of you and your friend…"

She tilted her head toward the sun.

"Mother Moriamo was wife to a king who had fought valiantly for his people. But she was the true hero in the end, an avatar master and protector when her husband could no longer protect us." Kayode and Tayo nodded along. "When it was clear that the Golden Wars could not be won, she instated this village, helped conceal those she could with nature's magic." The village mother brought a hand to her heart. "Late Queen Moriamo Tayshin, wife of late King Winsor Tayshin."

"Long live the Queen," said Kayode and Tayo, their fists to their chests.

"Long live the Queen," replied the village mother.

"Did you say… Tayshin?" mumbled Arianna, now on the edge of her seat. "You can't mean—"

The village mother let out a barking laugh that bounced between the high cliffs.

"You have just been traveling through the dark, haven't you, child?" She shook her head, clicking her tongue. "It's a wonder you've made it so far with such little understanding. The gods must really be handholding you, hmm? For you to stumble down such a path?"

Arianna stiffened, pursing her lips; the village mother laughed again, seemingly enjoying her frustration.

"Why, the last avatar master we know of was, *indeed*, the great-great-grandmother of Master Jon Tayshin, and he is my nephew."

Arianna thought she must be experiencing the effects of her earlier concussion.

"The Tayshin family is *long*-steeped in the Golden Age, child, as I'm sure you must know." The village mother gave a pat to her hair—it was wrapped up in a glittery fabric, white curls poking out. "Don't let my young looks fool you. I've been around a while, and so has he. That's why Jon was able to establish the Guardians of Gold in the first place."

Arianna opened her mouth to respond, but the woman never took a breath...

"*And* why they boast the symbol of the dragon. His great-great-grandmother's avatar was one of the last known dragons of Olleb-Yelfra. Though much of our knowledge of that history and of our ancestors was lost in the wars, her memory lives on with us."

The village mother gestured for Arianna to now speak.

She swallowed down a thousand questions, selecting a single one.

"What was her avatar's name?" she asked, thinking back to the grand lion at the base of the statue.

"His name was Evios, fallen in one of the final battles of the Golden Wars alongside his master. They died as one under attack by the Shadow Resistance," she said. "Though, not before she had sealed this village away from harm. After her death, the Tayshin family, and others close to them, vowed to carry on the legacy of Moriamo and Evios, until things could be set right again... one day, hopefully." She gazed fondly down toward the village. "It's been many years, but we're still here."

"If you're part of the extended Tayshin family, then why are you not a guardian too?" said Arianna, utterly perplexed.

"Because my legacy, my *duty*, is to this village," she said, waving her hand toward Kayode and Tayo. "These are my people. Jon's duty is to the Guardians of Gold, as was his choice. He was never one to sit around and wait for rescue. He's a great swordsman and sorcerer, so he chose action." She shook her head. "I cannot. It would leave Moriamo vulnerable. Nevertheless, we all stand on the same side."

Arianna was stunned into silence by this dive into history. She could think of no question other than "What is your true name? That is, if you trust me enough now to share it."

The village mother grinned, bowing her head slightly in introduction. "You may call me Mother Adunni."

She went back to her bowl, smashing the contents with a stone wand until there was not a lump in sight. Then she added a touch of what looked to be water but was surely something else—the paste-like substance began to smoke, transforming into a thick liquid that smelled of mint, leaves, and fire.

She signaled something to Kayode who knowingly plucked a small purple leaf off a bush that dotted these cliffs; Arianna had never seen a plant like it before, and hadn't noticed it anywhere else in this forest.

"It's called shadowleaf," said Mother Adunni, somehow sensing the question in Arianna's mind.

Kayode handed it over, and Mother Adunni crushed it between her wrinkled fingertips, sprinkling its dust into the potion.

Arianna eyed it with caution. "What does it do?"

"It frees up your mind, helps it to become unhindered by its worries and fears so that you can see clearly, the way you're meant to," said Mother Adunni. "Would you like to try it?"

Arianna took a mental note of this new piece of curious nature and magic to tell Demetrius about, if she ever saw him again.

"Is this why you called me here to meet you, then?" she asked, buying time as she considered what to do next.

"I called you here to see if you truly are the chosen one to fulfill the prophecy," said Mother Adunni. "To see what you're really made of and if you're worth our time."

"And?" said Arianna, throwing her hands into the air.

"I see that you could be… if you reach your full potential." Mother Adunni shrugged. "This, the shadowleaf potion, offers a taste of that. *Maybe*, if you realize what you're capable of, you'll get there faster on your own, before it's too late."

She pushed the bowl forward.

"It's your choice, avatar master."

Thinking of Queen Moriamo and Evios, the last of their kind, Arianna felt the weight of it now, what it really meant that she and Lessa had found themselves to be the masters of avatars—King Devlindor was outnumbered two to one.

Again, Talis and Keeper Kassime's advice rang in her mind.

There had been a time when she had little trust in, let alone respect for, Master Jon Tayshin, this woman's very own kin. But eventually, he had opened her eyes to even more possibility. Now, Arianna considered that man one of her dearest friends and a trusted teacher.

"Since you've done me the same courtesy, I'll give you a chance," she finally said.

"Drink every last drop," said Mother Adunni with a nod. "Your mind will need as much help as it can get."

She smiled, a tooth of gold shining through her lips.

Arianna brought the small pot to her lips and drank until it was empty.

"Now, close your eyes," whispered Mother Adunni.

The smooth liquid soothed her tongue and ran down her throat, tasting of smoke, bark, and spice. As soon as it hit her stomach, Arianna felt something retract in her mind, her thoughts instantly made sharper.

She understood in that moment why the key ingredient must be called shadowleaf—it felt as if cobwebs tangling her thoughts had been swept aside, the shadow spaces over her mind receding so that she could think clearly.

It was like an explosion of the senses; her eyes flew open.

Mother Adunni leaned away from her, appearing taken aback.

Arianna knew her eyes must be swirling with the smoky sheen of magic. She felt it coursing through her veins.

"Solza—I can feel her again!" she exclaimed. A tear rolled down her cheek. "I think she's all right."

"Your powers are stronger than you know," said Mother Adunni in a hushed voice. "An avatar master never loses connection with her avatar, no matter how far away. She is your soul now, and you can *never* lose touch with that. And as your avatar completes transformations, your powers too can extend to control those same natural elements. It's a shared bond, her magic yours to wield as you wish... if you can find it."

She laid a hand on her hand.

"You just need to focus," she insisted. "Try."

Arianna felt so alive, like a fog in her mind had vanished. She could feel her own energy and her powers so purely, as if they were as easy to command as lifting her fingers. It was like suddenly being able to understand the beat of her own heart or the flow of the blood in her veins.

All at once, she felt as if she could access everything.

Her thoughts were full of memories of Solza now, of her transformations and special powers over the elements.

Earth. Water. Air.

Earth was so easy—they'd both mastered that long ago.

Arianna pressed her palms to the ground. With barely a flicker of a thought, the dirt and rocks twisted around her fingertips like worms ready to do her bidding.

Mother Adunni held up a small mirror for her to look upon

her own face—Arianna saw her eyes flash a striking green before she let the dirt fall back to where it belonged.

She stood, her irises shining a deep purple now; the wind picked up all around them.

Arianna hadn't had much time to practice with this element yet. Solza's transformation to the grand owl had only been recent, but she felt the powers come easy enough when she concentrated; the shadowleaf was to thank.

Kayode could barely keep steady on her feet as strong gusts of wind began to batter the high cliff. She had to wedge her spear into the ground just to keep from falling.

Arianna let the winds die off almost as soon as she called them, for everyone's safety.

Her attention swayed to the ravine below, to the great waterfall that fed it. She admired that the water never stopped flowing for anything, forever falling down the sides of the cliffs.

"Stop," she whispered, lifting one hand.

Arianna felt the word roll off her tongue with a force of power she had never known existed inside her. Though, this was a true challenge—the weight and will of the water tried to resist her.

She recalled the first time Solza had shifted into the black and white dolphin that had graced the waters of Idris. Her avatar had been able to manipulate the sea so easily, bending it to her will around her; Arianna, on the other hand, had never felt anything like a 'master' when it came to water. Not like Lessa, who always had such a calling toward the sea.

Her connection to this element surged now, her eyes sparking to blue as the mighty waterfall froze all at once. It was as if a winter storm had stilled it to ice, or time had suddenly stopped.

"Do you understand now?" asked Mother Adunni. "Do you know who you're meant to be?"

Arianna released the waterfall, its roar echoing across the ravine as it came to life again.

"How long will this last?" she asked—she could feel the world around her with every breath, as if *it* breathed with her.

"I know what you're thinking," said Mother Adunni, shaking her head. "You cannot win a war by cheating. This exercise was only meant to demonstrate your capabilities."

She gestured to the bush Kayode had plucked the leaf from— not many other blossoms of the plant remained.

"Shadowleaves are rare and fleeting. We must use them with care and only to learn. The plant's magical properties prove to be just the same." She sighed. "The guise could *never* fool the King. It would wear off before you could even have a chance to touch him… if you even made it that close."

She snapped her fingers, and every fallen leaf or loose piece of dirt was wiped away from the vicinity with the strong brush of magic—Arianna was equally as impressed with her as she was with herself at the moment.

"Just imagine…" said Mother Adunni, "if you could one day achieve this level of control and strength on your own, no one could take it from you. But that day is yet far from now, I see."

She stood up, her bones creaking as she put all her weight on a cane to help her stand.

"Oh, and apologies, child, but you're going to feel like a boulder fell on your head once this is done." She smiled another toothy grin. "But now you know, Arianna Belvedor, what's really inside of you."

She turned to Tayo, holding out her arm for him to take.

"I think she's going to do just fine, wouldn't you say?"

"Never doubted her one bit given the fight she put up when we tried to help her," he said with a beaming grin.

He looped his arm through hers.

"Come along," said Mother Adunni. "It's time for a proper welcome to Moriamo. Best you meet everyone while you can still prove your worth."

She started down the hill with Tayo, Kayode and Arianna following obediently behind.

She felt as if she were floating, her entire body as light as the air around her. Lost in thought, she couldn't help but wonder if the King might have tasted shadowleaf in his past before; with the shadowleaf buzzing in her veins, Arianna thought she too could control the entire world, if only she desired.

RITE OF PASSAGE

"WHAT'S IT LIKE, THE SHADOWLEAF POTION?" asked Kayode, keeping pace with Arianna down the hill. She couldn't hide her fascination.

"It's hard to explain," she said, each word heavy with the weight of her own power. "I've somehow tapped into the greatest strengths I didn't even know I had. It feels like… like I could crush a king."

Her mind settled on that delicious thought.

"*Right,*" said Kayode, a little wary of her. "Just so you know, all those things I said earlier… we just had to be sure you were one of us before we bared all our secrets. We weren't *really* going to kill you."

"Or cut out my tongue?" said Arianna, narrowing her eyes at her.

Kayode chewed on her lip, speechless.

Arianna let out a haughty laugh. "Don't worry. I wouldn't

waste my energy on you now. You and I can duel on more fair ground later. I'd like to see if I can take you."

"I would like to see that too," said Kayode with a sigh of relief. She tried to hide her smile, and Arianna thought her pridefulness probably rivaled her own.

"I triple that," snickered Tayo from up ahead. "My coin's on Arianna."

"Oh, shut it, Tayo!" snapped Kayode, sending him a friendly jolt of magic to tickle his behind.

He howled in surprise, jumping into the air with Mother Adunni still holding tight to his arm; even in such a state, Arianna was stunned to see magic had found her once more.

Kayode turned back to her, dropping her voice low.

"Look, I heard everything you said to Mother Adunni, and… well, I'm ready to join the fight too. To leave Moriamo and help your cause… now that I know."

"Know what?" asked Arianna, still deep in the shadowleaf daze.

"That you're the chosen one," she said, matter-of-factly. "It's about time someone went up against the King again, and I always admired Master Tayshin for his efforts with the guardians. I would do *anything* for Moriamo. If we could remove King Devlindor from the throne, it would ensure our safety forever." She turned her attention forward, nodding to herself. "Master Tayshin was right about you."

"We don't know anything for certain yet," said Arianna.

"But we can hope," said Tayo from up ahead.

Arianna's heart pounded in agreement. *Down with the King.*

When they finally reached the bottom of the hill, Arianna felt like the shadowleaf magic was at a peak and she wanted nothing more than to test her power again.

"I don't think I can hold it in any longer," she said, the magic tingling her insides.

Mother Adunni flashed her brown topaz eyes at her. "You

can, and you will," she demanded. "Until the time is right."

Arianna complied, following Mother Adunni back past the statue of Moriamo and through the open doors of the beautiful, dome-shaped building that they'd passed earlier.

She had to pause to admire the archway entrance; her eyes feasted on the striking depictions of different figures, ones she faintly recognized, painted toward the top.

When she stepped through, a vast chamber opened up before her. It was decorated with portraits along the outer walls, and each displayed similar themes as had greeted her at the entrance.

It didn't take Arianna long to determine that this must be a temple dedicated to the gods of the earth, air, sea, and sun—their symbols were prominent at every angle.

Though King Devlindor had never deemed himself a 'god,' he might as well have, for he had never truly acknowledged the existence of any power greater than his own. There had been no teachings of gods in the Learning Center, nor literature to self-learn on the subject. Yet, somehow, whispers of higher beings had seeped into the districts and into the cities of Olleb-Yelfra, forever part of their world's culture and never to be eradicated.

'If the gods will it so,' was a common enough phrase among the Olleb's citizens, and Arianna had seen such symbols or similar depictions of gods before, in other parts of the world. But she had never stopped to think about what any of it meant.

Truthfully, she had assumed the meaning of 'gods' to be nothing more than the actual Olleb itself, to be the natural elements for which many of the gods were named.

Bearing witness to the grandeur of the room before her now, she saw clearly that, *here,* these otherworldly beings were idolized and worshipped with sincerity. To the people of Moriamo, gods had not been narrowed down to just a piece of common language or a pretty portrait—they believed they were real, existing somewhere out there beyond their reach and impacting life with incomprehensible influence over the Olleb.

Arianna couldn't help the thought that entered her mind next as she drank in the striking sanctuary.

If these elemental gods truly do exist, these supreme beings, where were they when the Olleb needed them the most?

She overheard Kayode giving orders to a guard near the archway.

Moments later, a horn sounded, its soft hum resonating loudly across the village. With its coaxing call, the swamp stirred into life. Men, women, and children of all ages rushed to gather inside the building behind them.

Arianna followed Mother Adunni and Tayo down a carpeted aisle; pastel-colored pillows covered nearly the total expanse of the floor. They were laid out purposefully to follow the circular design of the building, leaving only a bit of space toward the front.

There, a vast tapestry proved the clear focal point of the chamber. It hung down from the high ceilings, so long that it skimmed the floor.

Mother Adunni walked up to the front of the room and positioned herself on a small platform to face the gathering; the people of the village shuffled in eagerly, seating themselves upon the pillows.

Tayo and Kayode guided Arianna to sit with them at the front, in the row closest to Mother Adunni's low stage; Arianna sat cross-legged and fixated on the tapestry—it was directly behind Mother Adunni.

The designs and imagery on the large wall-hanging were depicted in meticulous detail through an immeasurable arrangement of dyed threads. She couldn't readily put them together to form any meaning. The spread was so massive that her eyes kept darting from one end to the other, trying to make sense of it as a whole.

The tapestry was doused in such vibrant hues of color that

Arianna was reminded of the enchanted murals they had discovered in the City of Undor. She even suspected that the images moved slightly, each thread dabbled with a hint of magic, she thought.

That, or the shadowleaf was truly messing with her mind.

She peeled her eyes away from the entrancing imagery and scanned the massive room—it had really begun to fill up.

The chamber buzzed with excitement, and she assumed nearly every person from the village had found their way here.

"That's her," she heard someone whisper.

Arianna turned to find a young woman wide-eyed and pointing as she gossiped with her friends. The woman blushed, shrinking into her seat when she saw she'd been overheard.

"Hush now. Gather 'round, everyone," called Mother Adunni, pointing to the tapestry with her cane; she too sat cross-legged on a pillow. "It's time for a story."

A quiet fell over the room.

"As many of you know, we call this the *Birth of the Dragon Rider*."

Arianna turned her back toward the people and put her full attention on Mother Adunni, trying to think of anything but the nerves trickling up her spine as the shadowleaf took full effect… and as the village mother's words sunk in.

Dragon rider…

"This tapestry was gifted to one of the very first avatar masters, long before even Queen Moriamo and Evios came to be," she said. "Eventually, as it was passed down through the generations, King Tayshin of the City of Lanzataré offered a hefty amount to one of its previous owners so that he could present it as a wedding gift to his queen. Together, they lived and ruled for many good years before their inevitable passing during a time of turmoil. May they forever rest in peace."

"May they forever rest in peace," the crowd murmured back.

Mother Adunni let her fingers caress the tapestry. "This depicts the greatest achievement of mankind… to completely relinquish one's soul back to where it began for us all, back to nature."

It seemed to be split into two sections. On the left side, Arianna noted depictions of people busying about with the traditional chores of human life. On the right was a beautiful landscape bursting with every kind of creature she knew to exist—from fish in the river to birds in the sky.

At the bottom of the tapestry, Arianna noted something more that made her take pause…

The nature side boasted a bear with its paw raised high, silver as the moon in the sky. On the human side, a man was rimmed in stitches of gold—he held a spear, as if preparing for a hunt.

With Mother Adunni's continuing narration in the background, Arianna raised her eyes to take in more detail. A forest stretched from one side of the tapestry to the other, connecting both the human and nature segments.

She lifted her gaze higher; the gold-rimmed man and silver-pawed bear were now in a deadly tangle with the forest as their battleground. The man was portrayed with the bloody mark of the bear's claw across his chest.

The very next section was all too familiar to Arianna—the silver-pawed bear and the gold-rimmed man had begun to morph into each other, essentially becoming one.

"—Then a brilliant, silver mark healed across his skin where the bear had before fatally wounded him," said Mother Adunni, recounting the historic events. "This is the first known depiction of animal transformed to avatar and man transformed to avatar master."

Arianna didn't need any further explanation. She understood exactly what this imagery chronicled now, and she couldn't look away. It was as if her own past experiences had been hung up on a wall for all to devour; her first encounter with Solza and the lasting silver scar she had earned from that day was still a fresh and painful memory.

As the figures continued up the tapestry, inching toward the center at the topmost section, the man and the bear seemed to twist through the elements—*earth, air, water.*

The bear, clearly of earth, morphed first into a stunning bird of the sky, shown in sleek lines of bright purple. Then the bird shifted to a creature of the sea, depicted in cerulean shades. Finally, as Arianna lifted her eyes to the top of the tapestry, the avatar had transformed into a remarkable red dragon, its golden eyes and silver claws coming to life in dazzling threads.

The beast's magnificent wings spread out across the entirety of the tapestry, and the gold-rimmed man now had eyes that swirled with silver and red magic, the fire essence of the dragon visibly within him. He was seated confidently atop his avatar, spear still in hand as the breath of fire rose all around them in bright orange and gold flames.

Arianna became so enthralled in the story depicted there that she thought she could even hear the fire crackling.

"It is said that all of the creatures *and* people of the earth came together in peace on this day, celebrating the first dragon and first man to tame fire and reach the sky. That is the story of how the first dragon rider was born," said Mother Adunni, shifting her focus now to Arianna, "and hopefully, one day, your story, child."

She pointed her cane to the dragon.

"The final transformation of an avatar and avatar master illustrates possibly the truest meaning of harmony in this world. It's the most literal and tangible depiction of the Golden Rule. Simply put, the humans that walk the Olleb are only as good as the world around them. Thus, if we're to continue to reap its benefits, the world deserves our utmost respect."

She lifted her arms up wide, turning her attention back to the crowd.

"Man cannot hunt, cannot survive, without the animals of

the earth and sea to feed him," she said. "He cannot thrive without the sun, cannot breathe without air." She slammed the butt of her cane to the floor, a piercing echo sounding across the chamber. "This place was once a breeding ground for dragons. They hid amongst the trees, soared free above the ravine, and drank from the riverbed. That is why Queen Moriamo founded this sanctuary for us here, so near to where magic once thrived."

She beckoned Arianna forward.

"Show us that you have a dragon inside of you, and we can follow Queen Moriamo's memory back into the war. You are her incarnate and the incarnation of every avatar master before you. Show us that our mother flows within you now, and prove to us that hope lives beyond our walls."

Kayode led Arianna to the stage, and Mother Adunni spun her around to face all the curious eyes quietly observing her, wondering what she might do.

She felt as if she had been in a dream the entire time she was listening to the story of the dragon rider. Now that the story had ended, all attention on her, the weight of the shadowleaf hit her again fully. With just the blink of an eye, she thought she could make the earth rumble at her feet.

"Show them," Mother Adunni whispered in her ear, this time pointing ahead.

Arianna followed her line of sight. There were four large glass urns at the back of the room near the archway, placed on both sides of the entrance. She felt drawn to them for some reason.

"Go on," said Mother Adunni, urging her forward.

Arianna walked back down the aisle, all heads swiveling to follow her every move. She stopped in front of the urns, peering inside of each—one was filled with water, another with soil, one seemingly empty, and the last glowed with flames.

She glanced back, uncertain; all those watching began to stand from their seats for a better look.

She felt her cheeks run hot with all the attention, but she

knew, in her heart, what she was meant to do.

Mother Adunni gave her a nod of encouragement, so she put her focus back on the urns.

It took nothing for Arianna to make their contents do what she wished—earth, air, water. Like on the hilltop before, she manipulated the natural elements into her grasp with ease, causing them to swirl together as one to the shock and awe of her audience.

The fire stayed put.

Try as she might, Arianna could not will the flame to move. It was unlike when she created fire through the sorcerer's spell she'd learned long ago; that was not the avatar way.

The power she exuded when she tapped into her avatar state came from a different part of her mind and soul. And it was much harder to get to when she wasn't under the influence of shadow-leaf potions or when Solza wasn't nearby.

She looked back to Mother Adunni for help but instead caught the eyes of another—a fierce-looking woman stood out among the gathering, her essence shimmering against the backdrop of the grand tapestry.

Her skin was so beautifully dark that it seemed tinted with hues of purple, and her head was piled with thin braids that hung long down her back, fading from black at the top to grayish-white at the bottom.

A robe so silver that it almost appeared transparent rested across her shoulders. And by her side, tail twitching with energy, sat a golden lion with the most intense stare.

What's more, the woman proudly wore a graceful crown atop her head.

Arianna had been forced to bow many times before, but only now did she feel compelled to do so of her own accord. She dropped to one knee and placed her hands on the floor.

"Queen Moriamo," she breathed.

The room stilled as the elements of earth, air, and water continued to whirl above their heads on strings of magic.

When she looked up, Queen Moriamo was floating directly in front of her, Arianna eye-level with the regal avatar lion she had only just learned about.

"You still have yet to find your fire, young one," said the ghost of the celebrated avatar master, observing her with great interest. Her voice rang out with deep wisdom and authority, filling the silence of the chamber. "When your time comes, do not fear its burn. You must wield it with courage. It will be gifted to you only when you're ready to accept the responsibility, and not a moment sooner."

Arianna couldn't find the words to ask any of the burning questions that had instantly flooded into her mind—it was a fleeting moment.

In all but a blink, the ghost of Queen Moriamo and avatar Evios had vanished without a trace, leaving her breathless.

She stood, the queen's powerful voice still swirling in her head.

That's when she felt it, a warmth welling up in her chest. It originated from somewhere deep down inside of her, as if Queen Moriamo had placed it there herself.

Arianna turned her attention back to the urn full of fire and grasped the flames in the palm of her hand. As she did, she saw her eyes streak with a bright flash of red in the reflection of the glass.

She guided the flame with only her mind, joining it with the other elements in a beautiful medley.

Mother Adunni spoke in a gentle voice, a hand to her heart. "Queen Moriamo lives. She watches over us still—"

Arianna turned to face her and saw a tear wetting her wrinkled cheek; she knew in just that one look that Mother Adunni also had the unfortunate, and extraordinary, ability to see ghosts.

I wonder what her stories of life and death might be?

"And so, it begins again," she said with a knowing smile. "May Queen Moriamo's spirit guide you to the end, child."

"I'll take all the help I can get," whispered Arianna, feeling the shadowleaf power finally ebb and her own tears of release come—she directed the contents of the urns back to where they belonged. "I'm going to need it if the King can do anything like this on his own…"

"Maybe," said Mother Adunni, calling Arianna back to the front to stand with her. She waved her cane out toward the on-lookers, the chamber exploding with claps and cheers of approval. "Though, it seems you're anything but on your own."

SECRETS OF THE SWAMP

AFTER EVERYONE HAD EXITED the temple, Mother Adunni asked Kayode to escort Arianna to her new quarters, this time as an honored guest and not a prisoner. The shadowleaf effects had fully worn off for her now, leaving a blazing headache behind, as was promised.

"Thank you… for all of this," said Arianna. "It's truly remarkable."

"You're remarkable, child," she replied, pinching her cheek, affectionately, before disappearing back inside the temple.

"Follow me," said Kayode, her long braids swaying behind her as she started down the hill. "Let's get you settled, shall we?"

They walked together back across the bridge, retracing their steps from earlier that morning.

"You all right?" said Kayode after a while, giving her a strange look. "You don't seem so good."

Arianna pressed her fingers against her temples to try to relieve the pounding ache—Mother Adunni had been right. There would never be enough time to defeat King Devlindor with such a fleeting boost.

Solza, I miss you.

"I feel like I've been hit over the head with a hammer," she mumbled.

Kayode laughed. "Well, that's not *my* weapon of choice."

Arianna groaned. "Do you have one?" she said, trying to focus on anything but the sharp, incessant pain stabbing at her forehead.

"Besides my spear?" Kayode shrugged. "I suppose I'm quite fond of swords and daggers. Speaking of…" She slid a blade out from a notch at her belt and presented it to her. "I think this belongs to you, no?"

Arianna felt a wave of relief come over her at the recognition of Aurora—the brilliant black, blues, and indigos, and the lightning-pierced jewel of the pommel. There was truly no match for this weapon.

"Thank the gods it wasn't lost," she said, accepting it.

"It's a rare find," said Kayode, nodding. "I haven't seen a weapon crafted from the Golden Age in a long time, aside from what we have stored here, of course. It's good to know there's more to be recovered out there than just this little piece of history we've kept hidden. The rest of your belongings will be waiting for you at home."

Home. Arianna wasn't sure if that label quite fit here. How could it be home without Jeom, Lessa, or Demetrius?

They continued walking.

"What do you know of the wars that brought the Swamp of Moriamo into existence?" she asked, tracing the wings of the dragon hilt with her finger. "Do you believe what Mother Adunni speaks of, about avatar dragons and whatnot?"

She averted her eyes, a bit afraid to voice her doubts.

"Sometimes it's hard for me to fathom this whole side of things…"

"Hmm," said Kayode, looking ahead. "Every person here is taught of the Golden Wars. All that came before and all that remains after. Dragons are, of course, a key part of our history, and avatar dragons are how they came to be." She looked to the sky. "They say that's how the Black Sand Desert was created, you know? That dragons killed themselves in a fiery rage rather than be subjected to King Devlindor's rule. Their sparkling ashes created the diamond-black sands."

Arianna grew quiet, thinking of all her time spent in that desert. Had they been journeying over the ashes of dragons all along?

"I'd like to see that desert someday," mused Kayode, lost in her thoughts. She studied Arianna from the corner of her eye, brow furrowed. "What is it that you don't believe? You of all people should understand what a world with magic is capable of."

"It's not that I *don't* believe," said Arianna, thinking of all she'd experienced this day. "It's just… all of this is a lot to take in. The surprises, the possibilities… they never lessen." She looked ahead to the village. "I wasn't born into this life like you were."

Kayode sighed.

"Ah, I think I understand where you're coming from," she said, seeming to relax. "I'm too young to have witnessed the truth of any of those stories Mother Adunni preaches. I've never actually *seen* a dragon. I only have my imagination to aid me." She frowned. "It's frustrating, really. To be caught in this 'in-between.' Somedays, I *hate* being stuck here… though, I know it's better than anything out there, in your world. At least here we're free."

Arianna nodded, understanding her sentiments all too well.

Still, she couldn't help but think to herself that hiding in a magically protected swamp wasn't exactly the type of freedom she was searching for. *Though, it is lovely here.*

They continued on in silence for a while, so she put her attention back to Aurora, mesmerized by the black jewel fixed to the pommel—the golden slash trapped inside of it glowed faintly in the falling sunlight.

"Arianna, may I ask why you came here alone?" said Kayode, pulling her away from her thoughts; all her muscles were tensed, like she was holding her breath for the answer. "When Master Tayshin came to speak of you, he said there were others… said there were four. What happened to your friends?"

She could sense the eagerness behind the question, though Kayode tried to hide it; it was obvious that she was desperate to know what it was like outside of this village and of the adventures that had brought her here, alone.

But Arianna didn't want to remember them now, not while she was still trying to wrap her head around all she'd learned from Mother Adunni. She didn't want to think of her lost friends, scattered across the Olleb, when she had no way of knowing if they'd ever meet again—and she didn't want to think of the ones she knew she never would.

"It's a long story," she said, her headache coming back in full force.

"Give me the short version, then," said Kayode, a plea in her voice. "I… I just want to understand."

She reminded her a lot of herself in many ways; Kayode seemed genuinely curious, and Arianna didn't want to let her down—she knew the frustration of always wondering, wanting *forever* for more answers.

Besides, it was nice to have someone to talk to who wasn't trying to test her with some bizarre magic or an unsolvable riddle. Right now, she needed all the friends she could get.

"All right," said Arianna with a soft smile, "but then I get to ask the questions. You do owe me, after all."

"Owe you?" screeched Kayode, taken aback.

"Yes, you abducted me," said Arianna, hands on her hips. "And you dropped me on my head!"

"Well, you *did* shock me," said Kayode, trying to keep herself from laughing.

"After you attacked me," she said, waving her dagger in her face.

Kayode responded with a mock bow, her braids touching the ground.

"Very well, Sorceress Belvedor," she said. "I accept your proposal."

Arianna shook her head in amusement and began retelling the story of how she came to stumble across the Swamp of Moriamo.

"Master Solomon Bell, a great warrior of Olleb-Yelfra, was once my master and friend," she said. "He's now my greatest enemy, sworn to the King's Guard and the Shadow Resistance. During our last unfortunate reunion in the Four Corners, he gave me a choice with his sword to my neck." She held Aurora up to her throat. "My friends' lives or mine—"

Kayode listened intently, drinking in every word.

"I relinquished mine, and he got me this far." Arianna felt her entire body sag, reexperiencing her defeat in that awful moment. "But, thankfully, a little meddling from some drifters allowed me to escape. I ran from him through your forest and got lost."

She considered her surroundings with new respect.

"I couldn't have wished for a better place to end up," she finished, gently touching the soul of the star.

"Master Bell…" said Kayode after a moment. "I *can't* imagine he could've fallen so far."

She shook her head, appearing truly saddened.

"You know him?" Arianna stopped midway on the bridge.

"Of course," she said, stopping too, always with a firm grip on her spear. "We all do. Master Tayshin was his master in magic, and he's been here before. Most guardians journey here at some point or another, after they've proven themselves truly worthy to Master Tayshin."

"How much more *worthy* do I have to get?" said Arianna—she rolled her eyes, knowing that Master Tayshin would surely respond that he had his reasons. "My friends and I were kept in the dark about this village. I had no idea…"

Kayode smiled, knowingly, continuing on.

"He would never take chances with Moriamo," she said. "*Or* with his auntie's wrath. I'm sure he would've brought you here sooner or later, under different circumstances." She sighed. "It's been many years since Solomon has been here, though. I was younger then, but I remember him well. His laugh mostly." She smiled. "He had *such* a big laugh, didn't he?"

"Yes, he did," she muttered.

She stared into the murky waters, ready to change the subject.

"It's my turn to ask the questions now," she called, running to catch up to Kayode—she had such long legs that Arianna thought she could probably outrun anyone. "How did you find me?"

Kayode tugged at her clothes, showing off the colors that easily camouflaged her against the wild wetland background.

"We all have our duties to ensure the safety and sustainability of Moriamo," she explained. "My duty is as a protector."

"A warrior," said Arianna, fixing her dagger into the band at her waist.

"Yes," she replied. "We use magic to reinforce the barrier spells that Queen Moriamo put in place long ago, and we patrol the outskirts of the trees from the cliffs all the way to the river. When someone gets too close, our magic sets off alerts and we bring them in for questioning. People can't 'stumble' into these parts of the swamp, so either they're completely lost or they're here on purpose. If they're searching for us for a reason, know that we exist, then we *must* ensure they never do so again, in the case that they don't prove to be allies." Her voice turned cold.

"Solomon Bell, for instance, will not be welcomed here again."

"And if one is truly lost?" asked Arianna, letting her fingers skim the wooden rail.

"It is inevitable, as you've so kindly proven."

Arianna chuckled.

"Over the years, several lost souls have wandered into our midst," said Kayode. "If they're deemed trustworthy, we consider them found. They're given a choice... to stay or leave." She caught Arianna's eye. "Nobody has ever left."

"What do you do with those who are not friends?" said Arianna, pushing the hair from her face. "What would you have done to me if Mother Adunni had found me less than honorable?" She stared ahead, the sun burning the last of its embers in the horizon. "What would you do to Solomon?"

"If one can't be trusted with the secrets of Moriamo, we can't risk letting them leave with them," said Kayode. "We erase their memories. Solomon would be no exception."

"I see," said Arianna, rubbing again at her temples. "Mind magic, then?"

Kayode nodded. "It's a good thing you can be trusted," she said with a wink. "Now you can stay as long as you like."

"I wish I could stay forever," she said. "It's really a paradise here, a dream..." Arianna thought of all the people she'd love to share this secret with. "But I'm afraid I can't stay long."

"I understand, although—" Kayode searched for the right words to say "—I know the fight you fight for, and that many believe you're the chosen one to lead it, myself included. But... how can you be sure you'll win, chosen one or not?"

Arianna felt the weight of her words atop her shoulders, heavy and unwanted. *How?*

Though Mother Adunni had tried to impress on her that she was not alone, she certainly felt like it. And that made the question all the more terrifying...

"I don't know that I'll win," said Arianna, meeting her eyes.

"I truly don't. But you're a protector of this village, Kayode… if you found yourself separated from Moriamo, knowing your people were in danger, wouldn't you do anything in your power to get back to them or protect them from afar, no matter what?"

Kayode returned a single nod.

"Every decision you make is with Moriamo's safety in mind," said Arianna, matter-of-factly.

She stopped, placing both hands on the rail, looking out to the water as the shadows of the night overcame the swamp; Kayode leaned over the rail of the bridge next to her.

"Just as you're a protector of this village, I have made it my purpose to be a protector of the Olleb," said Arianna, resolutely. "The people outside of this village are oblivious to the truth. They're slaves to a King even in citizenship and can't really see it, because they don't know of any other life. Somehow, my eyes were opened to the magic."

She spotted the light of firebugs twinkling far off in the trees, dotting the shrubberies with gentle sparks.

"Now that I know the possibilities, I can't just walk away from that and disappear. My friends are counting on me, whether or not they're with me now. And I know they'll show up to the fight, one or way or another." She let her head drop back, exhausted from thoughts of future battles to come. "I don't know where I'll end up next, but I won't stop until this is over, or I'm dead. As a sworn guardian, I have a duty to try and bring the peace you have in Moriamo out to the rest of the Olleb."

"You're a noble soul, Arianna, for someone who's grown up in the King's world," said Kayode, holding out her hand for her to shake. "As I've said before, I'm ready to join your fight, wherever it leads you."

Arianna considered her for a moment, thankful for her sincere support after being ripped away from everyone else she trusted; and when she shook Kayode's hand, suddenly she didn't feel so alone anymore.

THEY SOON CAME TO THE END of their journey, slowing in the middle of the village center. Kayode led her down narrow trails away from the main area and through the thick of the trees—limbs overhung many small homes in this quieter part of the swamp.

"Here you are," she said, stopping at the front door of a charming cottage overgrown with nature. "I imagine there are quite a lot of people eager to meet you later. Try to get some rest now… if you can. Tonight, we celebrate."

Kayode pushed open the door, stepping back to let her in.

Arianna heard a screech from inside and was abruptly enveloped in plump arms and a bush of bouncing curls.

"Arianna! Oh my, it's really you. Dear, I'm *so* glad to see you alive and well. So glad."

"Cyn?" she stuttered, peeling her face out of her bosom to confirm what she knew to be true. Her heart ached with happiness. "I can't believe it! But…" She beamed up at Kayode. "Did you know all this time?"

"It is my job to know these things," she said with a smirk.

She left, closing the door behind her.

Arianna shook her head of the shock. "I was so afraid that you—"

She choked on the words, not wanting to voice a single detail of the beachfront battle that had left them so scarred.

"Me too, dear. Me too," said Cyn, squeezing her cheeks between her hands to look at her properly.

She pulled her into another hug.

"Thankfully, most of us got out all right in the end."

When Cyn finally relinquished her, Arianna took her in fully—she seemed aged, so much worry and fear now etched on her face compared to the last time she'd seen her.

Arianna frowned; she couldn't stand seeing Cyn like this, so beaten down.

"It's been a rough couple of months," said Cyn, knowingly. "But we made it here not long before you arrived."

"We?" She looked past Cyn for the first time, praying to find Lessa and Eli also hiding somewhere in the cottage.

She froze, mouth agape.

"Surprised to see us?" said a husky voice from a chair in the corner—Master Tayshin observed her with a grin on his bearded face. He stood up and pulled her into a strong embrace before she could even utter a word.

With her arms wrapped around him, Arianna couldn't help but notice how much weight he'd lost. Clearly, the stress of being on the run had also done a number on him in his old age.

"So good to see you well," he said, sounding relieved.

"How could you not tell me about this place?" said Arianna, unable to quell the frustration in her voice. "And about Queen Moriamo, your great-great-*grandmother*, or something like that? An avatar master *and* a dragon rider! Left that bit out, did you?"

She glared up at him, though without much conviction.

Master Tayshin laughed, patting her atop the head.

"There's a time and place for everything," he said. "The Swamp of Moriamo is my best-kept secret. I planned to tell you young ones soon enough, to take you here, but then—"

"So this is where you and Gabriel came when you went on your little 'excursions' from the Greenhouse?" said Arianna, quickly changing the topic; she wanted to postpone the bad memories for as long as feasible.

"This was just one stop along the way," he said, pacing about the cottage with his hands behind his back. "More importantly, we told your story to pockets in cities still controlled by the King. Those are the people we need to hear us." He sighed, looking to the ceiling. "Moriamo already believes."

"Arianna!" came another voice as the door was flung open.

"Did you miss me?"

A short man stood in the entryway.

"Nico," she squealed and giggled as he tried, and failed, to sweep her up in his arms; he was so short that her feet never left the floor. "I just can't believe this."

Many of her Greenhouse hours had been spent training with him, amidst many jokes and laughs.

"Better believe it!" he sang, squeezing her shoulders. "Let me get a good look at you." He smiled. "Seems you've already made quite the impression here too, huh? Can't go anywhere without people making a fuss over you! Word around town is that we're due for some festivities tonight, in *your* honor, of course."

He put his hands on his hips, glancing to Master Tayshin.

"Nobody threw a feast for me when I showed up…"

Master Tayshin slapped him on the back with a chuckle. "You don't have as much potential, my friend."

"Oh, I do love a good party," said Cyn, clapping her hands. "It's about time we celebrate something around here, and an avatar master is as good as any." She tucked a strand of Arianna's hair behind her ear, looking at her with such admiration. "You did *so* great at the ceremony, dear. Such an epic thing to witness, really… the birth of a dragon rider."

She gave a little twirl of enthusiasm, hand over her heart.

"With any hope," said Master Tayshin, trying to hide his smile.

Arianna blushed. "You all saw that? I didn't notice any of you there…"

"We were hiding in the back," said Nico. "Didn't want to make a fuss in front of the entire village before Mother Adunni had her talk with you."

"But she told us what she intended to do with you and the shadowleaf potion," said Cyn.

Nico wagged his finger. "Yeah, she's a trickster, that one."

He plopped down on the bed in the center of the room, lying

back with his hands behind his head.

"Sorry for all the dramatics, but we were curious… wanted to know what she could pull out of you that we guardians hadn't already." He sighed in relief, shaking his head back and forth, as if in awe. "You *sure* were something, Ara."

"It was all very unexpected," she stammered, looking to her hands. "Mother Adunni taught me a great deal in just our first hours of meeting. My head is still spinning." She exhaled, leaning her back against the door. "Where do I even begin with all this?"

"Don't you worry. There's still plenty for you to learn, and now plenty of us here to teach," said Master Tayshin. "Nobody's expecting you to be the expert in centuries' old knowledge overnight." He crossed his arms at his chest. "I'm just stunned that the Olleb steered you right into Moriamo's arms with you none the wiser—"

"Magic works in mysterious ways," sang Cyn, pinching him on the arm.

He huffed, a smirk growing on his lips. "Very mysterious."

"Mother Adunni works in mysterious ways too…" Arianna grinned. "Maybe they're one and the same."

Master Tayshin snorted in laughter.

"Ah, yes, Auntie Adunni can be a bit stoic," he said, twisting a finger around his beard. "She's not one to delay a rite of passage, that's for certain."

Cyn pouted.

"Shame Lessa couldn't have joined…" She rushed to the other side of the room, pretending to be occupied with tidying something up—Arianna heard the sniffles.

There was a silence in the room; she readied herself for the difficult discussion waiting.

Master Tayshin lowered himself back into the chair and pulled out a pipe from his robes.

"*Solza ven immito,*" he whispered, giving the pipe a little flick of fire before inhaling.

Smoke rings began to rise to the ceiling with his next puff of breath.

Arianna was instantly transported back to her last peaceful Greenhouse memory. She lifted Aurora from her waistband, setting the dagger in plain sight atop a small side table.

"Has there been word?" she said in a whisper, too hopeful for her own good. "Of her, or Eli?"

Cyn came back over, her face splotchy with tears. "I'm sorry, dear."

"You probably know more than we do," said Nico, sitting up so that his feet dangled off the side of the bed. "I think you were the last to see them, and we haven't heard a thing since you guys… *poof.*" He threw his hands into the air. "You lot just disappeared."

"About that," said Master Tayshin, pointing his pipe toward Arianna. "Star magic?"

She nodded.

He leaned back in his chair, deep in thought.

"Its power is all used up now," she added, pinching the stone of her necklace between her fingers. "I used my last wish to get away from Solomon… though, just barely."

A coldness seemed to still everyone—Cyn and Nico exchanged fearful glances.

"Well, I'm glad you're safe," said Master Tayshin after a moment. "We stick together now. We'll find the others."

His voice was firm, as if he was reassuring himself of the same.

"There's no one else with you, then?" said Arianna, hardly able to push the sentence from her lips.

"I'm afraid we're it," said Cyn, head bowed.

Arianna took a deep breath, preparing for her next questions.

"All right then," she said, "tell me what happened on the beach after we disappeared. Please, just tell it straight."

She braced herself for the answers.

Cyn sighed, taking her hand.

"You had better sit down," she said, guiding her over to sit on the bed next to Nico.

Master Tayshin came to join them; they spent the next hour filling each other in on every detail they'd missed since their separation.

After Arianna explained about her narrow escape from Zambienth to the City of the Four Corners with Lessa and Eli, she detailed her journey south as Solomon's prisoner...

"I lost him at the waterfall thanks to this gem," she tugged at her star necklace, "and the rest is history." She let out a big exhale, leaning against Nico. "Your turn."

"After Talis—" Master Tayshin cleared his throat. "After you lot got away, the Shadow Resistance swarmed us. We could barely hold them back. It was everybody for themselves."

"Chaos," said Nico, shaking his head. "Just chaos."

"Rowina, we think she escaped into the city somewhere, in hiding hopefully," said Master Tayshin. "She knows every nook and cranny in the Burrows."

"Jon, Nico, and I barely got out with our lives," added Cyn. "Luckily, some of the city regulators who died in battle had come to the beach on horses, so we were able to make a run for it that way."

"We think Margery and Sergios made it out too," said Nico, "but we can't be sure. No idea of their whereabouts."

"And Vance, the poor lad," said Cyn with a whimper, "he didn't make it." She twisted a curl around her finger, absentmindedly—Arianna knew she was trying to hold back her emotions.

She remembered Vance well, such an intelligent man with a knack for mind magic...

"A terrible loss for us," said Master Tayshin. "We just weren't prepared."

Nico took a deep breath. "We lost Iris too," he mumbled, chin in his hands.

Arianna gasped. "Iris… but how?"

She had dueled with Iris many times in the Greenhouse, a fierce fighter indeed, so it was hard for her to fathom that anyone could've killed her that night—even taken off guard.

"She was protecting Rowina," said Nico. "Helped the old bat get to safety, and that was that." He snapped his fingers.

"I don't believe it," she said. "Dead? Really?"

Master Tayshin shook his head.

"No, not dead," he said. "*Taken.* Both her and Vance." He lowered his voice. "The only ones we know who died for sure were Talis and Tobias… may their souls rest in paradise."

"They will, as soon as this war is won," said Arianna, her fists balled in her lap.

She was immediately drawn to the glint of her twin swords sitting in the corner of the room. *Soon.*

"Is there any hope to rescue Vance and Iris?" she asked, afraid of the answer.

"They're as good as dead if the King has got ahold of them," said Nico, closing his eyes a moment. "If they're not on the other side yet, they will be soon."

Arianna looked to Master Tayshin.

"But why would he take them as prisoners? Why not just kill them then?"

No one responded—their silence told her all she needed to know.

"He's baiting us," she spat, both equally shocked and disgusted. "He *wants* us to come for them, doesn't he?"

"He's trying," said Master Tayshin with a curt nod. "Though, you and I both know that it'd be suicide to even try in the state that we're in. Iris… she was at the first failed siege on his palace and barely escaped with her life. Vance—" He bowed his head. "Let's just say we've all been through this before. They're smart enough not to hope for liberation, but they'll be loyal to the end."

Arianna's stomach churned at the thought of Vance and Iris

in the King's captivity, two people who had taught her so much. There was no telling the torture they'd have to endure, and the guardians were powerless to help them.

"What about Jeom, Demetrius, and Gabriel?" she said in a panic—their predicament suddenly felt even more dire. "Anything at all?"

Cyn laid her hand atop Arianna's.

"No one has heard from them since they escaped on the waters, but we can only hope for the best," she said. "At least, they got away. We've been waiting here… for anybody. It's the last of the guardian sanctuaries not fallen to the King, we think."

"It's some luck you found yourself here, Ara," said Nico, "since we hadn't gotten 'round to telling you young sprouts about it yet."

There were murmurs of agreement from the others.

"What can we do?" she asked, standing to face them all. "We *have* to find them. We have to help our friends."

"Arianna," said Master Tayshin, "the only way to help them now is to win this war. We have to finish what's been put into motion, and any guardians still alive today will know to put their focus on the same thing. We've made our choices, and our stance is known. None of us are going to give up until we see this thing through." He touched eyes with Cyn and Nico. "The Guardians of Gold may be divided now physically, but we all still bleed *gold*." He held up his palm. "Tomorrow we'll convene with Mother Adunni to determine the best way forward."

"Here, here," said Nico. "We aren't going to just sit back and wait for the King to pick us off, Ara. The war is happening now, and we will hit them back, hard." He gave a big, exaggerated yawn. "*Just*, not tonight, kid."

Arianna could feel her expression change from anger to annoyance. "But—"

"Tomorrow, dear," said Cyn. "You need to rest now. You've come a long way." She pulled a small jar out of her pocket and placed it into Arianna's hands. "In case you have trouble sleeping." She cocked her head to the side with a concerned expression. "You look like you could use a few hours without interruption. When you wake, it'll be time for the festivities."

She stood and forced a smile onto her lips, despite the certain worry wrinkling her face.

"Those were left here for you too." She pointed to a fresh pile of clothes that had been laid out on a bench. "For tonight."

Arianna couldn't possibly see how she could ever be in the celebrating mood after all she'd just learned; she swallowed the growing lump in her throat.

"We'll see you soon," said Master Tayshin, getting to his feet; he pulled Nico up with him.

Arianna couldn't help the uneasy feeling that settled in her chest as she watched Master Tayshin, Nico, and Cyn all leave the cottage. Even though she knew they were safe here in Moriamo, the moment felt very temporary.

When the door shut behind them and she was again alone, Arianna opened the jar Cyn had left her; she hoped its contents would help her forget everything. But the Guardians of Gold were so scattered, and much like her friends, Arianna's concerns were spread out in too many directions to fathom—it seemed an impossible feat to reel them in.

Before she could imagine even one more horrible ending for someone she loved, she dipped a finger into the jar, inhaling just a small amount of the blue powder.

THE CELEBRATIONS WERE IN FULL SWING when Arianna arrived later that night. She had bathed, twisted her curls up in a fancy way atop her head (like her attendant, Lily, had shown her back in South Luose), and dressed in the midnight blue robes Mother Adunni had left for her. Every time she moved, the glittery fabric sparkled just a little.

She held her head high, enjoying every second of the festivities—it was the first time in a long time that she felt less like a runaway and more like a person, even a highlife again.

She was seated before a roaring fire that burned quickly through the wood in a large pit. Its flames grew higher and higher, its smoke rising to the sky to mix with the wispy clouds above, all illuminated by a dust of stars.

Never in her wildest imagination would she have thought a place like this could exist in the present day—the children of the swamp danced around the fire with such joy in their eyes.

Some even practiced magic… as if it were the most natural thing in the world, zapping each other in good fun or making animals dance across the flames. *How truly wonderful.*

They knew nothing of a world without enchantment; Moriamo was the only home they'd ever known, and it was full of it.

An entire community thrived through magic here, just as sweet as any Golden Age history she'd ever studied.

But it didn't sit well with Arianna that the village lay on the edges of Saindora, right underneath the King's nose.

"Do you not fear King Devlindor or the Shadow Resistance?" she asked Mother Adunni as the festivities buzzed around them.

"Of course," she replied, poking at the sizzling wood with a stick—more embers sparked into the air. "We'd be foolish not to. Why do you think we hide so well?"

"Excuse me, Mother, can the avatar master play with us?" A young girl tugged at Arianna's hand, coaxing her away from her cozy seat by the fire.

Arianna looked to Mother Adunni for permission, not wanting to be rude; she was an elder she'd never dream of disrespecting.

"Oh, go on!" she said, sipping her drink. "I'm too old now to be bouncing around anymore, but don't let me ruin the fun."

Arianna obliged, and Master Tayshin took her place next to his aunt.

"Come," urged the girl, leading her away from the adults. "The others were too shy to say anything, but I'm the bravest."

She puffed out her chest, guiding Arianna to the other side of the firepit to join a group of children—they were dancing like baby birds learning how to fly, flicking magic tricks back and forth at one another.

As soon as they saw Arianna among them, they all froze, eyes wide and curious.

"Will you play with us?" the girl asked, looking up at her excitedly.

"What would you like to play?" said Arianna, feeling completely out of her element—she'd never played before.

"Can you do *this?*" said a boy, using his magic to make an elegant, winged creature soar across the flames.

Arianna shook her head. "I'm not sure…"

It occurred to her only now that she'd never called to her powers solely for amusement. Magic had been introduced to her under much different circumstances than those that these children had had the fortune of experiencing. To her, magic almost always went hand in hand with training exercises, fighting for her life, defending others, *or* proving a point.

"It's easy! We can show you." The young girl began concentrating very hard; her eyes gave off a flicker of silver that would surely grow even brighter with adulthood. "*Solza ven immito,*" she whispered in a small voice.

A tiny, pink flame grew in the palm of her hand; she grasped it there a moment, enthralled with her own abilities. Then she placed her other hand over it, seemingly smothering it into smoke.

As if praying for a wish to come true, her hands clasped as

they were, the girl closed her eyes and kissed her fingers, whispering another spell that Arianna had never heard before.

"*Morphiatis animo.*"

When she released her hands, a beautiful, fiery butterfly rose to the air on a smoky trail of magic. It fluttered all the way to the pit to join the firebird—they danced together across the flames.

"Just concentrate on what you want to see," said the boy. "It will come."

"All right, I'll try," said Arianna, holding out her palm—they all pointed in awe at her guardian mark.

She smiled, her heart warmed in the company of such innocence.

"*Solza ven immito,*" she said with confidence.

With hardly any effort, a large, pink flame grew in her hand; the children gasped in delight.

"Now, just cup your hands together, like this," said the girl. She placed Arianna's other hand over it. "And picture the creature you want to form with your flame."

She repeated the spell for her to speak aloud.

Arianna closed her eyes and thought of the only animal she'd ever wish to see again…

"*Morphiatis animo,*" she breathed, her magic tingling her tongue.

She brought her clasped hands to her lips, planting a kiss there; she felt her flame immediately expand within them, trying to escape—she opened her hands to let it go.

The children let out screeches of joy, and the entire camp stopped to watch as a detailed and exquisite form of a snow leopard grew from Arianna's spark; it pranced regally across the air, leaving a track of flaming pawprints behind until it too found a home among the other animals in the firepit.

And just as Solza ruled the animal kingdom in real life, this fiery snow leopard blazed a path to be followed—it was just so much *more* than what the children had been able to conjure.

Like everyone in the vicinity, Arianna couldn't peel her eyes away from the perfect representation of her avatar etched in fire.

"Again, again!" cried the children, pulling at her arms.

They practically climbed her like a tree in their excitement to see more magic.

Her whole heart opened up to these little lives who had yet to understand the dangers of the world, cared for and protected by their community. Without meaning to, without even really understanding why, Arianna knew she loved these children.

Just like nature—pure from the onset—they were worthy to be protected, merely because they existed. She loved the little girl who had been brave enough to ask her to play, and all the children in the village, in a way that made her want to fight even harder for their freedom. *They still have a future to save.*

She obliged without protest, sending bursts of beautiful magic into the sky. Sparks rained down over the celebration in strings of vibrant colors, similar to the magic she and Lessa had called upon to try to impress Eli in the desert...

She wished for both of them now, for a do-over. *Just survive.*

"Will you come to live with us?" asked the young girl; the sweet smile on her face was enough to persuade Arianna to do anything. "I can teach you more magic!"

"Maybe one day I could make this my home," she replied, beaming down at her. "I'm sure I could learn quite a lot from you." She gently tapped her on the nose. "But not to worry. We have time yet. I don't think I'll be leaving soon."

She thought to herself just how happy she was at that truth, for once—she felt safe and welcomed here.

The girl giggled, dragging Arianna behind her as she skipped around the fire. They twirled together to the music of a woman playing a flute to the beat of deep drums.

The sounds were so soothing that she disappeared with them, into her thoughts; she drifted to the last time she'd danced so freely. It was the same night of the Gathering Ball in Zambienth, the night before everything had fallen apart…

Eli had taken her in his arms.

Arianna wasn't quite sure when it had happened, in little moments over time that grew into something more, but eventually she had sunk into his spell.

Why didn't I realize it sooner? The love she held for that man.

She wished he was there now to dance with her again—in the most dreamlike of settings—the children of Moriamo spinning around her.

Arianna's thoughts took a sharp turn, the flames feeling brighter, hotter, uncomfortably warm; she prayed to the gods that somehow he and Lessa had made it out of the Four Corners to the safety of some similar paradise. But given that their first escape attempt from the Jar had been nearly impossible, it was hard for her to imagine a happy ending for her friends back north…

"Why the long face?" said Cyn, hopping over to join them in their dance. "Let me show you how this is done, dear. It's a *party*. Move over!"

She hip-bumped Arianna aside with gusto and took the little girl's hands in her own.

Cyn howled in happiness, spinning the girl around so fast that even Arianna was dizzy. "You can have rain, wind, grass, and fire, or whatever you feel like calling it, but this is *my* element."

She swayed back and forth with no rhythm at all, drunk and giddy from too much wine; the children fell into hysterics, taking a keen interest in her lively caretaker.

Arianna was fast to follow, hunched over in a fit of laughter. Cyn's happy nature was so contagious that she forgot her worries, forced to succumb to the fun.

If her caretaker had taught her anything at all, it was how to look on the bright side—even in the darkest of times, Cyn always seemed to drift toward the light.

Arianna slipped away from the children to let her have her moment, introducing herself to more of the villagers who were eager for the chance to entertain visitors and trade stories of the world.

She also spied Nico gossiping with a group of Moriamo protectors as they filled their plates with treats from the feast, Kayode and Tayo among them; Master Tayshin and Mother Adunni were still huddled deep in conversation.

Inevitably, she too let herself fully relax into this forever-fleeting feeling of peace.

As the night grew thicker—more wine and ale poured, more food served, and livelier music played—Mother Adunni and the people of Moriamo promised to teach Arianna all they could about the legacy of Queen Moriamo and how to tap into her avatar powers, without the aid of impermanent potions. In return, she promised to do all that was in *her* power to protect them, in honor of the avatar link she shared with Queen Moriamo and in honor of her vows as a guardian.

She wished Lessa and Sano, and Solza, too, could experience this new journey into the world of avatar magic with her, that they could learn all of this together, but right now that could not be; Master Tayshin, Nico, Cyn, and Arianna all agreed to stay in the Swamp of Moriamo until they could uncover the whereabouts of the other guardians and safely reunite...

Or until a moment came that felt right to infiltrate Saindora and attack the King.

They needed to heal and grow stronger. To exercise their magic, hone their battle skills, and restock their weapons. They *had* to stay vigilant, planning the way, carefully, forward.

And this time, Arianna would practice patience.

When the moment was right, they would strike again at the King's regime, with or without the other guardians by their side. Though, she was hopeful now that a moment *would* come when the Guardians of Gold might unify again... just as Moriamo had shown her.

She brought the soul of the star to her lips, believing fully in the endless possibilities of magic; when the children began to tire, slowly drifting toward their parents' laps, the adults took their place in dance by the fire, Arianna leading the charge.

FIRE REIGNS

ALTHOUGH SWAMP LIFE proved much less glamorous for Arianna than that of a royal palace or a big city, magic existed here. *Families* existed here, and the people here still believed in a world where they could exist again… everywhere.

Life had continued on in Moriamo without the influence of King Devlindor, and without the constant reminders of fear and death.

She had lived for weeks feeling as if she'd been born into the Golden Age—here, in the Swamp of Moriamo, time stood still, and she enjoyed every second of the rare opportunity to live in the wonderful, peaceful past. Magic flowed freely from her fingertips each day; there was no need to smother it for fear someone might see. And she could walk proudly through the streets of this village without hiding her face.

Arianna was a celebrated guest of Moriamo for as long as she wished to be, befriending many and trusting all.

Life was simple—nearly perfect if they needn't hide from the rest of the world—and she was more than grateful for her luck up to this point.

If not for so many things and so many people, so many chances, Arianna would have been dead before she even knew a thing about magic or the hidden wonders of the Olleb. How she had ended up being the 'chosen' one on this incredible journey, with the King at her heels, would always be a mystery to her—but this was the life she'd been handed.

No one could take it away, not even in death.

Her memories, choices, losses, and loves… they were all hers to claim, and she wouldn't trade them now for anything.

Arianna frequently shared stories with the villagers of her brutal upbringing in the Jar, of her adventures across the Olleb, and of all the exciting battles she'd overcome; it was as if she had fallen into a pocket of the universe where all the horrors of her former life had been wiped away, chalked up to an unspeakable bedtime story, a fictional scare.

But the brutality of Olleb-Yelfra was truer than anything; the safety net Moriamo had cast over her had never felt *fully* genuine. Not without Lessa, Jeom, Demetrius, or even Eli by her side…

She should have known the screaming would eventually find her.

Moriamo wasn't ignorant to what went on outside of their magical borders, of King Devlindor's cruel hand over the world, but they kept their heads down. Like the leaders before her, Mother Adunni was reluctant to pull her people into the messiness of Olleb-Yelfra, for fear this last bit of the Golden Age might not survive.

Arianna understood that wisdom clearly now as the screams of those she'd grown to care for settled in her ears—like the recurrent sound of the bell in the Warrior's District, heralding her into yet another cold morning, even in the warmest parts of the Olleb.

She wondered if there was a single action waiting in her future that could make that bell's far-reaching drone stop permanently.

No way of knowing until the end.

She collected her dagger and swords, running out of her cozy cottage and into the open, toward the sounds of the heart-wrenching calls for help.

SHE HAD TO SHIELD HER EYES from the sudden brightness that pierced the thick night. So many things were burning.

The ashes of Moriamo rose to the air as monstrous flames tore through everything, fiery arms reaching toward the night sky with a passion that wouldn't be contained; they consumed everything in their paths.

Arianna had to stop and stare, hardly able to register the chaos that had unfolded here, in the secret swamp. She covered her mouth as billows of smoke wrapped around her.

Her cottage went up in flames next, a burst of fire thrusting her to the ground. She stood to fight, trying with every effort to tap into her powers over the fire element, but it was fruitless; without Solza and without the shadowleaf boost, she couldn't grasp it.

She had learned a great deal more from both Mother Adunni and Master Tayshin during her time here, but her elemental magic just wasn't the same without Solza nearby. And out of all her avatar powers, unless she conjured it herself, fire wasn't hers to control—not yet.

"Run, Arianna!" she heard someone shout; he was a village protector, leading others to safety.

"What's going on? What's happened?" said Arianna, catching the man's arm.

"We're under attack," he said. "They've found us. You have to run!" He fled toward the trees, many others behind him.

Arianna did run, but not in that direction.

She could tell most of the commotion was coming from the very center of the village, so she started across the bridge. The closer she got to the heart of Moriamo, the louder came the screams—bodies were strewn across her path as more villagers ran past her in an absolute panic.

"Help!" A young woman was rushing toward her on the bridge.

She tripped and fell to her knees, tears streaming down her cheeks. A black-cloaked woman stood behind her, sword lifted high; Arianna knew a Shadow Resistance devotee when she saw one.

"*Levantis bora!*" she shouted without a second thought.

The woman flew into the air, sword falling to the ground. She tried to curse Arianna with a spell, but before she had the chance, she flung her over the rail to the mercy of the swamp.

The woman's cries were muffled by the sound of gurgling water; she was swiftly dragged beneath the surface by the scaly monsters who quietly lurked below, forever watching over the territory.

"Take this and follow the others to safety," said Arianna, helping the young woman to her feet and handing her the enemy's sword.

"Stay safe, avatar master," she said with a slight bow. "Our faith is with you—"

Arianna had already taken off at a sprint, the young woman's faith trailing behind her in smoke.

She ran the final stretch to the center of the village. On her way, it was impossible to even count those already gone. So many faces she'd gotten to know... now nothing but memories.

Death humbled her yet again as the ghosts of those who had fallen this night made themselves known; they lingered on the earthly plane, watching the havoc spread with forlorn expressions—there was nothing they could do but watch.

The translucent figure of a young boy caught her attention, floating at the end of the bridge. He'd taught her a game of hide-and-seek in exchange for stories of her adventures across the Black Sand Sea and of her glimpse of the giants.

His soul had now departed from his body, mangled on the ground, never to experience such adventures for himself.

The boy's father tried to shake him awake, begging him to get up; she didn't have the heart to tell the man that his son would never rise again.

Arianna paused for the child, shedding a single tear for him.

In a downward spiral, her mind sank into the Jar that had trapped slave Twenty-Two, back to a place where death had always surrounded her, stifled her… impassioned her to find a way out.

"No, not here," she whispered in a daze.

She willed herself to keep going.

When she came to the edge of the long walkway, the center of the village extending out in front of her, Arianna saw the true extent of the destruction brought by the Shadow Resistance; she readied her weapons, searching the chaotic scene for survivors.

Flames consumed the area, people struggling for their lives. Then she saw who she expected to see among them, fighting against them—Solomon Bell had returned to the Swamp of Moriamo, twin swords in hand.

His loyal shadows, those who probably posed as regulators or highlifes in the neighboring cities, scattered around the village in shining cloaks of black and gold, cackling with the joy of obliterating this beautiful sanctuary. They scorched everything in sight, from the temple of the gods to the surrounding trees on the hilltops.

"Solomon, stop this!" screamed Arianna, brandishing her weapons and racing toward him.

Her anger churned up a power inside her chest that was ready to blast out at any moment. Her magic sizzled and swelled from her hands, coiling all the way down to the tips of each blade.

Solomon didn't even flinch, an expression like amusement washing over his face as he laid eyes on her. Before she could even get close to him, his guards had stepped onto her path.

Arianna was forced to defend against them, under attack by magic and metal from all sides.

"*Ni passe!*" She crossed her swords at her front, using her magic to create a barrier of protection.

The shadows grew thicker, her opponents trying to get through—with a roar of effort, she pushed her barrier outward in one explosive movement.

Her attackers all flew off their feet.

But it was only a temporary relief. Dark magic spilled off her enemies like a wave of sickness, relentless in their hunt for her blood; Arianna knew, without a doubt, that she was the number one prize to be had from this massacre.

This is all my fault.

She used spell after spell to block the onslaught and managed to take a few of the shadows out with her swords, but it was too much. Her energy was already beginning to lag as the Shadow Resistance focused all their attacks on her.

"Keep it up. You're doing splendid," came a reassuring voice from behind.

Arianna turned to find Mother Adunni had joined her fight.

"I should have come sooner," Arianna said, spinning around to slay another shadow. "They've ruined everything."

"You couldn't have known, child," said Mother Adunni, leaning on her cane as she called to her own magic. "That's why they call it an ambush. We knew we could've never stopped Solomon from coming. It was inevitable he'd find his way back. Now, turn around."

"What—?"

"Turn around!" Kayode had launched at her from out of no-where.

She grabbed Arianna by the arm and spun her in the opposite direction, just as an explosive light grew from Mother Adunni's cane.

"Do you have to question *everything?*" she whined, stabbing her spear into the ground as they both ducked behind her shield.

Arianna heard the surrounding shadow soldiers shout out for help against Mother Adunni's strange attack. When it was safe to look, she found them all on their knees, scratching at their eyes in agony.

Solomon was nowhere in sight.

"Thank you," said Arianna. Then she registered Kayode's state; she was badly bruised and bloodied. "You're wounded."

Kayode sighed, lifting her shield. "Nothing I can't handle," she said, spitting the blood from her mouth.

"I'm sorry," whispered Arianna, helping her to her feet.

Kayode just shook her head. "For what? You didn't throw battle magic at me."

Arianna averted her eyes. *I might as well have,* she thought.

Tayo appeared in her peripheral vision, limping toward Mother Adunni. He hovered protectively nearby as she assessed her damage to their opponents—thanks to her, they all had a moment to breathe.

"What *was* that enchantment?" asked Arianna, gawking at how effectively Mother Adunni had cleared the area.

"It's her favorite trick," said Kayode, brushing the dirt from her clothes. She set down her shield. "Blinds the opponents temporarily *and* painfully. Will buy us some time to hit back."

She ran forward, impaling one of the blinded men with her spear.

"Did you think that Jon and I shared nothing between us?" called Mother Adunni—she swiftly killed an incapacitated shadow with the sharp end of her cane. "We are family, after all."

She moved slowly but assuredly, with skill rather than brute strength; Solomon would have praised her in another lifetime.

Tayo was by her side the entire time, guarding her; if anyone came near, they were tossed to the side in pieces.

"Can't say that I'm surprised," said Arianna—though it was a curious picture to see the gentle village mother with blood on her clothes.

Arianna wasted no time to join her friends. She spelled her own battle magic toward the blinded… men and women with blood streaming from their eyes, waving their weapons in the wrong direction; anyone who didn't die by her magic met Death by her blades. Mere minutes later, the vicinity was quiet.

It was the first time she felt no remorse at taking the lives of those who couldn't fight back.

"Well done, girl," said Mother Adunni as they all huddled together.

Arianna bowed her head, unable to acknowledge such gratitude—Moriamo was still burning down around her.

"Speaking of Master Tayshin," she said, wiping her swords clean, "have you seen him, by chance? Or Cyn and Nico?"

"I'm sure they're around here somewhere," said Mother Adunni, leaning on her cane. "They surely must've been alerted before us since they're housed closer to the center of the village."

She looked past Arianna, Kayode, and Tayo, seeming to suddenly recognize the total devastation to her home; her eyes glazed over in a look of disbelief. Then the tears began to well, etching lines across her soot-covered face as they flowed silently down her cheeks.

Arianna had to turn away, the guilt overwhelming.

"This is *all* my fault," she muttered, head tilted toward the smoke-riddled sky. "Solomon came here for me."

She squeezed the handles of her swords so tightly that she was sure her palms were bleeding.

Mother Adunni came around to her front, cupping her chin

in her hand so that they had to meet eyes; Arianna could hardly stand to look at her without crumbling.

"None of this is your fault," she said. "Do you hear me, girl? The Swamp of Moriamo could not have lasted in secret forever. We knew the risks we were taking, long before you were even thought of. But you found us with a mission in your heart, and one that affects us all, Arianna." She squeezed her eyes shut, as if the words that came next were made real once said aloud. "We will continue to stand behind that mission... even long after Moriamo is gone."

"But," said Arianna in a whimper, "what about all your people—"

"*Our* people," said Mother Adunni, resolutely, releasing her grip. "The only way to protect *our* people and the world we live in is to defeat the King. We can't do that by hiding in a swamp, as you have so politely put it before." She gave a nod of solidarity. "Today, our hand has been forced, and we will hide no longer."

She turned to Kayode and Tayo with a command on her tongue.

"Guide those you can to safety. You know what to do. We can't stay here now. They've outnumbered us, and more will surely come soon."

"What about you, Mother?" said Tayo, hesitating.

"Don't worry about me," she snapped, shaking her cane at him. "Worry about yourselves and the surviving villagers. *Go!* I'll be just fine."

He didn't budge, shoulders squared; Kayode seemed unsure of what to do.

Mother Adunni let out a heavy sigh, sagging under the weight of the difficult goodbye. She walked over to them, smiling warmly up at the two young protectors.

"Go," she said, resting a hand on Tayo's cheek. "I will not watch you both burn here as well. I *will* not. Save who you can, and don't look back." She looked them both in the eye. "That's an *order*. Can I count on you?"

"Yes, Mother," replied Kayode and Tayo with a low bow.

"That's more like it," she said with a big smile.

Mother Adunni leaned forward to whisper something in Kayode's ear that neither Tayo nor Arianna could hear.

With wide eyes, Kayode drew Mother Adunni into an unexpected hug—a bizarre thing to witness, given how closed off with her emotions she normally appeared.

Tayo barely noticed the quick exchange, his face splotched with tears; when Kayode released Mother Adunni, he took his turn to say farewell, planting a swift kiss on her cheek.

Arianna felt nothing but shame—one reason out of many being that she'd slightly underestimated Mother Adunni and the people of Moriamo. She'd always thought in the back of her mind that they had never *fully* comprehended the monsters that threatened their borders…

How wrong my assumptions had been.

The Swamp of Moriamo hadn't just been living peacefully or idly. They'd been prepared for a moment like this from the beginning, and now that moment was here.

Kayode grabbed Arianna's upper arm as she and Tayo made to leave.

"We'll meet again," she said.

There was no hint of a question in her voice.

Arianna nodded. "Don't let them catch you, all right? I couldn't live with myself if you—"

"Don't be foolish," she said with a smirk. "What *shadow* has ever bested a coyote? You don't let them catch you."

Arianna placed her fist across her chest, holding her head high.

Kayode and Tayo ran, shouting orders to other protectors and ushering families and friends to safety; Arianna and Mother Adunni watched together until they disappeared in a puff of magic, the swamp forest swallowing them whole.

Not moments after, the thin trees surrounding the village center sparked up in dense flames—the Shadow Resistance pursued those who had fled.

Please don't let them catch up to my friends.

The protectors still alive and in the vicinity stayed their ground to give the villagers time to escape; Arianna, Mother Adunni, and those left standing were soon surrounded again.

"How did you locate us after all this time?" said Mother Adunni, calmly, speaking toward the blackness of the only wooded area yet to burn. "How did you break the spell?"

Solomon stepped forth from the dark.

"Memory magic doesn't work on me," he said, walking out into the open to face her. "I never forgot."

Arianna became clouded with anger. She made to lunge at him with her weapons raised, but Mother Adunni held out her cane to stop her.

"*Hmm,*" she said with a nod of understanding. "A traitor through and through. We've been waiting for your return ever since the girl stumbled into the swamp."

Solomon cocked his head to the side.

"Is that so?" He chuckled. "Well, here I am. It's a miracle you've kept her alive this long. She has a knack for dying."

Someone barreled into Arianna; an arrow landed with a thud in the grass right next to her head.

"You have to remain vigilant!"

Disoriented, she looked up to find Master Tayshin standing over her, a sword in hand. He was drenched in sweat, clothes torn.

"Remember what I taught you," he shouted, blood dripping from a large gash on his arm, his face ghostly. "This is no practice duel. Do not let thoughts of revenge impede your better judgment."

He left her on the ground, stepping forward to be by his aunt's side; they were the only two people between Arianna and

Solomon. The rest of the village protectors had been swept back into battle, more Shadow Resistance swarming them from every angle.

"By the gods… oh dear," came a screech from behind. "Ara, are you hurt?"

Arianna rolled onto her back to find Cyn darting toward her, a thin, silver sword in her grip.

Nico was by her side, carrying an axe twice his size.

"Cyn, Nico! I'm so glad you're all right," she cried, shaking off the shock from her fall and pushing onto her elbows.

"Up you go," said Nico, offering her a hand. "Come on, we have to get out of here while we still have the chance."

"No, I can't leave now," said Arianna, getting to her feet. "They need our help."

Nico shook his head. "I have orders to keep you alive. There's nothing left to—"

He was suddenly drawn into a fight, a woman leaping toward him with her sword swinging.

Arianna yanked Cyn out of harm's way.

Nico wasn't anything notable with his axe, but he was truly something when it came to trickery; she and Cyn watched in admiration as he pretended to fumble with his weapon, just to land a sneak magic attack when his opponent thought she had the upper hand.

When all seemed clear again, they turned their attention back to Solomon, Mother Adunni, and Master Tayshin.

The three masters in magic were nothing short of enthralling to witness—two against one—battling to the death.

"You've gotten slow, Jon," coaxed Solomon; all his focus was on Master Tayshin as they fought sword-on-sword.

Mother Adunni was aiding her nephew with sharp magical strikes, as if she wielded her own blade from a distance.

Solomon thwarted them all.

"That's 'Master' to you, Bell," said Master Tayshin, swiftly maneuvering his weapon to counter the unending attacks.

Solomon moved with such a speed that Arianna thought she'd never truly even battled the real him before. *He's always been lying to me... I don't know him at all.*

Master Tayshin let out a roar of anger, his next swipe of the sword nicking Solomon in the neck. "How dare you show your face here again!"

Solomon pulled in a hiss of breath through his teeth.

"The King gets what the King wants," he mumbled, pausing a moment to consider his wound. "Right now, he wants Arianna Belvedor, and I must do my duty."

He turned his attention from Master Tayshin and threw a magical attack toward her—she and Nico blocked it together, its force knocking them to the ground.

"Oh, Solomon!" cried Cyn, tears filling her eyes as she moved protectively in front of Arianna and Nico. "Stop this, *please.*"

He gazed her way, but his expression was distant.

"I can't stop," he said. "I *won't.*" Fire grew in his palm, and he aimed it right at her.

Cyn was frozen where she stood, staring at him in horror.

Arianna barely had time to get to her feet. "Cyn, watch out!"

She called to her barrier magic, but before it could even form, Mother Adunni and Master Tayshin had blocked his attack together.

Solomon turned his sights back on them, evading attack after attack as they forced him back toward the trees; Arianna helped Nico up, and they focused their efforts on supporting the village protectors struggling under the expertise of the remaining Shadow Resistance.

For a moment, it seemed as if the Guardians of Gold and Moriamo united might send the shadows fleeing toward the dark...

Master Tayshin let out a yelp of pain. Then the sound of a heavy sword meeting the earth sent chills to Arianna's core—she whipped around, knowing that the tide had turned against them; Solomon had somehow gained the upper hand over the revered elders, his blade at Mother Adunni's neck.

Arianna realized too late that, despite her respected powers, Mother Adunni was not nimble enough to best someone as skilled in dueling and magic as Solomon. And Master Tayshin was much older than his famed apprentice, slowed by the aches of age—even together, they just hadn't been a match for the seasoned wolf with nothing left to lose.

Master Tayshin threw his hands to the air, yielding.

"Let her go," said Arianna, running forward without thought; Liam's final moments flashed before her eyes. "I will surrender to you. It's me you want, so take me! Leave them be."

She knew he would kill Mother Adunni if she didn't give herself over.

"Arianna, don't!" shouted Cyn.

Nico held her caretaker back from running after her; Arianna was sure Solomon would've killed her too—he would kill anyone who stood in the way of his goal.

The village was eerily quiet now, only the sound of crackling and consuming fires to be heard. Those still standing—both Shadow Resistance and what remained of Moriamo—waited with bated breath to see what Solomon would do.

"I will accept your surrender," he said after a torturously long moment. He lowered his weapon and signaled something to his followers.

The shadows nearest to Arianna grabbed hold of her, removing her weapons and immediately suppressing her ability to use magic; she didn't resist.

When Arianna was bound and trapped, no chance of escape, Solomon drove his blade through Mother Adunni's middle. Her blood spilled to the ground, and the earth gently caught her as she fell into its arms.

It had all happened in the blink of an eye, though Arianna

was sure, for the rest of her life, she would *always* see that image in her sight, no chance of blinking it away.

"Auntie, no…" shrieked Master Tayshin, falling to his knees, head in his hands.

Solomon turned to leave, blood dripping from his sword, without remorse; Arianna couldn't breathe, couldn't do anything, as she was dragged behind him and away from her friends, away from Moriamo.

"No, no, no, *please*," she stuttered, struggling against their grips. "I surrendered!"

In the distance, she saw Nico grab Cyn's hand as they locked eyes with her, a look of shock and despair splintering both their faces. Then they rushed to escape in the opposite direction before the battle could begin again.

Master Tayshin looked up too… there was something so haunting about his expression as they hauled Arianna away.

In that moment, looking upon her formidable master—the founder of the Guardians of Gold—she knew there was nothing he could do.

There was nothing anyone could do to save her now.

She relaxed into the arms of her enemies, numbed by this truth. *Struggling will only make it worse. This time, you really are on your own.*

"May we meet again," Arianna whispered—though her friends were already too far away to hear her hopes.

The Swamp of Moriamo vanished before her eyes, just the smell of smoke lingering in her nose to let her know it had ever existed at all.

THE KING'S LAIR

THERE WAS NO CAGE NOR CARRIAGE for Arianna this time, only horseback and saddle. Solomon held on to her tightly now, steering his steed toward the High City. They traveled back down the same winding path she had abandoned him on not so long ago, but she wouldn't be escaping him again.

The Shadow Resistance who had made it out of Moriamo alive trotted alongside them for added protection; her wrists were bound and dark magic stifled her.

For days, Arianna kept her eyes forward, never uttering a single word, as silent as Solomon. His followers taunted and tortured her with their victory all the way to the King's domain. And when they stopped to rest, they tortured her physically, beating her so badly at times that she wondered if she'd even make it to their destination alive.

She thirsted for freedom unlike she ever had before.

Then, one warm evening—the heat almost as smothering as

the enchantments persistently trapping her into obedience—the crisp view of the City of Saindora grew tall in front of them like a mountain in its own right. It was the only time she let a single tear fall on that journey, betraying her fearless face.

As the renowned city and palace finally materialized, Arianna was shocked to find that it looked nothing like how she'd always imagined it might be… she wouldn't have called it 'beautiful' at all.

The so-called 'silver-sanded' beach was peppered with filth from the city and seaport. There were too many boats to count, stacked upon each other like a horde of mindless fish that could go no further yet viciously kept trying to inch toward the land; Arianna could almost see the stink of it rising into the air, smacking her in the face upon arrival.

The palace towers which had once, supposedly, shone so white that they could be seen on the darkest of nights had certainly lost their shine, and the city that rolled down below mimicked the same bleakness before meeting steely, gray waters.

Arianna tried to match this Saindora together with what she'd read about in scrolls detailing the Golden Age, or from the tales that Syrifina Myr, the original mermaid of the Olleb, had fondly recounted to her and her friends. She'd vividly imagined this place to be crafted of blue skies, calm waves, and sparkling-white beaches. A thriving city surrounded by lush gardens and filled with music, magic, and laughter. The golden end of the world.

That world is clearly gone.

"Welcome to the City of Saindora," said Solomon. "Your dreams have finally come true."

Arianna remembered sharing such dreams with her Master Bell, of becoming a great warrior like him, dubbed with the honor of protecting their king here in the High City. Back then, never in her wildest imagination would she have thought she'd be standing where she stood today, so young, barely into her twentieth year.

She gazed upon the palace with contempt in her heart, forced to confront her naivety to have wished for such a future in the first place; the splintered golden gates of the city creaked open to reveal a plethora of paths that swirled up and around the palace in stacks.

"Master Bell," said a city regulator with a low bow. "How may we be of service?"

"I require additional escorts," he replied, curtly. "I have captured a *very* fine prize for our king, and we cannot risk losing her again. Gather 'round."

"Yes, sir." The man commanded more regulators into position behind and in front of them.

"Here we go," whispered Solomon into Arianna's ear. He snapped the reins, the decisive sound making her shudder. "Better hold on tight."

The procession started through the gates, and Arianna saw people had been awaiting them—word must've traveled ahead of Solomon. The streets were hectic, overrun with bystanders.

"Move! Out of the way," called the regulators, shoving the curious citizens aside with unnecessary force.

Most people had the good sense to swiftly get off their path as Solomon and his guards traveled with their prized prisoner up the main trail toward the palace.

Arianna was met with looks of shock, disapproval, anger, and even fear. She thought surely that seeing the face of the mighty King's prey turn from rumor to real was more than enough to send anybody here into an uproar.

Only now would the citizens of Saindora realize the hunt for Arianna Belvedor had not been a conspiracy nor a lie. This was reality, a new part of the Olleb's history to be recorded: a young slave from the districts had escaped through the Vanishing Tunnels and was—*years* later—captured alive by the King's faithful wolf, Master Solomon Bell.

A long time later, they reached what appeared to be the end

of public land and the beginning of the King's private territory; the tall, iron gates barring the palace away from the rest of the city stood wide open and waiting, like a mouth ready to be fed. A long, torch-lit path invited them to travel their last stretch in peace.

The procession of Shadow Resistance and city regulators came to a halt at the front steps of the palace soon after.

Arianna had to crane her neck to even glimpse the tops of the many towers that appeared to spiral up from the ground, stabbing toward the clouds with sword-like tips. From this angle, it was impossible to see more than a fraction of the colossal structure.

A palace regulator immediately received Solomon; he dismounted, pushing Arianna off the horse unceremoniously.

She was too weak to catch herself.

Her back slammed into the cobblestone and stars sprinkled her vision. From this viewpoint, the palace looked like the ghost of something inhuman that had escaped from the underworld, with countless glaring eyes; a wide, marble balcony with thick railings caught her focus. It overlooked the front courtyard where they had gathered.

A woman was staring down at her from it, her green eyes peeled open in what appeared to be disbelief. The silver, jeweled tiara sitting neatly on her head glinted in the light of the torches decorating the balcony, and she clung with long, polished nails to the banister.

"Never in a million years," Arianna said.

She forgot her distress as she gawked up at Her Highness, Princess Elisa—the King's very own sister, and the only other person in the Devlindor bloodline.

Seeing the Princess now—in the backdrop of the Palace of Saindora—made Arianna's quest, this journey she'd enlisted herself on, unequivocally real. Although in chains and at the mercy of those she deemed the villains of her story, she was finally right where she had set out to be after her initial escape from the Jar.

Down with the King... and anyone else who supports his claim to the throne.

A regulator gripped her arm and set her back on her feet, but she couldn't peel her eyes away from Princess Elisa. Her heart swelled to the challenge of having any chance at all at taking her and her brother down. *Maybe I still have a chance.*

"Get her inside," said Solomon, following her gaze.

"Right away, sir," said the regulator, shoving her forward.

As if triggered by Solomon's voice, the Princess seemed to snap out of her daze. With her lips pressed into a firm line, she spun around, her light-pink cloak and long mane of silvery-white hair trailing behind her in the wind.

She disappeared inside.

Arianna's eyes lingered on the balcony for a moment before considering what lay ahead…

Shining black double doors towered over her in such a way that she was afraid to know what was on the other side—the gold, coiled snake of the King's Crest stretched hideously from top to bottom.

The shadow soldiers were gathered around her, but the rest of the city regulators all left to return to their posts; Solomon barked orders to the palace guards to get the doors open immediately.

They slowly slid them ajar and a cool draft of air enveloped Arianna, her skin prickling with winter bumps even under the sweltering sun.

Everyone stepped inside to a grand foyer, boots clacking on polished tiled floors. Then, the doors closed.

Solomon gave leave to most of his warriors, to lurk wherever shadows did in such a dreadful place. However, Arianna had trouble believing that this could be considered any type of 'home' for anyone, even shadows; the gathering quietly dispersed to their respective duties around the palace.

But when Arianna really looked around, she suddenly understood why one *might* be able to find some joy within these snake-infested walls…

The main gallery opened up wide before her, sweeping away memories of the dismal exterior with something vibrant; colorful paintings covered the walls and brightly jeweled chandeliers dangled from lofty ceilings. There was even a window that created the entirety of one wall, the panes brushed with so many different shades of blue that Arianna thought the soul of the sea had been captured there, a living, breathing thing.

And everything, from the ceiling to the floors, seemed to be decorated in gold trimmings or laid in shining, white marble.

This is more like it, she thought.

Yet, despite the overwhelming grandeur that had engulfed her once she'd stepped through those palace doors, there was a coldness about this place—Arianna had never felt so frozen before in any given dwelling ruled by the King, including the Jar.

Palace attendants and staff scurried by with their heads held down, and no voice was raised above a whisper; it was as if fear had been stitched to the stale air trapped within these walls.

When Arianna again found the eyes of Princess Elisa, she saw that coldness there, too.

"Wait just a moment," she stated from atop a tall, velveted staircase that overlooked the foyer.

Everyone still in the vicinity immediately stopped, bowing their heads slightly as her voice filled the quiet space.

"Your Highness? We have to take the prisoner to the King," said one of the shadow soldiers.

"*Quiet*, Roland," she snapped.

The Princess's voice was such a smooth, tinkling sound but with an unmatched strength to it. Roland lowered his head like a dog in trouble and stepped back to Solomon's side.

Arianna saw she was beautiful, certainly, but she knew without a doubt that magic kept her looking that way. After so much time, so many years, not even the greatest concoctions in the world could stop the skin from furrowing or bones from creaking.

She had learned that, in the past, magic had been used to prolong life in an accepted, shared way. Not everyone opted for the extra years of youth, but many did—even Solomon, Talis, and Master Tayshin, she supposed.

The King and his sister, on the other hand, had abused the privilege, if only to rule a little longer.

Arianna, however, was confident that immortality could never be achieved for anyone. Even mermaids weren't entirely safe from Death's claim, so one day the Devlindors would *have* to relinquish the throne, whether or not it was taken from them.

She felt herself grinding her teeth as she considered the Princess. *One day you will be nothing but dust.*

Princess Elisa glided down the stairs to join them; Solomon and those still gathered bowed their heads again to properly greet her.

Arianna tried to refuse the gesture, but Solomon forced her head down by the nape of her neck.

"That's quite enough," said the Princess, her tone much gentler. She stopped directly in front of Arianna.

Obedient, Solomon released the pressure on her head, but he kept his hand firmly around the back of her neck.

The Princess studied her so intently that Arianna felt her skin burn hot under her scrutiny. She steered her chin upward with her finger as she examined her.

I cannot believe Princess Elisa Devlindor is touching my face.

Arianna was staggered by her presence once again, cringing away from the uncomfortable closeness.

"I see she's bruised… wounded," said the Princess with more sharpness than before.

She glanced to Solomon with a displeased expression.

"Not fatally," he replied with cold indifference. "It's nothing that could've been avoided. She's death to hold on to."

He squeezed her neck tighter, and Arianna gritted her teeth, forcing herself not to struggle.

Fighting won't do me any good right now.

"Very well. The King is waiting for you," she said, turning to leave. "He will decide what to do with her."

"Will he try to kill me today?" asked Arianna, unable to keep the question contained.

"Do *not* speak unless spoken to," barked Solomon. He took her tightly by the arm and spun her around to face him—he couldn't have looked more serious, so she decided not to test him further. "The next time, you'll regret it… if there is one."

"Try?" Princess Elisa walked back to Arianna's front, looking her over with something more of curiosity this time.

She gave a little chuckle.

"If the King wants you dead, that is what you will be," she said, playfully twisting the end of a gray, leather lash that was draped around her neck; Arianna didn't miss when a silver spark ran across the cords of the whip, just like when she channeled her own magic through her swords.

"The King can't have everything he wants," she retorted, infuriated to see even the slightest bit of magic emit from a Devlindor—together Princess Elisa and her brother had destroyed so many innocent lives just to hide and hoard it all for themselves.

The last word had barely left her lips before Regulator Roland struck her face so hard that her ears started ringing.

"The defiance that landed you here in your chains is apparent," said the Princess, placing a cool hand on Arianna's sore cheek. "I can respect that you desire certain freedoms. It's human nature. But the freedom you are searching for *is* unattainable in this regime, and 'desire' won't change who you bow to."

She dropped her hand, standing taller.

"I'm much more forgiving than my dear brother, child. You'll do well to remember that bowing is *still* bowing, even if you're forced—"

Solomon kicked Arianna behind her shins, and she fell to her hands and knees before the Princess—his sword at her back kept her there.

"And to answer your question," she added, staring down at her, "you'll be lucky if the King doesn't strike you dead today."

She gave a little shrug.

"Then *again*… as his prisoner, you'll be luckier if he does."

The Princess's statement left Arianna cold to her core as the consequences of poking the snake over and over again finally came to fruition. She knew one thing for certain—whatever the King might decide to do with her life wouldn't be lucky at all.

I have to escape!

"Take her to the throne room," said the Princess. Hand upon the railing, she started back up the stairs. "I'll be in my chambers if I'm needed."

"Yes, Your Highness," said Solomon with a bow.

She stopped halfway up the steps, glancing back to him.

"Yes, Princess Elisa?"

She gazed at the ceiling, sighing loudly.

"Oh, never mind," she said with the nonchalant wave of her hand, continuing upward. "It is done."

Solomon sheathed his sword and set Arianna back on her feet. They started down a long corridor.

Regulator Roland and other Shadow Resistance followers flanked them until they reached two heavyset, glass-paned doors; the guards posted here looked as if they were ready to march into battle for how much armor and weaponry weighed them down.

They swung the doors open, revealing the throne room.

As they entered the chamber, the clean, white tile of the palace shifted to a black granite; it covered the total expanse of the floor, like the Black Sand Desert had been locked there under glass.

Arianna gasped at the strange familiarity. *I've been here before.*

She remembered the striking ceiling—a kaleidoscopic mirror built over every inch of the room with a firelit and crystal chandelier its only embellishment.

It felt like only a fleeting dream, but she knew it had been real, a failed attempt at astral projection; here, in this throne room, had been the first and only time she had ever laid eyes on the King in the present day, even if only in a spectral state.

Only now did she note the statues lining the walls, gargantuan and ghastly things. And tall fires glowed in small pockets that lined the floor, casting an unnerving glow about the chamber.

A grand portrait of King Devlindor and his sister was the focal point on the far wall, and positioned directly below it was a thick, velvet carpet lining a platform of stairs...

Arianna sucked in a breath as her gaze traveled up the velvet steps, settling on a golden throne that appeared to be molded after fire itself, wild and destructive.

Just survive.

Sitting upon the throne was none other than King Devlindor, in the flesh, a decorated crown fitted to his head; one hand gently stroked a jaguar curled up at his side and the other held tight to a white staff with a ruby head.

Arianna barely had a second to comprehend this image. Bulky metal chains snapped around her wrists and ankles. Then Solomon dragged her down the aisle.

They reached the center of the chamber, its vastness seeming to swallow them whole; the King had yet to look up.

DIGNITY

ARIANNA HAD THOUGHT OF THIS MOMENT for so long. For nearly a lifetime, she had hailed to a king as part of her daily routine, her identity—to a man whom she'd never even met. And in a short span of time, she had made it her life's quest to *kill* that king.

Now, here she stood, only a few feet away from her target, utterly alone and utterly terrified.

This is not how I imagined this going.

"Kneel!" said Solomon, forcing her to her knees.

Her chains clashed with the tile, a piercing echo ripping through the quietness.

She glued her gaze to the floor, hair tumbling long over her face, as she gathered the courage to survive this moment; even with her eyes cast down, she could feel the King's on her now, contemplating her in silence.

He finally spoke. "Solomon, dear friend, you have earned

your name in history this day."

"It's my honor to serve you, my lord," said Solomon, placing his arm across his chest and bowing low.

"Leave us now, everyone," ordered the King. "I'd like a moment alone with the girl."

When King Devlindor's voice filled the chamber, solidifying him into something tangible for Arianna, she nearly lost her breath. She began to shake, involuntarily.

Solomon had one hand on her shoulder, keeping her down on her knees—she was sure he could feel her trembling, and a part of her prayed that he might never let go.

Don't be brave, little slave… Be a warrior.

Her heart began to beat faster. Despite all the damage he'd done and the threats he'd made, she realized that Solomon would have never considered 'dead' as an option in his mission to deliver her to the King.

At least, that's what she told herself in this moment, as Death's shadow loomed around her.

Since no one else she trusted could be with her now, she wished with everything that he would stay by her side. Even if he wasn't *her* Solomon anymore, the memory of her friend with his hand upon her shoulder was better than being left all alone with King Devlindor, in magic-resistant chains.

"As you wish, Your Grace," said Solomon.

He made to leave, and Arianna almost could have imagined that he gave her a gentle squeeze, as if to offer some sort of comfort in her final moments. Then, he pulled his hand away.

Arianna couldn't help the slight whimper that escaped her lips with the sudden release of pressure.

She turned her head slightly, watching the bottom of Solomon's cloak flutter away, back through the grand doorway.

The doors slammed shut and all was quiet.

Will I die today?

The sound of the King's shoes clicking across the floor filled

Arianna with even more dread, each step torturously slow until the tips of his boots came into her view.

He waited in stillness.

She took a deep breath, grasping the remnants of her courage to look up; they locked stares for what seemed like an eternity, and in that time, the fire in her heart that burned for justice returned in full force.

She saw within his pits of blackness the loss, and fear, and fight of her friends, of the Guardians of Gold… of her family.

I'm not here for me. I'm here for them. Do not give up!

As if she had to physically battle away her own self-doubt, Arianna cut the fear from her mind to make room for all her anger and all her valor, for the true warrior the King had forced her to become.

"Well, well, well," he said in an even voice, "look who finally decided to show up. You have caused quite the stir for one so young. I admire the fight in you, but it shall be punished severely." He finished in an almost gentle, reproaching tone, as if he were merely scolding a child for staying up past their bedtime.

Molten yellow eyes found Arianna from behind the King's legs—lurking alongside him was his famed jaguar companion, Raja.

The avatar had been confirmed as such by the guardians many moons ago, long before Arianna's time. But she had since witnessed Raja's transformative abilities for herself, and her extreme power over the elements; memories from the avatar's swift annihilation of the last of the giant race still haunted her.

Similar to Solza, Raja also appeared to prefer her earthly form.

I can only imagine what else she's capable of, after centuries of practice…

Just knowing the magical might Solza could tap into after only a couple years of training gave her good cause for concern; had Raja completed other transformations too, besides earth and air?

Raja is likely more lethal now than on the last day of the giant's history, whether or not she's made a third transformation.

"Do you have anything to say?" asked the King, breaking her focus on Raja and drawing it back to him.

Arianna nearly scoffed—*I have a lifetime of words to say to you! Where to begin?*

"You're a coward," she answered in a low voice. "If you wish to kill me, then be done with it. Or *fight* me and let me die with some dignity. That is, if you win."

She shook the chains at her wrists, glaring up at him.

Oh, if my friends could see me now!

She never let their faces out of her mind; they were the only thing giving her the strength to stand her ground against the King and his avatar, alone.

He made a noise that sounded like a mixture of shock and amusement—Arianna did not drop her gaze.

"A fight against me would not leave you with any dignity," he said, matter-of-factly. "It would only leave you with a rotting corpse as a prize. Is that what you want?" It was a rhetorical question. "Your confidence, for a slave, is entertaining but misplaced."

"A *warrior* never turns down an invitation to battle. That is what I am. What do you claim to be?" demanded Arianna, lifting her chin high. "We're taught in the districts, which *you* govern, that only warriors wear swords on their belts. Is that not a blade I see?"

King Devlindor's hand flew to the jeweled hilt of a sword hidden within a golden scabbard at his hip.

"If you deem me just a slave, then hand me my swords and fight me here and now. We will see if titles matter."

Arianna could tell she had struck a nerve with him, his calm demeanor shifting into something much harder. He circled her like she was prey, and she wondered if he might even draw his weapon and strike her dead as she knelt before him.

At least I'll die with honor.

"You think yourself brave?" The King clicked his tongue against his teeth, shaking his head back and forth. "Even as you are, before *me* in chains?"

He stopped at her front, his face growing dark.

"I am no warrior." He unsheathed his sword, pointing the tip of his blade so close to her face that she was forced to lean back or feel its sting. "I am your king!"

His voice came loud, a deep and guttural sound that left Arianna cold to her core.

"You're no king of mine," she said after the echo of his words had died away.

A low rumble grew from Raja as she inched forward from behind her master; Arianna thought she might lunge for her throat at any second.

"You're strong," said the King after a moment, considering her with a fragile calmness that made Arianna immediately think of Syrifina Myr. "That much is certain, just from looking at you… at the scars you wear. The unfounded courage in your voice. The *magic* that burns in your eyes, trying to get out."

He sheathed his sword and Arianna relaxed a little.

"Yes, your strength is quite impressive, I must say. If not for your defiance, you may have even earned yourself a place on my guard one day."

Arianna felt the remnants of her youth gasp internally at what her life might've been had she taken a different path. *I would've been a perfect fool in any scenario to serve such a man.*

"I'd rather keep the chains then, thank you," she said, meaning every word.

"Good," he replied, clasping his hands behind his back. "You were clearly born for them."

Arianna started breathing heavier, beads of sweat dotting her skin that she wished to wipe away. She struggled slightly against the metal binds at her wrists; they seemed to grow tighter.

"Strength comes in many forms, as does weakness," said the

King, "and the only thing I loathe more than blatant physical or mental weakness is disobedience." He patted Raja on the head. "You've been leaving quite the mess for me to clean up. One that, frankly, I do not enjoy doing. Now, it's time to pay the price for your misguided choices."

"Name it," said Arianna, digging her fingernails into her palms. "I'm ready to pay. Everything I've done up until this point has been worth whatever you have in store for me." She spat at his feet. "Like I said, you are *not* my king, and at least I tried to do something about it. Others will come to finish what I've started."

King Devlindor pulled in a deep breath through his nostrils, turning away from her; Arianna's stomach tossed with nerves, but she tried not to show it.

"What you think you know and what you've done on your… let me guess, *quest,*" he said in a hushed voice, "is only a fraction of what others before you have also tried and failed at, Twenty-Two." He whipped back around to soak in her expression, smiling at the crack in her confidence. "And that was when stronger, more potent magic still lingered in the air—"

The King flipped his palm upward, a ball of green and electric energy growing there; Arianna had no name for this magic, but it was certainly most beautiful and most deadly.

"I control it all now," he said, looking up; the green fire reflected eerily in the countless panes of the mirrored ceiling.

The ball began to float upward out of his hand, so high that Arianna wasn't sure anymore which enchanted emerald flame in the mirrors was the real one.

"You've only managed to scratch the surface of what it is that I possess. And, just so we're clear, the answer is *everything.*" He spread his arms out wide. "This palace, this city. Knowledge, power. The world, your life included, I will *never* give any of it up. No matter how much you try and fight me, no matter how far you run, I will always have you in my grasp," he glanced to his self-portrait, "because this world belongs to me. I have cured the Olleb of her inequalities so that everyone may have a fair chance at the same game of life."

"You're a mad king," said Arianna, tearing her eyes away from the entrancing magic. "You have cured nothing. All you've done is smothered a beautiful land in darkness so that light has no chance of spreading. The balance of life has never been more inequal with you draining all the goodness from its source."

"At least darkness spreads evenly, if that's all there is," said the King, coolly. "Light always seemed so… selective."

He knelt down so that he was level with her.

It looked as if a silver ring of fire had sparked around his pupils—hypnotizing. She could feel the energy radiating off him, so strong and potent that it made tears burn in her eyes.

Arianna felt suddenly sick to her stomach, her nerves tangling there in a way that seemed unnatural, like the King was literally toying with her emotions, spiraling them out of her control.

What is this magic? Is this magic… or am I just that terrified?

"In shadows or sun, Olleb-Yelfra will always bow to me," proclaimed the King with a smile in his voice, "and so shall you."

Arianna felt her head grow heavy with the weight of his words. In fact, her entire body felt so *unbearably* heavy that she couldn't help but fall to the floor as he loomed over her.

She tried to move, but it was as if a wall had tumbled on top of her back, pinning her to the ground face-down.

"I am the High King of Olleb-Yelfra. You are nothing more than an insect under my feet. Insult me again, slave, and I will crush you where you stand."

He stood, pressing the heel of his boot against her cheek so hard that she thought her teeth might shatter.

Arianna cried out, and the King laughed.

"Yes, you're so very brave," he cooed.

He gave another push, relishing the sound of her screams. Then he released his foot and his magic so that she could move.

"What will you do to me?" Arianna stuttered, cautiously pushing herself back up to her knees—this time, she didn't dare lift her gaze to meet his.

King Devlindor had succeeded in humiliating her into obedience. For now, she had no more cards to play.

"Oh, I do apologize," he said, "I must have misunderstood you before. I thought you wanted to die with, oh, what was it again? Dignity?" He put his hands on his hips. "Changed your mind that fast, *hmm*? I'm almost a little disappointed it was that easy."

Arianna looked to her hands, wanting so badly for her magic to come so she could truly show him what she'd meant.

Coward, she thought—she couldn't bring herself to say it aloud again.

"I won't kill you," he said, turning serious, "but by the end of this, you'll beg me for the mercy of death. That said, I make no promises. I have a long memory and don't forgive easily… I might just like to keep you around forever."

He scratched at the stubble on his chin as he pondered her fate, in the same way he probably pondered what to eat for dinner.

"My first priority will be to get to the bottom of *you*." He poked her in the chest, and she knew he'd felt her heart thrashing there in a panic. "I want to find out what makes your beating heart tick so fiercely that you were able to get as far as you have in the first place. I need to make sure that it may never happen again."

He tapped his temple, and suddenly Arianna understood what he meant to do.

I must not say anything to betray the guardians, no matter what magic he uses on me to pry it out.

But she wondered if she would even have a choice.

King Devlindor glanced around his throne room with an expression of sudden confusion. "Sir Vladamor tells me that you and your escaped friend have tamed avatars, but where is yours now?"

Arianna's mouth tightened into a straight line.

"What's an avatar?" she asked, tilting her head to the side—even she heard how unconvincing it had sounded.

She sighed. *Lessa would've gotten away with that...*

"Don't play games with me!" he snapped, taking her by the shoulders. "I know who you've been training with, those *disgusting* excuses for rebels. Solomon will forever remain faithful to me, and through his eyes, I've been watching the guardians for decades. I know everything you think you know and more—"

A sinister grin grew on his lips, like a horrible idea had popped into his mind. He let her go, turning his back to her again.

"Though, if you're truly unsure of what an avatar is, I'm happy to show you."

Raja let out a vicious roar, and Arianna squeezed her eyes shut, wishing to be able to cover her ears; she thought her eardrums might actually explode.

"Tell me where your avatars are hiding," screamed the King over Raja's roar, and over Arianna's howls of pain.

"I wish that I knew," she shouted back—that was the truth.

The King signaled Raja to stop, but before Arianna had time to feel any relief, he struck her so hard across the face that she toppled sideways; the jewels decorating his fingers dug deep into her cheek, ripping into her skin and lips.

She tasted blood pooling between her teeth and on her tongue—her ears were still ringing and now she was seeing tiny stars sprinkled across her vision.

"Tell me," he growled, his hand raised to strike again.

Arianna looked up at him from the floor as unbidden and silent tears began to fall; she hated that they did, but there would be no stopping them now that they'd started.

"Even if I did know, I wouldn't tell you a thing," she said

through haggard breaths, readying herself for whatever pain might come next—a smack from the King was the least of her worries.

"*Fine.* You needn't say another word," he said with a sigh of annoyance. "Your mind will tell me all that I need to know." He leaned over her, his shadow growing only larger from the flicker of flames everywhere. "And rest assured, once I've sucked your memories dry to my satisfaction, I'll make sure that you'll never be able to create new ones again."

Arianna mouthed 'no', but he only smiled.

"Until tomorrow."

The weight of his magic overcame her once more. She couldn't fight it any longer, his enchantments seeping into her bones and forcing her to be docile.

"Guards!" the King bellowed, stepping over Arianna like a piece of trash on the street—his silk robes swept over her.

A woman answered his call immediately.

"Get this filth out of my sight," he said. "Put her with the other resident slave of the palace until we can find a more permanent place for her body."

"As you command, my lord," she said.

King Devlindor left the throne room.

The next thing Arianna knew, she was again being thrust into the air by the hands and arms of strangers, her body numbed with magic. At least this time she knew who the enemy was.

The last thing she saw of the throne room was her reflection in the mirrored ceiling. She was surrounded by blackness, the granite tile melding into one vast pit.

Who is that wasted warrior? It was a painful image to see.

Arianna blinked and her reflection changed into something familiar—it was the girl from the mirror who she'd banished so long ago.

She didn't even have the capacity to be scared or surprised. *Will I ever wake from this nightmare?*

However, as she looked closer, something seemed different about her otherworldly reflection… she didn't appear to be born out of the darkness anymore, for she was encircled by a burst of brilliant light; Arianna was reminded of the ghosts of those about to transition on to their next chapters.

Is this the foretelling of my death?

The girl in the mirror shook her head, offering her a smile that she somehow knew she could trust.

She gazed down at her with sparkling eyes—*my eyes*—and a fierce expression full of hope; Arianna knew the girl in the glass was her *truest* reflection, the reflection of her spirit. One that was good, strong, and relentless. And that girl had destroyed the darkness more times than she could count.

The King cannot break me! He will have to kill me first.

As the guards dragged Arianna away to whatever fate awaited her, she kept her eyes glued on the girl in the glass; and she was confident that no matter the torture and pain, she *would* survive… if not in body, then in brilliant, beautiful soul.

THE DISTRICTS

LESSA STILL HELD THE FLAME of magic in the palm of her hand, warming her to the task ahead as they snuck out of the Dueling Arena. She felt empowered with such an energy that the pelting snow could do nothing to stop her, the pink glow of fire illuminating the swathing darkness of the blizzard.

"We're almost there," said Noah. "Gather your wits."

He guided them through the snowstorm, leading Lessa and Eli carefully down a winding street and away from the shelter of the sparring room. With Solza and Sano following closely at their heels, they traveled past the Stables and the Square, past the Learning Center and then the Pit, until finally they found themselves flush up against the mountainside.

Lessa had an urge to duck underneath the barracks; they were near the spot where she knew she'd find the firebug-lit path to the hot springs.

That life is gone.

She shoved the thought to the back of her mind.

There's no escaping anymore, no turning back.

She had found herself responsible for a key piece of the puzzle in trying to achieve her family's goal of bringing justice to the Olleb.

Talis gave his life for this.

And she'd risked her life over and over again, barely survived turning into a mermaid and back, *and* nearly lost her friends at every turn for this.

Everything the guardians had done was to just have a *chance* at standing squarely against the King; what happened next could put them on even ground with his Shadow Resistance, alter the future forever—and it was in Lessa's hands.

I must do everything in my power to make them believe.

They followed Noah to the door of the first set of barracks lining this street.

Lessa turned to look back down the path; not even their footprints in the snow were left as evidence of their trek. The storm had wiped everything clean. It was so dark that she couldn't even see what they'd left behind.

"Here's as good a place as any to start," said Noah, wrapping his arms around himself; the early morning was frigid here. "This is the only time I've ever been happy to be so cold… breaking the law." He laughed to himself.

Lessa felt anything but cold, her enchanted flame spreading warmth throughout her entire body as she focused on the opportunity before them. The sun would rise in mere hours, and—if they succeeded—with it would come a new beginning for the Four Corners.

Eli placed a hand on her shoulder, his expression so assured that she found herself pulling confidence from just his gaze.

"Everything will be all right," he said. "We can do this. We've made it this far. Now we just have to show them why we were crazy enough to come back in the first place."

"After you," she said, the flame flickering slightly with the onset of nerves.

Eli squared his shoulders. "Don't let that fire burn out until you see the belief in their eyes," he said, resolutely.

"Never," she said—her fire burned brighter.

"This is madness," said Noah with a slight giggle, unable to contain his excitement. "If Liam could see us now…"

"Who says he's not watching?" whispered Lessa with a wink.

Noah gave a small sigh, a softness in his expression.

"Right," he said. "Best we hurry, then. Once that storm clears, we'll lose our cover and the regulators will surely catch up to us quick."

"You two stand guard outside for now," said Lessa, drawing the attention of their avatars—Sano and Solza obediently positioned themselves outside of the door, a wolf and a snow leopard keeping watch.

Eli kicked it open, not wasting another second.

They all stepped inside, one after the other, the wind howling behind them and blowing snow about the room. There were murmurs of shock and surprise as the slaves of this barrack scurried to get as far away from the door as possible, fishing for their weapons.

It was a boys' barrack, and no one had been sleeping. Lessa was sure of it; all the commotion from the Free Falls had left them too riled to rest their eyes.

Terror shone on all their faces and nobody spoke, all surely trying to wrap their heads around this strange, unexpected disturbance in a place where strange and unexpected things never happened. The younger boys ran to hide behind the older ones.

Lessa knew they probably assumed them to be regulators upon first glance, trying to catch people up past curfew to punish.

That's what I would've thought.

She lowered her fist down by her side, her fingers clasped over the flame that burned in her palm so that no one could see the magic, not just yet. She moved slowly into the room behind Eli.

Noah followed behind Lessa and shut the door, locking the howling storm outside; the room fell unnervingly quiet.

"It's the ones from the Free Falls," mumbled one boy, breaking the silence.

"*Hush!*" said another. "You'll be tossed to the Pit."

"No, he's right. They're not regulators at all!" said a young man, flexing his muscles. "I saw them caged up by the general during my fight."

Lessa recognized this young man as a seventeenth year who had just won his freedom, his soul surely now scarred from taking the life of one of his own; she could see that pain already etched in the haunted look on his face.

"What are you doing here?" he growled. "What do you want? You shouldn't be in here."

He clenched his fists, stepping forward, and the rest of the boys began whispering in a panic—some prepared to defend themselves, gathering weapons from the undersides of their beds. Others kept their backs against the walls, terrified they'd be found disobedient.

Lessa didn't feel scared anymore, seeing how petrified these boys were of her. She'd faced far worse than warrior-slaves of the Four Corners during her time on the run.

She glanced to Eli, knowing he was thinking the same thing for how relaxed he looked; he had won his freedom from the Four Corners, fought with some of the best warriors across the land, and survived a year of torture in the Luose Dungeon.

These children were no match for him either.

Lessa and Eli waited, observing the boys observing them—they said nothing until they felt the right words come.

"Noah, mate, who are these people? Why are you with them?" said the seventeenth year when neither Lessa nor Eli spoke up.

"No, is that *Noah?*" gasped another young man, his back

against the far wall. "You mad, are you? What if the regulators come? What if they hear?"

"You know they won't come," said Noah, stepping forward. "That's why you're all up. You know the storm is keeping them away in their own quarters this night, and…"

"And you have some questions on your mind," interjected Lessa. "We're here to answer them."

The flame in her hand was still held low so that no one might have spotted the magic just yet. Down at her side, it could have been just a small lantern washing the room in a soft glow.

There was a long silence, then a smaller boy spoke up, poking his head out from under the covers on his bunk. He must have been barely a sixth year.

"What was that… out there? What did we see earlier?" he asked in a shaky voice.

A flood of questions followed, pouring out from every mouth. The barrack was suddenly filled with a rumble of chaotic sound as everyone let their worries spill free.

Lessa closed her eyes for a moment, overwhelmed at the sudden flurry of curiosity about the magic they'd witnessed yet didn't understand. *How not to lose any of them? How to explain?*

She thought of Jeom when they'd first journeyed through the Vanishing Tunnels—he'd reacted so frightened and furious to the unknown when she and Arianna had confessed their knowledge of magic. They couldn't afford that kind of reaction now, no time to debate truth versus fantasy.

Lessa was struck with a thought, *There's a key difference between these boys and pre-belief Jeom…*

She opened her eyes.

They've already seen magic.

Arianna had freed them of the King's spell, so—as Noah had already proved—most of them should have proof of magic within their own memories. And they'd *just* witnessed it again during the battle with Solomon.

They already knew that their eyes had seen something extraordinary and inexplicable… *All I have to do is give them an explanation just as extraordinary as what they witnessed.*

Lessa hoped it wouldn't prove a challenge, given all the magic she'd acquired since her time trying to persuade Jeom of it; she was better equipped now.

I can do this!

"Quiet down," said Noah, hushing the room with his arms spread out wide. "Lessa and Eli have come here, from outside of the Jar, to tell us everything."

"We're here to expose the truth," said Eli.

"The full truth," added Lessa. "A lie is the only thing you've ever known."

"What do you mean?" said the seventeenth year, the tizzy of questions starting up again. "What lie do you speak of?"

Lessa walked to the center of the room and opened her fist so that her magic was made visible—the pink flame of truth shone there for all to see.

The boys of the barrack were struck silent; this was an impossibility in their world. Lessa knew they could pull no explanation for this whatsoever from their minds, the most beautiful parts of the Olleb hidden from them.

"Do I have your attention?" she said, releasing the flame so that it began to float toward the ceiling—it shed light over the entire room, over her.

Her borrowed crimson cloak sparkled with icy, white flakes.

There were emphatic nods all around, everyone gawking back and forth at her and the floating fire, unblinking.

"Good," said Lessa. She used her magic to open the door, beckoning to Solza and Sano. "We can explain everything now, but we have to be quick. My friends and I have come here to free you."

With everyone's full attention, Lessa dived back into her

sharpest memories of magic, Sano helping her to produce beautiful things to prove their story. She healed those who had been injured during recent battles, and she levitated people who mocked her from their beds.

Solza also came to her aid, filling the gap Arianna had left by her side; she made the earth beneath the floorboards tremble with elemental magic, and she gave Lessa an energy boost to keep her magic flowing strong—not once did she let her flame burn out.

Eli didn't have tangible powers, but he proved maybe the most valuable asset this night. It turned out that his way with words was the strongest persuasion of all, a magic they hadn't seen coming.

Elijah Neve, a Warrior's District idol and survivor, was remembered among many in this room—every word he spoke seemed infallible to his peers, and his sheer belief in and loyalty to the Guardians of Gold was unshakeable.

Lessa stepped back to let him take the spotlight, and, in no time at all, the entire room had been turned into believers of magic and the guardians' cause.

When everyone seemed comfortable with the new plan for freedom, Lessa, Eli, and Noah left the boys of this barrack to gather their things and prepare for the rough journey ahead.

They headed back out into the storm, celebrating their first successful mission, though they still had many more barracks to go…

One by one, they visited all the slave quarters of the Warrior's District, sneaking through the snow like thieves in the night—stealing away loyal followers of the King.

The hours ticked by fast.

By the time the sun had begun to rise, every warrior-slave had heard the story of the Guardians of Gold and was ready and eager to learn more. In fact, by the time Lessa, Eli, and Noah were through, there were no Warrior's District slaves left at all…

Their unquestioning faith in the King had been shattered

with the undeniable proof of magic laid out before them. And with so much pent-up energy and anger toward the Crown for all they'd suffered, they were ready to destroy their inherited shackles and fight back.

The children of the Warrior's District bowed to King Devlindor no longer, and Lessa knew they would gladly die to prove it.

"Ready yourselves," was the warning that she, Eli, and Noah gave to all their new allies—they crept through the last remaining shadows of the early morning, guiding everyone to gather in the Dueling Arena. "For with the sun, we'll take this district. Then, we'll take the Four Corners."

WHEN THE STORM FINALLY SUBSIDED, the sun now high above the claws of the mountains, barely visible beneath the gray clouds, the bell sounded—its piercing ring reached every corner of the district.

Just like any other day over the last nearly three hundred years, regulators would burst through the doors of each one of the barracks, expecting to find their slaves ready and waiting. Except, today, they would find those quarters empty.

There would be no slaves to bully into a line or parade past the Pit. There would be no frightened children to corral into the Square… or to make hail to a King.

"Get ready," said Lessa.

She heard the creak of the large gate to the Dueling Arena opening. The regulators slowly poured in, weapons raised. Their sleek, black cloaks and shining weapons glinted under the sharp glare of sunrays trying to cut through the thick clouds.

Lessa readied her longbow—the blue and silver steel that had once belonged to Talis Churry gave her courage now.

"What do you think you lot are doing?" said the interim general—he had clearly been thrown into command after Solomon had disappeared without a word in the night.

He looked to his regulators for help, but they were all just as perplexed as him…

Lessa could tell they were still shaken up by last night's festival. Just like the rest of the district, they were sifting through magical memories that they didn't have the knowledge to comprehend.

She knew the regulators recalled the day she and Arianna had fled from the Four Corners, and the inexplicable catastrophe that had followed at the Free Falls Festivals just two years ago; Solomon Bell, the King's trusted servant, had taken out half of the regulators with swords of light that seemed to extend out from his body in all directions with no rhyme or reason.

They'd also witnessed Arianna's bizarre and explosive ending to Grinda Risso. And now, even the disappearance of General Ivo probably came back into question—was it linked?

Incomprehensible recollections swept the district, for regulators and slaves alike, and Arianna had made sure that the magic would never be forgotten again.

We can do this. We have the upper hand.

The regulators looked even more uneasy as they registered the avatars—Solza had transformed right before their eyes the night before. And they surely hadn't been expecting to find the girl with the bow and the boy with the tattoos who had fought side by side with Arianna Belvedor.

Their memories of magic were being confirmed, and illicit 'imagination' couldn't be to blame.

Lessa registered the regulators' collective panic, unsure of what to do next; every slave of Warrior's District had positioned themselves behind her, Noah, and Eli, an immovable wall of red, solidified as they stood together as one.

"Lower your weapons!" said the interim general.

"Not likely," retorted Noah, raising an axe.

"I'd stand down if I were you," said Eli, a sword in hand.

He stepped aside to showcase several district trainers who had tried to enter the Dueling Arena too early this morning—they were tied and gagged.

"You saw what happened. You saw Arianna Belvedor and her magic," he yelled. "This district no longer bows to your king."

Lessa said nothing, but the tip of her arrow became engulfed in pink flames; she hoped the magic in her eyes was bright enough for all the regulators to see clearly.

"We don't take orders from you anymore," shouted Noah. "And if you stand in our way—"

"We'll kill you!" said a small girl, standing proudly by his side.

Her name was Kiki, and she had a spunk that Lessa knew Arianna would love, should she ever get to meet her; she was to credit for helping Noah grow into the strong lad he'd become, when Liam and Arianna had had to leave him behind in the districts.

Kiki and Noah slapped hands before turning their attention forward.

"What say you?" said Eli, again addressing the regulators.

A few of them began to lower their weapons, whispering among themselves as they tried to make sense of this situation.

Many looked uncertain, but others appeared power hungry, not ready to lose in the face of the children they'd grown so accustomed to seeing cower before them; the interim general proved resilient, probably afraid to miss his chance at glory. He clearly had only one goal in mind—crush the rebellion.

He opened his mouth to speak another command, but Lessa was done with listening. *It's time to act!*

She released her fiery arrow before he could utter another word… only a scream.

She stopped it with her magic just before it pierced his skull; there was a collective intake of breath from both sides.

Lessa set her bow on the ground and left the safety of her peers to walk toward the enemy—Solza and Sano flanked her all the way to the middle of the Dueling Arena, their eyes a radiant silver.

There had to be at least two hundred regulators gathered at the gates, but there were thousands more on her side. Nobody challenged her yet, not with the arrow threatening the interim general's life in midair.

She marched right up to them, any fear she once had replaced with anger. *Down with the King!*

"Do not move even an inch," she whispered to the interim general—he would die instantly should she allow her arrow to continue on its natural path.

The flame was so near to him that he began to sweat profusely, his bulging eyes fixated on the sharp end of the weapon.

"I am tired… *tired* of all the killing," Lessa said with sincerity. "I'm a healer, not a warrior, and that is all I wish to be. I want to help and heal this land—"

She was full of so much rage and sadness that she didn't even know what to do with it. Such heaviness felt so unnatural in her heart, so she channeled it into her magic.

She lifted her hands, feeling immense power race through her veins, unconstrained and aided by the avatars; the broken weapons, arrows, and blades that were forever scattered about the Dueling Arena rose into the sky at her command, alive once more— they hovered in the air, steady with a purpose, each one pointedly targeting a regulator.

"But I *will* take the life of every single one of you should you continue to stand in our way and waste our time."

Lessa's face ran hot as she thought of everything she'd already lost, and all they hoped to gain if they could make it out of here in one piece.

"The King has lied to us all, yourselves included. You were

slaves once, too," she implored. "Remember that. Take this opportunity to help rid the world of that terrible fate, for all who come after you."

She grew excited, her voice pitching with both passion and power as she recognized the total control she wielded in this unthinkable moment.

"What you see now, and before at the Free Falls… it's called *magic,* and the world is filled with it, ready to be shared again with everyone. As is our right!" The weapons inched forward with her fervor, and all the regulators stepped back. "The King stole this right from you, buried magic under centuries of lies so that you don't even know what you've been missing. I'm here to tell you that a piece of you *is* missing, and we want to return it."

Lessa inhaled, and the weapons moved with her.

"King Devlindor stole our magic when we were all but children and forced this cold world upon us. Now we're going to take it back!" She narrowed her gaze, raising her hands higher. "You're either with us or against us, so make your choice… *now.*"

The weapons hanging in the air seemed to snap into place so that each regulator stared at their fate should they choose wrongly. With the obvious choice made clear, they all fell to their knees on the snow-covered ground in surrender.

All, except for the interim general.

"I said, choose!" yelled Lessa, tears in her eyes.

She stepped forward, the flaming arrow inching closer as well.

Breaking under the pressure, the interim general slowly sank to his knees, the arrow following him threateningly until his head was between his hands and his face was kissing the snow.

Lessa let the arrow drop to the ground in front of him, trying to hide her exhaustion; with a sizzle, its flame blew out, and the rest of the weapons rained back down to the ground as well, like a curtain falling.

"Tie them up," she commanded to Eli as he and others came to meet her. "We can't have anyone turning on us. We don't have time for that now. We have all the support we need."

"You did good, Les," he said, gently.

Lessa didn't move, staring, unblinking, at the arrow near the interim general's head; Eli grasped her by the arm and forced her to face him while the rest of their peers began to follow her orders.

"You did good. Now breathe," he said, taking Lessa by the shoulders.

He sucked in a deep breath, urging her to follow.

"I just hate being that person," she said, looking away from him. "It's too hard. You have to empty yourself, and it's so… hard to come back from that. I learned such lessons from Syrifina."

"You did what you had to do, and nobody died," said Eli. "I definitely wouldn't have been as generous."

He smirked, trying to draw a smile from her.

"If they hadn't backed down," said Lessa with a frown, "I would've killed them all, Eli. I would have had to. Arianna, she's had to make that hard decision for us time and time again so that we survive… I get it now."

"She's a warrior," said Eli with a knowing shrug. "We were raised to fight first and ask questions later. As you stated, *you're* a healer." He plucked at the fabric of her red robe. "Hopefully, one day soon, you won't have to put on the face of a warrior ever again, if that's not what you want." He tilted his head. "Though, if it is, you've certainly earned the color."

Lessa nodded, wiping her eyes.

"I can only fill her shoes for so long. We have to get her back."

"We will," said Eli, his expression hardening.

He opened his hand for Lessa to take, his dragon mark reminding her that she was not alone in this. They were both part of something much bigger.

She just prayed that Arianna and the others were able to do their part too—whatever it turned out to be now that fate had divided up their futures.

"Aren't you scared?" she whispered, resting her palm in his.

"Of course," he said with a soft smile. "It's scary… not having control of anything in this world. Our future is uncertain, the futures of our friends are uncertain, and we're all desperately searching for a piece of control." He squeezed her hand. "If all else fails, just remember that you can still control your *breath*."

He inhaled deeply again.

"Just breathe, in and out. Every single breath is you controlling your life. As long as you're breathing, that means there's still hope."

"How can you be so sure?" she asked, already feeling more relaxed with every word he spoke.

He patted Solza on the head as she nuzzled up against him. "How do you think I survived the dungeons for a year?"

Without another second of hesitation, Lessa inhaled deeply, letting the air calm her from the inside; Sano stood by her side, supporting her all the while.

"Good," said Eli. "Now, let's get out of here while we still can." He lowered his voice. "I doubt you could pull that little stunt twice, am I right?"

Lessa nodded—she needed time to recover her energy before her next show of force.

Eli turned to the gathering of eager young warriors.

"Listen up, friends," he called. "The time has come to leave Warrior's District behind. Everyone here has a choice. No one will make it for you. When we leave here, you can either head out into the world and go it on your own, *or* you can join us. Help us to free the rest of the districts and fight by our side in the war to come." He commanded their undivided attention. "I assure you, no matter if you leave us now or not, this war *will* find you at one point or another, so choose wisely. No one is getting out of this without a fight. A new age is upon us!"

Everyone raised their weapons into the air, roaring their approval with such a sound of hope, passion, and fight that it made

Lessa's heart leap for joy.

The start of a real army, she thought.

"Make groups," said Lessa, trying to show her kinder side after having to act so tough. "You will not be shamed should you wish to go your separate ways."

"Those of you who are with us, please escort the regulators to the private training quarters," said Eli. "Those who are not, move to the side."

Noah and Kiki stood to attention as Lessa and Eli gave orders, clearly making their choice known. Then, one by one, the newly freed warriors stepped forward to help.

When Eli and Lessa looked back to see who might be left, they found nobody there; even the youngest ones clung to their older mentors, ready to follow them into the world no matter the danger ahead.

Kiki walked toward the private training quarters with a big smile stretched across her face, shoving the interim general alongside her with a sword in hand.

"We're warriors," she called back. "No one's going to stay behind from *this* district. Maybe yours, healer." She nodded to Lessa, who couldn't help but laugh. "On to the next!"

All the former slaves of Warrior's District began to chant, "Down with the King! Down with the King!"

"Like music to my ears," said Noah, hands on hips.

"Here, here," said Eli, nodding along.

After they had procured an elder's map of the Vanishing Tunnels, they were ready to leave.

Eli took the lead, guiding the procession of freed warriors onward to the next district, Solza at his side; Lessa and Sano steered from behind to ensure nobody could get lost in the tunnels.

When the last person had disappeared into the Blancoren Mountains, Sano let out a heartwarming howl—it echoed throughout the now empty streets of the district, save for the occasional cook or caretaker who poked their heads out to spy. It replaced the shrill ring of the bell with something stronger, a warrior's cry that everyone was happy to rally behind.

Lessa glanced back to the Warrior's District one last time, hoping to never lay eyes on it again. She stroked Sano's head, his howl resounding in her mind.

Maybe by the end of this, it won't even exist.

PART TWO

KNOWING

THE SOUND OF WATER DRIPPING to the floor was the first to register as Arianna came to.

She was comfortable… too comfortable.

I must surely be paralyzed.

She lifted her arm and regretted the movement; everything hurt and her mind was in such a foggy state that she could hardly even consider her surroundings. With a moan, she rolled to the side, curling into a ball on a bed of soft, white feather pillows.

At least I'm still in one piece.

The King had let his regulators beat her senseless before tossing her here—wherever 'here' was—and they had been more than happy to do so.

"Lie still," came a soft voice.

Arianna jerked, trying to turn back over; a searing pain raced through her body. She let out a yelp, her voice echoing off the stone walls of this mystery chamber.

"I told you to be still." The voice belonged to a woman. "I see the King did a number on you. If you give him what he wants, the beatings may cease to be so painful."

Arianna felt the relief of a cool rag touching her forehead. She carefully maneuvered to see who was there; a young woman stood over her, with unruly hair and eyes she'd surely seen before.

She tried to place this stranger in her memories, but everything was in such a haze. "Who—"

"Am I?" said the young woman.

With piercing clarity, Arianna suddenly knew why she seemed so familiar.

"Your eyes... they look just like—"

"My mother's," she replied, matter-of-factly. "To answer the question sitting in your mind, yes... I am the daughter of Ophelia. My name is Odessa, also of the seer bloodline."

Arianna gaped at her. "Ophelia was your *mother?*"

She had learned a bit about seers in her studies of the Golden Age. The King had attempted to exterminate their bloodline, just as he had done with all the magical creatures of the world, keeping only what served him a purpose.

Ophelia, though, he had claimed for himself. She had become one of his most prized possessions.

It was a terrible fate for anyone, even this girl's wretched mother—if she spoke a truth—but it didn't dissuade Arianna's instant suspicion of Odessa; she wanted nothing to do with the daughter of the woman who had turned her world upside down. She had forced them to flee from South Luose and had gotten Liam and Keeper Kassime killed in the process.

"If you really are the spawn of that monster, then do not lay a hand on me," she growled.

With just one look at this frail girl, Arianna was sure she could snap her like a twig if she tried anything funny, even in her wounded and frightened state; she slapped the rag away.

Odessa flinched but stood her ground.

Arianna found her a tad eerie, the way she carried herself—
she swayed a bit, back and forth on her heels, as if she were following the dancing thoughts in her mind, keeping just one eye
on the present. It was reminiscent of the ghosts she'd seen who
still lingered in the Olleb, unfinished in the world of the living
yet not quite ready for whatever world came next.

"I know my mother tried to kill you and all the damage that
was done thereafter," whispered Odessa after a moment. "I know
all, though I wish I knew nothing."

"Then you know that if you put that hand on me again, you'll
lose it," said Arianna.

Odessa pursed her lips, defiantly placing the damp towel back
across Arianna's forehead.

"Just try and relax," she said, gently.

Arianna tensed but couldn't ignore how soothing it felt. She
closed her eyes, soaking it in. *Everything hurts.*

"My mother burdened me with the curse of sight," said
Odessa. "I think that's enough without you adding the consequences of her actions onto my shoulders." She gently dabbed the
cloth on her skin. "Children should never be judged by the
choices of their mothers and fathers. In a world where families
are now falling into myth, how can we be held accountable for
our origins, Arianna? Do you even know who your parents are?"

Arianna fluttered her eyes open, finding the seer's strange
gaze on her, waiting for a response.

She shook her head slightly.

She supposed there was truth in Odessa's words—no one
knew who their parents were in Olleb-Yelfra, save for those who
had formerly occupied the Swamp of Moriamo.

She quickly steered her thoughts in a different direction. "Are
you aware of what I've done to your so-called mother?"

"Of course, I am," said Odessa with an awkward, blank stare.
"I know *all.* I saw when you made the choice that ended my
mother's life, though I'd rather not dwell on that." She bowed

her head. "I've also seen all the choices and paths you've walked to lead up to this very moment." She looked up, an excitement in her expression. "I've had my eye on you… you're not supposed to be here yet."

She left her side, so Arianna shifted to be able to keep watch on her.

Odessa walked to the center of the room where steps appeared to lead up to a still pool of water inlaid in a marble platform. Thin, shimmering gold snakes had been painted across the steps, making it seem as if they slithered out from the water and down to the floor.

The seer seated herself on the side of the pool, running her fingers across the water, back and forth. She stared into it as if she were fixated on something, but Arianna could not see what it might be from her position; she began to grow uneasy with the silence.

"Are you not frightened of me?" Arianna called—she thought of how her arrow had plunged straight through Ophelia's chest.

How can someone who seems so compassionate be born from someone so dark? Is she playing a trick?

She remained cautious.

By gods, am I truly locked in a room with a seer? This is too much.

Her mind was so slow to catch up to her reality, churning over everything to try to find a sensible explanation.

I am, aren't I? That would be just my strange luck. But why on earth would the King think such a thing a good idea?

She was sure, whatever the reason, it wouldn't benefit her.

If it's true, then this girl is powerful. She probably knows every thought in my head.

Arianna felt everything click into place.

And that's just what the King desires…

Odessa turned to face her, and Arianna felt herself redden; smoky gray eyes, like stirring clouds on a stormy day, considered her—unseeing, yet seeing all—holding tight to so many secrets and truths.

"There are a good many things I've found troubling, but they're not *my* fears to be troubled by. The only person I am frightened of is the King," she answered with an airy quality. "The rest of my worries, I can see coming, and you are not my enemy. Not right now, anyways. Maybe tomorrow… or, maybe, not ever." She tossed her head back and laughed, startling Arianna a bit. "As it stands, you don't even have a weapon, and you're chained to a bed!"

Only now did Arianna notice the heavy weight of shackles on all her limbs, keeping her chained to the pillowed platform.

"I don't understand a word you speak," she said, lifting her hand to her head. *I can't believe I'm talking to a seer.* "You remind me of—"

"Master Talis Churry?" Odessa grinned, and Arianna felt herself frowning. "He was one for riddles, and I'm sure he would *implore* you to believe, yes? His was one of my favorite minds to follow…" She let out a little moan of annoyance. "Alas, such a pity."

"A pity, indeed," said Arianna, a bite to her tone; if she hadn't been chained down she might have slapped Odessa across the face for such a casual reference to the death of her friend.

She felt so vulnerable, as if her mind were spread out naked for this seer to poke around in, just as she knew the King would attempt to do soon enough.

Maybe this is his way of doing it entirely… through her. What secrets might she pry from my mind to feed back to him?

Arianna tried not to concentrate on her fears of the future or anything of importance to the guardians. Instead, she focused on the surprising fact that she still lived—King Devlindor had yet to rid her of her head, as she always imagined he would do should he catch up to her before she was ready.

At the very least, I'm still breathing. Just keep doing that and all will be fine.

"Don't count yourself lucky yet," whispered Odessa.

"I'm not," snapped Arianna. "I'm counting my lives."

"There's not many left to count, dearie," she said. "Most people only get one."

Arianna trained her focus on Odessa as she floated about the large chamber, trying to think of a way out of this; it was plain that the seer was playing out a sort of routine in this confined space.

In a way, Arianna could almost sympathize with her wicked mother now, seeing firsthand what life might've been like for her, before becoming Head of South Luose City Council… before experiencing freedom.

She knew that Ophelia had long ago sold her soul to the King, for just a semblance of liberty from the place he'd imprisoned her in—a place that Arianna imagined must've been a lot like this…

Did he keep her here, too? For how long? What was her treatment like? What does such captivity do to a seer's mind… let alone a less enduring human one?

Arianna could never even hope for selling her soul to King Devlindor for a trade as a worst-case scenario; he felt personally victimized by her mere existence and would never let her forget it.

He'll never let me go.

If she didn't find a way to escape or—by the will of the gods—be rescued, she'd never see her quest realized.

"You're not going anywhere anytime soon," said Odessa, pulling her out of her spiraling thoughts. "Not in those chains. Best get comfortable."

Arianna closed her eyes again, burying her face in the bedding to try to hide her fears. *It's useless! They're screaming out loud in my mind for her to hear.*

She channeled them instead through screams into her pillow. Then, she opened her eyes to face the seer.

"You should know," said Odessa, her expression twisted with concern, as if she shouldn't be revealing what came next, "when they decide to move you to your own chambers, you'll never leave this place again, just as I. Once that happens, it's over. They're fortifying your quarters in the Saindora Dungeon now."

Her words stunned Arianna into an even bigger panic; a bout of anxiety welled up inside her chest. *I need to get out of here. I can't die in here. I need to get back to my friends!*

She couldn't speak, her breath coming in sharp and haggard as she struggled against her restraints.

Odessa came back over to her, dabbing the cloth again, gently, against her forehead.

"Breathe," she said in a Lessa-like voice—the kind she would put on to reel Arianna back in from her edges. "That is just one fate I see for you now, but it's ever-changing. There are many other paths you could find. Not even I know what will come next for certain."

"Get me out of these," said Arianna. The walls were closing in on her. "Let me out!"

She fought against the resistance, but her magic wouldn't come—the oppressive enchantments had followed her here.

Just survive. Just survive. Just survive.

"Breathe," said Odessa, sitting by her side. "Just breathe."

Odessa's words seemed to seep into her thoughts to replace her panicked ones.

Just breathe. Just breathe. Just breathe.

Arianna sucked in one breath at a time, through her nose and then out through her mouth; her fluttering heart began to calm as the air filled her lungs, reminding her that the gift of life was still hers to claim.

"Maybe everything will be all right," said Odessa, patting her on the leg. "It's really up to you in the end."

She scurried away, humming to herself as she rummaged around a tall shelf, with countless bottles and books stacked on top of each other in no apparent order. When she came back to the bedside, she was holding three clear blue capsules in her palm.

"You should take these," said Odessa, placing them by her pillow—like wind trapped in a bottle, the contents of the capsules seemed to swirl with an almost hypnotizing effect. "Someone's left them for you. They'll help you heal quickly on the inside, but they won't wipe away the bruises and scars on your skin."

She went back to the shelf, taking care to place a lid atop a large glass jar; Arianna spied that there was a full supply of this magical medication inside.

Odessa hid the jar away, burying it among the knickknacks on the shelf.

Arianna turned her attention back to the capsules, mesmerized by the whirling potion inside. *Are they worth the risk?*

"I daresay you'll need a quick rest and recovery ahead of what comes next," said Odessa, earnestly. She tiptoed back with a cup of water. "Trust me. They work like a charm."

Arianna scoffed, finding the energy to slowly sit up.

"Why does it *always* come back to trust? What does trust even mean in this backwards world? I don't think I've quite put my finger on it." She was quickly transitioning from panicked to enraged by her predicament.

"You know, I really can't say," sang Odessa.

She lifted the long dress she wore, showing off small chains that connected her ankles.

"I've only witnessed the concept through the eyes of others, so you will probably have a better idea."

Arianna couldn't help but feel a bit guilty, averting her gaze.

She had been shackled for just a day, yet Odessa had been in chains probably her entire life. It made her wonder at just how long Odessa had been trapped under the King's eye; she appeared younger than Arianna, but there was no telling how old she truly was—if Syrifina had taught her anything, it was that ancient, enchanted bloodlines could age much differently than humans.

Nevertheless, Arianna was without Solza and her friends, without the ability to use her magic, and locked away in some lavish prison cell with the daughter of an enemy she'd finally removed from this world. What's more, Odessa knew everything about her—it was enough to make anyone cautious of their company.

Trust...

Arianna sighed, Talis in her head again.

She contemplated the small, marble-like pills once more and decided that the gamble was worth it, if only to feel just a little bit better in this dismal situation.

What's the worst that could happen now anyways?

She popped them into her mouth and almost instantly felt renewed as the potion worked, mending her internal wounds and stimulating her brain.

Arianna wasn't new to healers' magic, but this was the first time that she'd ever felt restored so quickly, save for Sano's unique abilities. She gasped at the strange, tingling sensation.

"Who did you say left this for you again?"

"I didn't," said Odessa. "But I did say that they were *meant* for you."

Arianna decided not to pry further, but something told her that somewhere in the Palace of Saindora there *could* be a person who might be the key to getting her out of this mess—there was someone nearby looking out for her. She ran through a short list of names in her head and suddenly felt hopeful that the captured guardians, Vance and Iris, may yet still be alive.

Had they escaped to somewhere nearby?

"Wonderful, aren't they?" said Odessa, observing her with a curious expression.

Arianna returned only a grunt of acknowledgment, but, admittedly, she felt better than her best days all at once—even though the bruises and surface wounds from her beating still remained.

Clever trick, she thought.

Whoever was able to concoct such a miracle remedy had to possess incredible power.

Arianna felt some of her optimism return.

She looked around, taking this moment of clarity to analyze her new environment; the small pool gave the chamber a softness that seemed misplaced here, considering it was a prison.

In fact, as far as prisons went, she found this one to be quite untraditional…

Even the bed she lay on now—a huge, round mattress flush to the ground and covered in white blankets and fluffy pillows—reminded her more of the quarters she'd once enjoyed in the Luose Palace than a dungeon cell.

The overall décor was simple but elegant, splashes of white, soft grays and blues giving the room a lightness; a tasseled rug that looked like a fluffy pile of snow covered the floor on one side of the room, with several large cushions scattered around it. And there were colored blocks strewn about the chamber that looked like they could belong to some sort of puzzle once stacked.

If not for the impenetrable stone walls and lack of windows, Arianna might have thought them in a regular wing of the castle.

But with the flicker of flames their only light source, it was not easy to forget that this *was* a dungeon hosted by King Devlindor—giant snakes, which appeared to be made of metal, coiled from the top to the bottom of four vast pillars that held up the ceiling, and the few spaces of wall not covered by sheer curtains to imitate a light blue sky were painted black.

But nature had found a way here too, giving life to a place where the King had tried to suck it dry; plants spilled out of round, stone basins in the corners, and vines crawled up the walls and ceilings, providing the chamber with a little fresh air—they were being fed by the pool, the tranquil focal point of everything.

A sudden wave of sadness washed over Arianna as she realized that this was a home…

"You've never been outside of this room before, I take it?" she asked, hesitantly, knowing the answer.

Odessa shook her head.

"Save your pity. My mind has been many places," she said, light-heartedly. "Besides, I cannot see."

Arianna almost rolled her eyes but refrained—she knew, somehow, 'seeing' or not, the seer would know. And she moved about the room as if she had perfect vision.

Odessa giggled, sitting back down next to her on the bed, seemingly excited by the conversation; Arianna scooted over to keep some distance between them, but with her ailments healed, she feared her less.

"And I'm not always chained," she added. "The King didn't want to take chances with a roommate such as you, and he *never* takes chances himself when he pays me visits." She shrugged. "I'm not sure why. What could a little lady like me do to someone as powerful as him?"

The coy smile on her face made Arianna raise an eyebrow.

I'm sure he has good reasons.

She scooted a little farther away.

"But often I'm relieved of my restraints when I'm alone, or when visitors of the palace who are aware of magic come to inquire of their futures." Odessa smiled, fluttering her eyelids. "I do enjoy visitors. They're always so kind. You will too… if you stay!"

There was a sincere hopefulness in her voice.

"I don't plan on it," said Arianna, firmly—it irritated her beyond belief that there were citizens of the Olleb who knew of magic, of people like Odessa, and still kept the King's secret.

Odessa sighed.

"Well, I wouldn't have thought so, really," she said. "You have many options ahead of you. I'm eager to see which path you choose, Arianna."

"What are the—"

"It doesn't work like that," said Odessa with a tinkling laugh.

"If I told you, it could change everything anyways. Or, maybe, it wouldn't change a thing, so what would be the point? Besides, only the King can demand anything from me."

Her tone changed, a sudden sharpness to it.

"He may own me and demand what he pleases, but I do not take commands from anyone else."

"Very well," stuttered Arianna—she had to respect that decision. "Keep your secrets. I have enough of my own."

But I do have many questions, too.

"That you do," said Odessa with a knowing expression. "But if you end up staying on, I sincerely hope we can become friends. I think the Princess *might* be my friend, but you can never be too sure these days, can you… of who your friends truly are?"

"If any Devlindor is your friend, then we can never be as such," said Arianna, curtly. "And if you really think Princess Elisa is your friend, locked in here as you are, then you must be out of your mind."

"Never say never!" said Odessa. "You cannot see the future as I." She laughed again, glancing to the waters. "But you're right on the latter. I suppose I am in a constant state of 'out of my mind,' being a seer and all."

She shimmied a little with joy, as if she'd just learned something new and it had been the most thrilling thing—Arianna assumed she knew everything, so she didn't know what to think.

Maybe she actually is out of her mind… or too lost in it?

"How does it work, exactly?" she asked, unable to dissuade her curiosity—if she was going to be chained to this bed for long, the least she could do was learn more about this bizarre Golden Age being. "Your powers, I mean?"

Odessa sat cross-legged now, playing with a thread on her robes. She had the same look as her mother, the same clouded eyes, but her face was youthful, with dark brown waves of hair framing lightly freckled skin.

Pippa flashed across Arianna's mind; with the memory of her

innocent roommate, tortured and slain, she wondered whether or not Odessa might need freeing just the same…

Seers have proven the ghosts of the Palace of Saindora for centuries, it seems. I'm sure she's ready to move on.

Her defenses came down a little more, brick by brick.

"No one has ever cared to ask me that," said Odessa, pondering over her answer. "I suppose, the King doesn't quite care as long as he can use the power… use me."

She pressed her hand over her heart.

"Have you ever gotten a feeling in your chest like you knew exactly what was going to happen next? What someone might say or do, or where you might end up, even if it was just from a mere second before? Have you blinked and thought back that, somewhere in your past, you had imagined you'd already been where you stood, already did what you were doing, or already heard the sounds filling your head? Like a memory, planted in your mind that you hadn't yet lived."

Arianna lay back as she chewed on these words, gazing up toward the high-vaulted ceiling.

"I *think* so," she said after a moment. "In my district, we call it déjà vu."

Odessa giggled, shaking her head.

"That's just a fancy word for magic," she said. "It's a natural magic of the mind, for the mind is a complex place and full of far more power than most people ever come to realize. Even I can't begin to understand it fully, though I'm a natural born master."

She squeezed Arianna's hand tightly, as if it connected her to the here and now.

"The women and men in my bloodline, for centuries, have been blessed and cursed with unlimited and uncontrollable access to our minds," she continued. "I am no sorceress, no witch, as you. I cannot make magic flow from my fingertips or levitate someone with just a thought or word, but I know all that will be and all that has been, if only I think it—"

With her finger, she drew in the air an incomprehensible picture.

"I follow the strings of energy down different paths to create the power of all-seeing, like a map of the entire universe within my brain, if I let all in. And seers can never fully shut it out." She cocked her head to the side. "*Maybe* for a second or two, for just a little peace and quiet, but even when we sleep, we dream of life. What has been, what could be… of everything. Always, I am everywhere. Time flows through me, back and forth." She ran her hand up the length of her arm. "I am its vessel."

"Someone told me once that destiny is set in stone," whispered Arianna, trying to comprehend such a life, such possibility as having all the answers she so desperately desired stored away for contemplation, "but that the choices we make decide if we realize our destinies or not—"

She took a deep breath, feeling the reassurance of the soul of the star against her skin—the glittering blue stone that encased the star's soul was just an empty shell now, but even a memory of such magic proved a powerful thing. It too was a vessel, one which had let her tap into powers not her own. It had given her hope in hopeless situations, and the memory of its magic gave her hope still.

"Is this true?" Arianna asked. "Is there no other path but one that was forged for us from creation?"

"Destiny is fluid," said Odessa. "You know that. I've watched you learn that lesson time and time again, as you decided on who you wanted to be. One's choices not only affect oneself but everything and everyone around them, creating chain reactions that make up our pasts, presents, and futures. And if you really think about it, destiny is just that… the sum of one's choices." She tilted her head back and forth. "To pursue that idea, to not. To choose something else entirely. It all starts with a choice. Whether an idea was planted in your head or created of your own volition, *you* decide if you'll grasp onto it. You get to choose whether it's worth uncovering further or going in a different direction."

She cupped her hands open like a flower.

"A choice can unfurl into so many greater things, into new knowledge and paths to choose from. When you reach your life's end, when we all do, then, and *only* then, will we understand our true destiny. For, at the moment just before death, one remembers that idea, that *one* choice which started it all, leading them to such a point as death in the first place—"

She leaned back casually, as if this was the most common knowledge in the world.

"Those who can go gracefully and without regret have achieved their destiny, even if they didn't really know what it was all along. But those who look back and wish they had made a different choice at one point or another, those are the ones who lose out greatly in the end... for they *decided* they did not complete their purpose. So, you see, Arianna, it's truly up to you to decide your destiny. A sense of completeness is unique to each and every soul, and one is never too young nor old to find it."

Odessa reached out to touch the tiny shell belonging to the soul of the star; Arianna was so enthralled by the conversation that she let her.

"Destiny may be written in stone... but even stones change slowly over time," she said, "however imperceptible to the human eye."

"Including mine?" asked Arianna, her voice small as she tried to grasp the simple meaning behind Odessa's complex answers. *In the end, I decide my destiny...*

"You have many choices in front of you. I know the paths for all," she repeated. "Though, it matters little. All lives end in death. There are no immortal souls in this world, save for the gods that put us here and who will take us away."

Odessa gazed again to the ceiling.

"However, as I've said, Arianna Belvedor," she released the

necklace, her voice suddenly steady and strong, "you're *not* supposed to be here yet. What happens next is entirely up to you."

Arianna was, once again, flabbergasted.

Speaking to Odessa was like speaking to a creature with a mouthpiece tied to the souls of the universe, both past and future. She couldn't even fathom such power as to know everything yet be able to *do* nothing. And she forever wore a dazed look, like someone unaware of their surroundings, lost in their mind.

Arianna supposed that all rang true.

She considered her with new tolerance—part of her couldn't help but pity this girl who had never felt the sun on her skin. Yet, when she spoke about what she saw, what she'd seen, and what she knew to be true, her voice came with the sound of old wisdom, as if Talis himself channeled through her from the beyond.

Not girl, woman… seer. She's right, she doesn't need my pity, but does she need my help? It was, so far, unclear.

Arianna found it in herself to empathize with Ophelia then too, who had probably birthed Odessa in captivity, traded in for a younger version so that the cycle could continue on; if Arianna could escape the King and finish what she and her friends had started, finish what the Guardians of Gold had set out to do, she would put that cycle to rest.

"Could you tell me… if my friends live? Jeom and Demetrius?" She wished she could conjure visions of the ones she loved to know their fates.

"I *could*," said Odessa. "But I've told you enough, and I won't let another sorcerer use and abuse my powers. You're slave to the King now, just as I."

"I don't wish to abuse your power of sight," said Arianna, sitting back up to confront her. "I just want to know if my friends are safe."

"And what could you offer me in return?" She twisted a lock of hair around her finger, transforming back to someone innocent and child-like once more.

Arianna held up her hands. "Nothing…"

She jingled the chains at her wrists and feet.

"Well, for nothing, I shall have to think about it," she said with a smirk. "We have plenty of time, so I'm sure we can come up with a better trade than that."

"If we're to be friends," said Arianna, understanding that this warped mind might also not trust so easily either, no matter how friendly she might appear, "trading power for power *isn't* part of that deal. That's not what friends are for. They lift each other up."

"So I've seen," said Odessa. "You sure have found a lot of great friends… lost many, too."

"That I have," she said through her teeth—it felt like she'd just been punched in the gut.

Her stomach churned; she had no idea how fresh some of those losses Odessa referred to might be. Maybe some she wasn't even aware of yet… *Jeom, Demetrius, Lessa, Eli?*

She shook away the thought.

"Knowing is not always the blessing it may seem sometimes, I assure you," said Odessa, softly. "Therefore, since I *see* that there's possibility for us to be friends in the future, I'll tell you only what you need to know, and nothing more." She squeezed her arm. "Trust me, Arianna. You can and you must. Right now, there's nothing you should focus on but you and *your* future… if you wish to have one."

As the wheels turned in Odessa's head, Arianna watching the sparks of silver sizzle across her misty stare, it was evident that this young seer could uncover for her everything she had ever hoped to know—not only about the safety of her friends but also of Ol-leb-Yelfra's future.

It was excruciating to dwell on the information that was being withheld, so she instead shifted her attention to what had already been revealed.

I'm not supposed to be here yet, and I need to figure out why.

14

NEVER FORGET

THE HEAVYSET DOOR OF THEIR DUNGEON chamber scraped against the stone floor as it opened, but Arianna hadn't fully been sleeping. The smell of food wafted in as a fresh gust of air filled the room from the outside. She inhaled deeply, relishing it.

The air circulating here tasted so thick and old that being shut in with no windows, even just for a single night, was torture enough—the plants did their best to create an imitation of the outside, but nothing beat the real thing. It reminded her too much of her time locked in the sparring room.

I can't go back to that colorless life.

Arianna ached for the freshness of the world she'd gotten to know on her adventures across the Olleb—she supposed Odessa's boundless sight was a blessing in that regard, for if she could only see what was sealed within these same four walls, day in and day out, she would've fully lost her mind long ago.

She blinked open her eyes, and immediately noticed that her

eccentric cellmate was no longer in the bed next to her; Arianna was still chained to it, so she had to twist around to locate her.

Odessa was on the far side of the room, back against the wall and head bowed low. Her hair covered her face entirely.

Arianna looked toward the door, knowing what she'd find—one of the King's many palace regulators stood in the doorway, surveying the room. He was a bulky fellow with wide eyes and a stern, chiseled face.

Regulator Roland, she thought with an exasperated sigh.

"Stand up," he barked. "Get over there, now."

Arianna lifted an arm, the weight of the chains holding her down.

"Would love to oblige, sir, but I'm a bit tied up at the moment," she said with a mock yawn.

"Do not speak again." Magic flared up in his eyes. "I'm sure the King wouldn't mind if I stitched your mouth shut. He only needs your mind."

With the snap of his fingers, her chains fell off.

Arianna felt a rush of relief at the sudden freedom to move her limbs. She practically flew to her feet.

And she realized with alarming clarity that this palace regulator felt comfortable enough to wield magic freely; she knew Regulator Roland was one of the King's loyal shadows. But how many others had he led into the dark? Secretly fortifying his power over those who knew nothing of magic, by sharing it only with those who proved faithful?

Even Solomon, she assumed, must've had an introductory lesson to magic as the King's obedient wolf—even if he *had* been already accustomed to it.

"Stand next to the seer, hands where I can see them," said Roland, coming into the room. His fingers itched toward the hilt of his sword.

Arianna was slow to obey the command, but she was in no position to refuse. She walked to Odessa, all her bones creaking and cracking as she moved; it felt so good to use her legs.

"You know what to do," he said in a bored voice.

Odessa brought her fist to her heart, standing up straight.

"Hail to the King. Hail to Lord Devlindor," she said in a small voice—Arianna's skin crawled at hearing the phrases she'd long since banished from her vocabulary.

The room grew frighteningly silent as Roland waited for her to speak next, staring her down.

"You must say the morning verse," whispered Odessa.

Arianna could feel her shaking, their arms touching as they stood side by side.

She didn't respond, struggling with doing what was easy versus doing what would surely earn her more bruises.

I have to stand up for my beliefs. I cannot let the King take them again!

"You heard the seer," said Roland. "*Say* it."

Arianna took a deep breath.

"I will not," she said, holding her head high. "I have no king."

Odessa whimpered, inching away from her along the wall.

Regulator Roland padded across the room, closing the distance between them. He raised the back of his hand as he came toward her, but this time Arianna tried to defend herself; she dodged his slap and threw a kick to his stomach.

Her heel landed in his ribs, and he groaned. But he had quicker reflexes than she'd been anticipating from such a large brute; he caught her foot midair, spinning her to the floor.

He pressed a knee into her back to hold her down, slamming her head into the stone floor with a heavy hand.

Arianna cried out at the sudden, dizzying pain.

"I *said*, say it, slave," he said, close to her ear, drool dripping onto her skin—he was seething.

"I will not," she said, tasting blood in her mouth, something that was starting to become all too familiar.

He pressed his hand down harder, and she thought her head

might burst open under his weight. She screamed, trying to shift him off, but he was too heavy.

"Release her, Roland," came a chilling voice from the doorway.

He did so without hesitation.

Arianna felt no relief, knowing whose face she'd find. Slowly, she pushed herself up to a seated position, hand to her forehead where a pounding ache had already settled in.

Odessa and the regulator had both dropped to their knees, heads bowed; King Devlindor leaned against the doorframe, considering Arianna with a hungry curiosity.

She got to her feet when he didn't say anything, trying to appear tall, brave. It was still so surreal to be this close to the man she'd thought so much about over the last few years. Finally, her imagination of the person she'd hated her entire life had formed into a real picture.

Arianna could see that the King could be considered handsome to someone ignorant of his actions—he had a thick head of swooping hair and a smirk that seemed to hide away the likely sinister thoughts in his mind. His crown looked freshly shined, and he carried the white staff with the gleaming red ruby fixed at the center. It looked as if he had dressed to attend a ceremony of some sort, doused from head to toe in what were probably his finest jewels and silks.

No amount of finery can hide your true heart.

King Devlindor was, through and through, an evil man.

After a moment, he slunk into the room, his avatar dutifully following behind him. They were accompanied by the full King's Guard, Solomon included.

As everyone flooded into the chamber to surround her, suddenly, the vast space became a lot smaller.

Arianna tried to make her powers known then, anything so that she could defend herself. But the forces oppressing her magic were still impossible to combat.

King Devlindor let out a loud, haughty laugh that echoed off the stone walls.

"Still defiant, are you?" he said, coming toward her.

Arianna backed away on instinct, until she felt a wall beneath her palms.

He loomed over her. "That will eventually be corrected. I'm good at teaching people how to bow."

With the tap of his staff on the ground, the floor shifted beneath her feet; she fell to both her hands and knees before him.

"Look, you're getting so good at kneeling!" he said with mock delight; some of the guards snickered.

Arianna pressed her fists into the floor, trying to stand back up—his magic was too strong.

"You can wield your magic on me all you want," she spat, buckling under his force, "but I'll never *willingly* bow before you."

Using the sharp end of his staff, King Devlindor tilted her chin up so that she had to look at him.

"You have proven an exciting conquest," he said, "but you've lost now. Your disobedience only hurts you, though it's something that I rather enjoy ridding from this world."

Arianna looked past him to Solomon. His face was like stone, as if he couldn't be less interested in this interaction between his former apprentice and the High King.

All her senses were clouded with rage.

"Funny, because I rather enjoy disobeying you," she said, keeping her eyes on her former master. "And if Master Bell couldn't rid me of that quality in years of study under him, I wouldn't bet that your chances are very good."

The King's lips curled up into a smile. He pulled his staff back, glancing to Solomon.

"Ha! Did you hear that, Bell? My, my, *my...* she truly is something," he said. "Why, I haven't heard someone talk to me in such a way in over a century, truly."

He let out an exaggerated sigh.

"Shame the guardians got to her first. What a waste."

"Yes, quite a shame," said Solomon, flatly.

"Well, we have plenty of time to try and tame this wild animal," he replied. He looked back to Arianna. "There's years and years' worth of discipline ahead of you, Twenty-Two, so I might just take those odds."

He turned on his heels, his cloak smacking Arianna in the face.

"Roland, you know where to take her." The King made to exit the chambers. "Solomon, walk with me now."

Everyone followed King Devlindor out of the dungeon just as abruptly as they'd come, Solomon falling in step with his master; Arianna was still on her knees, now at the mercy of Regulator Roland.

As soon as they'd all left, she made a lunge for the door.

"*Cementas cuerpa!*"

Her entire body froze, and she could do nothing but blink—it was her least favorite spell, to take away one's free will.

"Do you really think you can escape?" Regulator Roland was so close to her face that she could taste his sour breath. "The only way you'll ever be free of your chains again is on your deathbed!"

He continued to shout insults at her.

She found Odessa's misty gaze from across the room, focusing on the only friendly face she could.

"*Your paths are dwindling.*"

Arianna's eyes probably grew double in size as Odessa's voice filled her head, coming loud over the regulator's.

How did you say that? Her lips were sealed tight, but she had certainly heard her speak.

"*Soon, there will be only one ending for you to choose,*" she continued. "*May it not come to this, for all our sakes.*"

"*Is this mind magic?*" said Arianna, her thoughts replacing her voice.

"*Why, of course,*" said Odessa. "*Seers are the greatest masters of the mind, remember? And now, I've opened mine to yours.*"

"You haven't a chance here, girl," said Roland, pulling Arianna's focus back to him as he poked her in the chest. "You may know a sliver of magic, but the Shadow Resistance is all around you now. Our power is tenfold. And the magic your beloved guardians tried to cook up is nothing compared to what we control."

He released his spell, and she fell forward into his arms. Then he enchanted a rope to bind her hands behind her back.

"Time to go. Now, march!" He grabbed Arianna by the hook of her elbow, leading her out of the chamber.

Odessa stared after them, swaying in the odd way she did; Regulator Roland pulled the door shut, locking it behind him.

"*Don't give up,*" said Odessa, her voice still lingering in Arianna's mind.

"I won't," she whispered.

"What was that?" barked Roland.

Arianna focused on him as Odessa's voice faded away. "I said, where are you taking me?"

She struggled against him, though much less now with the seer's warning in her thoughts.

"To the morning commendation of our king," he snapped. "All citizens and slaves must recite the daily verse." He shoved her forward. "You're His Majesty's special guest this morning, so I'm sure he's prepared you a proper welcome." There was a sinister smile in his voice.

Arianna didn't respond, trying not to let the looming terrors in her future steal her concentration.

I need to memorize the way out.

REGULATOR ROLAND TOOK THIS TURN and that, the dungeon pathways a boring blend of bulky, gray stone; Arianna tried to remember every twist of the palace that led up to the main floor and to the outside—in case she should ever get the chance to escape.

She recalled Talis' story of when Solomon had helped him flee during the failed siege; there was a tunnel somewhere in the cellars here, maybe even near to her new quarters.

That could be an option too... If she could find it.

Why does everything have to be left up to chance?

From just one walk, the dungeon labyrinth was almost impossible to commit to memory. Everything below the main floors was a terrible maze before they even reached the steps that led up and out, the Saindora Dungeon a plethora of passageways that Arianna hoped to leave untraveled.

When they finally did reach the main level, Regulator Roland took her in such a roundabout way that the halls began to remind her of the Vanishing Tunnels—at one point, she considered that the pathways might *actually*, magically, be changing direction around them.

Anything is possible.

Her mind was now fully open to the endless creativity this world was capable of.

After a time, they exited the palace through an inconspicuous side door that Arianna had no hope of ever finding again on her own; thoughts of memorizing right and left turns were suddenly replaced by fresh air. She inhaled so deeply that she thought her lungs might burst.

The early morning was too bright for comfort after being shut away for so many hours. She couldn't see anything properly, forced to shield her eyes from the burning rays.

Save for the Island of Idris, Arianna thought she'd never been this close to the sun before.

She knew from her Learning Center studies that the South

was notably the warmest region in the Olleb; the North was known to be frigid and cold.

But experiencing Saindora sun firsthand was something else entirely—just as it was an impossibility to evade the touch of snow in the Jar, the only reprieve from the heat here seemed to be the cool breeze blowing up from the sea.

Sweat had already begun to gather on her skin, dripping down her back and tickling her arms in an unpleasant sensation; if this had been Idris, she would've already thrown off all her clothes and dived into the sea to cool down.

Arianna couldn't even wipe the sweat from her brow or pull back her hair, hands bound as they were. Barely five minutes outdoors and she had pinpointed the *one* positive thing about being locked in a dungeon with Odessa…

At least it's nice and cool down there.

It appeared to be a quiet morning in the city as Regulator Roland escorted her through the courtyard. So quiet that she could hear the subtle sound of waves splashing against the seashore, far away across the metropolis. *How long would it take me to reach those waters, if I could make a run for them?*

She longed for Solza.

Even if I made it there, I wouldn't last long against the sea.

Not without her avatar to help her navigate the unruly waves.

Her heart ached for her companion, so she put her attention on the streets that unfurled downward from the palace center. She tried to calculate how long it might take her to reach the city gates.

From here, Arianna had an aerial view of everything. And with every corner of Saindora splayed out bare underneath the brilliant sun, it was easy for her to spot its magic, hidden away in plain sight. *Never forget.*

Regulator Roland didn't let her enjoy the view for long, guiding her toward a striking black and gold carriage. It had the emblem of the King painted on both sides and two large steeds headed it up. The carriage driver was readying to leave.

Tobias, she thought.

She hated thinking of his final moments, but the only way to honor his memory now was to live. *Just survive!*

She stole a glance inside the carriage and spotted the King—his decorated crown caught the light each time he moved his head.

"Out of the way!" barked a palace guard, waving her sword back and forth as she cleared the way for someone.

Regulator Roland jerked Arianna to the side just as she laid eyes on the Princess.

Princess Elisa didn't even pause, continuing past them as if Arianna were nothing but a ghost on the wind; an attendant helped her climb in beside the King. Then she was followed by Solomon.

He's never far behind the Devlindors...

Arianna glowered after them.

The rest of the King's Guard headed up a small procession of regulators on horses, all lined up behind the royal carriage.

"Your chariot awaits, madam." Sarcasm laced Roland's every word as he shoved her forward.

He led her to another, much smaller carriage—or, more accurately, a cage on wheels—directly behind the royals'. It was barred, so Arianna was exposed to the outside for all to see, like some kind of wild animal the King wished to show off from a successful hunt.

She supposed, in a way, that was exactly how he viewed her.

As Regulator Roland steered her in, suddenly Arianna could think of only one thing... *Where is Sir Vladamor?*

The necromancer, Head of the King's Guard, was nowhere to be found.

Everything went dark as a blindfold was tied over her eyes. Then she heard the click of a lock.

With the darkness, Arianna's skin ran cold, even under the

hot sun—all she could focus on was the necromancer, a manipulator of death. He had nearly killed her and her friends in the Black Sand Desert and, subsequently, led the shadow army to ambush the Zambienth guardian sanctuary.

What's more, with the necromancer feeding information to the King, she knew that many of their secrets had already been revealed. *He knows I'm not alone.*

King Devlindor might hold Arianna's life in his hands, but he wouldn't be the King she knew him to be if he didn't still pursue those who had aided her.

Sir Vladamor is on the hunt again.

Since he wasn't lurking around the palace, she could only assume that the King had ordered his pet to seek out every last one of her friends, mercilessly. Until he was certain the Guardians of Gold were eliminated from memory—just as he'd promised.

The piece of her mind that always worried for her newfound family, her friends, exploded now as she imagined so many terrible possibilities for them. *Had Sir Vladamor caught up to Jeom and Demetrius? Lessa and Eli? Master Tayshin and Cyn?*

A long list of names ran through her head.

We barely survived him as a united front.

If that monster should catch up to any of them again, Arianna wasn't sure how they could survive. He wielded some of the strongest and darkest powers known to exist, and it was only by luck that they had escaped him before.

Lost in her worries, she almost didn't realize when the carriage started to move. It lurched forward, rolling down the sloping street and away from the palace. After a long while, it screeched to a halt and she was flung forward into the bars.

The door swung open, and she fell to the ground, scraping her hands and knees.

"Up!" Regulator Roland shouted.

She felt his sweaty palm wrap around her arm as he yanked her to her feet.

He guided her up a tall flight of stairs, never removing the blindfold; she knew they had reached the top when the ocean winds began to pick up, blowing harder with the height. The salty air scratched at her cheeks, and her hair whipped about her face.

For a moment, it felt good, a bit of a relief from the heat. Then, she was forced to her knees.

Her heart began to beat faster, nerves pinching her insides as she waited for someone to speak, for anything at all. She felt so vulnerable without sight, and she'd seen beheadings before in South Luose… victims being forced to their knees atop some kind of punishment platform was usually how they began.

The blindfold was ripped from her face before she had time to truly panic—she hesitated to open her eyes.

As bright light from the sun doused her skin, Arianna fixated on the inside of her eyelids, a glowing pink and orange. She lingered on the beautiful veil between knowing nothing and seeing everything.

When she found the courage to look, she wished she had been kept in the dungeons; there were thousands of people staring up at her with wide, curious, confused, and some even condemning stares. She had never witnessed such a massive crowd this silent before. And if she hadn't opened her eyes, she wouldn't have even known they were there.

Arianna clamped her lips tight, trying to lock in the scream that had erupted in her chest. Now was not the time to show fear—though she felt as if all the air had been knocked out of her.

From this height, it was evident that she was kneeling upon the platform in the center of Saindora where, each morning, citizens would gather to hail to the King, as was tradition in every region of the Olleb. Except here, on this day, the one they bowed to was with them in the flesh to receive his praise.

Arianna dared not search for his eyes. She knew they would find hers soon enough.

Instead, she peeled her focus away from the gawking citizens to inspect the rest of the area; this city center put the Garden in South Luose to shame.

Situated in front of the high stage and built as the centerpiece of a fountain was an incredible statue of King Devlindor, made entirely of gold—crown, ruby-headed staff, and all.

It was too large not to be considered garish.

The King's avatar companion was carved at his feet in shining black stone with golden eyes, reminiscent of the statue of Queen Moriamo. And the fountain itself was built of pure white marble, trimmed in abstract designs.

Arianna was shocked to find that—instead of water—a blazing fire filled its bed, adding more heat to the already sweltering day. The heads of snakes with gilt tongues licked the air all around the ledge, and strings of flames shot from their mouths in an alarming and disgusting display of dominance.

A vast mosaic of colored tiles extended around the fountain and statue like a disease inching across the paved ground; like moveable pieces in a game, four small, white stone statues stood on the edges of the design, each depicting a different district emblem of the Four Corners—each also engulfed in flames.

Arianna noted the mallet of the Creator's District, and another statue depicted open palms, cupping water... *Healer's District.*

She spotted the rose of the Agrarian's District, and, lastly—the most familiar of them all—the crossed swords of Warrior's District. *Home sweet home.*

Each statue was ensnared by the King's gilded snake to complete the district crests.

Arianna suddenly noticed a shadow growing over her from behind; she looked up to find King Devlindor smiling down at her. Raja was, strangely, not by his side.

Just as she began to wonder where his faithful avatar might be, a loud caw echoed over the silence. Arianna followed the sound—perched on the shoulder of the King's statue was a giant, black hawk, intently watching the stage. *Raja's air form.*

Arianna grimaced, averting her gaze to the ground.

King Devlindor cleared his throat, drawing the attention of the crowd.

"Citizens of Saindora," he said, arms spread out wide, "good morning, my friends."

He walked in front of Arianna, blocking her view; Princess Elisa and Solomon flanked him.

As if a highly trained army, the crowd bent to one knee in unison, fists to their chests. "Hail to the King. Hail to Lord Devlindor!"

Their voices were so forceful and loud that Arianna's ears were still ringing well after they'd finished.

"You may rise," he said with a satisfied voice. He clasped his hands behind his back as he nodded his approval.

Arianna thought he actually seemed ecstatic in this moment.

"I know that I don't normally come every morning to witness the loyal commendation from you all, but today is a special day."

He moved back to reveal Arianna again.

"Many of you may be wondering who this is," he said, gesturing to her. "Though, I think you know it in your hearts. Please allow me to introduce number Twenty-Two, the slave who tried to steal her freedom, who made a mockery of everything you have ever worked so hard to earn in your lives. You *might* know her better by the name of Arianna Belvedor."

Gasps and whispers began to snake through the crowd.

Arianna tried to look anywhere but at the faces scrutinizing her now; she spotted the 'Wanted' posters of her face and of her friends plastered all over the streets and buildings that grew tall around the city center.

Saindora rose high around this open area, giving way to tiny little streets and pathways, some of which she was sure led straight to the sea. She longed to run in that direction, to dive straight into the water and let the waves have her instead of the King.

But she knew she would never make it past standing up to even try.

"To your feet," barked Solomon, making her jump.

She obeyed, feeling his grip on the back of her neck; he walked her to the edge of the stage so that the people could see her clearly.

"Is there anything you'd like to say to her?" asked the King, stepping aside so that she was the only focus.

There was a moment of silence at first as everyone glared up at her. Then something flew toward the stage—she tried to duck out of the way, but Solomon wouldn't allow it.

It was a rock, thrown from the crowd, and it hit her smack in the leg so that she nearly fell.

Arianna let out a small whimper, blood already forming where the skin had broken; she quickly regained composure, trying to remain strong.

"Rest easy, sister," she heard the King whisper to Princess Elisa. "Looks like the prophecy will not come to pass after all. She's failed miserably at turning anyone to her side this far south. Those in the North and elsewhere will be dealt with in due time… if they don't comply."

As if fueled by the King's clear delight, the citizens broke out in jeers and taunts all at once, condemning Arianna for stealing her life back from the arms of this tyrant who had stolen everything from them all.

They didn't know any better, so she gritted her teeth and put on a straight, emotionless face, unwilling to cry or show anger at such a reaction from those so ignorant…

As ignorant as I used to be.

Arianna just accepted their shameful remarks and retorts, burying them away in a place that she would later use to fan her fire.

These poor people, they don't know a thing about the King they serve. They bowed to someone they feared, not loved.

King Devlindor did nothing for them, and she would make them see the truth of that. She would pull the veil from their eyes so that they could finally understand the lie they lived and feel for themselves. Not what *he* wished the world to feel.

Their city was crumbling, decaying beneath the surface; the most beautiful, carefully carved pieces that made Saindora such a worthwhile place withered away as the magic was drained from the air, suffocating its people slowly.

Creatures like the fairies had been erased from their beloved homes in the forests, and the majestic mermaids of the sea had long since fled, fearing the King's wrath; the dwarves who had helped build the castle, whose intricacies with magical creation had surely also shaped the winding streets of Saindora—*gone.*

There were no more elves, no more giants, and no more dragons. And soon, magic itself would wither away completely into the hands of malevolent sorcerers and necromancers, if King Devlindor deemed it so.

She thought again of the Shadow Resistance and the King's Guard. Sir Vladamor, Solomon, even the enslaved seer and Regulator Roland—magic was no stranger to those the King surrounded himself with. And if he were to hoard magic anywhere, it would be in the confines of his very own home.

Surely there have to be traces of it left inside…

Keeper Kassime's enchanted attic filled her mind, accessible only through a labyrinth of dungeons and locked away by a vault.

The King must have something similar. I just need to find it.

If she were able to get a sense of his full range of power—and if she could make it out of this alive—*maybe* this time spent in captivity would prove worthwhile to the guardians' cause.

"She is not the only traitor," announced the King, silencing the crowd after a moment. Arianna's head snapped up. "Others have aided her along the way, and their betrayal of our laws will not be tolerated. Do you agree her allies should be punished?"

Her throat ran dry as she tried to deny his statement. *Don't let this be true. Please, don't let it be.*

The crowd cheered, fists to the air to show their support.

"Saindora speaks," he bellowed. He glanced down to Arianna, a smirk on his lips. "Bring them!"

Solomon pushed Arianna back to her knees and gave an order; the regulators stationed farther back on the platform brought two people forward with bags over their heads. He guided them to stand on either side of her.

Arianna thought her heart might beat straight out of her chest for the terror she felt now. All the blood rushed to her face, burning. So many names ran through her head again—not one of them deserved to suffer whatever the King had in store.

No one should be here but me! Who does he have?

She didn't know the fate of any of her friends, of anyone who escaped Moriamo or the battle at Zambienth. *Who did he catch up with?*

"Remove the bags," demanded King Devlindor, the eagerness in his voice sickening.

Arianna felt nearly faint with fear as she craned her neck upward to see; slowly, the regulators lifted the bags from the heads of the captives and revealed their faces.

Her knees buckled, and she nearly toppled off the stage as she wobbled forward; Solomon grabbed her by the collar of her shirt.

Unbidden tears swam in her eyes as she shook her head back and forth in utter disbelief—there was no more holding her fear back. It was bared for all to see.

"Cyn, *no*," she choked out, the tears really coming now. "I thought you had escaped!"

Cyn, Arianna's loving-to-a-fault caretaker, since before she had discovered right from wrong, gazed down at her with a solemn expression—such an unnatural look for one who had never once shown anything other than optimism on her face.

She seemed resigned to what would happen next.

"Ara, be brave now," she whispered down to her. "This is

where it counts, dear. When you're more frightened than you're even able to admit. You *must* be brave."

"No," she screamed, looking back and forth between Cyn and Solomon. "Let her go. Please, you can't do this!"

Solomon had the decency to look a little shocked, maybe even ashamed. He stepped back, submissively, to the King's side, trying to hide his reaction.

Had he not known?

Cyn never took her eyes off Arianna.

"It's going to be all right," she said with a strained smile, voice shaking. "*You're* going to be all right, my dear."

Her face was bloodied and beaten, hair matted with gore; this was not the Cyn Arianna knew, and she couldn't bear to imagine what her gentle caretaker must have suffered.

"Don't give up your dreams for anything. Stay strong, darling. I love you."

"No, no, *no*," said Arianna, now straining against the ropes binding her hands at her back.

She wanted to run to Cyn and hug her, to feel safe again in her arms, but she could feel dark magic keeping her down, knees glued to the ground.

From the first day Arianna had been named as Solomon's apprentice, Cyn had been there as her personal caretaker. There wasn't a time that she could recall, even after escaping the Four Corners, where Cyn hadn't shown up to make things better; she had healed so many wounds, wiped away countless tears, and risked her neck every time she could to ensure Arianna's safety.

Now, Cyn needed saving, and there was nothing she could do. She'd never felt so helpless in her life.

But Cyn wasn't alone in her terrible position this day...

Arianna was stunned to also find Iris standing there; she had trained with Iris many times in Zambienth, an elder warrior who had had her respect on sight. She'd taught her invaluable lessons as an honored Guardian of Gold during their time together.

Arianna looked up at her with such sorrow in her soul.

Iris was stone-faced and emotionless, more of a warrior than she thought she ever would be; the prominent scar she'd earned from the failed siege on the King's palace, along with many new ones, proudly showed across her skin.

It was clear that Iris hadn't given up without a fight—and whoever had had the unlucky fortune to try to capture her was probably worse off, by the looks of it.

Arianna knew from her conversations in Moriamo that she *and* Vance had been captured together by the Shadow Resistance, during the battle at the beach; she couldn't help the pit in her stomach telling her that if Vance wasn't on stage with Cyn and Iris, he was, unquestionably, already dead.

It was all she could do not to be sick in front of everyone.

"Arianna," said Iris, sharply, drawing her attention. "There's nothing you can do but keep fighting, just as you inspired us to do." She nodded toward the cityscape. "Keep your eyes *open*, even when you're scared. That's the only way you'll be able to defend yourself from what's coming next… and there will be a next. We're counting on you to keep going, or to die trying."

"Then, die she will," said the King, interrupting the reunion. "When the time is right."

Arianna lost her voice to fear then as regulators fashioned nooses around the necks of her dear friends—the King paraded them across the stage to the dedicated punishment platform, their fates sealed.

She watched them go, her sweat and tears mixing together as one. She could do nothing but shake her head.

Cyn closed her eyes, silent tears falling as she bit down on her shaking lips; Iris just stared ahead, unblinking, no telling the thoughts going through her mind now—she held out her hand for Cyn to take in one last comforting gesture.

"You are hereby sentenced to death for treason against the High King," announced Princess Elisa. "Any last words?"

They squeezed their hands tighter.

"Hail to the World. Hail to Olleb-Yelfra!" they shouted in unison.

The ropes tightened, and the floor gave way beneath them.

"Stop!" wailed Arianna, pitching forward with her hands still bound, feeling a fire grow somewhere deep within her.

The ropes fell from her wrists in ashes, and her hands came free; she shoved the regulator nearest to her off the stage, and the crowd cried out as he smashed into those at the front.

Arianna crawled toward the punishment platform, trying to get to Cyn and Iris as they kicked and struggled for air, their faces bloated and red. She was able to reach out a hand and graze Cyn's leg, but bodies were on her before she could gain any more leverage; the little magic she'd exerted to free herself of the ropes had taken every ounce of energy she could muster under their oppressive spells.

She had nothing left to give.

Solomon had her now, his arms wrapped tightly across her shoulders and chest as he restrained her, pulling her back; Arianna kicked and screamed against him.

"Solomon, it's Cyn. It's Cyn!" she cried out, desperately praying to every god she could think of that her master and friend would break through this shell of a man and realize the error of his ways. "You love her! I know you do. And Iris, you fought by her side. Please, let them go. Please! *Please*, Master Bell."

An excruciatingly long while later, Cyn and Iris stopped moving and everything went quiet—only the hum of the excited crowd suggested anything had happened at all.

Arianna whipped around to look upon them, but she could barely stand to see; the light had been snuffed from their eyes, and she was sure the gruesome image of them swaying there, so vulnerable under the hot, beating sun, would forever be stained in her mind.

She pitched forward in Solomon's arms, sobbing hysterically.

"You did this," he said, dropping her to the ground in a heap as the regulators subdued her. "They are here because of you."

She could barely focus on anything other than her loss. King Devlindor knelt down beside her to whisper something in her ear.

"I want you to feel every bit of this pain as I relieve you of your humanity," he said. "When I'm through with you, you'll be even less than a slave to me. You'll be a mere speck of dirt on the great history I am writing, and your memory will survive only in slanders and foul remarks."

He tucked a strand of hair behind her head, and she almost collapsed from anger.

"In fact, I doubt your name will even be recalled in history once I eradicate the Guardians of Gold, your friends included." He nodded in the direction of posters depicting Demetrius and Jeom. "I daresay that Sir Vladamor should already be on his return with the heads of your male accomplices."

"You lie," she spat through the tears, her worst fears realized with his threats.

"Odessa has quite the talent. I'm sure you're already aware," he said, stroking her cheek. "She told us everything we need to know. Now that you're all separated, you'll be quite easy to pick off. And without your friends, you are truly *nothing*. If the sea didn't kill them, I'm certain that Sir Vladamor will enjoy doing it himself... if he hasn't already." He twisted his staff in his hand; the ruby began to glow a bright red. "He does whatever I say."

Arianna recalled seeing that same stone wrapped around the necromancer's neck when he had tried to kill her in the desert.

It must hold some sinister ability to link them through magic.

"He'll never find them," she said, shoving his hand away. "If he does, what makes you think your necromancer stands a chance, considering he's already failed to catch us twice?" She found her voice then, full of fire and rage. "Jeom *still* wields the Axe of Crissy, or don't you already know? Not even self-proclaimed kings can have everything they desire."

King Devlindor pursed his lips and stood.

"Get this filth out of my sight," he growled with the wave of his hand—she looked up at him with scorn as he gazed down at her. "Maybe a stroll across town will give you some time to think about your choices."

The King walked back down the stairs, and the citizens of Saindora bowed low in his honor—not out of love but out of fear that what had happened to her friends might very well happen to them next, should they stray from his rule.

Regulator Roland picked Arianna up and escorted her behind him. When they reached the ground, he proceeded to bind her hands at her front, attaching them to long ropes at the back of the King's luxurious carriage.

So absorbed in thoughts of Cyn and Iris, Arianna barely noticed how close she was now to the throng of people who had watched the events unravel this morning; they surrounded her, staring at her in abhorrence.

It took everything in her not to glare back at them.

She *had* to imagine that they envied her inside, craved to know what it must be like to try the thing most severely punished in this world, to risk their lives purely for freedom. She had to imagine that so as not to hate them, too.

If they did wish anything of the sort, they didn't show it.

King Devlindor disappeared into his carriage, along with his sister and Solomon; the rest of his guard flanked Arianna, not for her protection but so that she couldn't escape *or* get killed before her due time.

She turned to look back at the stage, trying to ignore the angry mob of people closing in on her—the bodies of her beloved friends swayed in the wind.

She swallowed back her screams. *Now is the time to be brave. Never forget!*

The horses pulling the carriage began to slowly trot forward. Arianna stumbled along, no choice but to walk.

15

PRINCESS ELISA

ARIANNA'S KNEES BEGGED to hit the ground when the entrance of the palace finally came into view at the top of the hill. The procession came to a stop.

Her tears had run dry some hours ago; she had been forced to smother her feelings while being dragged through the streets, vilified by the very people she had sworn to free. She was covered in filth, and she felt as if she might pass out, bruised, bloodied, and hungry to the point of pain.

They don't know any better, she had thought to herself as unimaginable things were said and wished upon her.

They don't know that wishes can come true. They don't know anything at all.

Arianna had never felt so disgraced, so alone and unloved in all her life. But over and over, she forgave the people who tortured her with their words, the people she had spent the last year of her life dreaming about saving…

But by the end of the long and torturous walk, she wasn't sure if she still had it in her to forgive. There was a sickness carving into her stomach, her mind, and her heart with every step the King forced her to take.

If only they knew, they'd turn their hatred towards him, she told herself.

King Devlindor's followers began to clamber off their horses, and the royal entourage stepped out from the carriage; Arianna's legs finally collapsed under the weight of her exhaustion.

The King barely glanced her way as he began up the pathway. Though, as he did, a spiteful smirk curled across his lips.

"Someone get the girl cleaned up," he ordered. "I don't want to have to smell this during our first session tomorrow."

"Roland," said Princess Elisa. "Run ahead and fetch my attendant. She can fix her up, if our king agrees."

King Devlindor tossed her a cautious look.

"As you wish, Elisa," he said with a nod. "I won't deny you another plaything, but don't get too attached to this one. She won't be around for long."

"Have I ever?" she cooed, cocking her head to the side—her tiara slid down her hair a little.

He scoffed, narrowing his eyes.

"I'll be in my study," he said, curtly. "No one is to bother me."

"Yes, Your Majesty," said the Princess with a curtsy.

He turned on his heels, cloak fluttering on the wind as he disappeared into the palace, flanked by two guards.

"Pick her up," commanded the Princess with a snap once her brother was out of earshot.

"You heard her," said Regulator Roland—he folded his arms across his chest as he waited for Arianna to stand. "On your feet!"

"I can't," muttered Arianna; her mouth was bone dry, her voice croaking out in barely a whisper.

Even if she'd wanted to, she could not pick herself up off the ground; she was utterly drained, both physically and mentally.

"Say that again!" he roared, spit flying from his mouth.

She looked up at the regulator from her knees, shaking in anger and humiliation as she considered him, all brute and no brain. Arianna wished any magic might flow to her fingertips to smite him where he stood—Regulator Roland was quickly making his way up her list.

"Roland, leave us and send for my attendant right away," said the Princess, sounding just as authoritative as the King.

He opened his mouth to protest but thought better of it.

"Don't *make* me ask you twice," she said. "I just can't stand the sight of you barking orders. Find something else to growl at, you worthless mutt."

She turned to Solomon, completely ignoring Regulator Roland's reddening face; his mouth fell open at the insult.

She waved her hand, flippantly. "Bell, handle her, please."

Regulator Roland puffed out his chest before giving a sorry excuse for a bow to Princess Elisa. He disappeared into the gardens surrounding the palace, leaving Arianna alone with the Princess and a wolf.

"What's next then?" asked Arianna, looking at Solomon with defiance—she wasn't fully broken yet, even if her legs had given up on her.

"Haven't you had quite enough?" he said, sliding a sword out from the sheath at his back—it was one of *her* swords.

She glowered up at him, feeling some of her energy stir anew at the sight of those glorious weapons; in all the turmoil since Moriamo, she'd not taken a single second to think of where her possessions might have ended up since her capture.

I want those back.

He cut away her bind to the carriage, the blade slicing through the rope like air.

Arianna's mind traveled back to her initial escape from the Jar, after completely throwing her Free Falls Festival; that fateful night, Solomon had revealed his magic to those none the wiser, using it against the district regulators in her defense. And after an astonishing battle, he had sent her off through the tunnels… with strong words of hope for her future and those very swords as a gift, a generous token to illustrate his faith in her as a warrior.

She had been over and over that night in her head, but nothing ever seemed to add up—how could a man so willing to risk his life to see her and Lessa safely out of the districts have been the enemy all along?

Arianna hated Solomon for his betrayals of the Guardians of Gold, and of her. Yet, the missing pieces in the story of his full transition to the dark side haunted her still.

She needed answers. And here, in the den of wolves, she knew they were right under her nose.

Her gazed followed her sword longingly; it glinted under the early afternoon sun.

She felt so naked without the weight of metal in her hand to ground her, too light and vulnerable here, tiptoeing around this maze of enemies without protection.

"Try to stand," said Solomon, his shadow looming over her.

Arianna's hands were still bound together, but she was relieved, at least, to be detached from the carriage. She dug her hands into the grass, getting to her feet.

"Walk," he said, pointing the sword toward the palace.

Arianna just stared ahead, too ashamed to meet his eyes; if she took one step, she knew she would crumple like paper to the floor.

"I cannot," she replied, unblinking as she glued her gaze on the palace doors.

She could hardly stay standing without extreme effort.

"Try," he said, sheathing the sword.

Arianna sucked in a deep breath, taking a step forward; her legs buckled, and Solomon opened his arms to catch her.

Princess Elisa sighed, impatiently.

"You'll have to carry her," she said, already starting through the gardens in the same direction as Regulator Roland. Guards never left her side. "We'll take her to my wing of the palace and get her sorted."

Solomon cleared his throat. "Are you sure the King—"

"Do as I say." Princess Elisa looked back over her shoulder, as if daring him to challenge her.

"Of course, Your Highness," he responded with a bow, following after her with Arianna still in his arms.

They circled the vast, outdoor courtyards, entering the palace from a different side.

Arianna couldn't help but gawk up at Solomon as he navigated the lengthy halls behind Princess Elisa. She wanted to understand him; he kept his chin high so as not to make eye contact with her, and his embrace felt cold and hollow, like being held in the arms of a stone statue.

"Set her down," said the Princess after a while. "I can take her from here."

They had stopped underneath a high archway; a silver door lay beneath it, vines of flowers engraved in the stone.

"You cannot handle her alone," urged Solomon, placing Arianna on her feet. "Do you always have to risk your neck?"

Princess Elisa turned her glaring, green eyes on him, sharp as the point of a dagger.

"Fine," he growled with a puff of frustration. "But do *not* let her out of your sight. The King will have both our heads if something should happen to her." He lowered his voice. "And if something should happen to you, I—"

Princess Elisa tossed her head back with a sugary laugh.

"Dear Solomon," she said, touching his arm, "out of the two of us, please let's not pretend that you're the strongest anymore." He didn't ease up. "Oh, relax! I have my personal protectors with me at all times. She's no threat here. Don't worry so much."

She smiled, playfully, and the sparkle of magic danced across the lasso draped about her shoulders—Arianna had yet to see her without it.

Solomon shook his head, resigned. "Just, be careful."

A strange expression crossed his face as he glanced at Arianna. Pity? Disappointment?

It vanished before she had a chance to decipher it.

He fortified the ropes at her hands and spelled her with another dose of the unbearable suppressive magic—something that she'd now realized was not unbeatable.

Iris and Cyn's deaths have to be worth something. There's still hope to get out of this.

As soon as she had the chance to recover her strength, Arianna was determined to put all her focus on breaking through that enchantment again.

"Come along, then," said the Princess as Solomon left them alone. "I trust you can get on now?"

Arianna nodded—not like she had a choice, with the guards pointing spears at her back.

"Lovely," said the Princess. She pressed her hand against the door. "*Operium undrio.*"

It clicked open, and they all stepped into a narrow foyer.

Arianna's focus trained on the tail of Princess Elisa's gown; fine silks of dark green with gold embellishments swept the floor behind her as she marched purposefully onward.

She was a spirited woman, that much was certain.

Arianna thought her unlike her brother in a way, more carefree when he wasn't around to watch. And while she possessed the same fair skin as him, the curious green eyes and striking silvery-white hair she'd inherited were so unlike King Devlindor's darker features; it made her appear much softer in comparison, at least on the eyes.

Arianna was not to be fooled by pretty appearances. She'd already witnessed this Devlindor's dangerous edges and knew she was from quite the same mold as her brother.

Princess Elisa started to gush about her personal collection of priceless artifacts, some even of magical importance, pointing things out as they walked; Arianna supposed she didn't care for pretenses, but it took her a moment to wrap her head around the situation—she was alone with the King's sister in her private quarters, and her personal protectors knew well of magic.

This part of the palace had sprung to life around them, much more vibrant in décor compared to the more public spaces Arianna had seen. In fact, as she really began to take notice, it seemed that this hall remained as a tribute to all that had been lost from the world after her brother had taken the crown.

It reminded Arianna of a small guardian sanctuary, this random assortment of memories from the Golden Age. Hidden away, only for the eyes of a special few.

Sculptures lined the foyer depicting ideas that were banned in their present day—people freely embracing in love, children playing, and sorcerers performing incantations.

There were colorful portraits of beautiful, sweeping landscapes... the magical kind that certainly weren't etched onto maps anymore. And Arianna even noticed strange, charmed objects humming with life that she didn't have names for; it all made her wonder if the elder guardians might even be too young to have a word for everything from the Golden Age, everything that the Princess had hoarded.

"Most of these things used to have a different home in the palace," she explained, after fondly describing each artifact. "Many of these statues filled the courtyards, and some of the portraits hung in the main galleries."

She sighed, caressing one of the sculptures of two lovers intertwined beneath an arc of what must've been magic.

"Times have changed now. The world isn't what it once was, but at least the memory of it remains."

Arianna couldn't help but scoff. "Well, it won't for long, thanks to you and your brother."

The Princess paused, back stiffening, but then she carried on without acknowledging her words.

When they reached the other side of the foyer, a tall door stood open and waiting, welcoming them into a vast, circular chamber; sun spilled in from all directions as tall, sheer-pink curtains fluttered in a gentle breeze from open windows.

The room was lined with softly colored carpets and sofas, and a large bed with a canopy sat at the far wall. Tall, vaulted ceilings were decorated with light trims of paint, and a grand chandelier with pastel jewels hung in the center.

Arianna's eyes were drawn to an enormous portrait framed in rose gold that reached from the floor to the ceiling; it depicted the City of Saindora, though surely a version from the past.

She couldn't look away. *This* was how she'd always pictured the High City, even as a child—and it was every bit as vibrant and magical as her imagination had predicted it to be.

"You may leave us now," said the Princess to her guards. "Have the cooks prepare a meal for two, and bring it to my chambers in one hour." She lifted her finger. "Not a word to my brother."

"As you wish, Your Highness."

The guards bowed and then left, traveling back down the hall—now, Arianna was really alone with the Princess.

A wave of anxiety washed over her. *What game is she playing with me that she doesn't want the King to know about?*

"Follow me," she said to Arianna.

She disappeared into an adjacent room, and Arianna cautiously shadowed her; she found herself standing in a much smaller room with shining floors.

It was decorated in garlands of light-colored flowers that made Arianna's own smell wash away in their delicious scent, and sun spattered the entire area, refracting against a bubbly glass awning that created the ceiling.

A deep, porcelain tub with bronze, claw-like feet rested along a wall of mosaic tiles. And the chamber was made complete with frilly floor mats and pretty glass figurines for added decoration.

Everything that the Princess surrounded herself with seemed to deliberately sweep away the overarching theme of 'darkness' that loomed about the palace; it begged Arianna to question if she must feel trapped, to have to hide from King Devlindor under the guise of material things.

None of this changes the truth.

"Jillian!" called the Princess.

An old woman with red, frizzy hair and a soft look about her scuttled in from around the corner.

"Princess Elisa," she said with a curtsy. "Roland told me to ready a bath?" She gasped as she laid eyes on Arianna. "Oh, my! Who—"

"This is the escaped slave from the Four Corners," said the Princess, matter-of-factly. She stepped aside so that Jillian could get a good look. "The King has requested her to be cleaned up. She had a rough day, and she is something of his… guest."

"Prisoner," said Arianna under her breath.

"Prisoner or not," snapped the Princess, "you cannot smell like cattle for a meeting with your king."

"I see, Your Highness," said Jillian. "I'll have her washed up straight away."

"Bring her to my room in one hour to dine," she ordered, heading for the door. "I have some questions for her before she goes. And, Jillian," Princess Elisa glanced back at Arianna, magic burning bright in her eyes, "Arianna Belvedor *is* a sorceress, a Guardian of Gold, so please keep your very best eye on her. You know how us magic folk have a tendency of playing tricks."

Arianna felt the ropes tighten around her wrists; she sucked in a hiss between her teeth.

"Just proving a point," said the Princess with a wink, the ropes falling to the ground in the next second. "Now that the secret's out, you might as well see all our cards." She narrowed her gaze. "Don't try anything stupid."

She left the washroom, leaving Arianna alone with her attendant.

"So…" said Jillian, a wobble in her step as she busied about the chamber. She gathered up a robe, towel, and other things to prepare for a bath. "You're *the* Arianna Belvedor? Quite the fuss you've caused around the palace, I must say."

"Have I?" said Arianna, hardly able to concentrate—it was a miracle she hadn't fainted yet. She rubbed at her wrists.

Jillian smiled, seeming so at ease.

Arianna could only imagine what her old eyes had witnessed over all the years as an attendant of a Devlindor.

"If Princess Elisa has her claws in you, you must be doubly in trouble," she added. "Two Devlindors fighting over anything has *never* ended on a good note." She chuckled to herself, as if she were musing about two loving siblings sharing a toy. "Alas, today you are here, and you're in great need of a bath, so get in."

Arianna walked across the room where steps led up to the remarkable tub. It sat beneath a cove of colored panels decorated with the outlines of what she thought must be mermaids.

Jillian trailed her, trying to pick out the chunks of trash and gunk tangled in her curls; Arianna thought of all the ways she could certainly kill this old woman and attempt to escape, even without magic. But she couldn't bring herself to hurt someone who had, so far, been nothing but kind.

Besides, I'm really in need of a bath.

She sighed, kicking her tattered clothes to the floor. She tested a toe in the water.

"It's freezing!" Bumps inched across her skin as she yanked her foot back. "I can't."

Jillian let out a cackle. "For a slave, you are quite demanding."

She scuttled up the marble steps and dipped her finger in the tub. She whispered a string of familiar words until the water hissed and steamed with heat.

"You have magic, too?" said Arianna, her voice pitching a little in surprise.

"I wouldn't underestimate anyone in this palace," said Jillian—if she didn't know any better, it almost sounded like a friendly warning. "Magic has always existed here, and it always will."

"I hope you're right," she whispered, carefully stepping in.

The heat was so soothing against some of her aches and pains that Arianna thought she'd been healed; she lowered herself fully underneath the water, wishing that the tub were a portal to the sea so that she could just swim away.

Unfortunately, she had to resurface and face the truth—Jillian watched and waited.

"Why would the Princess invite me, a slave, to bathe in her quarters?" she asked after a long silence, staring absentmindedly at the mermaid wall while Jillian cleaned her back.

"She's always had a weakness to soften the King's blow," said Jillian with a gentleness. "In fact, *she's* the only thing soft about him. Enjoy this while you can, for the King will not let it be a normalcy. Nothing ever happens without him knowing, but this is Princess Elisa's way of showing you a kindness... before you will never know kindness again."

The water seemed to grow cold around Arianna; she drew her knees into her chest. *So, she's trying to ease some kind of guilt for her brother's malicious practices...*

Arianna's stomach churned, sickened by the thought that she'd found herself in the middle of some kind of twisted tug-of-war between the two blood-sucking royals.

An hour came and went.

There was a knock on the door, and a man entered. As soon as he set eyes on Arianna, his stony expression fell into shock—she wasn't sure if it was because she was naked or because she was her.

"*Yes?*" said Jillian, eyebrow raised.

He cleared his throat, composing himself. "Princess Elisa is waiting in her dining area, ma'am."

Arianna had never heard an attendant spoken to so formally, though she was unsurprised; Jillian clearly commanded a high reputation here.

"Very well," she said, opening a towel for Arianna. "Out you go."

Reluctantly, she stepped out of the bath and dried off; Jillian brought over clean, dry clothes to dress her for dinner.

She slipped them on quickly, eager to leave behind her tattered ones from Moriamo—a reminder of her failure—though this thin, rough-spun material solidified her place as a palace slave.

Arianna froze as Jillian unfurled another garment.

"What's that supposed to be?" she shrieked.

The attendant held up a robe with the silver number twenty-two embroidered at the breast.

She shook her head. *Will I ever wake from this nightmare?*

It was as if she had been whisked away to her childhood, the chains of her past snapping back around her feet.

"The King has demanded you wear these from here on out," she said. "It's a little warm for this weather, but I'm sure it's much colder in the dungeons. Take comfort in it where you can." She shrugged. "That's really all you can do."

Jillian settled the cloak over her shoulders, and Arianna didn't protest, though the feeling of the cloth on her skin made her itch with anger. Its warmth and heaviness felt so familiar, but not in a good way—the cloak might as well have been made of needles.

But she was resigned to her unfortunate reality.

For now, she was the King's to torture in any way he saw fit, until she thought of a way out; and if Lessa had taught her anything at all during their risky escapades, it was not to do anything rash until she had a proper plan.

Currently, Arianna was nothing but flesh and bones against

magic and metal—she had to be smart.

I must wait for the right opportunity, or get my hands on a weapon before I can start pushing back.

"After you," said Jillian with a knowing sigh.

They left the washroom and returned to the main chamber.

Princess Elisa was lounging across a daybed, sipping a glass of wine. A table had been spread out before her, a chair on either end.

Arianna looked down at her with a blank stare, but Princess Elisa wouldn't acknowledge her yet…

"Bow," whispered Jillian from the doorway.

Arianna gritted her teeth but gave a small curtsy.

Princess Elisa accepted the gesture.

"You may sit," she said, swinging her feet down from the sofa.

The food before them looked so delicious that Arianna could barely keep her mouth from watering; she sat in the chair farthest away from the Princess, trying not to appear desperate or drool.

"Eat," she demanded from the daybed, not even bothering to join her at the table. "Don't let it get cold."

She sipped another bit of her drink, but Arianna didn't move.

"I *said*, eat," snapped the Princess, scowling at her from over her glass. "Don't worry, it's not poisoned." She tilted her head. "Although, that would be a kindness."

Arianna felt her hand jerk upward from her lap to the table by some invisible force.

The Princess had gone back to her wine, paying her no mind.

Reluctantly, Arianna brought a piece of bread to her lips— once it touched her tongue, she could hardly contain herself.

She began to shovel food into her mouth, caring nothing for etiquette. Every bite gave her energy, making her feel more like a person again. After she could no longer fit another morsel into her stomach, she leaned back in the chair, wiping her mouth clean with the back of her hand.

"Feel better now, don't you?"

Princess Elisa set her glass down and stood.

Arianna guzzled down the water in her goblet. "Why are you doing this for me?" she asked, slamming the empty cup down on the table.

"Don't be silly!" said the Princess, straightening out her dress. She seemed insulted or embarrassed. "I'm not doing *anything* for you. I'm doing this for me. What good is an unfed mind?"

"So, you're planning on performing mind magic on me now?"

Arianna braced herself, hands clenching the table.

Princess Elisa just shook her head.

"No, I won't be fishing for memories," she said with a sigh. "My brother will handle that soon enough."

"What does he hope to find, exactly?"

The Princess shrugged her shoulders. "Anything and everything, I suppose."

She walked around the table, circling her with curiosity in her expression.

"Once he gets what he wants from you, you'll no longer be useful to him," she said, as if to offer an explanation of how his warped mind worked. "At that point, his torturous games will not seek to humiliate you but to trap you in endless pain with no relief. What's ahead of you will not be easy."

"Fascinating," said Arianna, dryly. "Tell me then, what is it that *you're* after?" She looked around. "I can't begin to understand what we're doing here."

Princess Elisa came around to her side; they held each other's inquisitive gaze.

"You know, I really haven't decided yet," she said with a frown. "Either way, you're no use to anybody if your head isn't on straight." She walked back over to her glass, filling it to the top from a carafe. "Guards!"

The door to her chambers blew open, and palace regulators flooded in.

"We're done here," said the Princess, turning her back to Arianna. "Escort Twenty-Two back to the dungeons. She's in need of a good night's rest before her date with the King."

As Arianna was yanked from her chair and dragged away, the last thing she saw of Princess Elisa was her lifting her glass up as if to say 'good luck.'

"I DIDN'T THINK YOU WERE COMING BACK!" said Odessa, clapping her hands in surprise. "It's hard to tell what will happen anymore. So many things are unwinding."

"Well, here I am," mumbled Arianna. She ached for something to take away her pain, inside and out.

"Here," said Odessa, handing her one of the healing capsules. "It won't heal your grief, but it will help."

Arianna didn't hesitate to take it this time.

Between her royal bath, a full belly, and this magical curative, she almost felt like herself again… save for the gaping hole in her heart that had formed with the absence of Cyn and Iris.

"At least, this time they didn't bother to chain you down to the bed," said Odessa. "You're welcome to explore the room tonight."

"Oh, how my luck has turned," she muttered.

She did, however, use this opportunity to inspect her surroundings; she searched for anything that could be used as a weapon, but there was nothing very detachable here—except for the items on Odessa's shelf.

She eyed the thick, glass jar that held her magic pills.

It will have to do, she thought.

"Actually, this would work better," said Odessa, sneaking up behind her with a larger, empty one in hand.

Arianna jumped as the seer intruded on her thoughts. "By gods, would you please stop doing that!"

"Sorry… I really can't," she said, indifferently.

Irritated, Arianna snatched the jar from her hands and went to the center of the room; she slammed it against the side of the marble steps, the jar shattering into pieces with a piercing smash.

Her hand was bleeding, though she'd felt nothing—she assumed the magical medicine in her veins had numbed the pain from the cut. Or, maybe, she was just numb already.

With care, Arianna picked up the largest shard of glass and swept the rest under the rug. Then, she marched over to the bed to hide her makeshift weapon beneath one of the feather pillows.

Odessa skipped over to her.

"What's on your mind?" she asked, sitting down next to her. "You can say it."

Even though Odessa could not see, Arianna couldn't bring herself to look her in the face, knowing that she shamelessly read every thought that flitted across her brain.

"What's the point of me saying it if you already know?" said Arianna after a moment, plucking furiously at a pillow until she was surrounded with twisted, white feathers.

Odessa clasped her hands together in her lap.

"Well, there *is* no point in you saying anything to me," she replied. "Unless, of course, you would like me to say something back." She smiled with tight lips. "Don't forget, I may know everything, but you do not."

Arianna let out a howl of frustration, punching a pillow.

"Fine," she said, facing her, determined to get some answers. "Odessa… *tell* me what you told the King. He says that Sir Vladamor searches for my friends now. Is this true? Did you send the necromancer to hunt down my family?"

With each word, she grew more enraged; part of her wanted to take her anger out on the seer, though she knew in her heart that Odessa was not to blame for anything.

She's trapped, too.

Odessa stood.

"Follow me," she said, holding out her hand.

Arianna took it, getting to her feet—feathers fell from her lap to the floor. She let Odessa lead her to the top of the marble steps.

They both sat down by the ledge of the pool.

Odessa appeared to contemplate the water for a moment; Arianna looked too, unnerved by how still it was… if this pool had reflected her emotions, waves would be hurling as high as the vaulted ceiling.

"I told him what I saw," said Odessa, breaking the silence. "The only way I can keep my life is if I give the King useful information. What he wants now, more than anything, is to erase the Guardians of Gold from this earth, forever, and to regain control… to ensure the prophecy my mother gave him long ago can never come to fruition."

She tilted her head back and forth, as if looking for something.

She sees all. Arianna gulped, wondering what knowledge about the guardians she'd offered up to save her own neck.

"King Devlindor is worried, and even though he has you in his grasp, it's not enough for him to feel secure. What you and your friends have managed to do after all his centuries of control has shaken him to his core. This is what I see, indisputably."

"The King fears what all mortal men fear," whispered Arianna, considering her statement. "That's why he built the Four Corners in the first place."

She thought back through all she'd learned about the prophecy—in the King's narcissistic mind, he assumed it his own.

However, just like magic, the Golden Rule belonged to everyone. *The prophecy isn't his to control.*

And while there could be many interpretations of the Golden Rule, the clearest understanding Arianna had drawn from her experiences was that with life must come death.

Odessa grinned back at her.

"So you *have* been paying attention after all," she cooed. "Very good."

She gave a single nod.

"Yes, King Devlindor fears Death, more than anyone perhaps, and he's been evading him for an unnaturally long time." Odessa patted her on the head. "Enter Arianna Belvedor, the biggest reminder yet that he cannot run forever. He really cannot."

"Are you certain of this?" said Arianna, pushing her hand away. "Are you *positive* that he won't find a way to break the Golden Rule, despite the assumption that it's unbreakable?"

"The Golden Rule cannot be broken," said Odessa, firmly. "There is no tricking it, nor escaping it. It just *is*." She gazed in Arianna's direction. "It is not a question of whether or not one day King Devlindor will die... it's a question of when."

Arianna took a deep breath, trying to follow. "What are you wanting to say to me?" she said.

"All paths that I see for all living things end in death," Odessa replied—she began to swirl her finger in the water, the disturbance creating a rippling effect.

"Even the King's?" asked Arianna, watching intently.

"Even the King's," said Odessa, softly. "However, his grip on Olleb-Yelfra is strong. His dark disease is slowly eating away at her, and if things aren't set on a different path soon, she may die long before the King's due time, or right along with him."

A teardrop suddenly hit the water, breaking the sequence of ripples; Arianna glanced up to find Odessa's expression filled with emotion—it aged her somehow, underscored her years of experience, well beyond her own.

"If that happens," she continued in a low voice, "there will be nothing left to save. That path is where the future I see stops, completely and forever."

Arianna stiffened at this abrupt ending—she understood the Olleb's struggle maybe now more than ever.

"But… that's not the *only* path you see, right?" she asked. "Can he be stopped, before it's too late?"

"That depends," replied Odessa.

Arianna crossed her arms. "On what?"

She let out a little laugh, shaking her head. "Arianna, it depends on you. On you and *your* future."

Arianna looked away, feeling overwhelmingly powerless.

The weight of the world felt heavier on her shoulders each day that passed… so much so that sometimes she wished she hadn't even picked up the burden to begin with. How had she gotten so wrapped up in all this that something this significant could possibly depend on a single choice *she* might make?

She swallowed, her throat dry, as her mind churned with questions. She tried to change the subject, shaking the worries from her mind before they consumed her, before Odessa could see.

"Stop speaking in riddles and answer my question," she demanded. "What exactly have you told King Devlindor? What is he looking for right now? He's planning to search my mind tomorrow for more information to help him hunt down *my* people. What is it that he hopes to find within my thoughts?"

Odessa touched the water again, Arianna following her gaze; this time, a ring of ripples grew around her finger without any effort at all. More curious still, the ripples did not cease, but continued to grow and grow until the entire pool was bubbling under her enchantment.

Spellbound, Arianna couldn't tear her eyes away.

"I simply told him what I saw," said Odessa. "Battles on the beaches of Zambienth, friends riding the waves on the Sea of Saindora to escape. Watch, and you shall see, too."

Unblinking, Arianna felt as if the rippling water had taken over her senses. Soon, the clear pool grew cloudy—just like Odessa's eyes.

"I see something," she gasped as a blurred image fluttered

across the murky water.

"Keep watching," said Odessa, her voice thick with magic.

Sure enough, Arianna found that the ripples started to form into something tangible. "It's Zambienth... the battle at the beach. Is this—"

"A vision from the past," answered Odessa.

Arianna became enthralled by the horrific memory, wanting to reach out her hand and save her friends, steer them toward a safer path; it was strange to witness the happenings from another's viewpoint.

Sadly, though, there was nothing she could do but observe, throat choked in anger, as the Shadow Resistance swarmed the Greenhouse.

She had to relive Talis' untimely death as the city keeper impaled him with her sword, and she watched in fear as the boys— Jeom, Demetrius, and Gabriel—retreated on the waters.

Cyn and Iris were there, too, but Arianna could barely look upon them without screaming. And, ultimately, she witnessed the star magic for herself; she, Lessa, and Eli disappeared from the beach in a miraculous burst of light.

The misty image was swept away in a wisp, like steam rolling off a lake, and the pool was just a pool again.

"What happened after that?" asked Arianna, staggered as everything suddenly went back to normal. She splashed her hands in the water to try to make the visions return.

"I advised the King to go after the ones who escaped on the sea," said Odessa, calmly. "To try once more to secure the Axe of Crissy."

"How could you do that?" she stuttered. "Has the necromancer found them? Does King Devlindor know our plan?"

She began to grow frantic, trying to pull more details out of her.

"I did it to lure him away from you. I did it for the Olleb!" shouted Odessa, unexpectedly. "Don't you see? There *is* no more plan. With the Guardians of Gold so scattered across the Olleb as you are, nothing is as it should be."

She stood, shoulders heaving up and down.

"Haven't you realized this yet? I thought you were clever, but if you refuse to meet the change that is upon you, I'm afraid the paths you'll walk won't be pleasant." She waved her hands in the air as she spoke. "Wishing to return to the past and to find out the answers you seek about the futures of others will not lead you anywhere but to your death. You must focus on *your* future, Arianna." She leaned forward, forcing her to look into her eyes, silver and bright. "You're not supposed to be here yet!"

Arianna was taken aback, mouth agape.

"And yet, here I am," she said after a moment, trying to keep her calm. "Just… tell me what to do, please. You have all the answers, so what are they, Odessa?"

Her voice cracked, pleading now—all she could see was Cyn's tear-stricken face. She couldn't focus on her future when others she cared for no longer had one.

Odessa took a deep breath, their emotions seemingly mirrored.

"I wish… I wish I *could* give you the answers," she said, growing softer, "but it doesn't work like that. I would not be doing you any justice by sharing my sight with you."

"But—"

Odessa held up her hand for silence, and something about the gesture made Arianna obey; as eccentric and infuriating as she could be, this was a woman from the Golden Age with a power quite unlike anything else in this world—one that demanded respect.

"Do you know what is recorded about seers? Think back to what you've learned," she said. "It has been presumed for centuries that my kind tell half-truths or lies. Why do you think that's how we've been depicted in history…?"

Arianna knew she was not being invited to speak.

"Because," she continued, "as I've tried to explain, there is not just one future to be told. There are countless possibilities! Yet, humans have always had difficulty grasping this idea. When something foretold by a seer did not come true, they accused my ancestors of *lying*." She scoffed, curling her lip up. "While I may oblige the King by sharing visions of his future when he calls for counsel, to keep my own head, it does not mean that my predictions will always be realized. If that were true, he'd already have the Axe of Crissy, and you'd already be dead."

"Then, why does he bother to come to you for anything at all?" asked Arianna in a small voice.

"Now that's a very good question," said Odessa, seemingly impressed. "King Devlindor is wise enough to know that my predictions of the future may not always ring true, but *sometimes* they do. He lacks the courage to face his future completely blind, so he always asks. For him, it's worth the gamble."

"And yet, for me, you think it's not?" said Arianna, raising an eyebrow—a headache was forming.

Odessa hesitated, choosing her words carefully.

"The futures that I see don't truly exist until one makes the decisions that lead there," she said. "Thus, as I've *told* you, you must find the paths for yourself."

She placed her hands on her hips.

"What I've seen of the future that the King is fighting for can always be altered. And I'm praying that *you* will bring about that change, Arianna, just like so many others—"

She pranced down the stairs.

"Yet, if you are here as the King's slave, there's really not many decisions left to you. You see the irony?" She giggled to herself, but Arianna didn't find it in the least bit funny. "Ultimately, there is no future for any of us if you do not find your way again." She glanced back at her from the bottom of the steps. "You're not supposed to be here yet."

Arianna felt chills crawl up her spine.

"I don't care about some stupid prophecy or the futures you see," she grumbled, unable to keep composed any longer. "I care about my friends. Are they alive or *dead*? Lessa, Jeom, Demetrius, and Eli. Tell me if they live! Stop dancing around it."

Her voiced echoed loud around them, no escape in this windowless chamber.

"I have already given you too much," said Odessa, growing flustered. She paced around the carpeted area. "It could change everything. You have few choices left ahead, and I shall not influence any one of them more than I already have. This conversation is over."

She began to scoop up the blocks scattered about the room, stacking them in what appeared to be a nonsensical fashion; Arianna could practically see her using the activity to channel her racing thoughts.

She nearly roared in anger, wishing to chuck the blocks at her head.

"If that monster lays a finger on anyone else I love, I will ensure your soul never leaves this place!" she screamed at her from across the room. "Do you hear me?"

"I think that no matter which path befalls you, you would do everything in your power to ensure quite the opposite," said Odessa, focusing on the puzzle. "That's who you are, Arianna. Besides, soon, *very* soon, I think, you shall consider me a friend. Then you'll be worrying about my fate along with Jeom's, Demetrius', Lessa's, and… oh, who was it? Ah, yes—Eli's."

The way she said their names made Arianna know with certainty that they were floating at the top of her mind; if she could tap into any magic at all, she would've already unleashed it to try to get the answers she sought.

"It's a good thing you can't then, *hmm*?" sang Odessa.

Arianna dug her nails into her leg, staring back toward the pool until she finally felt calm enough to come down.

TALES OF REVENGE

DEMETRIUS' EYES SPRANG OPEN as a soft, warm wind tickled his face. He was in a small room, lying on an unfamiliar bed—thick vines ran across uneven walls of dark, unrefined wood. And sheer curtains fluttered in a large, open window.

For a second, he could've sworn he was back in the Greenhouse, that the battle of Zambienth and the wretched journey across the sea had been nothing but an awful dream. Yet, when he attempted to wiggle his toes to try to shake off the paralyzing sleep, he felt the shock of nothingness on his right side.

And so, the nightmare continues, he thought.

"Hello?" he said, cautiously, looking around. "Is anybody there?"

A tall, lean woman with a pointed face sauntered in from the outside; she wore loose yellow wrappings that made her seem like some kind of elegant bird as she walked.

"Ah, I see you're finally coming to," she said, placing her

hand gently on his forehead.

Demetrius flinched a little but didn't ask her to stop; he was too confused by the situation and too absorbed by her presence to focus.

The woman's bluish-silver hair was pulled back into a thick braid, tiny flowers weaved throughout, and several long chains of gold and silver dangled down her neck. She was a strange, stunning vision, not like anyone he'd ever seen before…

There was a sharpness in her expression that made him take extreme care.

"Where am I?" asked Demetrius—the more awake he became, the more he began to panic. *I can't run, I can't fight! Is this woman the enemy or a friend?*

"Safe," she replied. "Here, you must be parched."

She handed him a cup that appeared to be chiseled from raw stone.

Demetrius scrutinized the liquid inside, raising an eyebrow. "What is it?"

The woman smiled, the skin around her eyes wrinkling a little.

"It's good that you're suspicious," she said in a smooth accent; Demetrius found it slightly familiar but couldn't place it. "You'll last longer in this world. But don't agonize yourself further. It's only water from the springs."

She pressed her hands into his, forcing the brim of the cup to his lips.

"Don't worry, young one. I wouldn't feed my patients poison after such a healer's success. Drink up."

She laughed at his hesitation, a charming sound that he couldn't help but trust, despite his innate defenses flaring up; without thinking too much more about it, he gulped the water down.

"By gods," gasped Demetrius, relishing every swallow—it might've been the freshest thing he'd ever tasted, especially after experiencing life-threatening thirst.

I'll never take water for granted again, not as long as I live!

"Good, isn't it?" said the woman, refilling his cup. He gave a curt nod, suspicious still as he drank. "The rivers that run through here are some of the cleanest in the Olleb, nearly untouched from here to the sea."

"How's that possible?" he asked, feeling revitalized.

"They're very difficult to find for most humans," she said, setting aside his now empty cup. "The jungle is too dense to navigate."

She sat down on the edge of the bed, studying him intently with wide, curious, emerald-colored eyes; as she made to cross her legs, the sheets on the bed shifted…

Demetrius felt every nerve in his body come alert, his heartbeat quickening—the sheen of silver scar on the kneecap of his missing leg was suddenly made visible from beneath the covers.

With shaking hands, he yanked the sheet back in place. Then, he sat up, swinging his legs over the side of the bed next to hers.

In this position, Demetrius could imagine he was whole again, imagine that he might set both feet onto the sturdy floorboards and stand up straight. *I can't… I can't. It's gone.*

He sat with his imagination a moment longer before he spoke.

"Who are you?" he mumbled, head hung low as terrible memories began to flood his thoughts.

"My name is Diveena Lethander," said the woman with the casual confidence that he himself used to boast. "And you might be?"

"Demetrius… Demetrius Kane," he stuttered, trying to rub away the ache in his head. "Your name, it sounds so familiar."

"Well, Demetrius Kane, I don't see how that could be," she replied. "I am not yet your familiar." She placed her hand atop his. "But it is a pleasure to have your company. It gets somewhat lonely up here."

"And where is 'here,' exactly?" he asked, gazing around again.

The sun was high in the sky from what he could tell, light drenching the room. And he realized only now just how humid it was, the air sticky and sweet as it coated his skin with an extra layer; neither the Black Sand Desert nor the City of Zambienth had ever provided anything but dry, hot days and frigid cold nights.

We must be somewhere far off from those regions now.

"Your boat landed on the shores of what's known as the Impenetrable Forest," she said, pointing toward the window. "There's a city beyond the trees called Guanamara. Where we are now is halfway between the sea and the city." She tilted her head back, gazing toward the ceiling with a starry look. "Welcome to the jungle. It's miles and miles of untamed wilderness."

The curtains were drawn, so there was nothing but his imagination to aid him.

"A jungle?" Demetrius felt his brow furrow—he had never even heard of the Impenetrable Forest before, though the City of Guanamara sounded faintly familiar.

As he followed her gaze to the ceiling, he decided it almost looked as if they were inside the trunk of a tree—raw, with veiny cords of wood climbing over one another. *Where am I, really?*

"Your companions… what might they be called?" she asked before he could think of another question; the sharpness of her features became prominent again as she scrutinized him.

She's probably deciding if we are friend or foe, too, Demetrius thought. He wanted to be optimistic, but they had so many enemies these days.

He felt the panic rise up in his throat as he considered the fates of his allies, his brother. *Did they survive?*

"Gabe," he said, finding his words. "Gabriel was with me on the boat. Is he—"

"The dark one?" she interrupted, tilting her head with a squint in her eyes.

Demetrius shook his head.

"No, that's Jeom," he breathed, hardly able to speak his name. "He's my… brother."

He couldn't resist the shudder of emotion that overwhelmed him—everything came in a flood. He hunched over, burying his face in his hands as the tears finally came.

"There, there, child of earth," said Diveena, softening in such a way that he was reminded of Arianna's kindhearted caretaker. "All is as it should be."

"Are they alive?" His voice came muffled; he was afraid to look up.

"*Quite* so," said Diveena, patting him on the back. "You shall have a second chance with them soon enough, I'm pleased to say."

The tears flowed harder then as Demetrius let all of his feelings out of the bottle he'd locked them in. It was the first time since the incident that he'd really even acknowledged all that he'd lost—and his leg was only one small piece of it.

He had lost a part of himself; he'd lost his way; *and* he'd lost trust in the one person he had trusted most… *Jeom is alive.*

Deep down, he knew he couldn't survive the dangers of this world without his brother by his side, not after all they'd overcome together. But he couldn't bring himself to find forgiveness for him either. His heart was still so full of anger toward Jeom that he didn't see how he could ever love him the same way again.

He didn't even want to think about it—yet, the moment Jeom had brought down the axe over him was all he could see.

"Weep not for long," said Diveena, clasping her hands in her lap. "All wounds heal with time. Don't let the pain control you. Instead, you must learn how to wield it into power." She again looked toward the ceiling, as if she were looking into an endless sky—he wondered what she really saw there, in her mind's eye. "Pain is a feeling of the past, and the past is only meant to guide the future… not govern it."

Demetrius tried to compose himself; he brushed his long hair from his face and wiped his eyes with the back of his hand.

"Who are you, really?" he asked, more firmly this time, finding her brilliant green eyes again. "Where are Jeom and Gabriel?"

"You needn't worry over them just yet," she said, holding his stare, seeming to search for something within his expression—he felt himself redden. "They're still healing and will wake when they're ready. They were in much worse condition than you. It will take yet some time." She smiled. "You're very lucky, you know?"

"I don't see how," he mumbled, looking down at his leg.

Though, the part of him that wasn't still consumed by sadness *did* feel relief that this stranger promised his friend and brother were still breathing.

"Count your blessings, then," snapped Diveena, taking him aback. "You may have one less limb than you're clearly accustomed to, but at least you have your life. Your friend and your brother, on the other hand, nearly gave theirs to save *you*, from the looks of it." She studied him intently. "They were both almost dead from exhaustion when I discovered them. You were not."

Diveena's words came like a hard slap to the face, and poked at something inside of Demetrius he wasn't yet ready to confront.

"I was in shock," he retorted, angrily. He waved his hand toward the blanket. "I had just lost—"

Diveena held up her hand.

"You don't have to explain yourself to me," she said in an even tone. "I am not yet your familiar."

Demetrius bit down on his tongue, feeling emotions rise up inside of him, battling silently against one another; he couldn't be sure which would be the victor in the end, but the worst ones certainly had the advantage.

"*All right* then," he said, after a moment, growing more wary of her by the minute. "Well, how long have we been here... with you?"

He couldn't help but notice how much his hair had grown, even beginning to thicken on his face.

Diveena cleared her throat and her expression twisted into something calmer, as if to deliver the news as gently as possible.

"You've been asleep for nearly three weeks," she answered. "I found the older fellow in the jungle, Gabriel. Better yet, *he* found me… a feat in and of itself." She chuckled. "You and your brother I knew would be by the beach, for I had felt when you landed."

Demetrius gasped.

"*Three* weeks?" He pressed his hand to his temple, thinking of all that could've happened in the world in just three weeks. "How is that possible—"

"I gave you all a special tonic, a remedy to help you rejuvenate," said Diveena. She looked him up and down with smug satisfaction. "You should feel better than when you were several years younger, I'd imagine."

Demetrius did a self-assessment and couldn't deny that he did feel as strong and healthy as ever, save for his missing leg; it was as if he'd rested away all of his ailments and more.

"Sure, I suppose…" He continued inspecting his body for any hint of damage, besides his new kneecap of silver. Then he looked up. "Wait, what do you mean that you *felt* when we landed on the beach?"

His skin prickled—there was only one answer that immediately came to mind, but it was so outlandish…

Diveena sat taller, clearly excited to relay something further.

"I'm glad you asked," she said, a smile in her voice.

She unfurled her hands to present something.

"My compass!" he squealed in joy, reaching for it.

She closed her hands back over it. "Does this compass belong to you?"

Demetrius nodded, swallowing. "It was a gift from a good friend… Tobias."

His shoulders sagged; he'd never see that friend again.

Thanks to Jeom.

"And a very special gift at that," said Diveena with a knowing expression. "It has a gift all its own, doesn't it?"

She cocked her head, eyeing him strangely.

"How could you know anything about that?" he said, suddenly alert—despite all that had happened, he was still a guardian. *I still have to protect the Guardians of Gold.*

Diveena studied the compass with something of affection before she gave it to Demetrius.

He squeezed his hands around the cool metal, pressing it over his heart with a deep sigh. *Thank the gods this wasn't lost!*

"Because I'm the one who bestowed that gift onto this device," she replied. Her voice echoed with a prominence that it hadn't held before. "Along with several other guardian relics, at Talis' persistence."

Demetrius' mouth fell open but no words came out. He looked up at her, gawking; she gave a single nod.

"I was able to sense your arrival because I'm a guardian, too," she added before he could even utter a sound. "An honorary one, at least. I prefer not to make myself known."

Diveena took his hand in hers, tracing the outline of the dragon that was forever etched into his palm—a mark that *only* guardians could see. Then, she proudly offered her own hand.

Demetrius saw the same golden lines there, vibrant against her pale skin. *Not the enemy.*

He immediately relaxed, comforted to know that this strange woman was somehow a friend by default.

"You really know Master Talis Churry?" he breathed, still staring at her palm.

"Ah, so you're acquainted with him as well?" said Diveena, seeming more at ease herself.

Demetrius offered a shaky smile.

She clapped her hands, growing elated. "I thought as much! My intuition is hardly ever wrong. Oh, yes, he's a dear friend. My only friend, really." She laughed, winking at Demetrius, as if to say—*we'll see about you.* "I miss him terribly. I saw him last maybe half a century ago?"

The sharpness in her features, the weightiness of her voice, suddenly made sense—though Diveena appeared youthful on the outside, this woman was clearly to be respected as an elder.

"How did you both meet?" he asked, unable to hide his interest.

He couldn't help but to set aside his despair for a moment and bask in the intrigue of the conversation.

"I haven't thought of our strange beginnings in quite some time," she said with a soft smile. "It was such happenstance, but Fate has a reason for everything, of this I'm certain."

Diveena placed her hands back in her lap, staring into her past, a sereness washing over her.

"I mostly stay out of the affairs of humans, unless I absolutely need something from the neighboring city. But one day, by chance, I was surprised to find young Talis stumbling around my part of the jungle." Her gaze drifted toward the window. "And what a wonderful chance that turned out to be," she said under her breath.

Demetrius cleared his throat, so many questions caught there.
She turned her attention back to him.

"That was a *very* long time ago," she said. "He used to visit me here on occasion, when he resided in Guanamara, but the occasions have been less and less with the increasingly dangerous state of the Olleb." She shrugged. "Talis is such a lovely man, though, a prime example of what a man should be. Would you not agree?"

Demetrius didn't say anything, vaguely remembering the turmoil that had befallen them before their escape at sea. He wondered if Talis had survived… if anyone had survived the ambush.

"Talis Churry took no time to try and persuade me of the guardian's cause," she continued. "While I refuse to meddle in the way things have unfolded with the decisions of humankind, I don't pretend not to choose sides." Her expression hardened, voice firm. "Anyone who positions themselves against King Devlindor or *Vladamor*—" the name fell off her tongue like pure rot "—is the side I stand on. For that, I have provided many gifts to the Guardians of Gold over the years."

She gestured to the compass.

"All that I've asked in return is that my privacy is kept. Talis and the few guardians who know of my existence have never betrayed me. Thus, should he ever call on me again, I might be inclined to give a little more."

She beamed, leaning back on the bed.

"*Maybe.*"

"What other gifts have you created?" asked Demetrius, fingering the compass—the aura and ora stones peppered throughout the device sparkled in the soft sunlight.

"As I've said, your guardian trinkets have felt my magic," said Diveena. "They each have their own surprises, powers that lived within the dwarf-made creations and just needed a little more coaxing to come out. I daresay they will all reveal themselves in time, just as your compass has, should the owners prove as worthy as you." She smirked. "Though I'm *sure* Talis would argue that my greatest gift of all was bringing a little more life to his Greenhouse."

Demetrius couldn't hide his astonishment as he instantly understood the answer to a question that had sat in his mind throughout the entire year they had lived in the guardian sanctuary of Zambienth—*How could the Greenhouse exist?*

He had been completely enthralled by his beloved guardian refuge in the desert, a place where magic and nature had been one and the same, yet incomprehensible all at once.

"You don't mean to say that all the nature in the Greenhouse… *you* did that?"

Diveena nodded.

He let a drawn-out whistle, truly wanting that underground garden again.

"But no sorceress could be that powerful…" He raised an eyebrow at her. "*What* are you?"

Diveena sat up straighter, playing with her braid as they considered each other.

"Elves have always had a strong kinship with the God of Earth," she said after a moment, standing. "Our powers are derived from nature—"

She reached out to touch one of the many vines that had found its way into this room; a green, sparkling light emanated from her palms, and the vine began to wiggle with life. The magic spread so quickly that soon the entire ceiling was dangling with them, like bewitched snakes roused from a slumber—they began to sprout lavender flowers with soft petals shaded in white.

"My magic is particularly powerful among my kind," she added, "for reasons that I may reveal to you in time."

Demetrius pressed his hands to his cheeks, shaking his head in disbelief as he gaped at her.

"You're an *elf!*" he screeched after the shock had worn off.

A Guardian of Gold hiding out in a jungle was surprise enough, but this…

He leaned back to take her all in, his voice going hoarse with nerves.

"That tattoo on your wrist—" He hadn't missed the gleaming silver mark that twisted around her hand; he faintly recalled reading somewhere that it was the symbol of the Nicora Tribe.

Then it clicked.

"By gods, that's it!" If he could have jumped to his feet, he would have. "I remember why your name sounds so familiar. Master Lethander… he was your father, wasn't he? The King of Elves?" He clutched at the sheets, eager for her answer.

"The *Lord* of the Nicora Elven Clan, yes," replied Diveena, seemingly impressed with his knowledge—Demetrius barely suppressed another squeal of excitement. "I suppose he was a king of sorts... until he wasn't."

"I know the story well," he said in a hushed voice.

Demetrius could practically feel Diveena's energy shift into something darker; he trod lightly, almost forgetting his misery completely in the face of another great Golden Age secret to be uncovered.

"I'm sorry, but I don't quite understand." He averted his eyes. "I thought... I thought that King Devlindor wiped out the elven race during his siege on magic?"

Diveena turned her back to him.

"He tried," she said. "With the help of one of our own."

She began to breathe deeply, too controlled, fists clenched by her sides.

Demetrius reached out to touch her. "I didn't mean to—"

Diveena whipped back around to face him, eyes glowing with a magic and anger that was more than humbling, chilling even; the nature in the room seemed to react violently with her emotions.

He jerked back his arm and just listened.

"I am the last remaining elf from my tribe," she stated—the flash of magic in her eyes burned bright, then fell away as she found her calm. "Though, time may make known other clans who survived in different regions, hidden as I... with any hope."

She let out a long exhale, bowing her head; the nature settled back into stillness.

"I truly am sorry," whispered Demetrius, feeling his grief creep back in, twisting his stomach in knots. "I know what it's like to be betrayed."

"You're too kind," she said, softly. "Tell me, is this the result of the betrayal you speak of?"

She yanked back the blanket covering him so that it crumpled to the floor in a heap; Demetrius gasped, pressing his hands over his thigh to try to hide what was no longer there.

"Yes," he said with a quiver, unable to look at her.

"Then I'm sorry for your suffering, too," she said with sincerity. "But at least you live. At least, *we* live. And as long as that's true, we must practice forgiveness." She brought her hand to her heart. "Otherwise, our anger could consume us and turn us into something we may not recognize one day."

She tilted his chin up so that he had to see her.

"Do you understand me, Demetrius?"

A tear rolled down his cheek, but he quickly wiped it away, finding the willpower to hold his emotions back this time.

He took a deep breath. "But how? *How* can you forgive the monsters for what they did to you and your family?" His voice grew louder. "How can I—"

"There was a time that the land here rotted at my fingertips," said Diveena, her expression shadowed with pain. "Anger and thoughts of revenge turned my powers of life into destruction, death. I was becoming exactly what I despised." She looked at her hands, pursing her lips. "But when I met Talis, all of that changed. He brought peace again to my life through his sheer faith in a brighter future. He showed me how to channel my anger into something impactful."

She curled her hands into fists, and Demetrius saw a dark, frightening force sparking within the cage of her fingers; he sucked in a breath, drawing away from her. But when she opened her palms, there was only a beautiful, gentle magic floating there.

Friend, he reassured himself.

"I taught him a great many things, but I was yet his apprentice in the art of healing and hope. I'll forever call him Master."

She walked to the window, pulling on a string to draw the curtains back. An expansive, circular opening was revealed.

Demetrius nearly lost his breath, leaning as far forward as he could—without falling off the bed—to get a closer look.

A tangled green forest expanded out in front of him like a sea of leaves, birds and butterflies dotting his vision. And round hills rolled off into the distance for as far as the eyes could see. From this vantage point, if he squinted, he *thought* he could even spot what must have been the City of Guanamara somewhere far off, sprinkling the hills with strings of smoke to signify human life.

We must be incredibly high up!

"When I leave this earth," said Diveena, "I vow to leave a trail of life behind me that not even the darkest necromancer could destroy. The Impenetrable Forest is my masterpiece, my new home, and I've worked to grow and strengthen it, with Nicora forever in my heart." She looked back to Demetrius. "I've nursed this jungle back to health, as I have you."

"It's breathtaking," he said, unsure of where to look first—there was so much to discover.

As he drank it all in, he saw what looked to be several structures dotted throughout the treetops, constructed of the same dark wood as the room he sat in now—they appeared to be built straight into the mammoth trees themselves, almost as if they had strangely shaped limbs. Then he realized that this place was actually connected to the others in the distance, swaying rope bridges and stairs built straight into the bark.

He gasped in delight. "This is truly remarkable!"

As unfathomable as it was, he knew they must be at the highest height of this hilly jungle—birds and monkeys zoomed about at eye-level, zig-zagging between the trees, fearless and free.

"Yes, it's quite something," said Diveena, glowing with pride. "Come now, let me show you around."

"But I can't," he said, looking down at his legs, his cheeks burning hot with shame. "I can't walk properly."

"You'll find your strength soon," she said. "Until then, a little magic never hurt anyone." She placed her hands on her hips, a wry smile on her face. "I trust you can make it to that chair, no?"

She pointed to a seat on the other side of the room.

Demetrius balked at the challenge, shaking his head.

"Just *try*," she demanded.

In a way, she reminded him of Arianna, feisty and spirited, taking nothing but a 'yes' for an answer; he prayed for her survival, for Lessa's and Eli's, too…

The thought of them out there somewhere, surely still fighting, made him feel a flicker of the bravery he had embodied before the attack—he didn't want to let his friends down.

You can do this!

Sucking in a deep breath, Demetrius hoisted himself off the bed; he still had one good leg, but it was painful and awkward to maneuver without both. *Not impossible, though.*

Slowly, he hopped forward across the room until he met the chair. He felt slightly humiliated as he fell into the seat—and yet, slightly proud.

He smiled to himself, just a flicker.

Diveena came around behind him, giving his shoulders a squeeze.

"You will find your strength," she reassured him. "A new and better one, I imagine."

"One can only hope," he mumbled, breathing heavily.

"Hope is *all* there needs to be for something to eventually become a reality," she said, resolutely. "This jungle is proof of that."

With the snap of her fingers, vines from every angle started to twist all around Demetrius and the chair.

He shrieked, fighting against them as they strapped him down. "What in the King's—"

"Hang on!" shouted Diveena, throwing the door open.

A burst of fresh air smacked Demetrius in the face, whistling about the room as it flooded in.

Before he could wrap his head around what was happening, his chair was hoisted forward by the enchanted nature; he grasped onto the arms of the seat to keep steady, the vines churning in a fluid motion to propel him across the floor.

Holding on for dear life, Demetrius found himself gliding over one of the rope bridges behind Diveena—she skipped along with grace.

He bit down on his lip to hold in his screams, eyes closed and nails digging into the chair; he was sure he'd fall to his death if a bird flew too close, frightening him out of the safety of his seat.

"Open your eyes," sang Diveena.

Come on, Demetrius, you're braver than this. Open your eyes!

He slowly opened one. Then, they both grew wide, and he cracked his first real smile since fleeing Zambienth.

"Well, I'll be damned!" he howled into the open sky, a delicious adrenaline rushing through him.

His fear abruptly shifted into awe of the magnificent land that stretched out around him; it grew more beautiful still with every second he looked.

"Just lovely, isn't it?" Diveena called back. "I look forward to sharing it for once." She began to point out the different functions of this high-up haven she governed.

There was an alcove for everything—potion-making, weaponry, dining, and more; and with such an incredible tour of the treetops, Demetrius had no problem believing that she'd also had a hand in creating the Greenhouse.

"Your friends are in here," she said after a while; she stopped in front of a structure much like the one he'd awoken in and cracked open the door. "I had an inkling you'd wake first, so I kept you separate."

The rolling vines slowed so that Demetrius could see.

He peeked inside the room and found Jeom and Gabriel in a deep, peaceful slumber—a surge of relief escaped his chest as he saw his brother and friend safe and sound.

"They'll be just fine," said Diveena, hovering over him. "Come along. We don't want to disturb their rest."

She pulled the door closed, and Demetrius internally thanked the gods that he still had time to process things alone. *I'm not ready to face them yet.*

They crossed another bridge, stopping at a much larger structure, spanning the width of two trees; Demetrius let out a barking laugh at the surprise that lay inside.

"I'll be damned," he said with a wide grin. "I sure wasn't expecting to see you up here, ole boy!"

Phantom was munching on a mound of straw and looking as healthy as a horse had ever been—he was sheltered in a pen next to a stunning white stallion.

A horse in the trees? I must be dead or dying! If this isn't the strangest thing I've yet to see since the Jar...

He snickered again, silently relieved that all his humor hadn't been lost with his leg.

"Such a kind creature you have by your side," said Diveena, stroking the horse's muzzle. "I've enjoyed my time getting to know him. He might be the luckiest of you all. Your very own good luck charm."

"Phantom, you hear that? You're good luck, boy," said Demetrius with another laugh of disbelief. He looked up to Diveena. "It's true, though. He's got more lives than most."

Even rivals Arianna.

He shook his head of the wonder.

"Everything you have up here... so close to the clouds. There aren't words."

Diveena grinned.

"Fancy a ride? I'm sure he's dying to stretch his legs. Poor thing, I've kept him cooped up in here since I found you all."

Demetrius immediately wished to retreat back to his room, his happiness fleeing away in the face of his overwhelming doubts.

"I don't know if I can anymore."

"Don't you?" she asked, her face wrinkled with confusion.

"What did it ever take to ride a horse but sitting down and whipping the reins? And you've still got your voice, haven't you? The ability to move every other part of your body? Surely you wouldn't just slide out from the saddle..." She shrugged him off with indifference. "Alas, if you don't know, I quite understand. Phantom... is that what you call him? He certainly won't be able to decide for you. After all, he's just a horse."

She went to tend to the other, paying Demetrius no mind.

"It's just... everything is so different now," he mumbled, stroking Phantom's side; was it just him or did Phantom look at him longingly? "I don't know what to do."

Horseback riding had always come naturally to Demetrius, as a dedicated agrarian and ally to all animals, but he didn't feel like the same person anymore.

"When one experiences a change, difficulties originate when that change is met with resistance," said Diveena, as if reciting a story. "If the person is flexible and open to what fate has delivered, they learn to adjust and make accommodations until the change becomes as natural as was the first comfort."

"Not quite sure I follow..." said Demetrius with a smirk, starting to feel somewhat of his old self again—it was hard to remain sour about anything in such an extraordinary setting.

"I believe that you do." Diveena pointed toward the hills. "You may have one leg instead of two, but the world has stayed the same. Which means, you must change how *you* see the world and accommodate the new you, until you feel whole again." She started to ready the white horse for riding. "Frankly, it doesn't matter how many of anything you have. As long as your heart is beating and you can think for yourself, that is what you are... whole. You just have to believe yourself that way."

Demetrius took a deep breath, overcome by so many different emotions; he felt anything but whole, still teetering on the edge of the darkness he'd been drowning in.

But now that he'd had a gulp of fresh air—like a rope dangling toward him to grab onto before he truly slipped away—he was, at least, wise enough to know that the dark wasn't a great fit for him. *I want to feel happy again.*

The memories of joy were there, lingering in the back of his mind; he wanted to try to make them a reality again.

"I suppose… I suppose, I can try," he whispered into Phantom's side, resigned to taking some small step toward the man he was before this 'change' had been thrust upon him.

"I think that's a very wise decision," said Diveena—she tried to hide it, but he heard the approval in her voice.

She spoke a string of words that sounded foreign to his ears, yet familiar to his heart; Demetrius thought he must've heard Arianna or Lessa speak the words before in a spell.

The vines came to life again, guiding his chair onto a small platform with wooden rails outside of the pen. Diveena stepped onto the platform next to him, pulling both horses behind her.

Then, she closed a small gate to keep them secure.

As the enchanted words again fell from her tongue, thick vines and branches moved from the trees and wrapped around the platform—they began to move downward, lowering slowly from the treetops to the ground.

The trees grew taller and taller as the jungle swallowed them whole, the air getting thicker and muggier by the second; Demetrius was in a daze the entire time, as the forest floor rushed to meet them.

"Out we go," said Diveena, pushing open the gate and ushering them off once they'd settled. She repeated the spell, the platform shooting into the sky.

Demetrius followed it with his gaze for as far as he could, until it disappeared behind a canopy of leaves; any trace of Diveena's home in the trees was completely obscured from ground level—it proved the perfect hiding spot.

She held out her hand to help Demetrius into Phantom's saddle; it took significant effort for him to heave himself up out of his chair and clumsily climb onto the horse. But, when he was situated, a smile betrayed all his anxieties.

Diveena hopped onto the other horse, and they set off through the jungle at a slow trot.

At first, Demetrius felt oddly off-balance, but after a few minutes and a lot of wiggling, he started to find a normalcy in riding. In fact, having the ability to steer Phantom in the directions that he wanted to go gave him a wonderful feeling—as if he could walk again.

He realized in that moment that what he feared most about this change in his life was not the physical loss of his leg, but the loss of control; Phantom showed him there was control to be found in new places, if he cared to look.

He whipped the reins, starting to feel more like himself again.

DIVEENA AND DEMETRIUS SPENT HOURS trekking through the jungle on horseback—and the less he focused on how different he felt, the more he became enthralled by the maze of nature around him.

Giant, slow creatures roamed near a river, and brightly colored snakes drooped from tree limbs, blending in with their homes. Large apes flew from branch to branch, their voices echoing across the hills above their heads, and there were spiderwebs that could've been master works of art for how intricate they were—though Demetrius was smart enough to keep his distance as he admired them.

Even the flowers and plant life here were of a spectacular variety, the sheen of magic shimmering in the dew dripping off the petals and leaves—just as Diveena had said, this jungle was *her* masterpiece. And what a stunning creation it proved to be.

I can't believe all the beauty still left to uncover in this world.

They climbed to the top of a hill where a vast, open field spread out before them, the jungle receding for a bit until it reappeared some distance away, encircling the meadow.

"Ready?" said Diveena over her shoulder.

"For what—"

"*Yaaa!*" she screamed, pressing her horse onward.

She flew down the hill, a laugh trailing in her wake.

Demetrius raced after her, not allowing himself a second to overthink it; his eyes were filled with tears of joy by the time they both reached the bottom.

"How do you feel?" asked Diveena, guiding her horse toward his.

She sat tall and regally upon the white stallion, overseeing this stretch of nature just as surely as Syrifina had watched over the Island of Idris.

"I feel… so much better," he said after a moment of contemplation; he gently patted Phantom. "Thank you, buddy. I needed that."

"Wonderful." They slowed, pacing leisurely across the pasture. "A walk through nature always does the mind good."

Demetrius gave a grunt of acknowledgment, but on the inside he *did* sense the start of something new brewing, something stronger.

"Diveena," he said after a long silence, "would you have a way to help us find our friends again, the other guardians? We've been separated. There was an attack on the Greenhouse."

She pulled back on the reins of her horse, coming to a halt. "An attack?"

Demetrius nodded.

She pursed her lips and swung down to the ground. "I'm unsurprised," she said, solemnly.

He stopped, too. "You are?"

"Yes," she said with a pout. "Things have been so out of tune lately." She flicked her hand toward him. "Then you lot showed up, guardians for certain and on your last breath."

Demetrius cocked his head. "What do you mean, out of tune?"

"Nature is like an anchor to everything else," she said. "It flows into all, and all flows back into it." She moved her hand slowly across a tall patch of grass—Demetrius' eyes were glued to the area as sharp blades of green swayed back and forth. "If something disrupts it, *say*, something dark, the trees will react, the birds will scatter, and the flowers will hide. Darkness poisons by the roots, then it spreads throughout everything."

She looked up, emerald eyes glowing bright.

"Something's coming. I can feel it."

"Something has already come," said Demetrius, gravely. "We've been running a long time to stay ahead of it, of the Shadow Resistance. Unfortunately, they've caught up to us, and we can't keep running anymore."

Diveena's lips twitched up into the faintest of smirks, and Demetrius couldn't help the laugh that escaped him as he immediately understood why; he glanced down to his silver-capped knee.

"Well, shoot… I definitely can't run anymore."

He smiled back, wondering when that statement wouldn't sting so badly, wondering when he could really laugh about it. *If…*

"Go on," she breathed, growing serious.

"We were preparing to fight back when the ambush happened, actually," he replied.

"Are you telling me that the Guardians of Gold have risen from the dead?" Diveena tilted her face toward the sun, a definite smile there. "That is music to my ears, young one."

"Yes, I suppose we have," he said. "Though, I fear now that

many of us may have gathered in our graves too soon… It was a bloody battle, and there was nothing we could do but flee."

"You speak of the Shadow Resistance…" Diveena turned away from him, her tone darkening. "Do you also speak of Vladamor?"

She spoke in such a whisper that it was barely audible.

"Yes." Demetrius clenched his fists around Phantom's reins as terrible memories began to flood his mind. "I know he was behind the attack in Zambienth, commanding the King's shadow armies. That's how I lost my leg. Sir Vladamor… he took possession of my brother to try and gain power over the Axe of Crissy."

Diveena pulled a breath in through her teeth.

"I see," she uttered. "And your brother, Jeom, he controls the Crissy weapon now?"

"That he does," said Demetrius, his palms growing sweaty. "What do you know of it?"

"I know that only a king among dwarves has the power to wield such a treasure, so I'm not at all shocked that King Devlindor tried to steal this power for himself." She exhaled deeply, letting go of the tension in her shoulders as she looked again toward the sky. "Destiny has brought you right where you're supposed to be," she added, turning back to face him. "I've been waiting a very long time for you, Demetrius Kane. For you both."

"I don't under—"

"Come," she said, helping him down from his horse.

Demetrius had to lean all his weight into her to slide off; they both lowered down to the grass.

"What have you learned of Vladamor's story?" she asked, sitting cross-legged, observing him as he tried to find a new type of comfort in a seated position.

Demetrius groaned in annoyance, settling on just feeling awkward. "That he was once a part of your clan," he replied. "An elf."

"That was long ago," she said with a nod, "when the King

was only a wicked boy."

"He was banished and stripped of his powers because he had betrayed your clan's secrets to humans, one of you killed in the process," he added, finally finding a stillness in the grass. "Out of revenge, he aided the King in destroying your family as part of a strategy to steal the crown, vowing his soul to the darkness and to Devlindor." He closed his hands to mimic shutting a book. "The rest is history."

"Very good," she said, fingering a long chain at her neck. "You've read the scroll then, I take it?"

"*A Cursed Soul*," said Demetrius, thinking back to his studies. "Keeper Kassime had it in the Luose attic library. You're familiar with it?"

Diveena laughed.

"Quite well, in fact," she said. "I wrote it."

Demetrius lit up—*oh*, how he wished for Lessa, Arianna, and even Jeom to be with him now, to bear witness to such tales.

"I gifted it to Talis to add to the guardians' collection long ago. I had hoped he'd share my story and remember us."

"You're *really* the author of that scroll?" he stuttered. "You're E.D.?"

Her cheeks flushed slightly, a soft pink.

"Elf Diveena," she corrected with a little chuckle. Her voice softened. "Delira, the young female killed by the humans, thanks to Vladamor's greed, was my twin sister." She brought the pendant of one of her necklaces to her lips. "This was hers."

Demetrius' thoughts wandered to Jeom.

"I'm so sorry for your loss," he mumbled. "I can't... imagine."

"Thank you." She tilted her head to the side, studying him closely. "You're very compassionate for one so young. You remind me of Talis in many ways."

"That's a lofty compliment," said Demetrius, sitting a little taller. "But what happened after the..." He cleared his throat.

"How did you end up here?"

"As you well know, much time after my sister's death, Vladamor returned to the Nicora Forest seeking revenge. King Devlindor, then just a young lord, aided his quest. News of my father's death by Devlindor's hand had already reached our realm, so our clan was completely out of sorts when they attacked. It all happened so fast…" Her gaze lingered on the trees. "My entire family was slaughtered right in front of me."

She closed her eyes for a moment before she continued.

"I'm not sure what it was, but something urged me to run and hide in the trees during the peak of it," she said. "I survived, but I watched my loved ones burn. And then I had to bear witness as the rest of the Olleb followed—"

She twisted a piece of grass around her finger.

"After that, I went into hiding here, deep in the jungle. I've been fortifying this area ever since, and so far haven't been discovered by the King nor his soul-sucking necromancer."

"That's horrific," said Demetrius after a moment of silence. "I know what it's like… to lose a part of your family. Jeom and I are twins as well, somehow." He shrugged. "We have the same mother out there somewhere, I suppose."

"How could you know?" asked Diveena, raising an eyebrow.

"We just *do*, but we bear the same birthmarks, for one." He held up his hand to display one half of the six-pointed star. "When we were separated in the districts, Jeom a creator and I an agrarian, I always felt that a piece of me was missing." He balled his hand into a fist, staring at his mark. "I know he would say the same."

Diveena squeezed the pendant on her necklace. "And now you have him back."

Demetrius felt himself flush.

"I… I thought I did. Though it feels like I've lost him again," he whispered, tracing the dark, jagged line that ran from his thumb to his wrist.

The memory of their reunion long ago in the Vanishing Tunnels, by only the will of Luck and Fate, seemed distant now; he felt himself pushing it away, avoiding it.

"Love can overcome many things," said Diveena. "I suggest you find a way to forgive him, before you no longer have the chance."

Demetrius lowered his head, feeling guilty to have even admitted such feelings to her; she would never have the opportunity to see her sister again, save for the journey of death—it put things in the harsh light of perspective.

They didn't speak for a while after that, only the sounds of nature joined their thoughts as they basked in the sun.

"Demetrius…" whispered Diveena, looking toward him with something of caution in her expression, "you should know that the story of Vladamor is not only my own." She took a deep breath. "That story also belongs to you."

"*Me?*" he asked with a jerk. He blinked the sun out of his eyes to see her properly. "How do you mean?"

She spoke again in her strange, foreign tongue, one that sounded like musical notes dancing on the wind—this time, though, Demetrius knew exactly what they had meant.

'*My heart is your heart,*' she had said.

As those words rang out clear as day through his mind, Diveena reached out to touch him, pressing a glowing finger right over his heart.

Demetrius gasped, an irresistible warmth spreading throughout his entire body from where her finger met his chest.

"I can see *everything*," he breathed, tears instantly wetting his cheeks; he looked to the sky, feeling a delicious, inexplicable energy soar through him. "What's happening to me?"

"I have only shared with you a bit of my knowledge, so that you can begin to understand what it is I'm about to tell you. But it's hardly everything," said Diveena in a hushed voice. "I wouldn't wish that burden on you…"

Demetrius hardly noticed when she dropped her hand away, trying to make sense of any of the images suddenly swimming in his mind's eye.

"It was said among my people that when an elf died, his or her powers *could* be transferred into the next worthy possessor, so that elven knowledge may never cease to exist." She shook her head. "When Vladamor murdered our entire clan, I daresay that was his intention… to really put this theory to the test. And while he did receive his despicable powers back, I lived. Thus, our family's heritage flowed to me."

She rested her hand over her heart.

"I hold their memories, their magic, *everything*. My burden to carry until I can pass them on to someone worthy, or return them to the earth to be reborn again. It's a curse as much as it is the most precious of any gift."

Demetrius tried to focus on her words, troubled that she'd shared so much of her history with him; he knew how protective her kind were of their secrets.

"What does this have to do with me?" he asked—the sight she'd given him ebbed, the warmth fading slightly as he concentrated on her.

"Because," she replied, holding his gaze, magic swirling in her vision, "you, Demetrius Kane, are half-elf. You carry the blood of my blood."

She gave a firm nod in the face of his sheer shock.

"My sister's blood, my mother's, *and* my father's—the blood of the last Nicora elf lord—flows through you. I am certain of it." She reached for his hand. "You are my brother, in body and soul."

Demetrius gawked at her.

"You've been sipping too much of your magical spring water," he stammered, pulling his hand back. "What you're saying is impossible! I'm sorry, but your father would've died centuries ago… how could he have also fathered me?" He scoffed. "I know elves are supposed to be very wise and whatnot, but your mathematics might be a bit dated."

Diveena laughed—her voice seemed to echo across the field, swimming through the trees and wrapping around him on the wind, enchanted.

"Open your mind," she said. "Not all magical creatures are born the way humans procreate. Magic can also birth magic."

She leaned back on her elbows to gaze up at the drifting clouds.

"Long ago, during King Damas' time, peace settled among all peoples, magic-bearing or not. It truly was a Golden Age, if I ever lived one. But the Olleb's races weren't always known to have lived in harmony… least of all the elf, dwarf, and human kinds. King Damas brought us all together. Humans, elves, dwarves, and everything in between began to make alliances, to tolerate each other and even support one another through harsher times—"

She lay down on her back as she gave the history lesson of a lifetime; Demetrius had never been such a good listener before.

"Master Lethander, Lord of the Nicora Elven Clan, and King Undoriamus, ruler of the dwarves residing in the City of Undor, made a binding pact in the form of *life*. Not long before the murder of my sister, Delira," she noted. "That pact was acknowledged by King Damas himself, solidified with his own enchanted seal. And that was what allowed my father to form an alliance with the king in the first place…"

She let her eyes float closed, the sun beaming down on her.

"It was merely meant to be representative of good faith more than anything," she whispered. "No one could have ever fathomed that our lines would actually be destroyed one day." She sat up, her face splotched with tears. "Three of the most powerful leaders in all of Olleb-Yelfra summoned their strongest magic, with the gods as sure witnesses, to vow that if ever their kingdoms should fall or the last male heirs were taken, new life would be born again to carry on what they had built a lifetime toward... harmony. The elves, dwarves, *and* humans were never to be enemies again in the new age, and that promise was sealed in blood magic."

"Blood magic?" Demetrius croaked out, his throat dry. "What's that...?" He did *not* like the sound of it.

"It is such that can never be broken, undone, or fooled by anyone other than those who share the same blood—"

Diveena placed her hand over the earth and beckoned a flower from the soil, its petals unfurling to reveal a striking mosaic of colors.

"The ancient leaders combined their lineages through blood magic," she continued, "so that in their rebirth, should there *ever* come a day, they would be bound forever as brothers, with powers great enough to assume the thrones."

"What are you saying?" breathed Demetrius, pulling his fingers through his hair. When she didn't respond, he looked to his hands. "It isn't true... I have *no* powers. Jeom, he... my brother has the Axe of Crissy, but I have nothing. I'm not what you think."

"Quite the contrary," said Diveena, getting to her feet and offering him her hand.

Hesitantly, he took it.

As their palms joined, Demetrius felt himself being thrust upright—the roots of the earth filled the space where his leg used to be, lifting him up, sturdy and strong.

"I carry the weight of the Nicora Tribe, so you won't have felt the magnitude of what your powers could be," she said. "But I can show you more, as soon as I think you're ready. When you're stronger, I can teach you the ways of our clan. And in time, should you prove a *true* brother, your powers will come into fruition."

Demetrius was gaping down at his nature-made limb. "I haven't any magic. I'm telling you," he said. "I swear, I don't—"

"With certainty you do, dear child. The God of Earth has shown me." Diveena looked at him with a prideful grin. "You and your brother are the human embodiment of two of the strongest and noblest magical beings to have ever graced this land. You're one of us. You just have to believe."

17

JUST SURVIVE

TIME PASSED SLOWLY and excruciatingly for Arianna as a slave to the King. In his mind, he had won. Each time she was ripped from the chamber she shared with Odessa by someone from the King's Guard or a palace regulator, she knew he *thought* that he'd won.

It was nearing on two months now, and this dance was beginning to feel like a terrible routine.

The King squeezed tightly at her life and treated her like a rat found in the trenches of the dirtiest river. And she felt like one, too, hair forever matted with filth and clothes ragged and ripped; until, inevitably, Princess Elisa would demand her a comfort and force her to dine in her lavish chambers after her attendant, Jillian, had cleaned her up.

It was an endless cycle, and Arianna didn't know how much more she could withstand, the two Devlindors in a constant battle to claim some piece of her soul.

Over time, she concluded Princess Elisa to be a strange creature, with a twisted mind and warped way of thinking. She wasn't *innately* cruel, like the King, but she was complacent to his evils, making her just as bad. And when her mood was sour, she could be just as punishing.

Nonetheless, she fished for Arianna's respect in a much more pleasant way than her brother—the polish to the King's ruthless sword.

She might as well have said '*we're not as bad as you think*' while forcing her to bathe in a tub filled with rose petals or offering her delicacies beyond belief; Arianna never really played along, but she wasn't going to refuse those moments of comfort under Jillian's care, nor a full belly beneath the Princess's watch, if only to remain sane a little longer.

And the closer Princess Elisa allowed her to get, the more she could see straight through her beautiful exterior and into her heart—one filled with regret as she followed her brother into the darkness, forever burying her true feelings for the sake of her neck; Arianna presumed that those feelings had long since turned to cold memories now, subtle reminders of someone she would never know again.

She wouldn't be fooled.

She saw Princess Elisa for the coward she was, attempting to atone for her evils by offering her human moments; the King permitted his sister's behavior not only because he cherished her but because he wanted to stretch Arianna's life and tortures on for as long as possible…

There was nothing more torturous than enjoying simple pleasures, knowing that pain would soon follow.

Despite her hatred for him, Arianna could not deny that King Devlindor was a cunning man. Most days, he pushed her to the point of madness using mind magic, digging through her thoughts for any information to use against the guardians, or purely for pleasure. Then, before she could fully break, he'd allow the Princess to reel her back in and remind her that she wasn't dead yet, and wouldn't be able to die anytime soon.

Luckily for her, if there *was* any luck left in this situation, Arianna had learned mind magic from the best of the best. So far, she had been able to divert him away from anything that could truly endanger her friends or their mission.

Thank you, Keeper Kassime. The King has not yet won.

She wished, though, that her suffering would soon come to an end.

When Arianna wasn't enduring these terrible sessions, she had to endure everything else… relentlessly humiliated by the King and his loyal subjects; he loved to parade her about the streets so that his people had something to jeer at.

There was such a distaste for her presence in the City of Saindora that she couldn't see how they would ever come around to her side—if there even came a day to share it.

Her name passed between the lips of the highlifes and common citizens with revulsion; they pranced around the gold-trimmed palace halls with their silks and shining swords, or along the winding city paths to do their daily business, thinking they had it all figured out… that Arianna deserved her place at the very bottom of their society.

"There goes the girl who made a mockery of our world, of our precious freedom," they would whisper. "Let her rot! Let death meet her slowly."

You know nothing of the forgotten Golden Age!

Arianna held her head high and offered no bows nor curtsies to anyone—not unless there was a blade threatening the politeness out of her.

Saindora has no idea what the King has stolen from them.

Its people walked a formerly enchanted city that was impatiently waiting to come to life again.

She could sense the magic pulsating from the palace walls and trapped beneath the floorboards. She knew it had been buried away somewhere in boxes, lost hallways, and probably entire forgotten wings; the King had exerted every effort to control magic for himself, its existence wiped from the Olleb's memory.

Thus, every time his people spat at her feet or disgraced her with insults—made her bleed or scream—Arianna forgave them.

The first time, when they had dragged her through the streets after Cyn and Iris' brutal deaths, was so hard—the tears not to be withheld, the shrieks of pain not to be silenced. But after it was done, she'd found the strength to forgive.

It got easier every time... and there were other things besides hatred of the ignorant to fill her mind.

In the night, when the magicless citizens turned their eyes away, the Shadow Resistance crept out from dark corners to hail to the King, just as the world praised him in the day; the sheer number of his followers who were privy to magic was staggering—they were just as corrupt as him, and they were a great many.

Arianna had learned that there were thousands of men and women who made up the Shadow Resistance army, blending into the Olleb as highlifes, revered elders, or masters of their crafts; when darkness fell and their masks came off, they wielded their powers to carry out King Devlindor's dark biddings, tightening his authority over the land.

Arianna knew his priority at present was to wipe away any trace of magic that she might have let loose for wandering eyes to accidentally find, and to make sure something like this could never happen again...

The King ordered his followers off in this group or that, to hunt down the last remaining guardians and to destroy any evidence that they ever existed at all; his Shadow Resistance controlled their sanctuary in South Luose, had thwarted their plans in Zambienth, and now even probably controlled the Greenhouse.

Arianna didn't know for certain what had transpired with the rest of the guardians after all this time—almost six months having come and gone since she'd fled Zambienth—but she would do everything in her power to ensure that he could not gain another inch. Right now, that meant withstanding his mind magic to the best of her ability.

Fortunately, despite all the torments in her new daily life, Arianna enjoyed a small refuge—her imagination.

All she need do was close her eyes to travel to the sea or the sky; to swim in the warm waters of her utopia or walk through the towering trees of the Nicora Forest; to sit in the quiet of the Black Sand Desert or savor the seclusion of the Island of Idris.

And sometimes, she even tried to picture Saindora as she had once imagined it might be, based on old paintings and scrolls describing the Golden Age.

In her mind, the city's decaying buildings were painted a shimmering white with gold trims. And the dirty streets she walked in shackles were reimagined into smooth, clean stones, weathered down from when the waters had run too high.

A beautiful, magical place, she thought.

Alas, when she opened her eyes, her imagination would be wiped away and everything turned dark again.

Life in the Four Corners is no fond memory, but at least the snow covered everything in a permanent sheen of white...

Arianna had traveled far from that place now. She recognized that the darkness that plagued her first home flowed seamlessly from one corner of the world to the next, radiating straight from the City of Saindora.

Syrifina had been right. That which was once full of light and life was now blackened and corrupt—the closer one got to Saindora, the colder the souls grew.

The people here had also been beaten into submission more than most. Drifters kept to the outskirts of the city, and the punishment platform was sparkling clean; no one would dare do anything out of turn, knowing that King Devlindor himself would carry out the penalty.

Arianna felt sorry for them sometimes, their loyalties to the King aside.

There are more slaves in Saindora than even the districts, she thought. *And I'm trapped alongside them. I can't believe I ever wished to live here... to serve the Crown.*

"Are you ready?" came the King's voice, filling the air like a poisonous gas pouring into the room.

Her eyes flew open, her imagination flitting away.

She always got bumps on her skin when he spoke, the sound so smooth and sharp that it cut right through her bravery and made her fear resurface, just when she thought she'd wound it back in.

She was stretched out flat on a hard, wooden slab, her arms and legs uncomfortably bound with itchy rope. A large chain was also strapped across her stomach to keep her secure.

Her nails dug into the wood as she waited for him to start, for what seemed like the hundredth time since the first.

"You'll never find what you're looking for," she said, staring at a characterless and very familiar ceiling. "You never have, and you never will. Your entire existence is a history of searching for something *more*, which means you'll never find it."

"I always find what I'm looking for," he said. "I always get what I want."

King Devlindor stepped forward so that she could see his face.

A sickly smile grew across his lips, and his skin crinkled at his eyes and mouth, defying whatever magic he used to keep himself looking so young; this close up, Arianna could see plainly the years of hate and horrors piled up beneath the façade of a seemingly youthful royal.

"Do your worst," she spat, forcing herself to not look away.

He snickered. "Don't I always?"

Arianna balled her fists, every muscle in her body clenching as she readied herself—he dived into her mind.

His magic was resilient, but even the King didn't have an endless supply of energy to feed this type of enchantment. He couldn't last more than an hour of prying through her memories before he sent her away each day; and the more he used his magic on her, the better she was able to defend herself against it.

Each night, Arianna's mind healed. And each day, she grew stronger against his methods.

In fact, every minute the King kept her as a prisoner, her powers suppressed under this spell or that, his precautionary enchantments began to have less of an effect on her—little by little, she felt her magical energies building back up, seeking to overcome the relentless blockade.

So for that hour each day, when the King burrowed into her mind—like taking a knife to the deepest parts of her memories—Arianna raised more hope that her magic might one day resurface, against all the odds, and aid her escape.

Still, it was hard to keep the faith…

When they first started these sessions, the King had focused on gaining knowledge as to the whereabouts of other guardians, or how to try to thwart their next plan.

Then, his focused shifted.

Now he spent all his energy trying to understand *her* better—wondering how she worked, and fascinated with the powers she'd acquired in such a short amount of time, despite all the securities he'd established to prevent this exact situation.

He pored through her thoughts with an unending obsession—he wanted to decipher every choice she'd ever made…

From befriending someone like Noah (who, at one point in time, seemed destined for the Tunnel of Tombs) to giving her life over to Sir Vladamor for the sake of those she had chosen as family; Arianna screamed in agony as he flipped through her past like a picture book, her throat always sore and scratchy by the end of the hour.

She had to give him something, though.

She let the King see the little boy who had taunted her in her youth, before he was shoved into the Pit to his death—a reminder to be stronger. And, reluctantly, she allowed the King to steal away Liam's smiles from throughout the years.

Arianna let him know the love she had felt for Solomon Bell as he instilled in her both confidence and strength, and she allowed him to see the gaping chasm that Cyn's death had left in her heart.

Together, she and King Devlindor reexperienced her history, her great many fears and excitements.

Curiosity propelled them deep into the Vanishing Tunnels, her friends along for the ride, as they battled the monsters beneath the earth. He tasted the axe to her side as Grinda Risso stole her life during the Warrior's Challenge, and he felt the moment Talis Churry breathed the life back into her, the beginning of everything—he savored that one.

Arianna let the King all in, and the further he traveled into her past, the hungrier he became to learn more of the story behind slave Twenty-Two of Warrior's District.

It was painful to relive such private thoughts and moments, but it kept him from digging any deeper about the Guardians of Gold and the many different tactics they'd rehearsed for their shining moment against his armies; regardless, she knew that the Shadow Resistance would likely hunt down her friends soon enough—the King didn't need much from her to feel confident in that future. But she did what she could to hopefully buy them more time.

The things she had accomplished in life—to have walked such an interesting path for one so young, to even have had the opportunity to stand against the High King of the Olleb—were enthralling to him.

King Devlindor was of royal blood with extraordinary strength and power to his name—'*who is Arianna Belvedor but a slave amongst slaves in my world? Who is she to get her hands on an avatar… just like me?*

She could sense his thoughts merging with her own the deeper he dug.

"You know," said the King toward the end of their session, "the more I'm able to get to know you, I'm *so* thankful that you did cause such trouble for me. Now I can quiet any unsettled feelings I've ever had about my responsibilities to the Olleb."

He dabbed the sweat from his forehead with a handkerchief; hers dripped into her eyes.

"You, unsettled?" she choked out with as much sarcasm as she could muster.

"Nobody is perfect," he said with a sneer, straightening his crown. "Can you keep a secret?"

"Only if you sew my mouth shut," she said in a slur, trying to keep from crying out, his magic doing its worst.

The King tapped his chin, clearly considering the idea; Arianna focused on her breath.

(Inhale.) Just stay calm. (Exhale.) This will be over soon.

He eased his magic a bit to talk.

"I always thought that should my position ever be challenged and I lost the battle for the throne, well… fate is fate," he mused, "now isn't it?" He shrugged. "Alas, the Guardians of Gold have failed time and time again to take what is clearly, *rightfully* mine."

Arianna could hardly stand how smug he looked.

"You're vile," she said, spitting in his face.

Ever so slowly, he used the handkerchief to wipe the spit away. Then, he jabbed his finger into her chest, his voice thick with ire.

"You have managed to evade my system and try again under their tutelage—" He slid his hand around her arm, digging his nails into her skin. "And yet, here you are, a slave again and forever. The guardians have failed."

Arianna felt her insides curl, unable to hide her discomfort.

Just survive!

He smiled the more she squirmed.

"Your effort is to be respected, of course," he added, "but Fate has most clearly spoken." He released his grip on her, standing taller. "I *am* your king."

"And what do you know of fate?" asked Arianna, blinking away any hint of tears—she truly wanted his explanation of what she found to be the most complex subject of her life.

"Fate is knowing your place in the world," he snapped, his demeanor hardening like the lash of a whip.

Arianna recoiled, bracing herself for more pain.

He could have been Syrifina's emotional twin, but she would've given anything to choose between being a volatile mermaid's prisoner or his.

Syrifina, at least, has the remnants of a soul left.

King Devlindor's breath came heavier, his energy waning.

"I know mine," he said, leaning over her. "And with you here now, I'll ensure that it's never challenged again. Not by you, not by the guardians, nor anyone else who might prove to have an imagination outside the bounds of my regime." With a satisfied gasp, he fully released his mind magic. "Thank you for the challenge, though. I was getting so bored."

Arianna sighed loudly, that particular moment of relief always so overwhelming.

"As am I," she muttered, sweat drenching her entire body.

"Don't get too comfortable, then," he whispered, narrowing his eyes. "We're not done just yet."

A wicked smile crossed his face.

"*Memorium sequencia!*" His mind emptied back into hers.

She didn't even have a moment to catch her breath before she felt his agonizing magic grip her once more.

It was as if his dark spirit sank into hers, to take a stroll through her most personal experiences.

"Once I'm done with you," he said in clipped, concentrated

breaths, "I daresay you'll make a grand contribution to the Saindora Study. No doubt your body will be the best exhibition our Well Center Gallery has ever had the pleasure of hosting."

Arianna's fear amplified as she thought back to her first night in South Luose… exploring the vast halls of the city well center and hiding in what had turned out to be a room dedicated to the torturous experimentation on the bodies and souls of people deemed unworthy of life, or even proper death.

"People are just fascinated with the slave who made it so very far," he said, "who would dare to take something she hadn't earned."

He laughed, a sickening sound that reverberated throughout her head—as if his voice were that of her own conscience.

"Have you heard what they say? They'll remember you for a *long* time to come, but not in the way you had hoped, I'm afraid."

Arianna gritted her teeth, nails digging into her palms as she tried with all her energy to steer his direction, to keep him from taking her over completely.

"You're a monster," she said. "And you're wrong about your fate. Even if I'm destined to die here, I know all I've done has been for the good of the Olleb. You and your actions—" she screamed out in pain, breathing heavily "—driven by greed, fear, and power. You may have fooled the world for a long time, but your secret is out now and there's no putting it back in the bottle."

Her head spun as she tried to focus.

"The truth is spreading, and you can't stop it. Call yourself king as much as you want, but you didn't earn your seat on that throne, you *stole* it." She drew in another deep breath, panting. "Soon, everyone will know."

"So what if I did?" he replied in a low, menacing tone; he leaned over her, whispering near her ear, no chance to be overheard. "What if I murdered my cousin and manipulated my uncle to his deathbed, until there was nobody left but me to pick up the crown?" He stroked her hair as he contemplated her, his eyes disturbingly black. "And what if the guardians had succeeded and let this rumor spread, that I took the Olleb by sheer force? What then? Do you think it would change anything...?"

He sighed, shaking his head.

"Learn this lesson here and now." He straightened his back, his authority stifling. "I have *all* the power, and it doesn't matter how I got it. The only thing that matters now is that I have it."

His hands slid down from her head to caress her face; Arianna wanted to bite his fingers off but didn't have the strength.

"It's not about right or wrong," he continued, "or whatever moral quandary has sent you on this rebellious quest. In the end, strength always triumphs, and power *equals* strength. Right now, my living followers greatly outweigh the number of your guardians, dead and alive combined." She winced. "So yes... I have all the power, and you have none."

His hands found her neck, and he squeezed hard—she couldn't suck in any more air.

"There's no way out of this, Twenty-Two," he said, squeezing harder as she kicked. "Give up your hope and stop fighting me." Arianna felt her world spin, everything growing hazy. "Nobody is coming to save you, so you might as well quit struggling. Accept that *this* is your fate."

She thought of Cyn and Iris. *Just survive...*

The King let go, and Arianna gasped for air, coughing up a fit; her emotions swelled to the surface, the threat of oncoming tears weighing heavy on her chest.

"That's not true!" she said, beginning to fight her restraints. "There's more to ruling than just power." She tossed her head from side to side, trying to restrain her panic. "If the truth is uncovered, you'll no longer have the people's respect. They'll never keep following you after they learn what you've done. And without people to rule, your crown will mean nothing!"

Her head was pounding, her wrists chafing as she pulled up

against her shackles.

"Respect?" he shouted down at her, spit flying from his mouth. "Respect is earned through fear! And that I have in ample amounts." He shoved her back down. "The people believe what I tell them to believe, because they *fear* the repercussions if they don't. That is how I've kept the throne for nearly three centuries, and how I will keep it forevermore."

He stopped talking to concentrate, diving deeper into her thoughts—the searing pain of his magic carved away Arianna's sanity little by little.

"Fear is not the only way... to gain respect," she stammered— she shrieked as he pressed more. Then the tears finally came. "Centuries or not, the Olleb cannot sustain under your law. You've brought imbalance to our land, and it must be corrected." She clenched her jaw. "It's... the Golden Rule."

At this, the King took pause.

"So," he said, alarmingly calm, "you know of the prophecy then. Funny—" nothing about his tone suggested anything of the sort "—I haven't crossed this in your memories yet."

"Maybe you should've considered asking your questions politely rather than barging into my mind," she retorted.

"*Speak*," he said, narrowing his gaze.

She closed her eyes, turning her head to the side. *Keep it together, Arianna. No more slips like that!*

"Yes, I know," she said—the numbing pit in her stomach grew deeper, but it was too late to take it back. "I know that you created the Four Corners to keep innocent children from coming into their magic, because you were afraid of a prophecy you heard from a seer. Just like everything, you think you can control it, outsmart it." She shook her head, eyes flying open wide. "But you don't understand the Golden Rule at all! If you did, the Four Corners wouldn't even exist."

She glared into his eyes, the firelight in the chamber reflecting back at her through his dark pupils.

"You're no all-powerful ruler," she said with disdain. "Odessa was right."

The King fell silent; Arianna held tight to this bout of courage.

Now who has the power?

"No, you're just a scared little boy… everything you've ever done was in fear of not belonging and fear of death." She scoffed. "Does that not make you the weakest man alive? We *all* die someday. Chasing immortality is a fool's errand."

She laughed, dryly, her throat hoarse.

"You cannot control what is a rule of natural balance," she added. "You can try, but as you've said, the only thing that matters in the end is power. *Real* power. And how can you be truly powerful… if you're afraid of the inevitable?"

King Devlindor lunged at her like a viper; he wrapped his hands around her arms and whispered, "*Luzcora.*"

An excruciating shock ran through her entire body; all her muscles seized so that she couldn't even scream, and she felt every second of the pain so fully.

"Was that real enough for you?" he roared, releasing the torturous magic before it could kill her.

She struggled to pull breath back into her lungs, trembling from head to foot.

Her head lolled to the side, and she spotted Solomon and Princess Elisa spying on them from the doorway.

The anger she felt at seeing her former master in this moment overcame all else—she found the strength to lift her head as high as she could to look at him properly, fighting against the ropes and chains so hard that blood warmed her skin beneath them.

"Care to join us?" she called, seeing only fire.

She wished for Solomon's head even more than the King's sometimes—the weight of his betrayal grew heavier each day in this prison.

He did not speak as Princess Elisa entered the room, whispering something in her brother's ear.

"Yes, sister," replied the King with a nod. "If you must, but don't pamper her too much this time. She already thinks too highly of herself." He turned his attention back to Arianna. "You're chained by *me*, as you always have been and always will be. I own you, Twenty-Two. I gave you your identity, and my decrees granted that your life be allowed to grow and bloom in the place that I dictated. *I* am your beginning and your end, and I'll decide what happens next."

He squared his shoulders, eyes boring down into hers.

"No matter what prophecies are written, Olleb-Yelfra will always bow to me."

Solomon and Princess Elisa were nodding along in agreement.

"My friends will stop you," she said, her bravery building as the three people she hated most in the world looked down on her; she laid her head back on the table and put her gaze to the ceiling. "If I fail to stop you, they *will* come."

"There's no one left in your corner, Arianna," said the Princess, gently sweeping the hair from her eyes. "Your friends are surely dead by now if Sir Vladamor is any worth at all. I'm sorry that you're hurting, but it will be better if you stop fighting us."

"That's not true," she mumbled, lips quivering—she refused to look at her.

"Yes, it is," said the King, emphasizing every word. "I may have gotten sloppy, a little too relaxed in my rule if a place like Moriamo could exist right under my nose, but I'm awake now, and I do thank you for that."

He nodded with sincerity, a smile playing on his lips.

"And what you feel right now is only the beginning," he added with a repulsive gleam in his expression. "The magic that keeps me and my army young and strong will keep you so as well, just enough that you'll not die until I'm ready to let you go, and just enough that you'll survive whatever new tortures I can think of later." He grabbed her by the chin, forcing her to look at him. "You haven't even *begun* to know pain, but you soon shall. I'm going to rip all of the magic from you so that you won't even remember the taste of it."

Arianna's mouth pressed into a thin line, the weight of his words torture in itself. She drew in a deep breath, unwilling to let another tear fall for him to enjoy.

"What, nothing left to say?" He turned to Solomon. "She's not as much of a fighter as you led me to believe. How disappointing."

Solomon just shrugged.

"I'll leave you to your thoughts, then," said the King to Arianna. "You'll need some time to think about everything, to prepare yourself to become part of my... eternal family. And, evidently, you and *Odessa* are getting on too well."

Arianna's heart quickened—she'd let too much of the truth out, let him get to her...

"In a week's time, you'll be moved out of the seer's quarters and into something less comfortable, for I almost have everything I need. Then we can begin the real fun."

King Devlindor left the room, leaving Arianna in the care of Solomon and Princess Elisa, and with more anxieties still.

"The guards will take you to my chambers soon," said the Princess, too lightly. "Jillian will get you all cleaned up and fed. Don't you worry. Everything will be *fine*. My brother can be a little... extravagant, but he won't toy with you much longer, not once you're moved deeper into the dungeons."

She offered her a reassuring smile that made Arianna feel ill.

"Maybe we should let the girl rest a moment before the guards arrive to escort her?" said Solomon, opening his arm for Princess Elisa to take. "She probably has a lot on her mind, and I can hardly stand the stench of her."

"Hmm," said the Princess with a nod, linking her arm with

his, "though I'd imagine her mind would be quite empty at this point." She flipped her hair back. "It's about time we all move on."

They disappeared through the doorway, and Arianna was alone.

She wished Princess Elisa were right... that she hadn't a thought on her mind. But a numbing terror consumed her now in her solitude as she imagined what her life might look like should she become a more permanent guest of the King's. *If I don't find a way to escape soon, I won't even have to bother imagining it.*

Odessa would only see one future for her then, and it would surely be dark.

HALL OF MAPS

WHEN SHE LOOKED AROUND the dark chamber, lit only by the glare of a few candles, Arianna saw her own body, her chest rising and falling as she breathed in and out.

From this vantage point, she noted how long and unruly her hair had become, and she thought her features had hardened somehow; though she tried to stay strong beneath the weight of the King's tortures and her growing loneliness, the stress was slowly eating away at her, both physically and mentally. Her worries were carved into her cheekbones and the fresh scars on her skin—that's how she looked… when she saw herself sleeping.

This must be a dream.

She whisked closer to observe—Odessa was curled up like a child beside her in their bed.

Arianna thought her a child in many ways… but she knew she wasn't. She was surely fed magic to keep her alive, well beyond her years, so that her bloodline could continue to appease the needs of the King for as long as he wished.

Her hair was a deep brown, like her mother must've boasted in her youth, and her skin was so fair that it shone almost see-through under the light of the candles dotting the room. She looked so vulnerable and weak, frightened even in her sleep.

However, Arianna knew her to be strong in other, unimaginable ways.

In these past two long months, she had grown fond of Odessa. And while the seer was not without her oddities, she was the only person she trusted in this place.

Looking down on her now, Arianna realized that Odessa had been, unsurprisingly, right in her earliest predictions of their future relationship—she finally viewed her as a friend.

Even if she'd fed the King vital pieces of information that might one day lead to any number of awful outcomes, Arianna knew that she would forgive her. For, of all King Devlindor's victims, the hand Odessa had been dealt was by far the worst.

She knew what oppression could do to a person, and how freedom could change that; Odessa never even had a chance to earn her freedom like the rest of the world.

Arianna wished very much that she could give it to her, show her another side of life that she'd only ever seen in visions of the future. She shifted her eyes toward the door, wanting with everything to just swing it open so that they could both sneak away in the night—just as suddenly as the thought occurred in her mind, she found herself on the other side.

She was in a dark corridor lined with flickering lanterns.

A snoozing guard leaned against the door of their chamber, and she momentarily froze at the sight of him.

Then, she thought, *It's only a dream...*

Arianna might have first assumed this strange experience to be astral projection—if not for the fact that her magic had been smothered into nothingness in the confines of the palace, and because she didn't have her dagger to help guide her back to her body; if this was a walk through the astral dimension, she ran the risk of floating away to another plane altogether, a drifting spirit forevermore without the lights of the aura and ora stones to guide her back to her body.

Not to mention, she really wasn't skilled enough in such magic to do it by accident.

But it did *feel* like astral projection in every other way.

She deliberated over the potential consequences but, ultimately, was too curious not to lean into this… whatever this was.

This is very much a dream.

Cautiously, she decided to explore.

Gliding down the hall, she lingered on old, eerie portraits of people she did not recognize hanging on the walls, barely visible in the low lantern lights. Their beady eyes looked so lifelike and seemed to watch her every movement, as if spies of the castle.

She continued on with haste.

Arianna took turn after turn, exploring the paths she'd tried to memorize every time the regulators had taken her out to see the King; she wished to be on the main floor and out of this suffocating, infinite labyrinth.

With a *pop*, she found herself above ground, starting to comprehend her talents in the dream world a bit better.

In the dead of night, the palace was disconcertingly quiet, as if all the people had disappeared from it altogether; Arianna couldn't contain her eagerness to examine it freely.

She followed vast halls from one side of the sleeping palace to the next, roaming wherever her thoughts took her.

She admired the rich architecture, everything washed in the moonlight through tall windows, and she became lost in gold-leafed patterned paints and priceless décor.

She peeped into rooms of every function, each with high, vaulted, and picturesque ceilings glowing under candlelight, and she relished the gentleness of the countless courtyards and gardens, no guards patrolling the paths to taint the scenery—with such a perspective, it was easy for her to perceive the Palace of Saindora as a sanctuary for magic and not for the Shadow Resistance.

The enchantment is still here.

She could taste it—in the night, when nobody was looking, magic shone through.

After what seemed like endless hours of wandering, Arianna rounded a corner deep in the palace; an imposing dark blue and gold door stunned her.

It was constructed of thick, stained glass cubes that appeared as if drops of dye had been trapped inside of each before they could settle. Two thick chains had been strung across it, hiding away the room's purpose.

Arianna was drawn to it, compelled to rip the chains to the floor—she reached out her hand, but since she didn't have a physical body right now, her fingertips felt nothing and she stumbled straight through to the other side.

The deep echo of silence engulfed her as a lengthy hallway unfurled, paved in gold-trimmed, alabaster tiles. It extended so far out that she couldn't even see where it might stop at the other end. Dust swam in rays of moonlight shining through thin strips of glass windows along the ceiling and walls, light pouring in sporadically.

It was easy to gather that no one had entered this part of the palace in a long time.

Arianna could practically feel the pulse of magic swirling about in the air, locked away behind that door for probably as long as Kyrone Devlindor had called himself King.

Numerous massive paintings of what could only be maps covered the walls; they appeared to carry on down the length of the hall, each one as large as the Devlindors' portrait in the throne room.

Examining the first painting to her right, Arianna immediately recognized that these were not just *any* maps—they were magical, sophisticated, masterful works of art.

Fleetingly, she thought that, in another world, Lessa might've enjoyed such an honorable job as to paint life onto parchment like this. *So detailed.*

She began to walk farther in, craning her neck back and forth, up and down, to look upon each painting; the maps depicted every province and every city of Olleb-Yelfra.

Gold, blue, green, and silver strokes were the only shades used to make the world she knew come to life through paint.

Arianna thought that she'd never understood the Olleb so fully before now, all that there was to appreciate—the land bestowed unto them, to protect and honor, was laid out for her eyes to feast on through the most incredible depictions, so simply beautiful yet so complicatedly intricate.

She stopped in front of an illustration of a grandiose mountain range. Soft, snow-capped peaks curved inward and were surrounded by what looked to be fields of white flowers.

The Blancoren Mountains.

She lost her breath, gaping up at the painting.

For so long, she had wished to escape this place. Yet, whoever its artist may have been—whoever had laid eyes on what she knew as the 'Jar'—had at one time, undoubtedly, admired the land she loathed… in quite the same way that she'd learned to admire every piece of the earth after fleeing.

The portrait was labeled in gold, coiled letters: 'Damas Country.'

She gathered that the late, great king of the Golden Age, King Damas, must have once well-regarded these mountains, revered them so much so that the surrounding province had been named for him.

King Devlindor had torn that beauty away and turned it into something dark, something uninhabitable. Now, where King Damas had once seen beauty, Arianna only saw the Pit with the skeletons at the bottom.

As she considered this mesmerizing image of the mountains, this foreign picture, she struggled with her feelings toward them. She desperately wanted to let go of her hatred of what clearly had been one of the Olleb's most precious gifts of nature, but painful memories flooded over whatever good King Damas might've found there long ago.

She pondered, though, if one day she might come to understand his vision…

What was even more thrilling about the depiction of 'Damas Country' was that the dwarf kingdom of Undor had not been forgotten in its portrayal—busy beneath the Blancoren Mountains lay the magical city Arianna had navigated with Jeom, Lessa, and Demetrius.

Glittering gems and stones, familiar structures and statues, were painted across the vast web of tunnels that sprawled far below the mountains.

Eventually, she peeled her eyes away from where her journey had begun and lingered on the maps that represented the other homes she'd known for a short while.

There's so much magic here, she thought.

Each stroke of paint was charmed with life.

She found the Nicora Forest, bright and vibrant—dark red leaves and silver trunks bridged the way from Damas Country to so many other sprawling cities and lands; some she had names for and others she'd never even known existed in another time.

South Luose grew out from the trees, fine lines of gold tracing out the hilly streets all the way up to the stony palace, its towers poking out from the treetops. Arianna thought of Keeper Kassime and his longtime rule there, and of Tobias whom she'd also come to know, love, and lose. Of her doting attendant, Lily, who had been struck down too young, and of her dear Liam Black who had barely glimpsed the magic before he was gone.

Master Tayshin and Gabriel were the only friends she'd made in South Luose that she couldn't weep over yet.

Please don't be dead, too.

So much sorrow filled her then.

At least I'm alone and trapped in a dream. I can finally mourn for them all.

Her wall of control came tumbling down, and every emotion poured out—it felt so bad to feel so much pain… but it was also a much-needed release before she could move forward. She wept for a while, hand upon the painting, forcing herself to say the names of those lost from that chapter in her life.

READY TO MOVE ON, Arianna walked over to view the next striking display; directly across from the depiction of her first temporary refuge was a map of South Luose's twin city.

Enormous, curly letters spelled out 'The City of Crissy' across the top. But Arianna knew it by another name…

"The deserted City of North Luose," she breathed, drinking it in.

A cityscape, bordered by the Nicora Forest and waves of a hypnotic dark desert she'd become far too familiar with, towered over her. The Black Sand Desert portion of the illustration was even flecked with the diamonds she was sure existed in the sand, which made it sparkle in the impossible way it did.

An archway had been painted in at the point where the sand met the trees, serving as an open gate to what looked to be a bustling city on the outskirts of the forest—from there, the metropolis grew and grew, stacking tall into the sky as it sprouted upward within its defined territory.

Arianna had seen the bones of this city scattered at her feet, and had since learned briefly of its sad history; it had been wiped off the earth by the enchanted fires of the Three-Headed Dragon of Crissy—a result of wars between man and elf long before King Devlindor's reign.

She had never spent much time thinking about it.

Seeing it now, though, memorialized at a moment in time when the city had once thrived, she couldn't help but stand in awe of all that had been lost.

After paying her respects, Arianna made her way farther down the hallway of maps—she started from the beginning of her life in the Four Corners and traveled along the path she'd since chosen.

Despite the losses, hardships, and mistakes that had surfaced in each location, there was no other direction she could imagine that her life might've gone in… she couldn't readily perceive a wrong turn taken.

Where would she have stopped, if she had given up? What city would have become her permanent home?

Inevitably, she came upon the City of Zambienth, pyramids shooting toward the sky in sharp, silver strokes. As she considered her short time there—dancing under the moon with Eli and her friends, practicing magic and combat alongside some of the strongest and bravest people she'd ever had the privilege to know—Arianna wasn't sure where else she would've wanted to be.

What might she have done differently to not lose the ones who'd been lost? Would it have even changed a thing?

Odessa's words sprang to the forefront of her mind; each path she had chosen was hers to own, unfolding the way to some unknown future.

If she could go back in time and redo an action or choice for the better, it could potentially change everything else for the worse.

What would my life and memories, loves and losses, look like then? She shook her head of the riddle.

Everyone she had ever met, both good and evil, in each corner of the Olleb, had helped her to become the person she was today. Each choice, wrong or right, had shaped her soul in some small or large way; the world's gifts of nature—shocking her into silence with breathtaking scenes of oceans, oases, forests, deserts, and skies filled with starry magic—had impressed upon her the importance of every moment in life.

Take nothing for granted!

There were things she was proud of and things to regret, but fate kept propelling her forward regardless, down a path she should never look back on. Her past and her present made her uniquely *her*, Arianna Belvedor, and—just as the mask of Aridyn had taught her long ago—she wouldn't wish to be anybody else.

Motivated by this look back over her journeys, Arianna continued past Zambienth with pride. A portrait dedicated to the Sea of Saindora made her take pause.

If she looked very closely, the sea monsters and mermaids painted in the waters, and the brilliant ships chasing after them, seemed to actually rock back and forth on the silky-stroked waves.

By gods, if this isn't the most enchanting piece of art I've ever seen.

She passed more cities and provinces still; many she recalled from her long travels with Solomon and others she remembered from his Golden Age map—she prayed Lessa still held on to that.

She reached the end of the hall, and the last portrait.

'The City of Saindora' was scrawled out in bright gold letters at the top—it was the most spectacular map of them all.

Everything about this city, even through brushes of paint, seemed to be enchanted. It appeared as if magic itself had been depicted to originate from this very point of the Olleb, flowing to each corner of the land beyond like a nourishing river.

Maybe this is where magic started? Arianna would question Odessa on that later. *Where does it come from, really?*

The palace she stood in now shone like a radiant beacon on the portrait, welcoming to all. The Sea of Saindora splashed up alongside it, and dragons of silver and gold dotted the skies above.

Arianna could hardly grasp this warm, detailed image, trying to match it together with her cold prison.

As if struck by a bolt of lightning, she suddenly understood what Odessa had been trying to convey to her ever since her arrival.

I'm not supposed to be here yet!

Seeing it for what it was now—the sure epicenter of magic—she knew that in Saindora was where this would all end, whatever the conclusion. But unless she had indeed failed her quest to bring justice to the Olleb, *her* ending wasn't upon them yet.

She needed to find a way out and return at the ready, in order to see that this dreamlike Saindora had a chance to be reborn.

She drew in a deep breath as she let that thought simmer; on her exhale, she tilted her head back.

The entirety of the ceiling was brushed in soft blues to depict a dark, navy sky. Painted stars glinting with magic watched over this painted world, just like she knew them to do in her reality.

Arianna whispered the names of the stars Eli had taught them long ago on a cold desert night. She even found the South Star illustrated there, guiding the rest, the most important one of them all—it hovered directly over Saindora with a crown of light, making it unmistakable.

Further scanning the elaborate ceiling, she took a moment to admire the detail of its borders—small but complex depictions had been tucked away between the backdrops of the maps and the sky.

There, Arianna uncovered a brilliant new story… one which she thought she'd never fully understand.

The sharp faces of what had to be interpretations of the goddesses and gods of her universe stared down at her with piercing, lifelike eyes. Slightly different to what she'd seen portrayed in Moriamo, these beings were imagined with the bodies of humans with grandiose wings, each feather and scale adorned with detail down to the tiniest stroke; they came alive in glittering garments, jewels, and crowns of greens, purples, blues, and reds.

Arianna knew, without a doubt, that these were the faces given to the earth, sky, sea, and sun—though nothing could emulate their true form.

To her knowledge, no human had ever laid eyes upon a god-like creature of the Olleb. At least, not in a history that she knew to be recorded.

As the existence of Moriamo had proved to her, the belief in these beings had somehow carried on over time, regardless of the King's wishes, and regardless if they were real.

King Devlindor had been careful to ignore the teachings and histories of entities much more powerful than him, the philosophies of others curated long ago. He had silently squandered what had ultimately (if one believed) given him such power in the first place, going so far as to even ban 'imagination'… the actual freedom to *believe.*

Seeking to bury a hope that might try to claw its way out into the world and form into something tangible, he taught his citizens to fear, to quiet their inner callings and voices. All with the purpose of keeping them from realizing their true powers within, powers granted to everyone through the magic that is birth.

Arianna was beginning to understand magic better now.

It can have so many forms… Tangible powers, a manipulation of the elements, a talent or passion to be honed. Or even just the emotional capacity to laugh, love, and experience the wonders of the world. But no matter the form it might show up as, evil or good, every single person in Olleb-Yelfra deserved the right to *choose* whether or not they wanted to believe in magic, too… to believe in anything.

He cannot control it all!

The King had tried to squash the concept of belief and silence the prophecy, the Golden Rule—thus silencing the named gods and goddesses who perhaps instated the rule in the first place.

Earth. Air. Water. Fire…

Arianna considered the wonderful gifts that had been bestowed on her, just another district warrior-slave, by Olleb-Yelfra. *By the elemental gods and goddesses?*

For all she was worth, and for all she had seen of so many others with worth much greater than hers—her masters, teachers, friends, and family—she could not let them down.

She had to be worthy of their gifts. She *had* to prove herself worthy… or worthy would turn to waste, and waste would come to the entire world.

I am a slave no longer! she thought. *I am a warrior, a witch, and a Guardian of Gold. I'm a humble servant to the life I was granted… and I believe.*

She looked back down the hall one last time.

This is the path that I choose.

Bittersweet though it was to have her faith renewed in a buried jewel of the overthrown palace, Arianna held her optimism high; this hallway of maps, filled with enchanted timelines of Olleb-Yelfra, *remained.* It was a pure, real, timeless memory of what the world had forgotten, and that was something to be celebrated. *I'll make them remember.*

A window with a large ledge caught her attention at the end of the hall; Arianna moved toward it.

Peeking out, she was careful not to wish herself forward—she couldn't shake the growing feeling that this was no dream at all, no matter how much she tried to convince herself otherwise.

Master Tayshin's teachings grounded her in caution. *If it isn't a dream and I wander too far from my body in an ethereal state, I may never find my way back.*

Arianna contemplated the sleeping city; it unfurled like a rope away from the palace, until eventually buildings splayed out in every direction before stopping dead at the sea. There, the port consumed the shore, bridges stretching out through the water and connecting ship after ship to the harbor.

She felt the pressure of the silent night sink into her mind, waiting and wondering what might come with the sun.

Arianna felt so small compared to this world, so very trivial. But with the soul of the star as her witness, even in this ghostly state, she knew that the smallest of elements could sometimes make the biggest impacts.

She closed her eyes, unable to help the urge to impress her hopes and dreams upon her star necklace once more—when she opened them, she found herself in a different part of the palace.

SHE KNEW WHERE SHE WAS—she'd been in the main foyer many times before. The glass window that mimicked the ocean rose tall above her, and she wondered what it must have looked like without the sprinkle of magic erased from it.

She could sense it in her soul that the Palace of Saindora was steeped in magic just bursting to be known, to let its wonders explode from whatever suppressions weighed them down—just as the King weighed hers down now.

She could feel it in her bones that even just the tick of time might be enough to release it one day. And maybe, if she could uncover the seams with the loosest stitch, the easiest accessible magical proof, she could use it to her advantage in this war.

Then these last two months will have meant something.

She just had to stay alive.

Eyeing the staircase beneath the window, Arianna couldn't fight the urge to climb upward. When she reached the top, she looked down and saw the impressive entryway from a new viewpoint.

A short and stocky woman stepped out from the shadows, standing in the spot she had just left; she was covered in armor.

"Who's there?" Arianna called from the balcony, taken aback. *Who's here with me... in my dream?*

But if it was a dream, or even astral projection, whoever shared her space probably didn't know Arianna was there.

She let out an exasperated sigh, squinting to see this vision clearer in the dark.

"Why, you're... a dwarf!" She gasped, leaning over the rail—the twinkling jewel fixed to the woman's forearm made her certain. *She must be from the City of Undor.* "How odd."

She hardly realized she'd spoken aloud, not quite sure when she was speaking or thinking in this form.

"I am not the odd thing roaming about the palace tonight," replied what was, undoubtedly, a dwarf.

Arianna's mouth fell open. The woman was staring right at her.

"You *can* hear me? I thought—"

"That you were dreaming?" she said, nodding. "Yes, I heard you mumbling about that during your little adventure earlier. But afraid not, dearie. Ghosts don't belong in dreams." She narrowed her gaze. "Although, I'm not *quite* sure what you are... Have you died lately?"

Arianna just shook her head, completely dazed by the exchange with this apparition.

"I... don't think so."

It's hard to tell these days.

She felt a thread of panic unraveling in her thoughts.

It didn't come as a shock to her that she was talking to a ghost, nor even the ghost of a dwarf, but now she couldn't pretend that she was having some kind of hope-instilling hallucination.

This is real. I'm in the astral plane of the present day.

She thought back on her journey through the Vanishing Tunnels—the ghost of General Indra of the City of Undor had handed her the prophecy, her introduction to the Golden Rule.

'*Take this script in your heart and not in your pocket, sorceress,*' he had warned her, standing in the tomb of his fallen city.

Arianna wondered now if he had known then the incredible path he'd laid down for her to slowly discover. Had he foreseen that one day she'd be conversing with the ghost of a dwarf in the Palace of Saindora?

Before she could question who this dwarf might be, or even what *she* was herself in this moment, the ghost melted back into the shadows.

"Wait!" she shouted after her, but she was gone.

Arianna thought to follow her, but something in her gut told her to keep moving forward.

She began to explore the second level of the palace, all the while wondering what other ghosts might be hiding in its corridors—and why she hadn't seen them before.

Sure enough, more ghostly eyes and bodies started to creep out from the shadows, peering out from doorways and peeking around corners to spy. They were mostly garbed like palace workers, and there was a mix of humans, dwarves, elves, and others Arianna didn't have a label for showing their faces to her now.

Arianna didn't stop to inquire who the eyes belonged to, nor why they were silently watching her every move. But the farther she walked down this particular hall, the more ghosts she saw...

And more than once, she thought she heard someone whisper, '*Turn back!*

When she arrived at the end of the hall, she found a large, circular doorway with striking embellishments on the borders— the outline of serpents.

Without hesitation, she placed her hand on the handle of the door and simply appeared on the other side; her breath hitched in her throat. She froze.

She was standing in the bedroom of King Devlindor.

A sleeping snake is no less dangerous, she thought.

But Arianna dared to take one step into the room.

The King twitched under his bed sheets, and a silent scream escaped her lips.

Her eyes snapped open and that silent scream became loud.

Her shriek echoed all around the walls of her familiar prison chamber, and she found Odessa staring down at her in the bed that she thought she'd wandered away from long ago.

"I was curious when you'd develop your powers as an animancer," sang Odessa. "Your story just gets more and more interesting." She closed her eyes as if to savor the vision she surely saw. "Animancer magic can never be suppressed. It's far greater than anything that resides in this world, except for maybe a necromancer's." She twisted her mouth up to think. "I suppose, time will tell which is stronger."

Arianna was shaken at waking to her own screaming voice, sweat beading on her forehead with the sleeping King still a clear vision in her mind's eye. *Wait... an animancer?*

She opened her mouth to probe, but the seer's wicked smile stopped her before a question could even form on her tongue; Odessa wouldn't be giving up any more details tonight.

Sir Vladamor had accused Arianna of being an animancer during their desert battle; however, the more time that passed, the less and less she dwelled on it. Now she sat under the King's very roof, Odessa also naming her—the worries became renewed.

What could it mean?

Her mind stirred with the possibilities, its significance made greater with Odessa's statement.

"Return to sleep, Arianna Belvedor," she whispered. "All will unravel with time... if it is meant to."

Whatever an animancer might be, Arianna at least found some small comfort to know that she had *not* been dreaming. She stored all that she'd witnessed tonight in her heart—the locked door to the hidden jewel that she dubbed the 'Hall of Maps' was real and waiting to be opened, and there were ghosts of the Golden Age still lingering here with answers on their lips.

It just wasn't her time to take action, not yet.
Her eyelids grew heavy.
I'm not supposed to be here.

19

EYES WIDE OPEN

ARIANNA WAS DESPERATE FOR AN ESCAPE, and the thought of moving away from Odessa's quarters in less than seven days scared her more than any of the other threats King Devlindor had rained down. She knew herself, knew how she felt about being locked away—having company was the one thing that kept her grounded.

Odessa had become somewhat of a confidant to her; the seer was so concerned with her well-being and her story—both past and future—that Arianna hadn't been able to help but befriend her. She wanted to know what *true* freedom looked like, and the only way to do that was through the eyes of another.

Eventually, Arianna had stopped fighting Odessa's curiosity and allowed her to pry through her life; unlike the King's methods, the seer's caused her no pain at all.

Arianna narrated her story for her, too; in a way, she actually found these exercises therapeutic, to explore her life so intimately with another and to see her journey from a new perspective.

In exchange, Odessa taught her how to better control her mind—to understand and to trust it on another level, so that it could strengthen and grow.

During their lengthy lessons, she had learned how not to waste energy trying to hide anything from the King, instead distracting him from seeing what was most important; she had twenty years of life for him to explore, so it had been a while before he'd caught on to how much she'd been influencing his direction.

She had led him astray through the Black Sand Desert, let him feel her heart flutter during her first kiss with Eli, and given him a taste of her fear at being stranded on an island—but where was the epic battle between her and Sir Vladamor, or her first encounter with Syrifina? Where was the discovery of the soul of the star, otherworldly magic that he'd surely find of interest?

The King had also crawled through memories of her time as highlife Aridyn… although, she'd never allowed him to fully enter the guardian sanctuary that was the attic. To know of Keeper Kassime's wisdoms or the scrolls detailing about avatars.

And she *especially* never let him witness the many moments her and Solza had connected to conjure elemental magic that she didn't even yet understand; she thought that if he ever saw firsthand what she was really capable of, he might end her life then and there, for how frightened he was of the things he could not control.

King Devlindor had sent others to do his bidding throughout the course of Arianna's entire journey—he couldn't possibly know the extent of her powers, of her friends' powers, and of all their strengths combined.

Unless I make it clear, she thought. *If I ever get the chance.*

But Odessa's tricks hadn't lasted for long; the King had an inkling now that his seer was confiding too much in her, so now the true countdown to her imprisonment had begun.

Seven days…

"It'll be all right," said Odessa.

Arianna sat on the bed beside her, not saying a word.

She knew Odessa *knew* she was crying—not only because she literally had a view into everything that ever happened but because Arianna was only ever silent when there were tears or when she was sleeping, and she hardly ever slept these days.

Every other second in their dungeon was filled with storytelling, mind-magic training, and exercise to pass the time.

"Will it be?" she asked, turning away from her.

"It could be," she said with an airy hum. "I can still see that much, at least."

Arianna threw her head back and moaned.

"*Could…*" she repeated. She looked down to her hands. "There's nothing I can do anymore, is there?"

A moment of silence passed between them.

"No, there isn't."

"I've suspected that for a long time now," said Arianna with a heavy sigh; she plopped back on her pillow. "My fate must lie in the hands of another. In this place, I'm truly trapped. There's nothing left for me to choose. All I can do is wait for something to happen. For someone to do something, *anything* at all that gives me a chance to escape."

"You're very wise for one so young," said Odessa, not denying a word she'd said.

"I've had a lot of great teachers," she whispered, laying a gentle hand on her arm. "I was also taught never to rely on anybody else for handouts." She huffed, crossing her arms. "It's strange… knowing in this moment that I have *no* control over my future, whatsoever, something I've always sought. All I can do is wait for what comes next."

She stared at a flickering candle on the wall, waiting for something to happen.

"The King told me he will separate us," said Arianna after a while. "In a week's time. I know when that happens—"

"There will be no hope left at all." Odessa's words were so final that Arianna felt a chill skip up her spine.

She reached for Odessa's hand. "I'm scared," she mumbled. "I'm really scared this time."

"As is wise," she replied, giving her a supportive squeeze.

Odessa rarely let Arianna into her thoughts, but when she did, it was never quite pleasant.

She swallowed the lump in her throat. *What answer was I even looking for?*

Arianna hadn't needed Odessa to tell her that her odds weren't great anymore; she knew that if they locked her away alone, she'd lose her right mind and that would be that.

Seven days would mark either the end or the beginning of this terrible chapter, and it was a brutal wake-up call to know that it could all soon culminate in the King's favor.

THE WEEK CAME AND WENT, every day the same as the last.

On the seventh night, Arianna lay wide awake next to Odessa, thinking about her future and praying that her magic might come before the King found a way to destroy it for good.

She spoke Solza's name out loud—for the first time in a long time—just to feel as if she were near; she desperately wished that her avatar might hear her call for help in this lonely night, as Mother Adunni had expressed was possible.

I have no more wishes left.

Besides Solza's name bouncing off the stone walls of the chamber, it was so quiet that Arianna was sure time had frozen everything, save her heartbeat and her breath. It seemed as if she

were the only one who existed in the universe, alone and surrounded by nothingness, the way death felt…

Or, at least, one type of death she had come to recognize.

As she finally drifted off to sleep, she couldn't help but wonder what might await her after her *true* departure from this world,
and if it would be better than the life she fought for now.

ARIANNA AWOKE OUTSIDE OF HER BODY. She was back at the
top of the stairs in the main foyer, facing the circular door to the
King's bedroom. This time, though, she was prepared for what
she'd find as she stepped through to the other side.

King Devlindor was at the center of the room, fast asleep.

When the King had poked and prodded around in her mind,
she had been compelled to look at him many times… all the while
trying to hide how she focused her thoughts only on what she
wanted him to see; there had never been a moment where she had
been this close to him and didn't feel his eyes boring back into
her own, challenging her with his merciless power.

But this time, she was the one in control.

Not wasting the opportunity, she floated toward his bedside
and peered down on him—he seemed so peaceful as he slept,
much less monstrous than when his eyes were open.

His hair was slick and dark, falling to his shoulders, though
she could see bits of gray peeking out here and there; from afar,
he seemed young, with boyish, rounded cheeks, forever fooling
those he looked down on. But up close, Arianna always noted the
lines of age forming, cracking beneath the surface of his skin as
they tried to break free of their prison to prove who he was.

It was as if he wore a veneer to cover up the real Kyrone. After
all, aging was for the weak, so the King had to always maintain

that he was stronger than everyone.

Arianna saw him for who he really was, though, tangled in blankets, his arms and legs hanging off the side of the bed. *Weak.*

His muscled chest rose up and down, slowly with each breath. And if she looked hard enough—his skin practically colorless under the moonlight pouring into his room—she thought she might set eyes on his actual beating heart, finally determine if it was as black as his soul.

She wondered if she could enter the King's mind now and take control, as he had done to her so many times. Spy on the surely terrible things that occurred in his dreams, or maybe even discover his truest fears.

She knew the spell by heart, so it *was* possible. *I could… if I tried. He's just like anyone else.*

Except, he wasn't.

She stood at the bedside of the most powerful man in the world, with an avatar to his name—Arianna, on the other hand, was only a wandering spirit.

She took a moment to consider Raja who lay curled up, protectively, on the carpet at the foot of the bed. She was as beautiful a creature as any.

Arianna believed her god-touched, a sure gift from the magical realm, unlike any other species known to their world—rivaled maybe only by Sano and Solza.

But just as with Arianna versus the King, the difference between their avatars was experience.

Raja was the eldest known avatar in the Olleb, which meant her powers were certainly stronger and more adept; the King had put an end to an *entire* species with the aid of her magic.

She boasted black, shimmering fur as sleek as the hair on the King's head, and muscles rippled all the way from her head to her twitching tail.

As Arianna observed them together, a practiced unit, she knew they had been destined for each other. *Maybe even carved from the exact same mold, or thought up to exist as only a pair.*

Still, she just couldn't fathom that *this* had been the outcome in mind when the King and his avatar had been brought into the world; she would like to think that Fate and Destiny had imagined a different, nobler path of redemption for a young king and his avatar at the time of their creation.

Why else would Olleb-Yelfra grant him access to such power?

Odessa's wisdom pushed into her thoughts once more…

Finding true destiny lies in one's decisions along the way.

Fate could easily be altered with one wrong choice, and there was no all-powerful being nor enchantment that could change that. *It just is.*

She thought of all the good that she and Lessa had done with Solza and Sano by their sides—as avatar masters, they could certainly produce beautiful, great things, if they tried.

It led her to ponder… if the monster before her had been a different sort of man and not let his dark side get the best of him, would he have done good, too?

His powers were great. The King was, undeniably, *great.* Yet, he led the life of a tyrant and continuously used his magic to scar the Olleb.

She shook her head. *You could have been great.*

Arianna became fixated on his breath; it came slow and heavy.

She imagined that each one must be painful as he tried to circulate oxygen through to his blackened heart.

"If only this weren't a dream," she whispered to him, "I would smother you with a pillow here and now. Save the world from another sunrise sullied by your presence."

Of course, she knew this wasn't a dream.

But whatever state of being she was in—whatever an *animancer* may be—she didn't appear to have the ability to do the King any physical harm.

'Don't be naïve! Keep your eyes open, or the monsters will

destroy you before you even have time to blink. Face the situation.' She could practically hear Solomon in her head, the voice of the man who had loved her and taught her to be strong in a world filled with monsters.

His voice had long ago become that of her conscience and it would probably never change. No matter the other noble masters she'd praised in her life—Talis Churry, Jon Tayshin, Keeper Kassime, Mother Adunni—Solomon would always be the one who had given her the foundation to become what the rest had helped her hone.

"This is no dream, child," came a voice from across the room. "You know that. You've come this far. I'd think you'd be able to tell the difference by now."

Arianna shrieked, jumping back from the bed.

She looked up to find the most regal-looking ghost she'd ever seen staring at her from the other side of the King's bed; he was a tall, plump man with bright eyes and soft features twinkling in his ethereal state. He stood with a confidence radiating off him in torrents, as if he'd been standing watch in that very spot for his entire existence in the afterlife, and knew *exactly* what his purpose was in life after death.

"I couldn't agree more, Father," said the voice of a young man—with a *pop*, another ghost appeared right behind the first, hands in his pockets.

He was a replica of the older gentleman, just much younger with a much smugger face. And he was handsome, to say the least, with deep brown skin, jaw chiseled to perfection, and a golden brown stare that made her blush.

"She must not have had proper training," he added with a smirk, running his hand through his hair—it shimmered with his essence. "She's got the confidence, though."

"The confidence for what?" said Arianna, tensing; she certainly hadn't been expecting company over the bedside of the King.

The young man laughed, as if it were the silliest of questions.

"Not too quick, though, are we?" he said, tilting his head to look at her. "It's taken you *forever* to get here! And you sure showed up on your knees." He tutted at her, wagging his finger. "Not very kingly of you, if you ask me."

"I… what do you—"

"Cat got your tongue?" He snickered, nodding to the snoozing avatar.

Arianna pursed her lips, standing up straighter—ghosts didn't scare her anymore, but it had yet to feel like a normalcy to converse with them, or for her intelligence to be insulted by them.

"And who might you be?" she demanded, finding her *confidence*—she laid it on a little thick, her pride sneaking up on her.

"Just your friendly palace ghosts," said the young man, flashing her a bright, mischievous smile.

The man cleared his throat.

"This here is my son, Prince Neas," he said in a weary voice. "I apologize. He's developed a bit of an… attitude over the last century or so." He reached out his hand to Arianna and then gave an embarrassed chuckle, placing it back at his side. "I'm—"

"King Damas," she stammered, gaping at him.

Another *pop* and both the prince and the king were by her side; she jerked around to face them, suddenly overcome with nerves of excitement.

"At your service," he said with a kind smile.

The royal ghosts both bowed low—on instinct, she returned the gesture.

These were, after all, the *rightful* rulers of Olleb-Yelfra.

"King Damas and Prince Neas…" She could feel the foolish grin on her face but couldn't stop it. "I just don't quite understand."

Prince Neas scratched his head, as if unsure of what to say.

Arianna noticed then that neither of them wore crowns in their ghostly states; her gaze drifted over to the priceless, jeweled crown locked in a glass case next to King Devlindor's bedside—his grand prize for stealing the throne.

King Damas stared down at him with a grave expression. "Look at the mess you've made, son," he whispered.

Arianna thought a tear escaped his eye as he tried to sweep the sleeping king's hair from his face. But his hand was only a glimmer of flesh from the past.

King Devlindor tossed to the other side of the bed, pulling his covers in closer—she knew he must feel his uncle's presence, even if they were separated by different planes of existence.

"He's no son of yours, Father," said the prince, angrily, peering down at his cousin.

Arianna considered Prince Neas—no shirt, threadbare pants, sweat glistening on his skin, and a sword swaying at his hip.

It looked as if he'd just come home from a duel; she recalled the King's embellished version of what had happened back then from *Olleb-Yelfra the Fallen*; sadly, that duel had ended a long time ago, and he had never walked away from it.

Arianna could see the pure hatred burning in his eyes from sure centuries of watching his unrighteous cousin take all that might have one day been his… destroying the land that he had once loved in the process.

She remembered how the prince's story had come to an end.

The then young Lord Kyrone had struck him dead during a friendly sparring match out of jealousy and blamed it on Master Lethander. Poor King Damas had thus spiraled into a depression over the loss of his beloved son—Kyrone had taken advantage of a grieving father so that he could take power.

Prince Neas looked up, catching her gaze.

"Why have we never crossed paths before?" she asked, fervently. "I've seen others, but they wouldn't speak to me. And I've been here two months already, never seeing any ghosts before just recently."

"Ghosts cannot move freely in this place," explained King

Damas. "We keep ourselves hidden… out of the eye of the necromancer. But he's been gone a while now from the palace, so when you entered the astral plane, many of us were too curious to stay concealed."

Arianna was curious too, about a lot of things.

"I *know* this is not a dream," she said, her voice strong. "But how can I possibly be in astral form without my dagger or magic? It doesn't make any sense."

"Believe you me," said Prince Neas, haughtily, "you've no shortage of magic. Just a novice. Magic comes in many forms, or don't you already know that by now?" Another haughty smirk. "I'd say you've got a lot of work to do… and in very little time."

King Damas nodded his agreement, then his expression grew serious—he looked back to the King.

"I'm truly sorry for your pain and for your suffering," he said, speaking to Arianna. "The man Kyrone has grown to become was not the man I intended to raise…"

"It's not your fault," she said, reaching out to him.

"Then whose fault is it?" he asked, locking eyes with her. "Even kings have to take responsibility for their mistakes. A lesson he will never learn until death, and one that I learned too late. I should have seen his pain, and I should have shielded the world from it, tried to help him more instead of smothering him with banquets and material things."

He flashed a saddened stare toward the crown.

"Father, don't do that," said Prince Neas, his fists balled at his sides. "You were *wonderful* to him, to everyone! Nothing is your fault."

Arianna looked him over, her mind spinning with questions about the life he'd once lived.

"You must have truly been a great king," she said, her thoughts turned inward, "to still wear the burden of your people's suffering even after death." She glared at the crumpled man atop the bed. "But Kyrone Devlindor is a monster, and he does not deserve for you to take responsibility for *anything* he's done."

"Your compassion shows wonders, Arianna," said King Damas. "Just remember, monsters are not born, they're created. We all have darkness within us. It's the paths we choose that determine who we are."

"How do you know my name?" she said, skeptical.

"Your name has traveled far in this world, girl," said Prince Neas, with a dismissive flick of the hand; he puffed out his chest, his voice lofty. "Arianna Belvedor, the *daring* slave turned sorceress, on a quest to guide magic back into the world." His tone grew abruptly serious. "*You*, my dear, are the best hope any of us has right now."

"We all pay close attention to what unfolds in the present," added King Damas, "even though we remain in the past. And if there's one thing that every ghost in this palace can agree on, it's that we very much wish only the best for our beloved Olleb, no matter the era."

He didn't point at her, but he might as well have...

Arianna withdrew into herself a little—once again, she was being lifted into a shrine of hope that she had trouble trusting in at the moment. And this time, by the noble king of the Golden Age!

She didn't want to think about who had heard of her story, didn't want to focus for even a second on the burden of other people's hopes and wishes; she had a more immediate problem to deal with.

Not the dead, not the living, not the souls in limbo cheering her forward—it was too much hope to even bear at this point, when she knew with certainty that there was only a sliver left to cling to.

She tried to shift the conversation back to *her* burning question.

"How could I astral project without... help? How am I here right now?" she asked, opening her arms to the room. "I still don't understand the type of magic this could be."

"By gods, she doesn't know, Father," said Prince Neas with a mock gasp. "She really doesn't know!"

King Damas tried not to, but he chuckled. "Everyone must learn in their own time."

"Know what?" she grumbled, growing impatient.

"That you're an *animancer.*" Prince Neas rubbed his hands together—that smirk, *once* again.

"So I've been told," she said with a beleaguered sigh. "But what does that *mean*? Please, a hint. Anything."

She knew she'd never get another word out of Odessa.

Prince Neas was about to open his mouth with what Arianna was sure would be the answers she so desperately desired, but King Damas lifted his hand.

"All in good time," he said. He looked to Arianna. "It's important to discover these things on your own. That's the only way to truly learn to control one's greatest powers. And, Arianna, your powers are *great* indeed." He gave a reassuring nod. "Stay on track. You're not meant to be here for long. In fact, from the rumors I've heard, you're not meant to be here at all right now… and I think you know that."

Arianna glanced back to King Devlindor, wishing her body would solidify so that she might end him while he lay sleeping, rid the world of this monster and let it be done.

"Kill him now, and then what?" asked King Damas, guessing her line of thought.

"I don't know," she said through gritted teeth. "I just know we'd all be better off without him."

"*Hmm,*" he said with the cock of his head. "But what is your goal, really? All these quests you've been through since escaping the Four Corners, all that you've learned. What do you want to achieve at the end? I'm very curious to know what's in your head."

Isn't everyone…

"I want to kill the King," she said, resolutely—it seemed a silly question.

"But *why?*" he asked, holding her gaze.

"To… to free the people," she responded, a little more uncertainly. "To expose the truth, so that everyone may understand the injustice the King has done to them."

"I see," said King Damas, nodding. "A very noble stance." He tapped his finger to his lips, such a gentle expression. "Though, I *must* ask… how will the people know you've freed them from a lie and oppression, if you do not first show them that truth?"

Prince Neas couldn't have looked more smug if he'd tried, crossing his arms at his chest as she stammered.

"I—"

Her thoughts drifted over how much the citizens of Saindora had flaunted their hatred for her thus far—she couldn't readily think of a response.

"Death is a terribly frightening thing," said King Damas after a moment. "It's the unknown, really, that people fear the most. So much so that we continue to cling to life without hesitation." A shadow appeared to dim his ghostly sheen. "Even the death of a ruthless king would feed that fear… if not done properly or at the right moment."

He paused, glancing again to the crown.

"Who do you think might take power once the King is removed from his throne? Someone fair and kind, or someone worse?" His lips twisted downward. "Kyrone hasn't exactly bred kindness in this world, so you must think strategically, carefully, about your next move."

Arianna couldn't find the right words, her ethereal heart racing as she let his advice sink in—she'd never really thought past more than a grand battle that ended with the King's life leaving his eyes.

But then what?

Suddenly, she understood why the elder guardians hadn't always included her and her friends in their tactical discussions. Why they had pushed to hold off just running into battle, when she and her friends always felt like the time was *now*.

The Guardians of Gold had deemed Arianna a worthy leader in their fight and in magical potential. She had been made into a symbol that the people could rally behind—but they had wisely and often tempered her urges of rash decision-making.

"I never thought that far ahead, I suppose. I never thought of the future," she said, feeling a stab of stupidity. "I didn't ignore it. I just… never saw past the King's death."

With the guardians disbanded, maybe even dead for all she knew, who would think about those things now? Who would take the brute out of the equation to make room for the logic, the whole picture—a future beyond King Devlindor *and* beyond what Arianna could see with her young mind?

"It's quite simple," said King Damas. "Light is light and dark is dark, but never shall they live apart."

She blinked up at him, knowingly. "The Golden Rule."

He nodded, a soft smile playing on his lips.

"The only rule that has any true merit is the golden one, a rule of balance," he said. "The Golden Rule stems from the beating heart of the world, and for all its wonders and all its evils, that's the heart of us all. Thus, taking a life, even one as despicable as Kyrone's, may not accomplish anything positive if you don't first guide the light back in—"

Prince Neas held up a finger. "*Or*, at least have a plan in place to do so once he's dethroned," he said.

Arianna looked back to King Devlindor and then to her fists, trying to understand what she could in this moment, where leadership felt heavier and lonelier than ever.

"I will show them the magic," she whispered, nodding to herself. "I will share everything I know."

She had already used this same tactic to shake the Warrior's

District awake in her thwarted plan to gather an army—by releasing them from the King's mind magic.

But she'd never considered what the aftermath might've been… had her peers realized the error of the King's ways? Were they more frightened than impassioned to take back their rights and uncover the truth?

Even without those answers, Arianna was confident that this was the only way forward.

"I took a vow as a Guardian of Gold to protect the knowledge of the Golden Age," she said, resolutely, to the royals. "If we finally put a stop to the King, we won't have to hide our knowledge away any longer. The truth is there for all to witness, if they so desire to see. I *can* show it to them."

"Very well," said King Damas, approval ringing in his voice. "It does sound as if you've at least thought some of this through. But be careful not to lose your way. You wouldn't want the world to fear you, too."

He gestured to King Devlindor.

"I will be quite careful, sir," she said, humbly. "Thank you for the reminder."

"There you go, Lady Belvedor!" said Prince Neas, pounding a fist into the air. "I knew you'd live up to your reputation." He turned to his father, giddy. "Now can I show her? She's obviously in need of *some* kind of assistance. I've never seen a girl so lost."

"Yes," said King Damas, drawing in a deep breath. "Now is the time."

"*Finally,*" he hummed, an excited gleam in his expression.

King Damas glided nearer to Arianna, as close as he could get without touching.

"Go well, child," he said, gazing deep into her eyes. "No matter what happens next, just know that no one expects miracles from you. Your best will be good enough… and though we all hope for the best, it's truly *your* hopes that count the most in the end. For your own sake, don't let them dim." He offered her one last reassuring, kingly smile. "Whatever may come next, I know you can handle it."

"Thank you, Your Majesty," she said, bowing low. "Right now, my biggest hope is that I can aid in getting your crown away from the Devlindors and into nobler hands." She glanced to the sleeping snake one last time. "Until we meet again."

King Damas returned her bow. "Then my hopes in you are yet renewed."

Prince Neas held out his hand.

"If you please, madam," he sang with a slight bow of his own—for some reason she liked him, loathed him, and trusted him all at once.

Arianna timidly placed her palm in his, thinking that they'd merely melt into one another. *Pop!*

They reappeared in an entirely different corridor of the palace—one she had never seen before.

"Where are we?" she asked, trying to orient herself.

"Everything behind this door has been greatly protected since the Golden Age turned dark," said Prince Neas in a grave tone. "What lies beyond is what you need to show the world, should you ever have the chance."

Arianna found a magnificent door towering in front of her, a great golden snake forming the handle; it was coated in the blackest of black, the strokes of paint swirling in slow patterns, like a vortex to another world might form should they move any faster.

She could hardly think, hypnotized by the gate to... *What's behind the door?*

"Whatever happens now, Arianna, know that I believe in you," he stated, snapping her out of her daze. "In another life, I think I would've even liked to know you."

Arianna chuckled, thinking the same.

"Maybe one day we still can," she said, turning to catch the prince's inquisitive stare. "You never know what's coming next."

"Anything is possible," he whispered with a nod, gradually

vanishing before her eyes. "Good luck, and may the gods guide you safely through the rest of your journey."

When Prince Neas had gone and she was again alone, Arianna turned back to contemplate the door; even in her unearthly state, she could feel the heat of strong magic surging off it.

She was compelled to reach for the handle—the heat grew warmer, and she pulled back.

Unless she wanted to get burned, she could not get any closer.

Oh, what's there to lose? I'm not really going to get burned!

She squeezed her eyes shut and grabbed hold of the snakes.

The feeling that came next was quite like when Jeom had been branded with the Creator's Crest, she imagined. *Pop!*

Her eyes flew open, and she found herself again weighted down by her physical body, back in her prison; the image of the black door still swirled ominously in her mind.

"ARIANNA, GET UP!" SHOUTED ODESSA, startling her back to her senses.

She was standing near the bed, staring toward the door; her eyes grew wide, silver magic sparking there.

"Odessa," she stuttered, sitting up, "what are you doing awake at this hour—"

The echo of footsteps sounded in her ears.

Who else would be up so late in this part of the palace?

Thoughts of King Devlindor, the ghostly royals, and an impenetrable door consumed her.

"Get ready. They're coming," she replied, an unfamiliar excitement in her voice. "You must act now, or…" She grabbed her arm with more strength than Arianna had thought she had in her. "You must get ready."

Arianna shook out of her grip, crawling out of the bed—she was suddenly more nervous than she'd been when Solomon had left her alone with the King in his throne room.

"Who's coming?" she said, watching the door with caution. "Get ready for what?"

Odessa didn't respond; however, Arianna knew it in her gut that if she messed this up, whatever *this* turned out to be, she wouldn't be getting any more chances.

"Who's coming, Odessa?" she urged again, readying herself the best she could.

"Someone you've condemned for their past choices," she finally replied. "But people can redeem themselves when you least expect it."

She faced her then, her expression as eerie as ever.

"I wasn't sure which choice would be made, but now it's safe to say that you have a plethora of choices of your own again." She gave a satisfied smile. "This is your sliver of hope, Arianna. You better grasp it tight. It's now or never."

Arianna let out a groan of frustration, tugging at her hair as her heart pounded in her eardrums. "For once, can't you please be straight with me!"

Odessa laughed and, unexpectedly, gave her a strong hug—Arianna hugged her back without hesitation.

"Good luck to you," she said, planting a kiss on her cheek. "It was such a blessing to know what a friend truly is before I go."

Arianna was at a loss for words as Odessa released her, shooing her forward. "Odessa, but what—"

There were several thuds at the door and something that sounded like a muffled scream. She heard the jingle of big keys— the keys to her cage. The lock clicked open.

20

DISLOYALTY

ARIANNA STAGGERED BACKWARD as the King's very own sister loomed in the doorway. Her face looked as fierce as ever, a determination there. She was illuminated by the light of a torch she held in her hand—her fingers were stained with blood.

Princess Elisa paused only a moment to survey the room, holding the torch higher. Her gaze steadied on Arianna.

Arianna peered past her to see if anyone else may have followed. This couldn't be the savior she'd been waiting for…

But when her eyes found the regulators in a pile at Princess Elisa's feet, she had no choice but to believe; the lingering smoke left by a trail of magical attacks rose off their armor.

"You?" stuttered Arianna. She instinctively tried to take another step back, but the Princess lunged forward, clasping her free hand around her wrist.

"We don't have time for a discussion!" she said, forcing her to stay put; with the snap of her fingers, the shackles fell away from Arianna's feet. "We must hurry."

Arianna pushed away all her doubts and worries to ready for battle, knowing full well that she must try to escape, no matter the cost... no matter *who* aided her. She nodded her understanding, so the Princess released her grip. Then she dashed to the bed to collect the shard of glass she'd hidden long ago for just such an occasion.

"It's too late," said Odessa, shaking her head; she stood toward the back of the room. "They're already here."

As soon as the last word left her lips, more guards rounded the corner.

Arianna placed herself protectively in front of Odessa.

"It's going to be all right," she said, angling the shard of glass just right.

"I know it is," whispered Odessa—Arianna wasn't as sure, but she clung to her friend's faithful vision nevertheless.

"Your Highness?" said one of the regulators, his voice pitching too high; he was clearly shocked to find her there. "I must ask you to please step away from the prisoner. We have strict orders from the King that this slave cannot leave the premises... unless by his command."

"You have orders?" she replied, coolly. "Try this for an order... *Solza ven immito!*"

The spell slipped off her tongue like sure silk, and the lasso forever draped over her shoulders grew ablaze with a pinkish flame—Arianna hadn't quite appreciated the true power behind this magic until now.

The flame and lasso moved like water, the way Princess Elisa wielded it with such skill. It seemed as if the King's beloved snake symbol had snapped into roaring life as she whipped at the regulator who had addressed her, striking him in the chest; blood spilled from the place he'd been hit, and he fell to the ground.

The other palace regulators flew into a panic, leaping out of harm's way and drawing their weapons.

"Call for the King's Guard!" one woman shouted. "We cannot let the girl escape."

Princess Elisa grabbed Arianna by her wrist again, this time dragging her behind her as she made a run for it.

"Wait!" Arianna dug her heels into the ground, stopping in the doorway; she looked back to Odessa, calling her to run toward them—but she wouldn't budge, merely swaying back and forth like a trapped ghost. "Please, Odessa. I promised I'd free you! This is our chance."

Bursts of deadly magic suddenly raced toward them from all directions, blasting the walls and ceiling; Arianna and the Princess had no choice but to dive through the doorway, scurrying around the corner to avoid getting blown to pieces.

They'd left the chamber and Odessa behind.

Arianna tried to turn back for her friend, but the Princess wouldn't let her.

"There isn't time," she urged, dragging Arianna farther down the hall along paths she'd finally come to memorize; powerful blasts shook the walls and shattered the palace fixtures all around them, debris sprinkling down on their heads at every turn. "If you want to live, we must go and not let them catch us. It *has* to be now. We cannot go back. The seer has made her choice."

Arianna felt her heart constrict, knowing that Princess Elisa was right.

She's finally made a choice.

Even with Princess Elisa's magical prowess, they were sorely outnumbered by the Shadow Resistance suddenly swarming the castle. And Arianna still didn't have access to her own magic to help.

We cannot go back... Odessa, I'm so sorry.

Suddenly, the seer's voice filled every space in her mind.

"*Death is but another chance to live,*" said Odessa, her words drowning out all else. "*It's time for an adventure all my own now, for once to discover what is unknown without knowing. It's tantalizing to even consider, but this is a type of freedom, too. You'll do well to remember that."*

She laughed a sound like wind chimes singing in her ears.

"Choose wisely, Arianna Belvedor. Every choice matters, for we cannot change the pasts we create. We can only carve the future. Right now, I see that yours may yet be the brightest future of them all... if you stay true to your heart. Goodbye, and good luck to you, my friend."

Her voice faded away into nothing, and Arianna knew that Odessa's life would soon follow. However, her soul would, hopefully, prove as boundless as her mind.

"Let's go!" shouted the Princess, running forward.

She sent a blast of magic soaring back down the hallway as the King's shadows started gaining on them; the whole palace was awake now.

Arianna threw her hands over her head and followed, keeping pace behind her.

"Where are you taking me?" she called as they ran along the dark pathways—the light of the Princess's torch bounced between the stones, creating monstrous shadows over every surface; it looked as if the shadows were literally chasing them at their heels.

If we stop, we'll surely be swallowed whole by the dark.

Arianna ran faster, but a regulator leaped onto her path as soon as she rounded the next corner; he cut her off from the Princess.

Arianna yelped, thrusting her hand forward—she was still holding the shard of glass.

To her surprise, she also felt the muscles of her magical mind begin to stir. She felt it flowing anew through her veins, gradually filling her as if a sudden rainfall were healing an empty riverbed with much-needed water.

It was weak still but growing fast; it seemed that the farther she got from the confines of her suppressive prison, the quicker she felt like herself again. Her powers were starting to break free all at once.

The regulator stopped dead in his tracks as the shard entered his stomach. He scratched at her hand to try to pull it back, but it was too late—a spell entered her mind, and Arianna felt the magic come without resistance.

"*Cementas cuerpal,*" she breathed.

A striking silver flooded her eyes, reflected in the glass.

The regulator stilled like stone, unable to move a muscle; she released her grip on the makeshift weapon and left him there to die.

Her palm was bleeding from where she had gripped the glass too tightly, so she thought the spell to heal…

Helthra saludis emencia.

Her skin stitched together like new.

Arianna jogged to catch up to the Princess; she was waiting for her at the bottom of one of the tall dungeon stairwells that led to the main floor.

"Let's pick up the *pace,*" she said, waving her hand.

Arianna had never seen her look so disheveled before, anxious.

Understandable, she thought with one quick glance back behind her—more shadows were coming.

They climbed the stairs two at a time until they were on the first level. The halls here expanded out in front of them like a maze of marble, beautiful stone pillars, and chandeliers with candlelight spilling down; Arianna was still in disbelief as she trailed the Princess up another flight of stairs, her silvery hair sharp and brilliant against the black of her cloak.

They tiptoed through the halls for a while, careful not to make a sound with the regulators crawling about. Then, Princess Elisa guided her into an open room and shut the door.

Arianna finally opened her mouth to speak. "What do—"

"Here," said the Princess, hurriedly. She pulled something out from a large box hidden away in a cupboard. "I thought you might want these back."

Arianna's eyes lit up as she tossed her Solomon's twin swords and her old sheath.

"How did you get these away from him?" she gasped in delight, snatching them up—immediately, she felt whole again.

"I have my ways," said the Princess, still digging through the closet. "Oh, and this belongs to you, too, I believe."

Arianna felt even more relief wash over her. "Aurora!"

Princess Elisa handed her the dagger and its sheath.

"Take care of these items," she said, averting her eyes. "They're precious, really. More than you know."

Arianna strapped her swords across her back, feeling all her confidence slip into place with them.

"Why are you helping me?" she demanded, glaring at her. "I don't understand why… why *you?*"

"Sometimes it's not necessary to understand why," she replied, still shuffling in the cupboard. "Sometimes, you should just graciously accept the paths that open up to you."

She pulled out one last thing and then turned to face her.

"Take this, too. It's a gift from Jillian," she mumbled. "She thought it might be just your color."

Princess Elisa tossed Arianna a brilliant cloak fit for a highlife, pools of red silk spilling to the floor.

She unfurled it for a proper look and found that it did not have a twenty-two stamped on the breast. And the Warrior's Crest did not rest at the back. Instead, a sleek, gilt dragon was embroidered where normally the King's mark should be, and it was lined with sun-gold silk.

As she clutched the cloth in her hands, something suddenly clicked.

"It was you who left the magical healing capsules for me, wasn't it?" she said, not really grasping this moment. She looked up. "If the King finds out you've helped me, he'll kill you." She chewed on her lip, wanting answers. "Why are you doing this? Why have you betrayed him for me?"

Princess Elisa softened, staring so intently at her that it made her blush.

"I have had the opportunity to make many choices in my lifetime," she finally said, "and each one has been worse than the last. I've done unimaginable things in the name of my brother, my king, in fear of his wrath and in hopes of a more secure future… for myself." The Princess then took the cloak from Arianna and draped it across her shoulders. "I have lived long enough. If my life should end tonight, I'll know that my greatest kindness to the world was giving back yours."

She shrugged, seeming so defeated.

"At least this choice may do some good in the face of all the damage I've helped create."

"I suppose I owe you a thanks, then…" stuttered Arianna, hardly able to process such a surreal conversation.

Never in her entire life could she have imagined she'd be thankful to a Devlindor for anything, let alone her freedom.

"Listen to me," said the Princess, gripping her by the shoulders, "within the walls of this palace, magic is remembered, practiced, and revered. You've learned this now… but what you probably don't understand is that not all those who wield magic on behalf of the King have *willingly* bent to him."

She took a deep breath, letting her go.

"As your journey comes full circle, remember that, won't you? Not everyone can be as brave as you, to find the courage to try and fight back. Some of us just survive the best we can."

"But you're a powerful sorceress, a royal by blood and birth," said Arianna in a low voice. "What could be more powerful than that?"

Princess Elisa let out a small laugh that had no happiness in its echo. "Oh, you mean besides a ruthless brother and monarch?"

Her lasso lit up again in flames; Arianna jumped back, reaching for the hilt of her sword.

"Fear," she whispered, her eyes glowing dangerous with magic. "It rules this land, and it rules inside these walls just the same." She let the flame extinguish, and Arianna let go of the breath she hadn't realized she was holding. "I may be the King's sister, but blood and birthright mean nothing anymore in this world. Kyrone has taken all that away, and I have felt the sting of his laws just like everyone else."

"But... you're basically the King's right-hand. How could you fear—"

"We both know who the King's right-hand is, and it isn't me," she retorted.

Arianna's mind wavered to Sir Vladamor.

"When I was but a child, family was the backbone of everything," said the Princess, staring back into her past. "When that was taken away, the darkness really poured in." She sighed, looking to her feet. "That, I believe, was the cruelest law of the King, forcing children apart from the ones who might raise them for the better."

She locked eyes with Arianna.

"If you do live..." she said, "and if you do return here one last time, please just remember, there are slaves here too. However convincing they may seem as loyal followers to the King."

Arianna gave a curt nod.

"I'll try," she said, securing her dagger into place. "Though, I make no promises to *you*. Everyone has a choice."

In her heart, she had trouble empathizing with Princess Elisa's clear plea to pardon the pretenders.

The Princess returned a tight smile. "Truer words have never been spoken," she whispered. "Come, it's time for you to go."

She led Arianna into the adjoining room, and a gust of fresh air immediately hit them. A low-hanging balcony stretched out toward the night sky, and white draperies fluttered in the wind.

She stepped through the curtain and saw that the balcony looked over the front courtyard of the palace—she couldn't wait to leave it all behind.

I'm so close to freedom.

A loud bang echoed from down the hall, and they both spun around, looking toward the door.

"You must go, *now!*" said the Princess, squeezing her hand for only a moment; Arianna pulled away. "Run, and don't look back."

She went to the edge of the balcony, glancing down—it was a long drop to the ground.

With a deep breath, she placed both hands on the banister and threw herself over, praying her magic would not falter.

Levantis bora!

She landed gracefully in the grass with a muffled thud, controlled and steady; but unable to fight the urge, she did look back.

Princess Elisa was standing on the balcony, watching her go—just as she had watched her arrive on her very first day.

The same look was plastered across her face, one mixed with terror, resentment, and curiosity, as if she were tossing with the decision she'd already made. And, if Arianna didn't know any better, her green eyes even sparkled with what might have been tears.

"Survive," she saw her mouth before she disappeared inside.

Without wasting another second, Arianna took off toward the palace gates as fast as she could. *I must survive!* She raced through the streets of Saindora, following the paths she'd memorized from the King's cruel excursions, deep into the city.

All too soon, she heard what could only be the sound of a stampede of horses, not far behind and catching up fast. There was nowhere to run except forward; the seaport came into view.

This time, the Sea of Saindora proved not a beacon of hope but a wall she desperately wished to climb over, to get to the other side and away from this gods-forsaken city. But Arianna knew she couldn't win against the ocean with only her swords.

She drew her weapons, feeling the delicious weight of magic and metal again at her fingertips. With no other options left to her, she turned from the water to face the city, and the army of shadows that swarmed it.

FINDING FIRE

"THERE'S NOWHERE TO RUN ANYMORE," said Solomon, his voice bellowing out across the distance separating her from the Shadow Resistance. "You're cornered!"

Arianna stood there, swords in hand, expressionless as her hair whipped around her face in the violent winds. Though Solomon had a hundred men and women on horses at his back, all she saw was him.

He sat atop his steed, a sleek black cloak flapping out behind him—Arianna faintly thought a storm was surely coming, bowling over the waters. *How appropriate.*

She gripped her swords tighter, the wind blowing harder, as if it had been generated from the fires of her heart; she racked her brain for the best strategy.

"Lay down your weapons, and we might let you live!" he called again, his horse pawing at the sand.

She snorted, knowing it was an empty offer.

"You can pry them from my hands when I'm dead," she said—that was the *only* way she'd ever surrender to him again.

"So be it," he said in a low growl, his expression darkening.

His followers were itching to attack, but before he gave the order, a loud howling wind caught everyone's attention. It sounded unnatural.

The gathering shifted their gaze to the sky, searching for something; as the sound grew closer, the wind picked up even more.

Arianna felt a nervous excitement tingle her insides as some empty part of her suddenly filled with a wonderful and warm spark—a part of her that was reserved for only one thing… *Solza!*

Her heart yearned for her avatar so much that she thought it might explode. *Am I only imagining this feeling?*

She thought that maybe she'd snapped, conjured up the memory of their bond in this drastic moment of need. But her gut told her otherwise.

She spun around to face the sea, her back to Solomon and his army—and there Solza was, as real as could be, in her air form of a great white and black owl.

Arianna watched in shock, awe, and elation as she soared over the waters, the dark clouds chasing after her. She flew faster than possible, avatar magic surely aiding her on the wind.

Before Arianna even had a chance to process anything, Solza had landed next to her on the beachfront, instantly transforming into the striking snow leopard that she knew best.

She fell to her knees, dropping her swords in the sand.

"By gods, you found me!" she cried. She wrapped her arms around her neck and hugged her close. "You couldn't have had better timing, my friend. I'm *so* glad you're safe."

Arianna could sense the happiness her avatar shared in the reunion as she nuzzled against her chest.

She squeezed Solza tighter, feeling her own powers amplify each second they were together again, like a cover had been peeled back to reveal all the magic that had been hidden away inside of her. Arianna was teeming with power.

Her courage renewed, she glanced back up the beach to see Solomon ordering his army to march—the Shadow Resistance slithered down the sandy bank and closed in.

"This is going to get dangerous," she whispered to her avatar. "I don't know if we'll make it, just the two of us."

Solza shook out of her hold and roared her response, glaring toward the King's soldiers; Arianna felt her resolute answer, electric and sure in her bones.

She recalled the scroll detailing the unbreakable bond between avatar and avatar master and finally understood the power in it—as certain as she was connected to her soul, Arianna knew that Solza would *never* leave her side again, not even in death.

They turned to face the enemy as one, and Arianna picked up her swords. Then, the battle was upon them.

Solza quite literally pounced on the nearest attacker, knocking her clean off her horse. She sank her teeth into the soldier's face, claws into her belly, before she even had a chance to utter a single magical word. Then, she moved on to the next opponent, her nature-linked powers giving her the advantage on this sandy battlefield.

Arianna cut her way through the onslaught, keeping Solza always in her line of sight. She welcomed the challenge like fresh air as a wave of shadows engulfed her.

The pulse of magical attacks rolled off her back or caught the blades of her swords, making them sizzle and spark like flashes in the night; she pulled all her powers to the surface, and it seemed as if nothing could touch her.

After having her magic suppressed for so long, she thought she had never felt so strong before. And Solza's unique energizing magic gave her the boost of a lifetime.

She froze soldiers on the spot, cutting through them before

they could even try to weaken her magic, and she dodged offensive spells with ease.

She sliced straight through the middle of the shadow army, battling up the sandbank with one goal in mind. *Solomon Bell.*

Arianna had all but forgotten the sheer impossible number of Shadow Resistance that she was up against, blinded by her burning desire to destroy her master—he waited and watched from atop his horse, until she finally broke through his line of defense.

"You cannot win this fight," he said, jumping down to face her.

"Watch me!" she shouted back, leaving a path of bodies in her wake.

Solomon crouched low, double swords in hand and teeth bared. He beckoned her forward, and Arianna offered a slight bow.

They ran forward, master versus apprentice.

She slammed into him, slashing her swords with a fury that she'd been dying to release since the last time they were ripped from her hands; he blocked every bite of her blade, parried every swing.

But Arianna kept going, her energy never waning.

I just need to tire him out. He didn't have an avatar to keep his attacks and defenses ever-enduring, but she did.

The battle felt good, right somehow, sword-on-sword with no magic yet played; she couldn't stop the flashbacks that screamed through her mind of days so far gone that they seemed almost like fake memories, dreams even—such as Solomon showing her the proper warrior stance, the basics of training.

Even now, fighting him to the death on the beaches of Saindora—no wooden weapons this time—she felt her back straighten.

But even after all those years of practice for duels such as this, he still drew blood.

Arianna let out a scream as his blade sliced into her wrist; she released the grip on one of her swords.

"One down, one to go," he said, circling her—it sounded less like a threat and more as if he spoke of the inevitable.

She recognized in one humbling breath that it didn't matter, all she'd learned, or the list of names now gone from this world which she held him responsible for… Solomon Bell was the Great Wolf of the East, one of the King's most revered warriors. And despite everything that gave her hope to beat him in this moment, it just wasn't possible.

He was a master swordsman for a reason, and never before had he let Arianna walk away from a duel without reminding her of that. Why should now be any different, when she was outnumbered a hundred to one?

Yet, if he bested her on this beach, with the Shadow Resistance as sure witness, Arianna wouldn't wake up after a stint in the well center with dear Cyn to coax her back to life—she just wouldn't wake.

Had all our lessons been for this?

Here she stood with the unfathomable realization that she'd never be able to best her master, not even with the swords he'd declared she'd rightfully earned from him years ago.

"I'll make this easier for you to stomach," said Solomon with a knowing look, "now that I see you understand. I would give you that… at the very least. A fair match to the end."

He threw one of his swords to the ground and placed his free hand behind his back. Then he undid his cloak so that it floated away on the wind.

Arianna's bravado wore off just as suddenly as it had come.

She peeled her focus away from Solomon—the beach had grown utterly quiet, save for the sound of the waves crashing at the shore.

Every man and woman still standing, restless shadows, surrounded them, waiting for her blood to spill; her panic soared as she couldn't spot Solza.

Solomon inched forward, and Arianna took a step back, giving him again her full attention. As she assessed the situation with more of a 'Lessa point of view' and less with vengeance in her eyes, she recognized the loss.

She grasped the hilt of her sword with both hands now, pointing it toward him with shaky hands—oh, how she wished for a sip of the shadowleaf potion to help her tap into her strongest avatar powers. What she was able to reach on her own clearly wouldn't be enough to undo him.

He lunged forward, and she faltered under his skill. He danced around her with effortlessness, nicking her shoulder, then her arm, still not even bothering to use magic—though Arianna tried desperately to call to hers.

The more hits he landed, the less confident she became… the less focus she had to coax her magic to come. *Why won't it come?*

From the corner of her eye, she noticed the shadow soldiers in deep concentration; the air seemed to be pressing out of her lungs.

She recognized the strange, heavy feeling suddenly choking her insides—they were trying to suppress her magic again.

Arianna let out a roar of anger, thrusting her sword with as much force as she could muster. But their magic weighed on her, like something was muffling her energy.

This will remain a sword-on-sword battle to the very end.

The duel didn't last much longer after that… soon Arianna found herself with no sword at all.

She let out a small gasp as her blade touched the sand, and even Solomon seemed to take pause.

They considered each other for an agonizing moment that seemed to tick on forever.

The Shadow Resistance had, at some point, encircled them. They let out a blood-curdling cheer, sending celebratory blasts of dark magic to the sky—just like the audience of a true Warrior's Challenge, they were cheering for her to die.

Solomon slowly lifted his weapon, and Arianna felt as if she were staring at the sharp end of her destiny.

Is this really it? No… this can't be it.

It was the first time that she'd ever seen his sword hand shake; his blade was pointed right at her heart, and there was nowhere to run.

With an earsplitting growl, Solza leaped into the circle to stand beside her, clearly wounded from her own trying battles.

Arianna looked down at her with so much love in her heart.

At least we are finally together again.

Whatever resistance or doubts she'd been holding on to melted away, and the avatar state engulfed her entirely.

There was a collective gasp from the surrounding army as Solza's eyes began to glow, like they'd morphed into stars. And Arianna was sure hers appeared just the same.

With only a thought, she called the sand to shoot up from the earth in an unsurpassable barrier that took Solomon's sword with it. His eyes widened in disbelief, and she *swore* she saw the flicker of a smirk before he attempted to utter a spell in defense.

However, no mere spells could stop them now.

Arianna felt as if she were floating above it all, Solza's magic quenching a thirst quite like she had gulped down the shadowleaf concoction; but it was different than the time where she'd nearly demolished the Black Sand Desert during the battle with Sir Vladamor—she didn't feel overcome by the magic, but one with it.

She fully accepted her powers, and in turn, they fully accepted her…

She sent Solomon flying backward with a gust of wind so strong that he wouldn't have survived the landing had he not used magic to cushion the blow. And a guttural growl ripped from Solza, the ground rumbling in response with such intensity that the shadows were all forced to their knees.

When the avatar-induced earthquake had died down, Solomon got to his feet atop the small hill where he'd fallen. A swirl of black magic coiled around him like an inky shield; the Shadow Resistance followed his example, all calling their deadliest spells to the forefront.

"Avatar magic or no powers at all, you will not win here tonight!" he shouted down to her, letting his magic explode around him—it hissed through the air, hunting for blood.

It hit them like a punch, and Arianna and Solza were thrown backward.

Arianna glanced to Solza as they shook off the attack, feeling herself growing warmer from the inside out—the streak of electricity in her avatar's eyes burned brighter than ever before.

The Shadow Resistance released their magic as a united and deadly force; it was oddly beautiful, dark magic pooling in their palms, merging together as it rose into the sky. Arianna thought if not for the aid of the moon washing their battlefield in a subtle, white light, she wouldn't have been able to see it at all on such a dark night.

A cloud of black formed over her and Solza, crackling with power. *Will our magic be enough to withstand whatever rains down from that?*

Solomon and his gang had them cornered with their backs against the sea.

Solza surely felt her doubts, for she began to inch toward the water, compelling Arianna to fall back alongside her.

When Arianna felt the spray of water on her skin, she hesitated, but Solza kept going until her body was halfway in the sea; she wasn't sure what to do, though she could sense Solza urging her to follow.

"There's nowhere to go!" said Solomon, marching toward them. "If you try to swim away, we'll stop you before you have time to come up for air."

Arianna wasn't sure what to do; however, she could sense

Solza's urgency… as if to say 'trust me.' She took a deep breath and turned away from Solomon just as he and the Shadow Resistance released their enchanted rain.

Solza transformed into the elegant dolphin she'd come to know well during their sunny Idris days, then together, they attempted to escape under the sea.

Without any further reluctance, she allowed Solza to pull her downward, dodging the blasts of magic that chased after them; the waves softened the blows a little, but not much.

Daring to open her eyes, Arianna looked toward the surface—spells hit the water like exploding stars falling from their home in the night sky to meet the sea in a deadly battle. The bottoms of ships docked at the surrounding port burst into flames as the magic landed, creating a rush of debris that sank to the depths of the water along with them.

Solza suddenly jerked as she changed direction. *Wait, you're going the wrong way!*

Arianna barely had a second to be afraid before her face broke through the surface of the water and she tasted delicious air again. She was still in the avatar state, but it was beginning to feel like something else, otherworldly—as if the dangers from before were inconsequential in the face of what had to be a new kind of magic they'd tapped into together.

The warmth inside her grew, engulfing her like a shield of invincibility, a beautiful light that nothing dark could ever dim; that light seemed to sink into her body to physically fuse her together with Solza.

Then, she realized that they were still going up.

Arianna could no longer feel the water on her skin as the cool night air surrounded them, the wind drying her soaked clothes. She couldn't see what was happening below either, but it didn't matter anymore—all that mattered now was what she could *feel* happening to her and Solza.

Are we changing? Inside this bubble of light, which had

formed around them, encased them, something entirely new and glorious was surely being birthed.

Arianna was familiar with what happened when avatars underwent a transformation, but this was without words; Solza's body grew wide beneath her while she held on tight.

She ran through the avatar elements in her head as her mind slowly caught up to what was happening. *Earth. Water. Air…*

"*Fire!*" came a booming voice that rang throughout Arianna's mind.

The voice was strong, compassionate, and commanding all at once, and there was not a doubt in her soul about who it belonged to—*Solza!*

Arianna was utterly astounded to find that connection they shared had somehow solidified into actual, tangible sound and words. *How can it be?*

The bubble of light fell down around them in a sparkling shower, the daze of the transformation fleeing with it; she realized they hovered just above the water with the harbor in their sights.

Solza then released the most entrancing sound that she'd ever heard any creature of the Olleb make. A thunderous roar echoed across the skies.

Arianna could hardly breathe for how excited she was. *This is it. By gods… I can't believe this is really happening.*

The ultimate dream of the Guardians of Gold was finally shaping into a reality. Solza had completed her final transformation. And in that moment, a new age of Olleb-Yelfra was born—the age of the dragons.

Just as the story stitched into the grand tapestry in Moriamo displayed, the birth of a dragon and a dragon rider had been achieved; Arianna and Solza were now truly one.

Solza's power embodied Arianna completely then as she tapped into her every thought—she wasn't just warm now, she felt as if her heart were ablaze with new life.

"Olleb-Yelfra speaks!" she shouted with spirit, relishing the fire that surely burned bright in her eyes, and ran through Solza's belly. "Hear her now. King Devlindor's reign has come to an end, and anyone who continues to stand in the way of the Guardians of Gold shall meet their ending as well."

Solza beat her mountainous wings and propelled forward on a wind of her own making; Arianna held on tight.

The Shadow Resistance scattered as they landed on the shore.

Arianna manipulated her power over the air to cushion her jump from Solza's back to the ground, a great height indeed. She knelt down to retrieve her swords from the sand.

When she looked up, her weapons again in hand, she found Solomon staring after her—the mixed shades of disbelief played across his face. It was the first true emotion she thought she'd seen him conjure in a while.

She looked up as Solza's new shadow engulfed her; a large, electric blue eye stared down at her adoringly.

Just like Solomon and his army, Arianna was struck silent by the sight of a dragon, *her* dragon.

Solza had transformed into a terrifying yet enthralling creature to behold, with shining black scales and a bright white belly. Her claws dug deep into the sand, like striking silver stakes in the ground, and a spiky tail, as thick as a tree, impatiently twitched back and forth. She craned her long neck and massive head to the sky.

"*Get back on!*" Her voice took over Arianna's thoughts again. "*And hang on tight. We're getting out of here.*"

Solza lowered her head to the ground, and Arianna climbed back up, magic aiding her way; she found a nook between her shoulders and the white horns that lined her spine, the scales oily smooth yet as hard and steely as any armor, enchanted or not.

"*Let's go!*" thought Arianna, finding a good grip.

Solza let out another mighty roar and spread her giant, leathery wings; veins of silver streaked the midnight black of her skin, like slivers of electricity that flickered through a dark rainbow of color, catching the moonlight with every movement.

As Syrifina had exposed to her, Arianna knew these veins to be Solza's actual lifeblood—and they showcased the strongest of all the elements in the world, come together as one.

It begged her to wonder… *If I were to change into a mermaid again, would my lifeblood have changed too?*

Arianna was certainly someone, *something* new; just as Solza had wholly transformed, so had she.

Solza's bone-shuddering roar came again, frightening even Arianna this time; she felt the buildup of something searing hot come with it, deep in her dragon's core—Solza opened her jaws and fire rained down on the beach, scorching everything in sight.

The night was lit up like the morning.

Solomon blocked himself and anyone near him from the fiery attack, but those too far from his protection were incinerated on impact; it was the first time that Arianna had ever seen the *true* strength of what fire could do.

She also had the terrifying knowledge that the creature now under her control—who had pledged infallible fidelity to her— could level thriving cities.

She thought of the bones of North Luose… and so did Solza.

A jolt of fear raced through both their minds.

"*We can't lose our way,*" Solza said. "*We must protect the Olleb. We must save her.*"

"*Then go. Go now!*" urged Arianna, seeing Solomon's power bubbling at the surface just as she felt her own slipping away— she let the deep avatar state fade, and her energy waned just as quickly.

Solza flapped her wings and launched into the sky with in- credible force and speed, but Solomon was determined. His magic pursued them into the clouds, so Arianna used the last of her strength to shift the sands and waters of the beach; wielded together, they created a barrier strong enough to withstand him.

When the elements of the earth and sea fell away, showering

their enemies in a powerful sheet of magic, Arianna and Solza had already escaped high into the sky; she glanced back only once as Solza circled the beach, deciding their direction.

Was it just her imagination, or did she see the hint of a smirk again cross Solomon's lips—a shadow of the smile that she had once known before? And did she dare think that she heard the booming echo of laughter chasing after them, his swords flung to the air to cheer them on? *Or* was he cursing her name, daring her to return and face him once more?

"*His smiles are only memories,*" she heard Solza whisper.

Arianna gripped her dragon tighter, knowing that she was right—whatever else may happen, the next time she found herself face-to-face with Master Solomon Bell would be the final battle for them both. This, she knew with conviction.

There will be a next time. I will not let him stand in my way again.

"*Down with the King!*" Solza sang.

And down with Solomon.

She hoped that he'd seen the golden dragon stitched on the back of her cloak as they flew away.

ARIANNA WAS COMPLETELY DRAINED, her mind overwhelmed with thoughts of all that had just occurred as she soared across the night sky. Together, she and Solza flew high above the clouds where no one might spot them, the world racing by down below.

She thought she could nearly touch the stars now and wondered if such a thing were even possible… *if we flew high enough?* With this astonishing view, she couldn't help but contemplate what new secrets the world must hold tight to. How far the skies might stretch. *Is there even an end?*

Though its magic was now spent, Arianna thought she could even feel the soul of the star growing warmer against her chest, like being closer to its former home had revitalized it somehow.

Maybe it had.

There was something reassuring about the feeling, as if it were a spirit, alive and strong, guiding her in the right direction and with her always, until the end. Now here she was, one with the stars—a dragon rider of Olleb-Yelfra.

Solza rose higher, and they both savored the unbelievable star-kissed sky in a wonderful silence.

If Keeper Kassime could see me now…

Arianna remembered the day she had learned of avatar dragons, an avatar phase which seemed impossible at the time as Solza had curled by her feet in her first form.

Nothing is impossible, she thought, truly believing that now.

Solza had evolved into a mighty beast of the skies, never to be tamed… not by anyone other than Arianna, her loyal master and friend.

"*Where do we go now?*" she asked after a long time of quiet, hugging herself closer to Solza as she glided gently through the air.

She thought that this high up she should have felt cold, but she was nothing but warm.

"*That's up to you, Master,*" said Solza, the beautiful hum of her newfound voice echoing delightfully across her mind.

Arianna couldn't be sure if she had just conjured it herself or if it was *really* what Solza sounded like in her language—and she was certain there was no explanation that anyone could give her.

It was like a sensation that had solidified into something tangible, something that she'd always known had been there all along.

Was it still *just* a feeling? Or was it real?

It honestly didn't much matter, for now Solza had a voice—

and it would never be silenced for as long as Arianna lived.

"*Let's just get as far away from this madness as possible,*" replied Arianna. Then she remembered something that felt important, as if from a dream. "*I think we need to find someone by the name of Diveena. Master Churry… he told me so, when I was on his astral plane.*"

Upon using his name, she could sense Solza mirror her own sadness over the loss of a great mentor.

"*Where can we find her, this Diveena?*" she asked, the warm, deep sound resonating in her mind in such a reassuring way that Arianna couldn't imagine life without it.

"*I don't know…*" she said. "*I wish that I did, but in all the time passed since that moment and now, I've learned nothing of anyone with such a name, nor how they could even help our situation.*" She sighed with a little laugh. "*But even in death, I trust Talis Churry to give me a riddle worth my time.*"

Again, there was silence.

Arianna felt Solza's mood shift, her mind tracking to a different emotion that she couldn't quite place; she was trying to hold something back from her.

"*You came to me when I called,*" said Arianna, softly, guessing the topic of worry. "*I didn't think… that was very brave of you to travel so far to find me.*"

She patted her gently on the side.

"*Yes, I journeyed far for you, Master,*" said Solza, an edge to her tone. "*I had waited a long time for that call. I searched for more than a month. You should have called me sooner—*"

There was a slight pause.

"*Didn't you care?*"

Arianna laid her body against her dragon's back, tears escaping her as the whirlwind that was this night finally broke through for her to feel.

"*Of course I cared,*" she mumbled, not even wanting to dwell on how broken she'd felt when they were apart all that time. "*I will always, until the day I die, care for you in a way that I care for no one else. For whatever reason, the universe has intertwined our stories, and your soul is now a piece of mine. I would have called sooner, if I'd thought you could hear.*" She sniffled. "*I'll always care for you, Solza, no matter how far apart we may be. I'm so sorry you ever doubted that.*"

"*I didn't, not truly,*" she said, matter-of-factly—Arianna could tell she was trying to appear untroubled, and it made her swell with contentment.

We're more alike than I imagined, she thought with a giggle. Solza sighed. "*I just… I just missed you.*"

"*I missed you, too, dear friend,*" she said. "*But I'm also glad you weren't around for what happened in the King's palace.*" Her mind darkened. "*They tortured me, Solza, used mind magic on me to gain our secrets. I fear we haven't much more time. They're coming for us all.*"

"*No one, not even the King and his avatar, will separate us again,*" said Solza, her voice powerful, angry—she beat her wings harder. "*Let them try! We live together, or we die together.*"

Arianna closed her eyes.

"*Let's put our focus on life for tonight,*" she said. "*I've spent too much time troubled over dying. Now tell me, how did you find me?*"

"*I was with the others for a while,*" mused Solza. "*I left them to search for you. I couldn't bear it to be apart for so long. Then I heard your call, just some hours ago. I was, thankfully, nearby, for I had assumed you'd be somewhere near Saindora. I had just been waiting for a sign, not far off from the shores of the High City.*"

"*You were with Lessa and Eli before?*" said Arianna in surprise, desperate to know if they were safe.

"*Yes, Master,*" she said. "*We journeyed together across the sea. They search for you still, but I left without any goodbye. I think Lessa will understand, though, for Sano would do the same for her. He makes a grand companion."*

"Can you take us to them?" she asked, ecstatic. *"Could you find them again?"*

"I traveled far… and it's been many moons, but Sano and I share a strong connection too," said Solza, mulling it over. *"Avatars can sense each other, you know?"* Arianna felt Solza's confidence grow. *"Yes… I should surely be able to locate them, if I can pick up his scent."*

Arianna had never known this for certain, though she and Lessa *had* pondered on occasion if avatars shared some kind of link of their own. Either way, it was clear to anyone that Sano and Solza had a strong bond, as true friends do—just like her and Lessa.

"Yes, please take us there!" said Arianna, overjoyed at the prospect that some of her family may yet live. *"We're stronger together, and we need to reunite. If there's a Diveena out there to find, we can locate her later, with our friends by our side."*

Solza veered in a new direction with the waves as her guide; Arianna had no idea where they traveled toward, but she trusted her avatar with everything.

And she knew—as the City of Saindora shrank behind her—that the King would not be far behind.

With only an endless, peaceful sky ahead, a song resurfaced in her thoughts from her childhood, steering her mind away from the King's shadow; it took her back to memories of a person she could no longer claim to be, of a person who had since grown into someone far better:

I see you down below,
As I'm flying in the sky,
Up above the mountains
To the other side.
The air here is sweet,
And it's warmer by the sun.

Nobody can catch me,
No one, no one.

Can you see me so far up,
As I'm soaring 'cross the sea?
Higher I go,
No jar can keep me.
My hope keeps me lifted,
My wings help me fly.
I am free,
I'm free in the sky.

Now I only see ahead,
As I'm sailing with the clouds.
Drifting with the wind,
Happiness I've found.
Free and alive,
Goodbye, I've left my past behind.
It is my dream,
Finally, I am free.

The song stirred up harsh memories, years of pain and suffering, and of searching for a way out; she accepted that those memories would always remain with her, dull reminders of what 'growth' meant for her—this was her life, and she owned it.

But Arianna could now also let it go.

She could forgive herself for her mistakes, for her selfishness. For her lack of confidence in times when strength had been needed. She could let that person die to make room for someone better—someone she had *chosen* to be and had already since become.

No one could grant happiness to anyone, and no one could dictate just exactly what happiness was; each person had to find that out on their own journey.

Arianna fully embraced hers now, the best of the Olleb as her guiding witness.

The moon stayed dead ahead in their sights, in a backdrop of pearly stars, and white, cottony clouds rolled by beneath them; it seemed as if they flew straight toward that bright shining orb, following the light through the darkness once and for all.

And as Arianna soared across the sea of clouds—the stars as her company and a dragon as her protector—she *was* completely and utterly happy. A sense of sureness washed over her, and she thought that if she had ever been on the right path toward something, it was now.

COME WHAT MAY

"BRING ME THE SEER!" shouted King Devlindor from the seat of his throne, seething with fury; Raja paced back and forth by his feet, as if to exude her master's restlessness.

A regulator stumbled forward from the gathering, dragging Odessa along with him by the elbow. He threw her before the King and then hurried back to his place.

She wore chains at her ankles, forced once more to kneel.

"Where is she? Tell me now or so help me, you *shall* suffer!"

The walls practically vibrated with the sound of his voice, magic lacing every word.

The room remained quiet, heads bowed low and fear palpable on this dark night; it made the King feel even more powerful.

Odessa looked up at him with a smile on her lips—he was certain that she could see him clearly.

He gripped the arms of his throne, wanting to rip the answers from her mind, bleed them out of her.

That smile… It twisted his stomach in knots.

He stood and marched down the steps to meet her. He gritted his teeth and smacked her so hard that she flew backward across the room.

The crowd scampered out of his way as he went to where she'd landed.

She was crumpled in a ball on the floor, so he crouched over her, voice heavy with the weight of his rage.

"Tell me now, seer, or I swear by the gods—"

"You know *nothing* of the gods," she spat, wiping the blood from her lips. "But I know them." She laughed, a sound so sharp and cutting that the King felt his heart flutter with the memory of fear. "And they certainly know you."

His eyes widened. *There's no such thing as gods in my world!*

He grabbed her by the neck and lifted her up from the floor, so high that only her toes skimmed the ground.

"You *will* tell me everything you know," he growled, tightening his grip so hard that he could feel the bones in her scrawny neck.

"How about I show you all that I know," she choked out, blood staining her teeth.

"Show me wha—" His voice was lost to a shriek as Odessa pressed her hands to his temples.

Her eyes lit up like stars, and with one glance to the mirrored ceiling, he saw his were too. His head thrust back from the sheer power of sight that was suddenly being shared between them.

King Devlindor made a gargling noise, the bystanders watching in terror.

"Should we do something?" he heard someone mutter.

The answer was lost to the excruciating pain that seared through him with Odessa's visions.

He went rigid, nearly convulsing under her hold—she may have been scrawny, but he'd never felt such strong magic grip him like this before.

Finally, he found the strength to push away her mind, letting go of her in the process.

Odessa fell back to the floor in a heap.

Then, she stood to face him.

"No, no, no." He squeezed his eyes shut, trying to rid himself of the visions. "Take back these lies!" he roared.

They could not be unseen.

"One cannot take back one's choices," she said in a deeper voice than he'd known her to have—it echoed somehow, still in his thoughts. "You cannot change what has already been, and what's already been will decide all that is to come, including your fate, young king. It never mattered how much you thought you knew. The future cannot be tamed and belongs to *no* one." She swayed back and forth on her feet, in the strange way she did. "You really should have never tried to interfere with Fate. She's not kind to those who do."

The King's breath came heavy now, his head filling with his own dark thoughts, *dark* magic. He visibly shook from what he hoped everyone assumed to be fury, fists balled by his sides.

Not fear... No, I'm not afraid of visions! Lies!

He became so enraged, so amped with power that it would only be seconds before it exploded.

All lies! I decide the future. He just couldn't contain himself.

It didn't matter that Odessa was believed to be the last of her kind, the last of the seer bloodline. She *would* die tonight, and one didn't need to have future sight to know it.

ODESSA CLOSED HER EYES, exhaling a breath ladened with all her burdens, shifting all the weight of the world from her. The last vision that flickered through the streams of her mind was of

Arianna Belvedor, twin swords in hand and a magnificent dragon at her back as she stood her ground against an impossible storm of enemies.

"*Choose wisely,*" she whispered, knowing the words would reach Arianna's mind, a distant reminder that would hopefully keep her on the right path until the end.

It was then that the King's magic and anger, *and* fear, seemed to overflow from him, exploding out in such a way that Odessa, and those standing anywhere nearby, were obliterated in a horrific yet spectacular display of power.

Her mind lingered, for a moment, though, curious as to what her future held.

KING DEVLINDOR TEEMED WITH SUCH AN ENERGY that even many of his followers hadn't seen in lasting memory. They all dropped to their knees, no one even daring to look at him.

I am the High King for a reason.

And he had just reminded them all just exactly why that was—the ruthless serpent had finally awakened from its slumber, ready to sink his fangs into his prey before they even saw what they'd stepped on.

King Devlindor opened up his hand, and his staff flew into his palm. He slammed the butt of it down, and a glowing apparition of the necromancer, Sir Vladamor, appeared before them, his golden mask and all.

"She has escaped!" said the King. "Where are you? What is taking so long? Return here at once with the heads of those who aid her. We take no more prisoners! The guardians will leave not even a golden smear when I'm done with them, and Arianna's body will bleed dry along with them."

"As you command, Your Majesty," said Sir Vladamor with a low bow. He fingered the ruby of his necklace. "I believe that I've found the ones they call the Kane brothers."

King Devlindor tapped his foot. "Go *on*," he said, curtly.

"I remember the taste of the one who claims the Axe of Crissy, Your Highness, so they were easy to track. But they're being assisted by someone... *powerful.*" Sir Vladamor nodded to himself, eyes like black marbles plucked from the Black Sand Desert. "I wasn't able to pick up their scent, until now. For *some* reason, they've come out of hiding and left their enchanted protection. Barring there's no surprises, I should be able to easily eliminate them both and return soon to help the Shadow Resistance finish off the rest of the guardians. We shall put an end to this nonsense."

"Do *not* fail me, Vladamor," said the King, his muscles bulging for how tightly he gripped his staff. "I will not be merciful should you prove unsuccessful again. I have been silent for too long..." He shook his head. "See how the people rebel and take advantage of my kindness? It's just like before." He looked around the silent room, his loyal servants cowering before him. "Hear me now. I will be merciful no longer!"

They bowed lower, bellies on the floor.

Sir Vladamor bowed again.

"Yes, my great king," he said. "I shall not fail you again."

King Devlindor tapped his staff on the floor once more, and the apparition vanished. Then he smiled, an unexpected laugh escaping his lips. *This is all... quite thrilling, isn't it?*

The cat and mouse game had truly begun as King Devlindor finally stepped out from the shadows, lured by Arianna's sheer bravery, no matter how unfounded. His excitement sizzled with a dark fire, lit by the audacity and sure luck of this girl—a slave who had made it so very far from her chains that she'd practically walked right into his arms for punishment... only to escape again on the back of a dragon.

I'm ready to play now. I'm coming for you, Twenty-Two.

He was no longer willing to leave this chase up to his weaker followers.

The King surveyed them, everyone still on their knees.

"Well, what are you waiting for?" he bellowed. "Find her and kill her! I want a report every hour." He took a deep breath. "And bring my sister to me at *once.*"

His voice seemed to echo across the land as Raja's roar joined his command—just the thought of Princess Elisa made his blood boil after what she'd done.

Just remember, she has always been conflicted. Try not to kill her. Try not to kill her…

He made no promises to himself.

The men and women in the throne room immediately began to scatter about the castle and the city in search of a runaway princess and the one they called 'slave,' yet who seemed to always slip out of her shackles; King Devlindor left the chamber behind them to oversee the search.

When he came to a dark hall, he was compelled to stop in front of an abyss of a black door with a golden serpent for a handle—it led to the cellar.

He'd placed a protection spell on it long ago, when a young man, a Guardian of Gold, had escaped through the tunnels with a precious item from his vault. *Olleb-Yelfra the Fallen…*

He'd memorized every word of that scroll and he remembered each one now; it contained the story of his Golden Age past, and the first prophecy he'd ever learned of his future, a prophecy he'd just witnessed again by way of Odessa's mind magic.

Puffing out his chest, King Devlindor knocked on the door only once.

"*Who goes there?*" asked a voice that seemed to echo only within his thoughts. "*Answer at your own risk.*"

The enchantment speaking to him now was one of the

strongest known to exist—a protection spell derived from blood magic.

No one could release the secrets locked behind this door ever again, save for him and his sister.

"It is I," stuttered the King. "A once noble man, born of noble blood… to a once enchanted land and noble kingdom."

The magic answered. "*You may proceed, Kyrone Devlindor.*"

He simmered with annoyance, unable to help the shiver that always ran through him upon hearing this statement—even though the voice emerged through a spell he had conjured himself, the magic still had a mind all its own.

And this magic had *never* acknowledged his crown.

King Devlindor grasped the head of the serpent handle and pushed the door open. As he descended the long staircase, Raja loyally at his side, he thought to himself, *I could use a challenge.*

The cellar door slammed shut behind him, and he stood for a moment in the dark, relishing the way it wholly surrounded him.

Dear Dragon Rider

You've come a long way! I'm honestly shocked you left the High City alive, and even more so with a dragon to your name. You've made a true enemy of the King now, and things can only get more fired up from here.

First things first, you must reunite with your friends and fill them in on all that they've missed.

Which stop on your travels with Solomon left you with the most exciting tale to tell?

Share your stories on

You're nearing the end of your quest, young adventurer. I pray you'll prove strong enough to survive King Devlindor's wrath.

Sincerely,
Ashleigh B.

Acknowledgments

Originally, this story was published on February 22, 2020, as parts one and two of *Belvedor and the Golden Rule*, the final installment in the series. I had predetermined a long time ago that the *Belvedor Saga* would only be a four-book series (*hello*, Four Corners). However, during the revision process for the new editions, I came to the realization that I had forcibly combined two stand-alone books in order to make that happen.

Thus, *Belvedor and the Trail of Fire* was born (officially released on 2-22-22… I couldn't help myself!), and I'm both surprised and thrilled that it was. The story definitely deserved a voice of its own. Now, on to the acknowledgments.

My father insists that he 'advised' me to divide the 750+ page book from the beginning; my memory is a bit blurry on this, but knowing it will be years before he ever actually reads the book (he's partway through *King's Curse*), I'll give him *some* credit for the big idea. As always, **thank you for your unending support, Dad!** Father's sure know best (and read super slow).

To my mama—thanks for not disowning me over Cyn's downfall. And thank you for loving every word that I write, in every draft. Even when something's incomprehensible, you always *insist* that it's amazing. Your encouragement has done wonders for my soul and my goals, and I'm lucky to have a mom like you.

To my best friend, Lisa—I know who the real ones are! Your support has never wavered over the years, even when my confidence has. Thank you for always being in my corner, no matter how far apart we are in this world.

To my big sister, the agrarian in the family—thanks for loving me through thick and thin, and for supporting my writing journey through all of it.

To my talented editor, Hannah McCall—you really showed me the true value of the age-old lesson 'less is more.' I've learned to *love* making cuts. And with every one we make, I feel like the best of my writing has more room to breathe. Also, POV is *everything*! Thank you for teaching me to hone my craft.

To the Belvedor design squad—**Mirella Santana**, I've been waiting years to get a dragon on the cover of one of these books! Such a fantastic fiery addition to the saga. **Jessica Khoury**—Arianna and her friends are sure city-hopping now. Whatever would we do without the map you designed to follow along on their journey?

To the Belvedor Bookworms—I can't wait to share the last installment in this series with you. So many surprises to come! As Arianna nears the end of her quest, we'll be greeted by some new faces and some old, and there will be no shortage of magic or bloody battles for you to devour. As always, thank you for reading and sharing my stories. I can really feel the love!

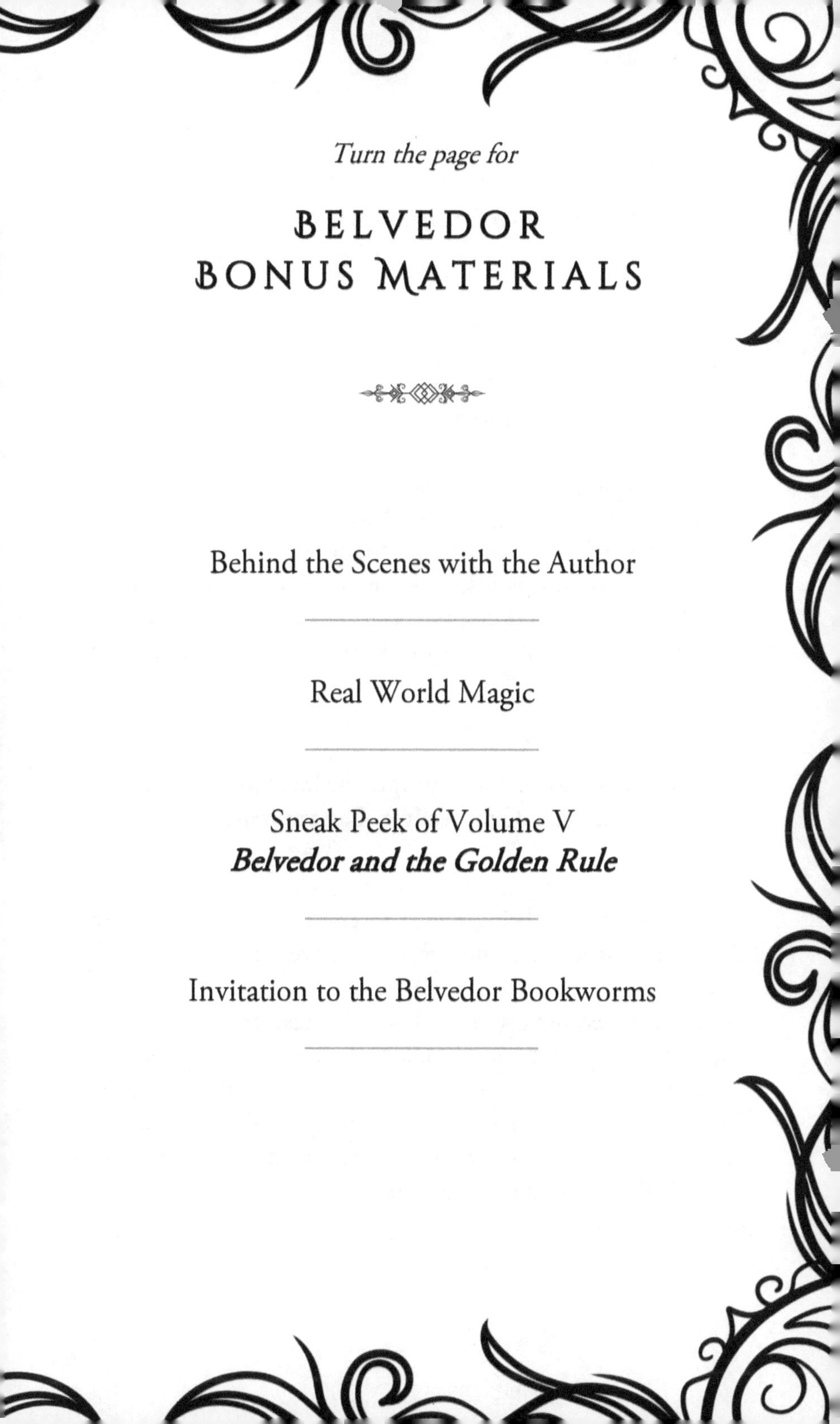

Turn the page for

BELVEDOR
BONUS MATERIALS

Behind the Scenes with the Author

Real World Magic

Sneak Peek of Volume V
Belvedor and the Golden Rule

Invitation to the Belvedor Bookworms

BEHIND THE SCENES

Have you always wanted to be a writer?

Not at all; however, I *have* always enjoyed writing. I excelled in those classes growing up, and I wrote creatively off and on, just for fun (poems, songs, short stories, diaries); Arianna's quest for freedom was just a blazing idea that popped into my head by chance. I felt compelled to put it to paper. But with every word I wrote, her story just kept evolving—she made me into a writer.

Arianna has lost a lot of people she loves on this quest (*umm…* Cyn, really?). Can you relate?

Yeah, *sorry* about Cyn. That one was hard for me to write. In fact, it's difficult to bring myself to end the lives of any of the characters that Arianna and her friends have come to love.

I don't do it because I want to. I do it because, realistically, without such loss, Arianna just wouldn't be the person she is at the end of the story. She'd have no motivation to continue fighting. She grows through the pain, learns to cope with her losses, and turns her hurt into power for the betterment of her world—I think that's a very human reaction to loss. And experiencing loss is also very human.

As for me, well, my grandma was an angel in disguise while she lived. Cancer took her too young; it felt so unfair when it happened, and it still does, but over the years I've found that she's stayed with me all this time, in different ways. I just had to see past my sadness and recognize that her love was enough to last a lifetime, even though she's moved on to her next chapter.

What was your favorite part to describe in *Trail of Fire*?

Definitely the *Birth of the Dragon Rider* tapestry scene. I felt like I could really see every stitch in my mind's eye. I loved creating it, and exploring the rise of the avatar and avatar master on a deeper level.

Solza has had a lot of shocking transformations. How did you decide what animal forms she would take?

Very easily. First of all, what young girl didn't wish she could have one of the big cat species for a pet growing up? Jasmine (from *Aladdin*) was living the life! As for the dolphin phase, I had a serious obsession with them in my youth; it got so out of hand that I had to make a formal announcement to friends and family that I no longer wished to receive dolphin-related items gifts.

Finally, the owl… I honestly don't know a lot about bird species (we really only have pigeons in Brooklyn, NY), so I was very limited in my imagination there. I might have partially been influenced by that cute movie *Legend of the Guardians: The Owls of Ga'Hoole*, or the fact that Hedwig from *Harry Potter* was just my favorite. RIP.

REAL WORLD MAGIC

Africa certainly influences some of the new places we visit in *Belvedor and the Trail of Fire*.

Moriamo really came to life after I traveled to Nigeria for the first time to meet family (my father is from Lagos); the ravine and waterfall that Arianna dives into were inspired by a trip to Livingston, Zambia and the Victoria Falls (a massive waterfall that borders Zambia and Zimbabwe)—it's one of the seven natural wonders of the world! And for good reason.

Fun Fact—the area of still water on top of the waterfall referred to as 'Fate's Pool' in this book is actually based on a real area of the Zambezi River called the 'Devil's Pool'. Google it.

It sits right on top of the waterfall, and you can actually swim to the edge to look over as the water thunders down all around you. *But*, if you swim outside of the safety bounds, the current might take you over the waterfall!

It's definitely for the thrill seeker and was one of the most exhilarating things I've ever done… except for maybe bungee-jumping from a 100-year-old bridge over the river. That was madness, so of course I had to push Arianna off a bridge as well. ;)

Photo from the top of Victoria Falls. Livingston, Zambia (2013).
The rainbow! Such magic.

I also can't leave Italy out. *The Hall of Maps* chapter was one of my favorites to write because I was super inspired by a solo trip to Rome (2017) where I visited the Vatican—inside, there's a wing called the 'Gallery of Maps' with giant artworks of countries and cities decorating a long hall.

I remember everything being sky blue and gold, from floor to ceiling. I was so enchanted by that walk. Look it up! My pictures don't do it justice.

And get this, the Gallery of Maps is located to the west of the *Belvedere* Courtyard (lol). Close enough that a fantasy version was clearly meant to be part of Arianna's story.

Turn the page for a sneak peek

BELVEDOR AND THE GOLDEN RULE

THE IN-BETWEEN

AN EXCERPT

IT HAD ALREADY BEEN SEVERAL MOONS of searching for their friends.

Arianna's hands and legs ached from clenching so tight to Solza's back for hours on end. But after a while, she began to crave it, the deafening silence. She could live in the sky, she thought—just the calming sound of the wind beating in her ears, and the stars twinkling forevermore in her sight.

Arianna and Solza had never been so connected, and the skies were starting to feel like they belonged to her now too, just as much as they belonged to her avatar.

Solza made a grand avatar dragon of Olleb-Yelfra, clearly born to fly.

After completing her final phase of transformation, she was now able to manipulate all of the elements. She confidently wielded her power over the air to create speed on the winds beneath her expansive wings, putting as much distance as possible between them and the City of Saindora.

They rested and replenished during the long, hot days, and flew only with the cover of the dark.

At the end of the seventh night, the sun finally started to rise again in the sky, hovering like a plump orange over the sea; Solza gradually began to drop lower; they emerged from a large, puffy cloud in a burst, as if a dandelion's seeds had been blown apart with a *whoosh*.

Moments later, they were hovering so close to the water

that Arianna could feel the soft sprays of the ocean tickle her skin. A twinge of excitement ran through her every time a new sunrise came—it meant that they were nearing their destination, that they could possibly reunite with Lessa and Eli.

But what if Solza loses Sano's scent? Or what if he's been separated from Lessa and Eli? What if they're all…

Arianna could feel Solza's mind press into hers, urging her not to worry. She shook her head, pushing away the anxious thoughts, focusing instead on the lull of the water…

It was mesmerizing, this endless bright, rippling turquoise.

The reflection of Solza's white belly shimmered atop the waves in line with the glistening sun; it appeared as if a silver beast lurked just beneath the surface of the sea, following them always and about to emerge at any moment.

With a giant, arching splash, something *did* break through the waves from below.

Arianna gasped as a true dweller of the underwater world surfaced to greet them—it was a fraction of the size of Solza's shadow.

"A whale!" said Arianna, pointing ahead.

A jolt of happiness made all the hair rise up on her arms, the sea gifting them with such a rare sight today—she'd only ever witnessed this creature in her studies. She stretched out her fingers to try to graze the gentle beast, but it sank beneath the waters before she could.

She was sad for only a moment—Solza veered to the left just as a pod of dolphins gracefully jumped up to welcome them into their domain.

"*Hmm… they're like me?*" Solza mused, slowing a bit to observe them.

She was equally as enthralled with all the peculiar life that flourished with the water's blessing.

"Nothing like you," said Arianna, knowing that she referred to her dolphin form. *"You are so much more."*

"Beautiful, though," said Solza in delight—she made strings of delicate water dance around her kin, zigzagging between the pod as if she swam alongside them.

"As are you," replied Arianna in awe.

The dolphins raced after Solza for a while, but they were no match for an avatar dragon. They soon fell behind.

Arianna turned around to try to glimpse them one last time.

She froze, eyes wide open, trying to decide whether or not what she saw was real or just a distorted image from the waves; the dolphins were gone, but something had appeared in their place. *Someone* was watching them.

"Syrifina?" Arianna's voice was carried off into the salty breeze.

Solza took a sharp turn, forcing her to look ahead and focus on her grip. *"She's here?"* said Solza.

Arianna didn't miss the anxiety in her voice.

When they were steady, she turned back around, staring at the same spot—nothing was there.

"I think I was just imagining it."

"Hmm..." said Solza, clearly unconvinced.

It *could* have easily been a trick of the mind, her thoughts merely wandering over the witches of the water.

And yet, it rarely ever is just my imagination... not these magic-filled days.

Had the mother of mermaids been spying on them all this time? After all, the Sea of Saindora *was* her domain, and they had been following it a very long way from the High City.

"Do you think that we're close?" asked Arianna, growing impatient with the journey.

The last thing she or Solza desired was a reunion with Syrifina Myr, or any of her water-bred minions, not before they located their friends. And never again would also be fine.

"*I think so, Master,*" said Solza, sensing her unease. "*You have to trust me.*"

"*I do. I'm just…*" Arianna couldn't bring herself to finish her thought.

"*I'm scared, too,*" murmured Solza, "*but I left them in good hands, so I pray that 'good' is what we find.*"

They glided at an even slower pace now, keeping their eyes peeled for the next daytime campsite.

"*I see land!*" roared Solza. "*I thought they'd be sailing still, but they must be around here somewhere. I think we've made it.*"

"*Are you saying what I think you are?*" said Arianna in a steady tone.

She felt Solza smile.

"*Yes, Master. I can sense that Sano is very close.*"

Arianna felt so much nervous energy rush through her then.

"*Are you sure?*" she said in a shaky voice. "*I don't see anything…*" She tried with everything to squash her exhilaration down, not wanting to be disappointed; she'd had enough experience with the ocean to know that it could certainly play games on wary wanderers—all she could see was an infinite stretch of water.

"*Quite,*" said Solza. "*Use your magic. Your eyes unaided aren't nearly as strong as mine.*" She flapped her wings harder, aiming for whatever land she claimed lay ahead.

"*You wouldn't mind?*" asked Arianna, chewing on the idea.

Her anticipation grew, but she remained hesitant. She just couldn't bring herself to be hopeful until she saw the proof for herself.

"*My sight is your sight,*" said Solza, matter-of-factly.

Arianna closed her eyes. Then, she emptied her mind, just like Mother Adunni had taught her to do in Moriamo.

The avatar state of being was easier to call now. In fact, after spending so much time under the blanket of suppressive magic during her imprisonment with the King, Arianna found that it had become second nature to summon; it was as accessible to her now as conjuring her regular magic, if she concentrated and Solza concentrated too. They had come a long way since their bonding in the Nicora Forest, and so much time apart had only reaffirmed that they were much stronger together.

Arianna gave a long exhale, letting Solza's magic flood through her. When she opened her eyes, she could *really* see—a new world expanded out in front of her, washing the old, dull version of the Olleb away in a blink.

She glanced to the waters; the varieties of blue and green hues she found there were so striking that she lost her breath momentarily. And when she gazed forward, her sight stretched much farther than her human eyes could have ever hoped to attain.

Arianna let out a little scream of joy.

"I see it!" she said as a distant terrain came into view.

Trees shot up around a hilly base for miles; it was possibly the most enchanting green she'd ever seen, like a lake of emeralds glittering against the shore underneath the sun.

She beamed. "It looks like a jungle."

"*Told you so*," said Solza.

Arianna rolled her eyes.

"And look! There's a city there, too, beyond the trees," she said, drinking it all in. "Do you think that's where they are?"

"*I don't know, but we're going to find out*," said Solza, flying faster toward the trees. "*Sano is here.*"

Arianna held on tight, praying to every god and goddess she could think of that she might find her friends soon, hiding somewhere in these mysterious hills—the air grew thick with a sweet, sticky taste as they drew nearer, and the fresh scent of nature hit them in a burst when they came upon the shore.

THE BELVEDOR SAGA

By Ashleigh Bello

Find the completed series on Amazon.
Follow the Magic!

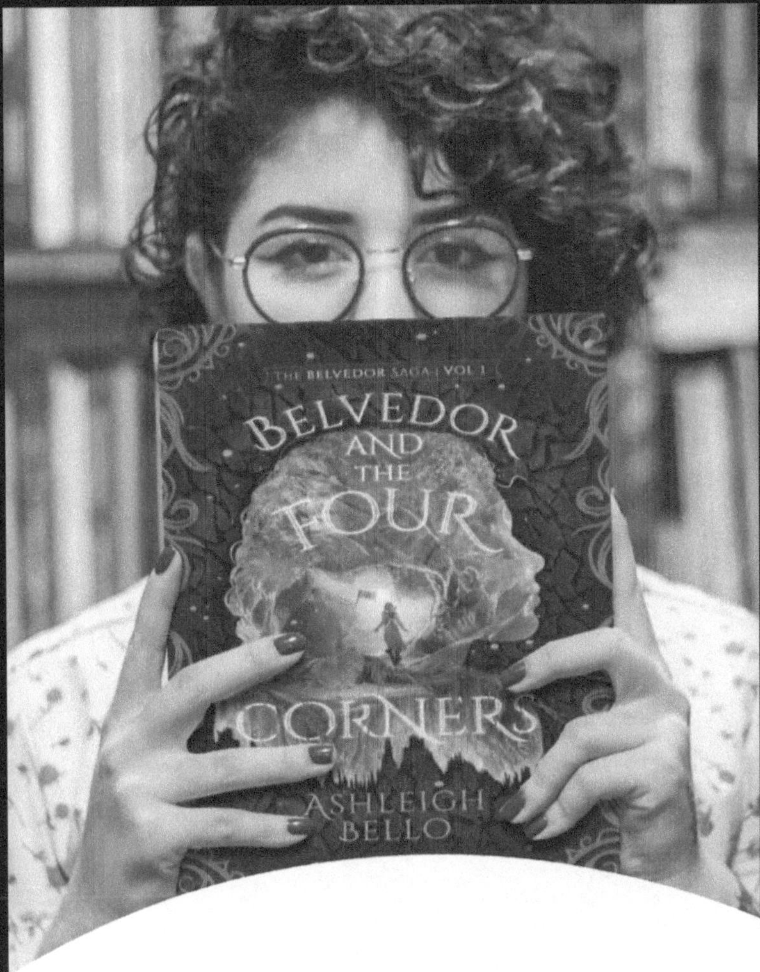

A S H L E I G H   B E L L O is the author of *A Myrmaid's Kiss* and the *Belvedor Saga*. She graduated from the University of Missouri-Columbia and currently lives in Brooklyn, New York. She also teaches and practices vinyasa yoga in her community and is the co-founder of Yoga Block Party, a female-owned yoga events and retreats business. She enjoys spending time with friends and family every chance she gets and is always daydreaming about her next novel. Her endless passion for travel and spontaneous adventure continues to be her inspiration for future works in the enchanting world of Olleb-Yelfra and beyond.

Connect with the Author
www.ashleighbello.com
@ashleighbello

Follow her on TikTok!
Scan the QR code to visit her bookish social account